THE MAN WITH THE LOCKED AWAY HEART

BY
MELANIE MILBURNE

SOCIALITE... OR NURSE IN A MILLION?

BY
MOLLY EVANS

THE MAN WITH THE LOCKED AWAY HEART

BY
MELANIE MILBURNE

First published in Great Britain 2011
Harlequin Mills & Boon Limited,
Eton House, 18-24 Paradise Road, Richmond, Surrey TW9 1SR

© Melanie Milburne 2011

ISBN: 978 0 263 88581 1

Harlequin Mills & Boon policy is to use papers that are natural, renewable and recyclable products and made from wood grown in sustainable forests. The logging and manufacturing process conform to the legal environmental regulations of the country of origin.

Printed and bound in Spain
by Litografia Rosés, S.A., Barcelona

The domestic scene made her feel as if she had stepped over a boundary way too soon. It was intimate, and yet he was a perfect stranger.

She was sharing this big old house with a man she didn't know, and yet for some reason she didn't feel afraid. She *did* feel on edge, but that had more to do with her reaction to him: his touch, for instance. What was that all about? Why had her heart started to race like a greyhound when his fingers had pressed down over her wrist? His dark brown gaze had locked her just as firmly in place—those bottomless eyes that saw so much and gave away so little.

She made a business of preparing the coffee, when in reality she would normally have settled for a teaspoon of instant. But Italians loved their coffee, right? She breathed in the fragrant aroma as the percolator did its job, her mind wandering as she thought about how long the sexy sergeant would be in town.

In her house.

Melanie Milburne says: 'One of the greatest joys of being a writer is the process of falling in love with the characters and then watching as they fall in love with each other. I am an absolutely hopeless romantic. I fell in love with my husband on our second date, and we even had a secret engagement—so you see it must have been destined for me to be a Harlequin Mills & Boon® author! The other great joy of being a romance writer is hearing from readers. You can hear all about the other things I do when I'm not writing, and even drop me a line at: www.melaniemilburne.com.au'

Melanie Milburne also writes for Modern™ Romance!

'THE FIORENZA FORCED MARRIAGE
by Melanie Milburne: insults fly, passion explodes,
and it all adds up to an engaging story
about the power of love.'
—*RT Book Reviews* Bookclub

CHAPTER ONE

'THERE'S someone here to see you, Gemma,' Narelles, the receptionist at the clinic, informed her as she popped her head around the consulting-room door.

Gemma looked up from the patient notes she was filling in before she left for the day. 'Not another last-minute patient?' she asked, trying to ignore the sinking feeling in her stomach. She had been working twelve hours straight and could think of nothing better than driving back to Huntingdon Lodge to catch up on some much-needed sleep.

'No,' Narelle said, and cupping her hand around her mouth in a conspiratorial manner added in a stage whisper. 'It's a police sergeant.'

Gemma straightened her slumped shoulders like a puppet suddenly pulled up by strings. 'A sergeant?' she asked. 'Why? What's happened?'

Narelle's eyes danced. 'He's the new cop. You know, the one we've been waiting for to replace Jack Chugg? He's in the waiting room. I guess he just wants to make himself known to you. Do you want me to hang around while he's here?'

Gemma pushed out from the desk and got to her feet. 'No, you go on home, Narelle. Ruby and Ben will be missing you. You've already stayed way past your usual time. I didn't realise Nick Goglin's transfer to Brisbane would take so long.'

'You think he's going to make it?' Narelle asked with a concerned frown.

Gemma hiked her shoulders up and down. 'Who knows? With head injuries it's always hard to predict the outcome. The neuro team in Brisbane will let us know as soon as he is assessed. All we can do at this stage is hope and pray he comes out of the coma with all his faculties intact.'

'Yes, well, all of Jingilly Creek is behind him, and of course Meg and the kids,' Narelle said. Her hand dropped from where it was holding the door ajar. 'I'll send your visitor in on my way out. Have a good one, Gemma.'

'Thanks,' she said as she quickly straightened the files on her desk. 'You too.'

Gemma heard firm footsteps moving along the corridor and then there was a brief hard knock on the consulting-room door a moment or two later.

'Come in,' she said, fixing a pleasant but professional smile on her face.

As soon as the door opened she felt her eyes widen involuntarily and her smile falter. For some reason she had been expecting a slightly overweight, close-to-retirement-age cop, someone who would take up the remote Outback post until they finally hung up their badge for good. She had pictured in her mind's eye a mid-height man with a balding pate and a belly that overhung his belt, similar to the recently retired Jack Chugg. She hadn't for a moment conjured up a tall, broad-shouldered, slim-hipped, dark-haired, gorgeous-looking man in his early to mid-thirties with a body that looked as if it would look even better without the covering of the blue denim jeans and white casual shirt he was wearing.

'Dr Kendall?' He moved across the floor to her desk in a couple of strides—most people took at least three or four—and held out his hand. 'I am Sergeant Marc Di Angelo.'

Gemma put her hand in his and immediately felt as if he had zapped her with a Taser gun. Electric jolts travelled from her palm along the length of her arm. And even more shocking, disturbing and totally inexplicably, her heart gave a funny leap and skip and trip movement behind the wall of her chest. 'Um—hi,' she said, feeling her professional front peeling away like shedding skin as she met his dark-as-espresso, coffee-brown eyes.

'I'm sorry to disturb you at the end of the day,' he said. 'But I have not long arrived in town and thought I should drop by and introduce myself.'

'Um…would you like to sit down?' she asked, waving a hand towards one of the two chairs she had positioned beside her desk so as not to intimidate her patients. Now she wished she had the barrier of her desk between the sergeant's long legs and hers. It seemed far too intimate a distance when he sat down soon after she had taken her own chair. If he moved his legs even a fraction, they would touch hers. He had powerful-looking legs, long and strong with well-developed muscles. She tried not to look at his quadriceps as they bunched beneath the fabric of his jeans but her gaze felt drawn to them as if pulled by some invisible force. She quickly fixed her gaze on his and her heart did another funny little stop-start. His eyes were so dark she felt compelled to stare at him. They were so dark and secretive, mysterious, closed off, locked down, as if he had seen too much and was not prepared to let anyone else catch even a glimpse of what it had done to him. 'Welcome to Jingilly Creek,' she said, working extra-hard at keeping her professional poise on track. 'I hope you enjoy your time here.'

His gaze was unwavering on hers and his expression—like just about all of the cops snthe had met in the past on business—was completely and utterly unreadable. 'From what I have seen so far, it is certainly going to be a change from the city,' he said.

In spite of his casual attire, Gemma could see the slick city cut to his jeans and shirt and the totally urban look he had in terms of grooming. The thick dark locks of his wavy hair were controlled by some sort of hair product, and his lean, fashionably unshaven jaw hinted at the potent male hormones surging around his body. She wondered why he of all people had taken such a remote post. She wondered too if he had brought anyone with him, a wife or girlfriend perhaps. She sidestepped her thoughts, annoyed at herself for even thinking about it. His private life had nothing to do with her. 'Yes, well, it's generally pretty quiet out here,' she said. 'But we have our moments.'

'How long have you been in town, Dr Kendall?' he

asked, leaning back in his chair slightly, as if settling in for the rest of the evening.

Gemma shifted in her seat, her eyes flicking to those impossibly long, strong legs before returning to his dark, inscrutable eyes. 'I've been here three years,' she said. 'I came up from Melbourne. I wanted to do my bit for the Outback. There's a shortage of doctors in regional areas. It's obviously much the same for your people. We've been waiting for a replacement for Sergeant Chugg for nearly six months.'

He gave a slow nod. 'And what keeps you here, Dr Kendall?' he asked. 'It seems to me to be a rough, lonely sort of place for a young single woman.'

Gemma frowned at him. 'How do you know I'm single?'

His eyes went to her tightly knotted hands in her lap before coming back to hers. Was that a hint of mockery she could see in his darker-than-dark gaze? 'You're not wearing a ring,' he said.

'So?' she said, shifting again in her chair but in an affronted, agitated manner this time. Did she look as desperate and dateless as she sometimes felt? It had taken her the best part of her first year out here to put her heartbreak behind her. She was over it now. Well and truly over it. Or was there something about her appearance that shrieked lonely single woman? She knew she wasn't wearing any make-up to speak of and her blond hair was in need of new highlights, not to mention her roots, and she didn't even want to think about how badly her eyebrows needed a pluck. She would have done it last night but she had fallen asleep in front of the television.

'I might choose not to wear jewellery when at work,' she said. 'A lot of doctors don't.'

An upward movement of his top lip suggested it was about as close to a smile as he was used to giving. 'Point taken,' he said.

The ensuing silence was intimidating but, then, Gemma wondered if he had intended it to be. He was obviously assessing her, summing her up for his mental database. Most cops did it. They were trained to read people, to decode even the most subtle body language and subtext of speech. She suspected he was a master at it. She sat it out as determinedly as she could. She crossed her arms and her legs, a lightning strike of sensation rushing through her when her ankle accidentally brushed against one of his. She thought she saw a flash of primal male interest in his gaze but he just as quickly went back to deadpan.

'You currently live at a property called Huntingdon Lodge,' he said. 'Is that correct?'

'For someone who's only been in town a matter of minutes, you seem to have done your research, Sergeant Di Angelo,' Gemma said with an arch look.

He gave a lift of one shoulder, a careless, casual movement she knew instinctively was a guise. 'In a town this small I don't think it will take me long to get to know everything there is to know about everyone.'

He said it as if that was his goal and Gemma could well believe he would achieve it if he set his mind to it. There was a steely determination to his personality. She could see it in the chiselled strength of his jaw, the Roman nose and in the firm, intractable line of his unsmiling mouth. Here was a man used to getting his own way in every facet of his life, she thought. The hint of arrogance in his persona, the aloof, brooding set to his features and his unmistakable attractiveness was a powerful and deadly combination she would have to take care to guard against.

'I've lived there since I came up from Melbourne,' she said. 'Gladys Rickards was a patient of mine. She ran the homestead as a boarding house and farm-stay property after her husband died. I ended up staying on with her rather than finding my own place. She was lonely and liked the company. We became very good friends. I guess that's really one of the reasons I've stayed on for as long as I have in Jingilly Creek. I didn't want to leave Gladys. She became rather dependent on me towards the end.'

His gaze was still locked on hers. 'Mrs Rickards died not long ago, correct?'

Gemma shifted a little in her chair, her hands untying and then reknotting in her lap. She felt uncomfortable that he knew all that about her already. What else did he know? 'Yes. It was very sad,' she said. 'She was one of the mainstays of this community, everyone loved her. She will be greatly missed.' She let out a sigh and added, 'It's been just over a month and I still can't quite believe she's no longer there when I go home.'

The same brow lifted up, slightly higher this time, interest and intrigue there in that single movement. 'What did she die of, exactly?' he asked.

Gemma felt another frown pull at her forehead. 'She was eighty-nine years old, Sergeant. She had a long history of kidney problems associated with her type-two diabetes. She went into renal failure and at her request died at home.'

Dark, bottomless eyes, steady, watchful, assessing. 'You were with her?' he asked.

The question seemed loaded with something she found disturbing. She felt her back come up at what he seemed to be implying. 'Sergeant Di Angelo, I have been with a number of patients when they die out here,' she said. 'Jingilly Creek is a long way from dialysis and transplant facilities, any facilities, in fact. Even if those were options Gladys could have had, she chose to die at home. She felt she had lived a long and productive life. She wanted no further intervention. I felt it was a privilege to have taken care of her. She had been extremely kind to me when I first arrived in town.'

'She must have thought very highly of you,' he said, still watching her with the gaze of a hawk. 'Huntingdon Lodge is now yours, is it not?'

Gemma sent her tongue out over her lips again. Who on earth had he been speaking to? Ray Grant, the only other cop in town, hadn't even mentioned the arrival of the new sergeant and she had been with him just an hour ago at Nick Goglin's place. The only thing he had mentioned, and that had been at least a couple of weeks ago, had been that he was still waiting to see if the guy in mind was going to take up the position so he could have some much-needed time off. 'Look, Sergeant Di Angelo, I am not sure what you are suggesting, but I had no idea Gladys had written her will that way. It came as a complete surprise to me. I had not expected her to do anything like that. It was certainly never something we discussed.'

'How did her family feel about her bequeathing everything to you?' he asked, still with that cop-like gaze fixed on hers.

'Gladys and her husband Jim lost their only son forty years ago,' she said, trying not to fidget under his unnerving scrutiny. 'There are nieces and nephews and second cousins and so on, but no one who visited or kept in touch regularly.'

'So you were the lucky one to inherit all of her considerable assets.' It was neither a statement nor a question but more leaning towards an accusation, Gemma thought.

'Huntingdon Lodge is like a lot of old properties around here—quite rundown,' she said. 'It needs much more money than it produces in order to keep things going.'

'What have you decided to do with it?' he asked. 'Keep it or sell it?'

'I—I haven't quite decided,' she answered, which wasn't exactly the truth. As much as Gemma loved Jingilly Creek and caring for the locals, Huntingdon Lodge, although beautiful and with masses of potential, really needed someone with a farming background to run it properly. But for the first time since her mother had died she had a place to call home. But selling up and leaving so soon after inheriting the property could easily be misinterpreted by the locals. She had decided to make the best of it until enough time passed to make other plans.

'No immediate plans to head back to the big smoke?' he asked.

Gemma pursed her lips before she responded. He was watching her with that steady cop-gaze, quietly reading her every word and movement to see if they were in sync. 'I am not sure what these questions have to do with your appointment here, Sergeant. I should warn you that if you subject every person you meet in Jingilly Creek to the same inquisition you have given me, you might find your stay here is not as pleasant or productive as you might have wished.'

He gave her his brief version of a smile but it didn't involve his eyes. 'I'll risk it,' he said as he rose to his feet. 'Thank you for your time.'

Gemma stood up but her legs didn't feel as steady as she would have liked. The consulting room seemed to have shrunk considerably as it accommodated the sergeant's tall, authoritative presence. She could even catch a hint of his lemony aftershave and late-in-the-day honest male sweat. It wasn't unpleasant, certainly not as unpleasant as that of some of her hard-working, hard-drinking, hard-smoking patients.

Marc Di Angelo smelt of a man in his prime: sexy, virile and dangerously potent. 'How long are you planning on staying at this post?' she asked out of a politeness she didn't really feel.

'I am not sure at this stage,' he answered. 'It depends.'

'So, you're like doing a locum or something?'

His eyes gave nothing away. 'Something like that.'

'Have you had a chance to meet the other officer?'

she asked. 'I was out on a call with Ray Grant earlier but he should be back at the station by now. He didn't mention he was expecting you today.'

'I spoke to him by phone a short time ago to let him know I was here,' he said. 'I'll head back there now to introduce myself in person.' He reached into the breast pocket of his jacket and handed her a card. 'My contact details in case I'm not at the station any time.'

Gemma took the card, which was still warm from being so close to his body. She put it on her desk, and faced him again. 'Where are you staying while you're here?' she asked, not just out of forced or fabricated politeness this time. Accommodation was limited in Jingilly Creek and he didn't seem the type to rough it at the local pub.

'The department has booked me in at the hotel for the time being,' he said. 'I believe it's called The Drover's Retreat.'

'Yes, well, it was a long time since it was anything like a retreat,' she said with a wry expression. 'You'll get a bed, a shared bathroom and a cold beer and bangers and mash, but that's about it.'

'Do you have somewhere else you could recommend?' he asked.

Gemma hesitated. Sharing Huntingdon Lodge with Marc Di Angelo was not something she was going to put her hand up for even if she was keen to get some regular boarders in to meet the cost of the repairs Rob Foster was helping her with. 'Um...well, there's not much around here. You'd have to go to Minnigarra for a motel but that's over a hundred kilometres away.'

He looked at her for an infinitesimal pause. 'So you're not currently taking in lodgers?'

Gemma knew her face was pink but there was nothing she could do about it. 'Um…I'm in the middle of repairs and renovations at present…' It sounded like the fob-off it was and the look in his dark eyes confirmed he recognised it as such.

'I'll give the local place a go before I make other arrangements,' he said. 'Thank you again for your time.'

Gemma let out the breath she had been unconsciously holding once he left the clinic building. She had a feeling this was not going to be the last time she was going to be cross-examined by the determined and rather delicious-looking sergeant.

The drive out to Huntingdon Lodge, especially close to sundown, never failed to inspire Gemma. The sky was a brilliant backdrop of orange and yellow against the red dust of the open plains. It hadn't rained for months but the last showers had been enough to fill the tanks and rivers for the first time in a decade. The pastoral area surrounding Jingilly Creek was still struggling to get back on its feet after such a difficult time but the locals were hopeful of another solid rain before winter arrived.

The long driveway to the stately old Victorian-style mansion was lined by old poplar trees, whose just-starting-to-turn leaves rattled like bottle caps in the evening breeze. A flock of corellas and sulphur-crested cockatoos called shrilly from the red river gums down by the river running through the property. It was a picturesque setting and yet Gemma felt a rush of loneliness when her gaze went to the empty rocking chair on the veranda.

Flossie, Gladys's old Border collie, came limping down the steps to greet her. Gemma crouched down and hugged the old girl around the neck. 'Hiya, Floss,' she said. 'I miss her too.'

The dog gave her a melting look and followed her into the house. Gemma fed the dog, and then, after a quick refreshing shower, she poured herself a cool drink and went back out to sit on the veranda to enjoy the last of the sunset. A couple of kangaroos were grazing in the house paddock, increasingly brave now that Flossie's eyesight and sense of smell and speed were not what they had once been.

A thin curl of dust rose from the road in the distance but Gemma couldn't make out if it was a neighbour or a tourist. Jingilly Creek hadn't exactly been a tourist destination since a bypass to the town had been built in the eighties, but very occasionally a visitor would find their way to the isolated community if they headed inland off the main highway. Gladys would always give them a warm country welcome, fill them with a good hearty meal and offer them a bed for a night or two. Gemma had enjoyed watching her landlady entertain 'city folk', as Gladys had called them. Gemma had reminded her that she too was a city girl, but Gladys had always insisted there just had to be country blood in Gemma's veins because she fitted in so well in the community. Gemma suspected Gladys had known how much she longed to fit in anywhere after so many years of feeling adrift. The Jingilly Creek community had become like an extended family to her. She felt loved and appreciated and valued and yet just lately it wasn't quite enough.

Within minutes another curl of dust appeared but this time, instead of continuing down the road, the car creating the plume turned into Huntingdon Lodge. Gemma got off the wrought-iron seat—she couldn't quite bring herself to sit in Gladys's chair—and held onto the veranda post as the gunmetal-grey car rumbled over the cattle grid. It continued on up the serpentine drive until it finally came to a halt in front of the grand old house with a spray of gravel as the brakes were applied.

She felt her chest give a little flutter when the tall figure unfolded himself from the car, and her hand around the post tightened. He had undone a couple more of the buttons on his shirt, revealing just enough of his tanned chest to make her breath hitch in her throat. She suddenly was aware of her femininity in a way she hadn't been in years. She couldn't think of a time when she had met a more attractive-looking man. She used to think her ex-fiancé had cornered the market in good looks but Marc Di Angelo took it to a whole new level. 'Good evening, Sergeant,' she said as he crunched across the gravel towards the veranda. 'Taking in the sights, are we?'

His dark gaze ran over her pink T-shirt with 'Princess lives here' written across her braless breasts before slowly coming back to her eyes.

Too slowly.

Deliberately slowly, Gemma thought. She felt something in the air between them, something heavy and pulsing. She didn't want to think about just what it was.

'This part of the Outback is certainly worth a second look,' he said with a ghost of a smile playing about his sensually contoured mouth.

Gemma wondered how many female mouths had enjoyed being kissed by those sinfully sculpted lips. Her eyes surreptitiously went to his left hand and saw it was ringless. She wasn't sure why her belly did a little flip turn. Maybe she had spent too much time in the bush alone. 'What can I do for you, Sergeant Di Angelo?' she asked in a deliberately cool tone.

By this time his right foot was on the bottom step of the veranda and his right hand was holding the railing. Flossie lumbered over, with her tail going from side to side, and he bent down and gave her a gentle ruffle of her ears, and the dog—shame on her—sighed as if in ecstasy. Gemma could see the muscles and sinews of his tanned arms liberally dusted with dark masculine hair that went all the way to the backs of his long fingers. His olive skin, along with his name, hinted at his Italian heritage, so too did the way he accented certain words, which suggested he spoke Italian fluently, although from his perfect colloquial English he was most certainly Australian born.

'Apparently there's no room at the inn, so to speak,' he said.

She frowned. 'That's ridiculous. Ron always has rooms free. He's always complaining how he hasn't had full occupancy for years.'

'Not this time,' he said. 'He told me I should ask you for a bed as you now own a guest house.'

Gemma's heart flipped like a pancake. 'Um…I'm not quite set up for guests…' She faltered. She waved a hand vaguely towards the house behind her. 'I'm still stripping the paintwork and refurbishing the place. As you can see, it's very rundown.'

His gaze moved past hers to take in the house. 'It looks fine to me.' His eyes met hers again. 'I'm prepared to pay my way. I can even help you with some jobs about the place in my spare time. I'm good with my hands.'

I just bet you are, Gemma thought with another furtive glance at his broad spanned hands. 'Um…well, then, I guess you can stay.' Not that I have much choice, she thought. She decided she was going to give Ron Curtis a piece of her mind next time she called in at the pub, and a very big piece at that.

She let the post go and brushed her damp palms down the sides of her faded trackpants. 'It's probably not what you're used to. I mean, it's a basic bed and breakfast and I can do an evening meal when I'm not out on a call or out on the plane with the Flying Doctor service.'

'You sound like you work long hours, Dr Kendall,' he said.

'I do, but, then, that's the Outback for you,' she said. 'I'm the only doctor this side of Minnigarra and the one there is semi-retired. The nearest hospital is Roma. All the serious stuff gets sent to Brisbane.'

'Do you have anyone else staying with you at present?' he asked.

'Er—no,' she said, suddenly wishing she had a

house full of guests to dilute his disturbingly masculine presence.

He stepped back down from the veranda. 'I'll get my things from the car,' he said.

Gemma pushed her hand through her still-damp hair. Good grief, why hadn't she blown it dry and done her eyebrows while she'd had the chance? Had she even put on deodorant? And when was the last time she had shaved her legs, for pity's sake? That was the trouble with being single for so long. You stopped making the effort because there was no one worth making the effort for.

She watched as Marc Di Angelo popped the boot of his car, his biceps bulging as he lifted out a gym bag, a smaller suitcase and a laptop. He hooked one of his fingers through the neck loop on a leather jacket and draped it over his shoulder as he came back to the steps leading to the house.

She stepped aside to make room for him as he came up the stairs of the veranda. 'Welcome to Huntingdon Lodge, Sergeant Di Angelo,' she said, hoping Gladys wasn't turning in her grave at the insincerity in her tone.

Marc Di Angelo's dark brown eyes glinted with something indefinable. 'Thank you, Dr Kendall. I am looking forward to seeing what fringe benefits the bush has to offer.'

CHAPTER TWO

GEMMA showed him into one of the guest rooms, the one that was the most presentable and coincidentally the one furthest away from her room. His little comment about fringe benefits had made her awareness of him heighten. She felt the magnetic pull of his presence, the allure of his aloof, unknowable personality—a heady mix for a girl who hadn't had a date in close to four years.

She pointed out the main bathroom further along the hall on the second storey. 'Although we had fairly decent rain a few months ago, it's best to keep showers short,' she said. 'You never know out here when the next rain is going to fall. The meteorologists don't always get it right.'

'I am well used to water restrictions,' he said. 'Although I've lived in Brisbane for the last couple of years, I originally came from Melbourne.'

'Oh, really?' she said. 'What part did you come from?'

'I grew up in the outer suburbs,' he said. 'My parents ran a restaurant in Dandenong.'

'Were you stationed in the suburbs?' she asked.

'No, I was based in the city,' he said. 'Homicide.'

There was something about the way he said that word that made Gemma's skin prickle. 'So, what brought you up to Brisbane?' she asked.

'I wanted a change of scene. A new challenge. A new climate.'

'Yes, well, Brisbane and Queensland in general will certainly give you that, compared to Melbourne,' she said.

'Do you miss your family, living so far away?' he asked.

Gemma thought of her father with his new wife and young family. He had remarried within four months of her mother's death in an accident. She still hadn't quite forgiven him for it. Her comfortable childhood home had been completely renovated and extended into an unrecognisable showpiece that had been featured in several home magazines. It was as if her stepmother had wanted every trace of Gemma's mother eradicated. Gemma's childhood bedroom had been knocked down to make room for a third bathroom no one ever used. 'No, not really,' she said. 'We pretty much live our own lives. If you'll excuse me, I'll make a start on dinner while you settle in. There are fresh towels in the bathroom if you'd like to freshen up before we eat.'

Gemma darted back to her bedroom and changed into jeans and a cotton shirt, this time with a push-up bra underneath. She ran a brush through her hair before pulling it back into a ponytail rather than leaving it hanging limply around her shoulders. She put on some deodorant and some perfume. She plucked out a few strays from her eyebrows and then gave her lips a quick swipe with some lip gloss. She could hear the shower going in the guest bathroom and tried not to imagine Marc Di Angelo standing naked under the spray of water.

She gave herself a vigorous mental shake. He might be gorgeous-looking but he was a cop. Most cops had control and power issues as far as she was concerned. Sure, they did a good job and there was certainly honour in protecting others at the risk of your own life, but she was not going to even think about getting involved in any way with a guy from the force. Besides, he was there as a professional and so was she. How would she appear to the locals if she launched into a red-hot affair with the first man who came striding into town? Desperate and dateless, that's how. She was already tired of the broad hints about her approaching thirtieth birthday and her single status. It seemed every patient thought it their mission to get her hitched before she hit the big three-oh. So far the candidates presented to her had done nothing for her. But Sergeant Marc Di Angelo was something else again, even if he was too attractive, too arrogant and too controlling for her liking.

She was in the kitchen, watching over the chicken pilaf she was cooking, when Marc Di Angelo came in. He had changed out of his shirt and was now wearing his blue denim jeans with a black T-shirt that clung to his perfectly formed biceps and pectoral muscles like a second skin. His abdomen was so flat she instantly sucked in hers. 'Dinner's not quite ready,' she said.

'Would you like a drink? I have wine, beer or soft drink and fruit juice.'

'What are you having?' he asked.

She gave the pilaf a good grind of black pepper. 'I had a mineral water just before you arrived,' she said. 'I was thinking about having a glass of wine.'

'Are you on call?'

Gemma met his gaze as she put the pepper grinder down on the bench. 'I am always on call. That's the way it is out here. I am the only doctor in a radius of about two hundred kilometres.'

'Must be tough, not being able to let your hair down occasionally,' he said.

She shifted her gaze from the piercing intensity of his. 'I'm not much of a party girl in any case,' she said. 'I've seen the damage binge drinking does to young people. Lives can be changed in an instant and they can't always be changed back.'

'We see a lot of that in the city,' he said. 'I'm not a big drinker but I will join in you a single glass of wine.'

She chanced another glance at him. 'So you're not currently on duty, Sergeant?'

He gave her a quick movement of his lips that again was not quite a smile. 'Not at the moment. I came a week early just to get a feel for the place.'

'First time in the bush?' she asked.

His dark eyes glinted. 'Does it show?'

'A bit,' she said. 'But, then, I can't talk. It took me weeks to get used to everything. Time is slower out here. No one rushes unless they have to. It was frustrating at first but after a while you get used to it. Would you prefer red or white wine?'

'Red if you have it, but white is fine if not.'

'I'll…er…get some from the cellar,' she said, putting her wooden spoon down with a little thud.

'You have a cellar?'

'It's not mine—I mean, I didn't have it put in or anything,' Gemma explained. 'It's been here since the house was first built. In a climate as hot as this, it's too warm upstairs to keep good wines.'

'Mind if I come with you?' he asked.

Gemma would have refused his offer, except she absolutely loathed going down to the cellar. Gladys had always gone down there in the past, and then, when she had not been well enough to do so, Rob Foster, the handyman-cum-gardener, had always brought wine up for Gemma on the rare occasions she'd wanted it. The dark dank atmosphere of the cellar made her flesh crawl. It hadn't helped that on the first and only occasion she had gone down there alone a mouse had scuttled across the earthen floor right in front of her feet.

'Sure, why not?' she said, carefully disguising her relief. 'I might need your help in any case to lift up the trapdoor. It's over here at the back of the kitchen.'

Sergeant Di Angelo took over the opening of the trapdoor, lifting it as if it was a sheet of cardboard instead of solid timber with iron hinges. Gemma found the light switch and then she hesitated.

'Is something wrong?' he asked after a moment.

'Um—no,' she said, taking a deep breath and fixing her gaze on the sandstone steps.

'I'm happy to go first,' he offered. 'There might be spiders down there.'

Gemma felt her pride take a dive. 'Actually, that would be great,' she said with a tremulous smile. 'I'm not all that fond of spiders.'

She stood at the top of the steps as he went down and then once he'd given the all-clear she followed, but she stayed on the last step. 'I think the red stuff is over here,' she said, pointing vaguely to the left-hand side of the cellar.

Marc Di Angelo looked at her. 'Are you claustrophobic?'

Gemma rubbed her upper arms with her crossed-over hands. 'A bit, I guess.'

'You go back up,' he said. 'I'll get the bottle of wine. Is there any one in particular I should or shouldn't take?'

'No, just whatever,' she said, scooting back up the steps and hovering at the top. 'I don't think there's any Grange Hermitage or Hill of Grace down there.'

'You never know,' he said dryly, and bent at the waist to check out the labels as he pulled out various bottles.

Gemma couldn't stop looking at the way his jeans hugged his taut behind, or the way the muscles of his arms were so well formed. She was used to seeing well-used muscles out here in the Outback. The men were all toned from hard work on the land, but something about Marc Di Angelo's body made her feminine senses switch into overload. He was so damned attractive. Those eyes of his, so dark, like rich chocolate, and those lips of his, so sensual, and that strong, uncompromising jaw that gave him that don't-mess-with-me air.

Her insides did a funny little dance as he came back up the steps, carrying a bottle of wine. 'Here you go,' he said, handing her the bottle. 'I'll put the trapdoor back down.'

She watched as he closed the trapdoor, again lifting it as if it was a diet wafer before shooting home the bolt. 'So,' she said with an overly bright smile as she clutched the wine against her middle, 'no spiders?'

'None that I could see,' he said, dusting his hands off on his thighs.

She bit her lip. 'Um—you've got dust on your forehead.'

He wiped the back of his hand across his forehead. 'Gone?'

She shook her head. 'No, it's still there.' She balanced the wine with one hand as she pointed with the other to just above his left eyebrow. 'There.'

He gave his face another wipe but he somehow still missed the mark. 'All gone?'

Gemma felt his eyes lock on hers. The space between them was suddenly no space at all. He was standing so close she could see the darker circle of his black pupils in those incredibly brown eyes. She could even see the pinpoints of stubble on his jaw, the way it outlined every masculine contour of his face—his forceful chin, his firm upper lip, his fuller lower lip and the slopes and indentation of his lean cheeks. She could smell his cleanly showered smell. She could smell man and citrus rolled into one, fresh and sharp and dangerously tempting. Her breath hitched to a halt in her chest. Her mouth went dry. Her heart started to hammer and her legs felt strangely unsupportive.

'Here,' he said, and handed her a clean and folded handkerchief from his pocket. 'You do it.'

Gemma swallowed as her fingers curled around the fabric. Still clutching the wine to her chest, she lifted her other hand and wiped at the smear of dust on his forehead. Touching him, even through fabric, was like touching a live wire. She felt the kickback right up her arm. He must have felt something too for she saw his nostrils flare like those of a stallion and her heart gave another little stumble. 'I—I think that's it,' she said, in a voice that sounded like she was about fifteen years old.

'Thanks,' he said, stuffing the handkerchief into his back pocket.

Why doesn't he move? Gemma thought. She had nowhere to go; she was practically up against the wall in any case.

'Is there anything I can do to help with dinner?' he asked.

She suddenly remembered the simmering pilaf she had left unattended. 'Oh, my gosh,' she said, and thrust the wine at him. 'You open this while I check on the chicken. There's a corkscrew in the second drawer.'

'This one's a screw top,' Marc said.

'Oh, right.' She gave him a flustered sort of look as she lifted the lid on the dish she was making.

The smell of chicken and rice and Moroccan spices filled the air and Marc felt his stomach rumble in anticipation. The salad sandwich and instant coffee he had picked up at a roadhouse three hundred kilometres out of Jingilly Creek seemed like a long time ago.

But then his whole life seemed a long time ago.

That's how he saw things now: before and after. He was stuck in the after and there was no way he could replay his decisions and stay in the before, even though everything in him wished he could. A stint in the country was supposed to reset his focus. Get him back on track. Make him feel the buzz he'd once felt when going to work.

Make him forget.

The trouble was he didn't want to forget. The continuing nightmares about Simon bleeding to death in front of him were his punishment and he took it like a man. Simon's wife Julie's devastated face was another main feature during his dark, sleepless nights. And then there was his godson Sam, little innocent Sam who still didn't quite grasp that his father was never coming home. Marc dreaded the day when Sam would find out what had happened the day his father had died. How would the boy look on him then?

Forgetting was not his goal and neither was forgiving himself. That just wasn't going to happen in this lifetime. But distracting himself was something he needed to do. And this place looked about as far away as any place could be from his previous life as a city cop.

As soon as he had driven into this Outback town he had felt as if he had been in a time warp. The place looked like something out of an old movie, with its general store with its tall jars of old-fashioned sweets in the windows and its faded ice-cream cone advertisements on the walls outside. The one and only service station had a similar appearance, although its worn sign was well out of date with its petrol prices. He knew exactly why there had been a sudden shortage of rooms. Places as small as this soon got talking. A hot-shot sergeant from the city was not a welcome guest in a local watering-hole— bad for business. Everyone would think they would be nabbed for drink-driving or causing a disturbance or affray. No wonder Ron Curtis had sent him straight out to Gemma Kendall.

Not that she was all that welcoming either. She had grudgingly let him stay but it was pretty clear she was uneasy about it. Her recent inheritance had had his alarm bells ringing as soon as he had heard about it via the woman at the general store when he'd enquired about local accommodation options. It all seemed above board. No one in town suspected anything untoward, but Marc hadn't been a cop for thirteen years without having seen just about everything there was to see in terms of human greed.

Gemma Kendall was a cute little blonde who had supposedly come out here to do her bit for the bush, but she had just collected a windfall that by anyone's standards was a little unusual. Sure, this place was as she had said, a little rundown, but with a coat or two of paint and a few quick repairs it would fetch a fine price on the currently overblown property market. How had she done it? How had she got an old lady to rewrite her will in the last days of her life, leaving everything to her? Gemma Kendall was one smart cookie, that was for sure. Her innocent façade was convincing, a little too convincing, he thought as he watched her stir her delicious-smelling dish.

'So, what do you do out here in your spare time?' he asked after he had poured them both a glass of rich red wine.

She took a tentative sip before answering. 'I haven't had much spare time until recently,' she said. 'I'm usually pretty busy with the clinic and station visits, but then Gladys needed me almost full time by the end. Narelle—that's the community nurse-cum receptionist you met this afternoon at the clinic—helped when she could. She's a widow with two kids. Her husband died four years ago. She juggles their property and her part-time work with me. Her mother helps but it's not easy for her.'

Marc took a small sip of the wine, which was surprisingly good. 'What happened to her husband?'

'Car accident,' she said, adjusting the heat setting on the cooker. 'He rolled his ute out on a back road. There was no doctor here at that point. He might have lived if there had been.'

'I suppose that's the problem with outlying areas,' he said. 'Time and distance are always against you.'

'Yes, that's true,' she said as she set out two plates and cutlery on the large kitchen table. 'We had another accident earlier today. A local farmer, Nick Goglin, came off his all-terrain bike. He's in a coma with head and probable spinal injuries. His wife and kids will be devastated if he doesn't make it. There's no way Meg will be able to run that cattle property on her own.'

'It's certainly a tough life out here,' Marc said, 'which makes me wonder why you've stuck it out for so long.'

Her grey-blue eyes met his across the table. 'Three years isn't all that long, Sergeant.'

He gave an assenting gesture with his mouth. 'Maybe not.' He picked up his fork once she had done the same. 'This smells great. Do you enjoy cooking?'

'Very much,' she said. 'What about you? Did your parents insist you work in the family's restaurant from a young age?'

Marc picked up his wine and gave it a swirl in the glass. 'I spent a lot of time learning the ropes. There was certainly some expectation I would take on the business but my heart wasn't in it. My younger sister and her husband run the restaurant now.'

'Your parents are retired?' she asked.

'Yes, they travel a lot now,' he said. 'I have another sister who lives in Sicily. She's married with a couple of kids. My parents love spending time over there with them.'

She leaned her elbows on the table as she cradled her wine in both hands. 'So, what about you, Sergeant?' she asked. 'Is there a Mrs Di Angelo or Mrs Di Angelo-to-be back in Brisbane, waiting for you to come home?'

Marc held her gaze for a fraction longer than necessary. 'No rings.' He held up his left hand. 'No wife, no fiancée, no current girlfriend.'

Her grey-blue eyes rounded slightly. 'You are either very hard to please or hell to be around.'

His mouth twisted wryly because both were true to some degree. Even his sisters had told him bluntly he wasn't a nice person to be around any more. As to dating…well, he could certainly do with the sex, but he could no longer handle the expectation of commitment that so often went with it. He was a drifter, not a stayer. If you stayed too long, you got emotionally involved and that was the last thing he wanted. Not professionally and certainly not personally. 'What about you?' he asked. 'Is there a man in your life at present?'

She put her wineglass down, a delicate shade of pink tingeing her cheeks. 'Not currently,' she said.

'Too hard to please or too hard to be around?' he asked, his eyes gleaming.

'Too far away,' she said with a rueful expression. 'This place doesn't offer the greatest dating opportunities. The men out here tend to marry young, while most women my age have three or four kids by now. I'm not interested in being involved with someone just for the sake of it. Anyone can do that. I want more for my life. I want to feel connected intellectually as well as physically and emotionally.'

Marc leant back in his chair. 'So you're a romantic, Dr Kendall?'

Her eyes challenged his. 'Is that a crime?' she asked.

He leaned forward and picked up his wineglass again, frowning as he looked at the red liquid. 'No, of course not,' he said. 'It's just that sort of package doesn't come around all that often.' He sat back and met her eyes. 'You might be waiting for a long time for someone to come along who ticks all those boxes for you.'

'Better to have five years with the right one than twenty-five with the wrong one,' she said.

Marc felt a hammer blow of guilt hit him in the chest. Simon and Julie had been married five years. He had been their best man. He remembered the day so clearly. He had forgotten the rings and had had to get a colleague to bring them to the church in a squad car. Everyone had laughed, thinking it had been a set-up. So many memories. So many images of happy times he had shared with them both. Marc still remembered the day Simon told him he was going to be a father. He had been so proud and excited about building a family with Julie. There had been photos of Sam and Julie plastered all over Simon's desk at the station. Their anniversary had been the week before Simon had been killed. Marc had taken all of that away from them: their future; their hopes and dreams; their happiness.

The silence was measured by the sound of the large wall clock ticking near the pantry.

'What about you, Sergeant?' Gemma asked. 'Do you want to settle down one day?'

His eyes met hers but this time it looked like a light had gone off inside, leaving them like an empty, dark room. 'I am Australian born but, as you have probably guessed, I have a strong Italian background. Family is supposed to be important to us Italians, but I must be an aberration as I don't see myself settling down.'

Gemma pursed her lips. 'So you're a bit of a playboy, then, are you?'

He gave her that sexy not-quite-a-smile again, the

glinting light back on in his eyes. 'I always make an effort to leave no casualties in the love stakes.'

'Have you ever been in love?' Oh, God, why did I just ask that? Gemma thought with a cringe of embarrassment. She took a quick sip of wine so she could bury her head in the glass.

'No, not unless you count the time I fell for my kindergarten teacher, Miss Moffat,' he said. 'I didn't miss a single day of my first year at school. My mother was very disappointed it didn't last. I had to be bribed to go most days, right up until I left high school.'

'School is often an issue for boys,' Gemma said. 'A lot of the boys out here drop out. It's sad to see the waste of potential.'

'What sort of social problems do you have out here?' Marc asked.

Gemma toyed with the last of her food, pushing it around with her fork as she thought of the heartbreaking situations she had handled in the short time she had been in town. 'The usual stuff,' she said, 'drinking and violence and vandalism. It's a real problem with the indigenous youth. They're caught between two worlds. They don't really fit in either one at times. Some make it, like Ray Grant, for instance, but others don't. But it's much the same for the whites. The youth around here are bored as there is simply nothing for them to do if they don't work on the land. I try not to be overwhelmed by it but sometimes it's hard not to get involved. Clinical distance works a lot better in the city when you don't see past the name on the patient information sheet. Out here you know the patient personally and their parents, and the brothers and sisters. They're not just patients. Most of them become your friends.'

'You sound like you really care about your patients.'

'I do,' she said. 'Being a doctor in a small community is a huge responsibility. People depend on you in so many ways. But that's what I like about the job. You get to make a difference now and again. It's very rewarding when that happens.'

Gemma realised she had poured her heart out much more than she would normally do to a person she had only met just hours ago. It made her feel a little uncomfortable. He had much more information on her than she had on him. 'What do you love most about being a cop?' she asked.

'The long hours, the crappy pay, the criminals and the cold coffee,' he said.

She gave him a droll look. 'Very funny.'

His mouth tilted slightly. 'Did I mention the endless paperwork?'

'You didn't need to,' she said. 'It's the same in my profession.'

He put his knife and fork together on the plate in the correct I-am-finished position. 'Serving the public in law enforcement is always a challenge,' he said, his gaze momentarily focused on the wine in his glass. The light went off again. A shadow drifted over his expression, like a cloud over the face of the moon, but then he blinked and the shadow disappeared as he picked up his glass to add, 'You can't fix everything that needs to be fixed. You can't solve every case that needs to be solved.'

Gemma fiddled with the stem of her wineglass. 'So why Jingilly Creek?' she asked. 'Why not some resort town on the coast or somewhere more densely populated?'

His chocolate-brown eyes met hers, but apart from a tiny tensing movement in his jaw his expression remained unreadable. 'I felt like I needed a complete change,' he said. 'It seemed as good a place as any.'

'Did you throw a dart at a map?' she asked.

That brought a flicker of a smile to his mouth, softening his features for a moment. 'Just about.'

Gemma wondered if there was much more to his move out here than he was letting on. He had an air of mystery about him; an aloofness she suspected went much further than him simply being a cop. 'So you'll be the one in charge now at the station?' she asked.

'Yes,' he said. 'Constable Grant can now resume his regular duties.'

Gemma wondered how the new broom was going to fit in the broom cupboard down at the small station. In remote areas more junior officers often had to take on more senior positions due to the chronic shortage of staff. There would most certainly be an adjustment period. Jack Chugg had been strict but fair with the locals before he'd retired. Ray Grant had a much more laid-back approach, especially when dealing with other local indigenous people with whom he had blood ties. It would be interesting to see if Marc Di Angelo adopted the same live-and-let-live approach that Ray did. 'You might have to feel your way a bit,' she said. 'Ray's been used to handling things his way.'

'I'm here to do a job,' Marc said. 'Not win a popularity contest.'

Gemma studied his expression for a moment. 'It would be nice to do both, though, don't you think?'

He gave her a cynical look as he leaned back in his chair. 'Maybe I should take some lessons from you, Dr Kendall, on how to charm the locals,' he said. 'Who knows what bonuses might be out here for me to collect?'

Gemma set her mouth and began to rise to gather up their plates. Marc's hand came down over her wrist and held it to the table. The smile fell away from her mouth, her heart picking up its pace until she could hear it instead of the ticking clock. She felt the slow burn of his touch in his long strong fingers, so dark and masculine against the soft creamy texture of her skin.

'No,' he said. 'Let me clear away. You cooked. It's only fair that I get to do the dishes.'

She slipped her hand out from under his, her face so hot she felt like she had stuck it in the oven on full fan-forced heat. 'Th-thanks,' she said. 'I'll make some coffee. I don't have any dessert. I mean, nothing I've made especially. I have fruit and yogurt, if you'd like?'

'Coffee is fine,' he said.

Gemma let out the breath she was holding as she opened the fridge to get out the ground coffee. The kitchen suddenly seemed far too small with Marc Di Angelo standing at the sink with his wrists submerged in hot, soapy water.

The domestic scene made her feel as if she had

stepped over a boundary way too soon. It was intimate and yet he was a perfect stranger. She was sharing this big old house with a man she didn't know and yet for some reason she didn't feel frightened, or at least not in a physically threatened sense. She did feel on edge but that had more to do with her reaction to him: his touch, for instance. What was that all about? Why had her heart started to race like a greyhound when his fingers had pressed down over her wrist? His dark brown gaze had locked her just as firmly in place, those bottomless eyes that saw so much and gave away so little.

She made a business of preparing the coffee when in reality she would normally had settled for a teaspoon of instant. But Italians loved their coffee, right? She breathed in the fragrant aroma as the percolator did its job, her mind wandering as she thought about how long the sexy sergeant would be in town.

In her house.

Sharing the kitchen, the living spaces, the cutlery and crockery, his lips resting on the rim of the same cup she might have used the day before, his lips closing over a fork she had put in her mouth previously. It had never felt like this when Gladys had had guests staying before. The middle-aged couple from Toowoomba, for instance. They had stayed for two weeks and not once had Gemma thought about the towels that had wrapped around their bodies in the bathroom, or the water that had cascaded over them in the shower, or the sheets that had covered them while they'd slept.

The mere thought of Marc Di Angelo in the shower had sent her pulses soaring and this was only the first day. What would it be like in the morning? Would she hear him shaving, or perhaps singing or humming to himself, or was he one of those grumpy types who didn't properly wake up until ten in the morning or until a double shot of caffeine hit his system?

'Where do you want these put?' Marc asked, jolting her out of her reverie.

'Oh…' Gemma said, flustered again and unable to disguise it in time. 'Um…the cutlery goes in that top drawer over there and those plates in the cupboard above.'

She watched as he reached up and stacked the plates, his arms so tanned, so strong, so arrantly male. She swallowed when he turned his head and locked gazes with her. 'Is something wrong?' he asked with a quizzical look.

She shook her head, running her tongue out over her lips. 'Um, no, not at all,' she said. 'I was just thinking how I have to stand on tiptoe to get into that cupboard.'

His hand closed the cupboard while his gaze remained centred on hers. 'You seem a little uptight, Dr Kendall.'

'That's ridiculous,' she said, folding her arms across her middle but just as quickly unfolding them as she realised how her body language was contradicting her denial. 'Why would I be uptight? This is a guest house. You are a guest.'

'Maybe you should call me Marc as we're going to be living together,' he said.

Gemma felt her cheeks heat up again. Did he have

to make it sound so intimate? Had he done that deliberately, knowing it would unsettle her? It worried her that he was seeing so much more than she wanted him to see. Those eyes of his were so penetrating and dark, his expression so level and composed, while she was sure she was giving off all sorts of clues to her discomfiture. 'Marc, then,' she said, forcing a stiff smile to her lips.

'Am I your first house guest since you inherited the property?' he asked leaning his hip against the counter.

Gemma reached for the coffee cups, embarrassed at how she betrayed herself yet again by allowing them to rattle against each other as she put them on the bench. 'Yes, the first since Gladys died, that is. We had a run of guests a few weeks before she went downhill. The rains we had in the spring brought a few extra tourists our way to see the wildflowers.'

'Do you mind if I call you Gemma?'

Hearing her name on his lips sent a shower of sparks down her spine. It was like a rolling runaway firecracker bumping against each and every vertebra. 'Um...of course not,' she said. 'No one stands on ceremony in Jingilly Creek.' She picked up the tray she had put the coffee and cups on. 'Would you like to have this outside on the veranda? It's probably nice and cool out there now, or at least cooler than inside.'

'Sure, sounds good,' he said, and took the tray from her.

Gemma stepped back, her fingers burning where his had brushed against hers in the handover. She told herself to get a grip, but it didn't really work. Her eyes kept going to the taut shape of his buttocks as if drawn by a magnet as he walked out to the veranda.

He set the tray down on the table between the two wrought-iron chairs, politely waiting until she sat down before he did so. The sound of Flossie's toenails clip-clipping along the floorboards as she came out to join them was the only sound in the still night air.

The night sky was dark as ink, thousands of stars peeping through the velvet-blanket canopy. An owl hooted from one of the sheds and a vixen gave her distinct bark in the distance as she signalled for a mate. Flossie pricked up her ears but then gave a long drawn-out too-tired-for-all-that-now sigh, and rested her greying head back down on her paws.

Gemma shifted forward on her chair. 'How do you have your coffee?' she asked.

'Just black, thanks.'

She poured it for him and handed it over with a wry smile. 'Sorry I haven't got any doughnuts.'

The light coming from inside the house was soft but it was enough to see the glint of amusement reflected in his gaze. 'Not all cops live on coffee and doughnuts,' he said.

She sat back in her chair, carefully balancing her coffee cup in her hands. 'It's a tough job,' she said after taking a sip. 'It must be awfully stressful and heart wrenching at times.'

He paused before he spoke, and again she saw that fleeting shadow pass across his gaze before it shifted from hers. 'Yes, it is but no one forced me to do it.

I chose it. And I will stick with it unless it becomes obvious there is nothing left for me to achieve.'

Gemma gave her coffee an unnecessary stir. His statement seemed to be underlined with implacability. There was a steely determination in his character she found both attractive and a little unnerving. She couldn't think of a single person she had met before who was quite so determined, quite so focused and quite so disturbingly, dangerously attractive. She could imagine him working on a case, uncovering information that others would surely miss. His sharp intellect and his ability to read people and situations would make him a formidable opponent for any criminal deluded enough to think they could outsmart him.

The owl hooted again, the swish of its wings as it flew past the veranda on its way to the shearing shed sounding exaggerated in the stillness of the night.

'This seems a rather quiet appointment for someone who has worked in a busy city homicide department,' Gemma said. 'We haven't had any murders out here for decades.'

He took another leisurely sip of his coffee before he spoke. 'I am sure I'll find plenty to do to pass the time.'

The sound of the phone ringing indoors brought Gemma to her feet. 'Excuse me,' she said. 'I'd better get that. I'm waiting for news of Nick Goglin's progress.'

Marc put his cup down, stood up and walked to the edge of the veranda. Leaning on the railing, he looked up at the twinkling stars of the Milky Way. At the funeral he had heard one of Simon's relatives tell his little boy Sam that his daddy would always be watching out for him up there in the night sky, no matter where he went. 'Which one are you, mate?' Marc asked, but of course there was no answer.

CHAPTER THREE

'GEMMA.' One of the volunteer ambulance officers, Malcolm Gard, was on the other end of the line. 'We've just got news of a roll-over out on the Bracken Hill Road. A passing motorist called it in. We're on our way now but it might be best if you meet us out there. It sounds bad.'

'I'm on my way,' she said, and hung up the phone.

Marc came in from the veranda with his mobile phone up to his ear. 'Right, I'll go with Dr Kendall,' he said, and hung up.

Gemma snatched up her doctor's bag and mobile phone, which she had been recharging on the kitchen bench. 'Was that Ray?' she asked.

'Yes, he'll meet us out there,' he said. 'Would you like me to drive?'

'No, I'd better drive. I know the road better than you do,' she said. 'Flossie, come in, girl.'

The dog obediently came in and settled on the doggy bed near the back door, next to her bowl of water.

Gemma didn't like admitting it but it was rather re-assuring having someone with her on the journey out to Bracken Hill Road. The road was unsealed and interspersed with potholes and, of course, out here there were no streetlights. Although the night was clear, the bush seemed dark and threatening as it loomed either side of the winding road. The thought of breaking down out here, even with a mobile phone with her for back-up, was a little frightening. She didn't feel quite so unsafe with Marc Di Angelo on board, although he threatened her in other ways. She was acutely conscious of him sitting in the passenger seat, his long legs taking up far more space than any other passenger she had carried before. He'd had to put the seat back to its furthest position as soon as he'd got into the car. She could smell his aftershave now he was a little closer to her than when they had been sitting on the veranda. The lemon-based scent teased her nostrils, making her think of how the rest of his body would smell even closer up.

'You drive well, considering,' Marc said.

'Considering what?' Gemma asked, instantly bristling. 'That I'm a woman?'

'No,' he said. 'Considering this road is rough and there are kangaroos and wombats, possums, dingoes and foxes in that bush.'

'I know they are there,' she said. 'I've seen three kangaroos so far.'

'Only three?' he said. 'I counted four.'

Gemma didn't chance a glance at him as that particular stretch of road took every bit of concentration she possessed. As she rounded the next bend she could see the lights of a car turned upside down against a tree about half a kilometre ahead. Another car was pulled over to the other side of the road. The driver, she assumed, was the person who had reported the accident.

'How far away is the ambulance?' Marc asked, checking over his shoulder.

Gemma glanced in the rear-view mirror and breathed out a sigh of relief when she saw the glow of lights coming around one of the bends in the distance. 'Not far now,' she said. 'Malcolm's not the fastest driver out here. He's one of the older volunteers. He doesn't take too many risks.'

The person who had called for help was a local, Bill Vernon. He was visibly shaken by coming across the accident and rushed over as soon as Gemma and Marc got out of the car. 'I found her like that,' he said, pointing to a girl lying on the gravel roadside. 'I reckon she's hit a roo and rolled the car. She can't have been wearing a seat belt.'

'Thanks for staying with her, Bill,' Gemma said, as she set to work assessing the patient. 'Do you know who it is?'

'Nuh, never seen her before,' he said. 'She's only young.'

She was at that, Gemma found out as she examined the girl. Aged about nineteen or twenty, she was unresponsive so Gemma put on a hard collar, privately relieved that Bill Vernon hadn't moved the girl in case she had neck or spinal fractures. The ambulance had arrived so within a few minutes Gemma had oxygen running and with assistance from Marc and Malcolm and the other volunteer, Dave, who was even older than

Malcolm, they got the girl on to a spinal board, and Gemma established IV access.

While the ambulance drove back to town, Gemma rode in the back and worked on resuscitating the patient with Dave's help. Ray Grant had turned up just as they had been leaving the accident site. He stayed behind to conduct the accident investigation with two officers on their way from Minnigarra, who Marc had called as back-up. Marc had offered to drive Gemma's car back to the clinic and was leading the way.

The patient didn't respond to voice stimulus and Gemma could see she had right facial abrasions and a scalp haematoma. There was blood at the girl's mouth and her breaths were shallow and short at fifty per minute.

Gemma got Dave to take the girl's pulse and BP and put on the pulse oximeter and ECG dots while she redid the primary survey. The patient was clearly developing an obstructed airway so Gemma got Malcolm to stop the ambulance, and with Dave stabilising the patient's neck she loosened the cervical collar and intubated the patient. There was no ventilator in the ambulance, so Gemma had Dave hand-ventilate the patient while she pushed the IV fluids.

Once the patient was transferred into the clinic treatment room, with Marc assisting the older men, Gemma was better able to assess the level of injury. There had been a progressive drop in blood pressure after the patient had been hand-ventilated, but there was no apparent blood loss to account for it. She cut off the patient's T-shirt and bra to reveal an extensive left chest abrasion and haematoma. There was bony and subcutaneous crepitus, indicating a flail segment. When she listened to the chest with a stethoscope, there was no air entry on the left, which had become hyper-resonant to percussion, the trachea was deviated to the right and the neck veins distended, indicating she had developed a left tension pneumothorax. Gemma had deliberately done EMST, or ATLS as it was better known abroad, before she'd come out into the country—unrecognised and untreated tension pneumothorax was one of the killers in the 'golden hour' after severe trauma.

Gemma inserted a large-bore cannula into the front of the left chest and air hissed out, with rapid improvement in blood pressure and ease of ventilation.

She got Dave to assist her as she inserted a left chest drain to complete the immediate management of the chest injury, talking him through it as she knew he wasn't all that confident. It was at times like these that she thought of the well-equipped and super-trained paramedics she had met while working at a large city teaching hospital in Melbourne. They were so adept at handling just about any situation that by the time the patient got to the resus bay at the hospital they were stabilised and ready for definitive care.

Out here, with just volunteers and minimum equipment, Gemma sometimes felt as if she was all alone in the Outback. Patients lived or died according to her expertise and calm in the face of panic-ridden situations, even though at times she herself felt very much like panicking. This was nothing like playing doctors and nurses with friends in the back garden when she had been a kid. This was about real people's lives and real futures in her hands. People who had loved ones, families who would be torn asunder by the loss of their son or daughter, husband or father, wife or mother. Gemma had felt it herself when her mother had been struck by a car while crossing the road. One minute your loved one was alive and breathing and the next they were dead. Gone for ever.

She caught Marc's dark eyes as she reached for more IV fluid to run in saline at full bore, and got ready to insert a second IV cannula. 'You were a great help out there,' she said. 'You've obviously worked in Traffic at some stage.'

'Yes,' he said. 'Seen a lot of things I wish I hadn't seen.'

'Yeah, I know that feeling,' she said as she glanced over at Dave. 'Pulse and BP, Dave?'

'Pulse one-thirty and BP ninety over sixty,' Dave informed her.

The patient began to respond to painful stimuli and Gemma's further examination revealed tenderness over the left upper abdomen.

'What do you think?' Marc asked.

'It's hard to say with any certainty but I think she might have a ruptured spleen,' Gemma answered. 'But we don't have any imaging facilities here.'

'So what happens now?' he asked.

'I'll do a secondary survey to exclude other major injuries,' Gemma said as she prepared to insert a nasogastric tube and urinary catheter. 'And then she will have to go to Roma. They've got a general surgeon there, and ultrasound—if she's got a ruptured spleen she'll bleed out without a laparotomy before they get anywhere near Brisbane. When they've stopped the bleeding, she'll go to Brisbane for neurosurgical assessment.'

Gemma had relayed the clinical details to Arthur Rogers, the general surgeon in Roma. Once the patient was back in the hard collar and supported by sandbags and a spinal board, Gemma supervised the return to the ambulance. However, Malcolm was complaining of tiredness and Dave too was dropping not-too-subtle hints about the trip to Roma.

'How about I drive the ambulance while one of you guys rides in the back with Dr Kendall?' Marc said. 'Constable Grant is still at the accident site with the Minnigarra guys.'

'It's all right,' Gemma assured the ambulance volunteers. 'He's the new sergeant. He knows how to drive.'

'Yeah, we heard about him from Ron Curtis,' Malcolm said, exchanging a quick look with Dave.

Gemma was soon in the back of the ambulance with the patient and Dave as back-up. Via the ambulance radio, she relayed a clinical update to the hospital at Roma. She was also able to give the girl's name so the family could be contacted as Marc had found her purse in the overturned car and got the information from her licence as well as her mobile phone. Gemma had been impressed by his calm, manner of working in the background. He had helped where he could, but he had also switched into cop mode, making sure the road was clear of debris and that everyone had put on their fluoro vests in case of another car coming around the bend without warning. He had also delegated responsibilities to Ray without taking over completely. And he was driving the ambulance with the sort of competence that was sadly lacking in the regular volunteers. The trip would normally take a couple of hours but after a quick peek at the highway sign they had just passed, Gemma thought they might take thirty if not forty-five minutes off that.

Once the patient was handed over at Roma, Dave expressed a desire to spend the night at his daughter's house. She only lived a few streets away from the town centre. Gemma was pretty sure it wasn't because he felt uncomfortable around Marc. She thought it had more to do with some sort of matchmaking attempt. The looks Malcolm and Dave had exchanged back at the clinic seemed to suggest something was cooking. She gave Dave a questioning look but he pointedly avoided her gaze. It was only as he got into his daughter's car once she had pulled up in front of the hospital that his expression became sheepish.

Marc turned to her with a twitch of his lips. 'Was it something I said?'

Gemma gave her eyes a little roll. 'I think it has more to do with me, actually.'

'Oh?'

'Yes,' she said, deciding it was better to have it all out in the open. 'Ever since I've been in Jingilly Creek the locals have taken it on themselves to try and find me a husband. It's apparently absolutely appalling to them that I am twenty-nine years old and still unattached.'

'So I am to be the current candidate, is that it?' he

asked with an amused look as he opened the ambulance door for her.

Gemma's gaze moved away from his as she got into the vehicle. She waited until he was back behind the wheel before she said, 'Look, if you just ignore it, they will soon get the message. It's embarrassing, I know, but they mean well.'

'I'm not the least bit embarrassed,' he said, pulling away from the hospital.

She swung her gaze to him. 'You're not?'

He gave a one-shoulder shrug. 'You're a dedicated doctor, a very skilled one, I might add— I've seen a few bumbling their way through accident scenes. And you can cook. Oh, and you're not all that bad in the looks department.'

Gemma arched her brows at him. 'Not all that bad? What is that supposed to mean?'

He gave her another twitch of his lips that was all she was going to get in terms of a smile. 'I think you know what I mean, Dr Kendall.'

Gemma sat back in the seat and mused over his comment. At the time her ex-fiancé's betrayal had hit her hard. And although she liked to think she had mostly put it behind her, the knockout punch to her confidence had left its mark. She still found it hard to find anything but fault with her looks. Like a lot of women, she had issues with her body. She would have liked to have been taller than five-six and she would have liked fuller breasts and a flatter stomach, but generally she was content to have a healthy body, which was more than a lot of people had, even at her age or younger. She had never forgotten a young patient of sixteen during her training who had been diagnosed with osteosarcoma. A keen athlete with her whole life ahead of her, Madison McDougal had died after extensive treatment, including the amputation of her leg. It had made Gemma thankful for her own health and strength, and whenever she felt herself preparing for a pity-party over her broken dreams she recalled that young girl's courage to regain perspective. She wasn't sure what to make of 'not all that bad in the looks department' but it was certainly gratifying to know Sergeant Di Angelo had taken a second look.

The trip back to Jingilly Creek was over before Gemma realised it. She felt the ambulance come to a halt outside the clinic and jolted upright. She blinked her sleepy eyes and sent Marc a rueful look. 'Sorry, I must have fallen asleep.'

'Just as well you weren't driving,' he said with a wry expression.

They drove back to Huntingdon Lodge in Gemma's car, and again she let him take control. She was much more tired than she had realised after treating the accident victim. The level of concentration and sense of responsibility had zapped her energy, especially on the back of Nick Goglin's accident earlier in the day.

It was now well after midnight and Flossie barely lifted her head off her paws when Gemma and Marc came in.

'Would you like a hot or cold drink or something?' Gemma asked, pushing back her hair, which had worked loose from her ponytail.

'No, I'm cool,' he said. 'You look exhausted. Is this a usual day for you out here?'

'No, thank God,' she said, reaching for a glass to have a drink of water. 'Mostly it's pretty quiet. The clinic days can be hectic, of course, but it's not usually as crazy as today has been.'

'What time do you head into town in the morning?' he asked.

'I have a clinic that starts at eight-thirty,' Gemma said. 'I have a couple of house calls in the afternoon—elderly patients who can't always make the trip to town.' She put her glass down on the draining-board. 'Please help yourself to cereal and toast and whatever in the morning if I'm not here. Everything is in the pantry over there or in the fridge. I'm sorry I can't offer the sort of service Gladys was renowned for. She would have cooked you a full breakfast.'

'You don't have to wait on me,' he said. 'I am quite capable of looking after myself.'

'Right, then,' she said, tucking another loose strand behind her ear. 'Well, goodnight. Oh, and thanks for your help tonight. It was much appreciated.'

'Glad to be of service,' he said.

There was a beat or two of absolute silence. Even the clock on the wall seemed to have stopped, as if the second hand had frozen.

Gemma dropped her gaze from the dark intensity of his and slipped out of the kitchen, her heart beating a little too fast and too jerkily as she made her way upstairs to her room.

* * *

The moon was behind a cloud when Gemma woke from a deep sleep. She usually had no trouble getting to sleep—it was staying asleep that was the issue. It had been worse since Gladys had died. The big old house seemed so empty, and the various creaks and groans of the timber floorboards or staircase had made her wish more than once or twice she had more than an elderly deaf and almost blind dog for company.

She lay on her side and looked out of the window, waiting for the cloud to pass over the face of the moon, her thoughts drifting to a few doors down the hall where Sergeant Marc Di Angelo was sleeping. She had given him the king-sized bedroom, figuring with his tall body he would need the extra length. She couldn't stop herself imagining him there, perhaps lying on his stomach, the sheets draped over his taut buttocks, or maybe he was a back sleeper, his arms flung out wide, his muscular chest rising and falling as he slept. She wondered if he slept naked. Her mind conjured up his tanned toned body in all its glory. She had seen her fair share of male bodies, in all shapes and sizes, but she had a feeling Sergeant Marc Di Angelo's body would be cut and carved to perfection.

She rolled on her back, taking one of her pillows with her and hugging it to her chest. She blew out a sigh of frustration. Why couldn't she just switch off her brain and go to sleep? It was always worse after a late-night emergency. She would ruminate over the whole scene, checking and double-checking she had performed the correct procedure or followed the right protocol. She thought of that girl's parents, how they would feel to be informed their daughter had been badly injured in a car crash. She could just imagine the worry they would feel, she had seen it so many times in ICU back in Melbourne: the haunted, haggard faces of loved ones who could only hope and pray for their child or relative to pull through.

Gemma turned back to look at the moon, which had now peeped out from behind the cloud. She closed her eyes and began to relax each of her muscles in turn as she had learnt years ago in a yoga class. Her toes, her ankles, her shins, her knees, her thighs—

She sat bolt upright in bed, her eyes wide open, her heart beating like frantic wings inside her chest. She listened as ice-cold fear dripped drop by drop down the entire length of her spine.

There was a faint scratching sound behind the wainscoting of her room. And then she heard a tiny squeak and then another.

She flung off the bedclothes and bolted out of the room, calling out for Flossie as she went. 'Flossie? Floss? Come here, girl.'

'Is something wrong?' Marc appeared from his room, a towel draped around his hips, one hand holding it in place.

Gemma pulled up short, her heart still drumming a tattoo behind her ribcage, but now it went up another notch. 'Th-there's a m-mouse in my room,' she stammered. 'Actually, I think there's probably hundreds in there, maybe even a plague of them. I heard them behind the wall. I have to get Flossie.'

Marc frowned as he tightened the towel about his

hips. 'I'm not sure poor old Flossie is going to be much help. Do you want me to have a look?'

'Oh, would you?' Gemma asked with wide, grateful eyes.

'Have you had a problem with mice before?' he asked as he led the way back to her room.

Gemma kept well back in case any of the little pesky rodents took it on themselves to head out into the hall. 'Gladys always dealt with it in the past,' she said, hovering in the doorway. 'But mostly when we had them they were downstairs in the kitchen or the laundry, but then Rob filled in the holes where they were getting through.'

'Rob?' Marc asked as he bent down to press his ear against the bedroom wall. 'Who is Rob?'

'Rob Foster. He's the local handyman,' she said. 'He's been doing work out here for Gladys for years.' She watched with bated breath as Marc listened intently. After a long pause she whispered, 'Can you hear anything?'

He let out a breath and rose to his full height. 'Not a thing,' he said. 'Do you think you might have been imagining it?'

Gemma felt her face heating because of what she had been imagining before she'd heard the squeaks. 'Of course I didn't imagine it,' she said with an affronted toss of her head.

'Maybe you should sleep in another room,' he suggested.

'Yes.' She rubbed her upper arms as if it was twenty below zero. 'I think I'll do that.'

His eyes meshed with hers, a stretch of silence pulsing like electricity along an invisible wire that seemed to be connecting her to him, pulling her inexorably closer and closer.

Gemma felt her belly turn over itself, a flicker of feminine awareness travelling downwards all the way to the apex of her thighs. In case he could see what effect he was having on her, she quickly lowered her eyes from the searing intensity of his to stare at the muscular perfection of his naked chest. He had a masculine covering of hair that went from a fan over his broad chest before it narrowed down his abdomen, ridged with muscle, disappearing below the towel he had slung around his lean hips. Her eyes widened a fraction and her throat threatened to close over. There was a hint of arousal behind the fabric of the towel and the tension in the air suddenly skyrocketed.

She slowly brought her gaze back up to his, something in his eyes reminding her that she was standing before him in a satin tank top and shorts pyjama set that was outlining every single contour of her body. 'Um…I'm sorry for disturbing you in the middle of the night,' she said, stepping away from the door to stand out in the hall.

He followed her, closing the door of her room behind him.

She licked her lips and rambled on, 'I suppose you think it's terribly cowardly of me to be so scared of a tiny mouse but I just can't help it. I can't stand them.'

His expression was back to deadpan. 'Maybe you need to think about getting yourself a cat.'

'Yes,' she said, biting at her lip. 'I guess I should.'

'I can set a trap for you if you'd like.'

'I can get Rob to do it,' Gemma said. 'You're not here for pest control.'

'Not those sorts of pests perhaps,' he said dryly.

She gave him a tight smile. 'Well, goodnight, then,' she said, stepping back and cannoning into the antique washstand. 'Ouch!'

Marc stepped towards her, his hand coming down over her arm, his long fingers wrapping around her wrist. 'Are you all right?' he asked. 'You hit that pretty hard.'

Gemma felt clumsy rather than bruised, although her rear end had taken rather a knock. But it was her face rather than her bottom that felt like fire, and her wrist where his fingers were holding her burned like it had been branded with his touch. 'I—I'm fine,' she said.

His eyes locked with hers in another moment of silence. She saw the flare of his pupils, she felt the subtle tightening of his hold, as if he sensed she was about to pull away. Her breathing rate escalated, her heart rate creeping up as the silence stretched and stretched and stretched.

She wondered if he was thinking about kissing her.

She was definitely thinking about kissing him.

She could just imagine how that firm mouth would feel pressed against hers.

Was he thinking about kissing her? It certainly looked like it. His dark chocolate eyes had flicked down to her mouth, lingering there for an infinitesimal pause. She saw the slight movement of his jaw as if he was preparing his mouth for the descent to hers. Her belly imploded with the thought of his tongue slipping between her lips, thrusting into her mouth to tease and tangle with hers.

'You really should watch where you are going,' Marc said, suddenly releasing her wrist. 'If something happens to you, what will happen to the community of Jingilly Creek? It could be weeks if not months before they find another doctor to replace you.'

Gemma blinked herself back into the moment. 'A bruised behind is not going to kill me. I've suffered much worse.' Like the bludgeoning of my ego, she thought. Why hadn't he kissed her? Had he downgraded her from 'not bad in the looks department' to 'quick, cover all the mirrors in case she cracks them'? She decided she had been in the bush for too long and for too long alone. She was fantasising about a man she had only just met. What on earth was wrong with her? Even when she'd lived in the city she had never been one to develop silly crushes or infatuations. Her one serious relationship had developed slowly over time. She had enjoyed having someone to go out with, although at times she had found the intimate side of things a bit of a chore. She hadn't felt much passion with Stuart, but she had always blamed it on the long hours she'd worked. It had been a vanilla relationship, as one of her friends had called it after the break-up in an effort to cheer her up, after finding Stuart was to become a parent with one of the oncology nurses.

Gemma couldn't imagine anything vanilla about Marc Di Angelo. Everything about him suggested there would be blistering passion and heat and fire in his arms. All she had felt so far had been his fingers—twice now—and her flesh was still tingling. When she looked into his eyes, as she was doing now, she felt as if he was heating her up from the inside out. She felt tremors of desire deep and low in her body, ripples of want that refused to go away. Her breasts felt sensitive under the satin covering of her shortie pyjamas, her nipples tight and erect. Her tongue slipped out to deposit a film of moisture over her lips and she held her breath as his black-ink eyes followed the movement.

'Things could get very complicated around here if I do what I think you want me to do right now,' he said in a deep, rough-sounding tone as his eyes locked back on hers.

Gemma put up her chin haughtily even though she knew her hot face gave her away. 'What makes you think I want you to kiss me?'

'You know you don't have to pretend there's a mouse in your room to get a man to sleep with you,' he said. 'There are other ways to get his attention.'

Her mouth dropped open as wide as her eyes and it took her a moment to get her voice to work. 'You think I would sleep with you when I've only just met you?'

His brushed the broad pad of his thumb across the fullness of her bottom lip, a little half-smile playing about his mouth. 'I'm damn sure you would. At the very least you'd like to kiss me right now.'

Gemma rubbed at her buzzing lip as if he had burnt it, which it felt like he had, but that was beside the point. 'Your confidence is misplaced, Sergeant Di Angelo,' she said in a prim manner. 'I have no intention of kissing you, either now or some time, any time, in the future.'

'Fine. You're not going to kiss me, I'm not going to kiss you.' He stood looking down at her for another pulsing beat of silence. 'Do you want to put money on that?' he said with a glint in those black-as-pitch eyes.

She put her hands on her hips, her chin still high. 'How much?'

'How much are you prepared to lose?' he asked.

Gemma was incensed at his arrogance, incensed and a little bit excited too, which was really rather disturbing when she came to think about it. 'I'm not going to lose, Sergeant Di Angelo,' she said with some misplaced arrogance of her own.

'We'll see about that,' he said, and before she could spin on her heel and make her outraged-female-stalking-off-with-her-chin-in-the-air exit, he had gone back to his room and closed the door.

CHAPTER FOUR

WHEN Gemma came down to the kitchen in the morning she saw through the window, as she filled the kettle, Marc's tall figure running up the driveway. He was dressed in T-shirt, shorts and trainers, each of his long strides kicking up a little puff of dust as he went. He looked magnificently fit. Lean and strong, and although as he drew closer to the house she could see he had worked up a sweat, he looked nothing like she would have done if she had tried to cover even a quarter of the distance he had run.

She drew in her stomach and sighed. She couldn't even remember the last time she had gone for a jog. It was usually too hot for her to do much more than walk, and because Flossie always wanted to come too, it wasn't exactly a pace that got her heart anywhere near the training zone. She decided it was time to get back into the pool, or at least in the river in the case of Jingilly Creek. Before Gladys had become so unwell Gemma had swum almost daily at a watering-hole she had found along the river running through Huntingdon. It was like an oasis in the middle of the bush, lush and green, the pendulous branches of the willow trees that fringed the curve of the river offering both privacy and shade. There wasn't time for her to swim now but she made a promise to herself to get back to it this afternoon once she got home.

Marc came in the back door, bringing with him the smell of the bush and vigorous exercise. He stopped to ruffle Flossie's ears before straightening to look at Gemma. 'Off to work?' he asked.

'Yes,' she said. 'I've left a key for you on the bench so you can come and go as you please. Flossie has a pet door but she only uses it if no one is here to let her in and out.'

'Fine. I'll be off once I've had a shower,' he said. 'I thought I would to go to Minnigarra to introduce myself to the officers there. I should be home about six.'

Home.

How domestic and intimate he made it sound, Gemma thought as she scooped up her keys and purse and sunglasses. 'Have a good day, Sergeant,' she said.

'Didn't we decide to drop the formalities, or are you worried it might blur the boundaries for you?' he asked.

She raised her chin. 'Have a good day, Marc,' she said with pointed emphasis.

'You too, Gemma,' he said with his first real smile. 'Don't work too hard.'

Gemma couldn't get his smile out of her head all the way to town. Or his eyes. Those dark-as-chocolate eyes that seemed to see through her clothes no matter what she was wearing. She had felt a little exposed last night dressed in shortie pyjamas, but this morning she had felt exactly the same dressed in a cotton shirt and trousers.

The first-name thing was dangerous, she thought. It added another layer of intimacy she wasn't sure was wise given they were already sharing a house. The bet they had agreed on worried her too. For some reason, possibly because it was forbidden now, she wanted nothing more than to feel his mouth on hers. She wanted to taste him, to taste the maleness of him, the potency and power she could sense he had in full measure. She found herself wondering who and what sort of women he had dated in the past. Work colleagues or women he had met casually? Was he a casual sex person or a serial monogamist? She didn't have to stretch her imagination too far to know he would be a monumentally satisfying lover. Not that she had a lot of experience compared to other women in her age group, but something about his aura of command and competence and confidence made her certain he would know his way around a woman's body like a maestro did a Stradivarius violin. She felt the pull on strings of desire deep and low in her body every time he looked at her. God only knew what would happen if he took her in his arms and followed through.

Narelle was at the clinic, setting up, when Gemma came in. She looked up from booting up the computer and grinned delightedly. 'So the sexy sergeant is staying out at your place, is he?'

Gemma narrowed her eyes resentfully. 'Only because

Ron Curtis pretended he didn't have a room.' She dropped her purse and keys on the desk with a thud and a clatter. 'Can you believe that? He's got fifteen rooms. He's always complaining no one uses them any more. I'm going over there as soon as I get a chance, to tell him what I think of him.'

Narelle swung back and forth on her ergonomic chair. 'You have to admit it's a whole lot nicer out at Huntingdon Lodge than at the pub.'

'That's beside the point,' Gemma said. 'If Gladys was still alive, it wouldn't be a problem.'

Narelle's tawny brown eyes twinkled mischievously. 'So you think you need a chaperone, do you? What, has he made a move on you already?'

Gemma felt her face flush and bent to put her keys and purse in the drawer under the desk to disguise it. 'Of course not,' she said crisply. 'He's not my type, in any case.'

'Come on, Gemma,' Narelle said. 'He's every woman's type. He's tall and gorgeous to look at and you only have to look into those sleep-with-me eyes to know he'd be fantastic in bed.'

Gemma schooled her features into indifference, even though those strings inside her body twanged yet again. 'I'm not interested. He's too arrogant for my liking.'

'It seems to be he's not so much arrogant as sure of what he wants and how to get it,' Narelle said, and she reached for the phone as it began to ring.

Which is exactly my point, Gemma thought as she went through to the consulting room.

* * *

Gemma worked her way steadily through her list of patients before she headed out of town to a property called Hindmarsh Downs, owned by the Hindmarsh family for six generations. Elizabeth Hindmarsh, the matriarch of the family, was in her early nineties and suffering from dementia. The family wasn't keen on sending her to a care facility several hundred kilometres away, but it was clear that looking after a frail and confused old lady was taking its toll, particularly on Janine Hindmarsh, Elizabeth's daughter-in-law.

'How is she today?' Gemma asked as Janine met her at the homestead door.

'Irascible as ever,' Janine said with a worn-out look. 'I found her out in the veggie patch stark naked except for her slippers this morning. Just as well none of the stockmen were around.'

Gemma held back her smile at the thought. 'It must be so trying for you, keeping an eye on her with all the rest of the stuff you have to do.'

'Tell me about it,' Janine said. 'Joe helps when he can but he feels uncomfortable dressing or helping his mother in the bathroom, so just about everything falls to me.'

'Have you thought any more about a rest home for her?' Gemma asked.

Janine shook her head. 'Joe won't hear of it. His grandparents died on Hindmarsh property and so did his father. He wants Elizabeth to be buried in the family plot in Jingilly Creek too. I just have to cope.'

'Maybe we could see if there's someone in town who can come out and help you on a daily basis,' Gemma suggested. 'I can ask around or a put an ad up in the café or the pub. You never know, there might be someone who would be grateful for a few hours' work.'

'I guess that could work,' Janine said. 'Even if someone was to help me shower her a couple of times a week, or just sit with her and listen to her hark on about old times. She tells me the same story over and over again. It's so draining to have to pretend you are interested.'

'Yes, that is a pattern of age-related dementia,' Gemma said. 'Typically the past is recollected in accurate detail but when it comes to what she did yesterday or five minutes ago, she will be vague or not remember a thing.'

Janine led her through to the large family sitting room where Elizabeth was sitting staring out of the window, muttering to herself.

'Mother, the doctor is here to see you. Dr Gemma,' Janine said. 'Do you remember her from the other day? She had a listen to your heart and your breathing.'

Elizabeth turned her snow-white head and glared at Gemma before she addressed her daughter-in-law. 'I don't want to see any doctor. And I'm not going to answer any of those silly questions either. Fancy asking me what day it is or what the Prime Minister's name is. Does the silly little chit think I'm off my head?'

'Mrs Hindmarsh, I just want to check your blood pressure and listen to your chest this time,' Gemma said. 'Would that be OK?'

The old woman shifted in her chair like an old broody hen ruffling her feathers. 'I'm not sick,' she grumbled. 'I haven't been sick for a day in my life. I haven't spent a day in bed, not once, not even when I had the children. I was back in the kitchen, cooking the meals for the workers, you ask Henry. He'll tell you. Get him in here, Janine. Get Henry to tell this young lady I don't need any fancy pills or potions.'

'Mother, Henry's been gone for ten years,' Janine said rolling her eyes at Gemma.

'Gone?' Elizabeth frowned. 'Gone where? What are you talking about? Of course he's not gone. I was speaking to him just this morning about the cattle in the river paddock. They'll have to be shifted in case it rains.'

'It's not going to rain, Mother,' Janine said in a long-suffering tone. 'Now, just let the doctor listen to your chest.'

Gemma took out her stethoscope and warmed it in her hand for a moment before she raised the old woman's blouse to listen to her heart. There was a faint murmur and when she moved the stethoscope to Elizabeth's back to listen to her breathing she could hear the sound of fluid at the base of the lungs. She straightened and put the stethoscope back in her doctor's bag. 'I think we'll have to keep a close watch on your chest, Mrs Hindmarsh,' she said. 'There's a possibility you could develop pneumonia if that fluid builds up any more.'

'Phffft,' Elizabeth said with a scowl.

Gemma put the blood-pressure cuff around the old lady's bony arm and watched as the portable machine recorded the figures. 'Your blood pressure is a little bit higher than normal but nothing to be too worried about.'

Elizabeth tugged her arm away almost before the cuff was off. 'Told you I'm not sick.'

'I'll come and see you tomorrow, OK?' Gemma said.

'Do what you like,' Elizabeth said, still scowling. 'But don't expect me to count backwards from a hundred.'

Gemma said goodbye and followed Janine out to the kitchen.

'Would you like a cuppa?' Janine asked.

Gemma wanted to get going but she was sure Janine was desperate for company, or at least for company other than that of a demented and difficult old lady. 'Sure,' she said with a smile. 'That would be lovely.'

Janine filled the kettle at the sink and then carried it over to the bench to plug it in. 'I've heard the sergeant's quite good-looking,' she said as she reached for the teapot and cups. She turned around and smiled at Gemma. 'I also heard he's boarding out at Huntingdon Lodge.'

Gemma pursed her lips. 'Yes, well, it wasn't my idea.'

Janine put some home-made cookies on the table. 'But I thought you wanted to take in boarders? Wasn't that the plan to help with the upkeep of the place?'

'Well, yes, but I have a lot of work to do before it's ready for guests,' Gemma said.

'Isn't Rob helping you with that?'

'Yes, but he's not able to do the heavy stuff with his back being so touchy,' Gemma said. 'He promised to come around today and do some stripping back of the paintwork in the hall. That will be a big help.'

Janine smiled as she handed Gemma a cup and saucer. 'Maybe the handsome sergeant will help you. Joe said he's a strong, fit-looking man. How long's he staying with you? Do you think he will get his own place eventually?'

'I'm not sure,' Gemma said, pushing the image of Marc's strong, fit body out of her mind with limited success. 'I get the feeling this is an interim thing for him. I can't see him sticking it out here in the bush. He has city cop written all over him.'

Janine sat down and leaned her elbows on the table and rested her chin in her hands. 'You're what, nearly thirty, right?' she said. 'Don't you think it's time you went looking for a husband? Before you know it you'll be forty and it will be too late to have kids, or too late without help. You don't seem the single, career-driven type, Gemma.'

Gemma felt an all-too-familiar pang when she thought of the possibility of spending the rest of her life alone. It wasn't that she was still pining for Stuart. She had come to realise over her time out in the bush that their relationship would not have lasted the distance even without his infidelity. It was more about where she was in her life now. She wanted to settle down, to have a family with a man who loved her, a man who would be faithful and true to her. She knew that by staying out here in the bush she would be reducing her chances of meeting someone, yet she couldn't quite bring herself to leave. She felt at home here, and that sense of belonging was going to be hard to give up, and even harder to find in a big city if she did. 'It's not exactly raining men out here, Janine,' she said, picking up her cup and taking a sip of the hot, refreshing brew.

'That's true enough,' Janine said, handing over the cookies. 'Is the dashing sergeant single?'

Gemma took a cookie from the plate, renewing her vow to swim that afternoon. 'Apparently.'

Janine's brows waggled up and down playfully. 'You never know, Gemma, he might be the one for you. Anyway, even if he's not the one, a little fling with him wouldn't hurt. God knows, you've had no social life out here. You've got to take what comes along when it comes along.'

'Would you be suggesting I have a fling with Marc Di Angelo if he was nudging retirement or twenty years older and divorced with adult children?' Gemma asked.

Janine chuckled as she topped up their teacups. 'He must be more gorgeous than Joe let on. Go for it, Gemma. He's hot, he's hetero and he's here. Make the most of it, my girl.'

Gemma drove back to town to pick up some supplies for dinner. She was across the road from the pub at the general store when she heard shouting. The doors of the pub burst open and two local men fell brawling into the street. They were followed by some of the other drinkers, including the owner/manager of The Drover's Retreat, Ron Curtis.

'Break it up, you two,' Ron said. 'I won't have no fighting in my pub, d'you hear?'

There were a couple of grunts from the two men

while a few more punches were thrown. The dust was being stirred up so much it was hard to know who was getting the worst end of the deal. Gemma winced as yet another wildly flung punch was thrown. She could see where this was going to end. Her day would be made longer by having to stitch up someone's face or splint a couple of broken fingers. Alcohol was a real problem with some of the locals, particularly the younger ones. Although they were legally able to access alcohol, they had yet to learn there were limits. It frustrated Gemma to see them abuse their bodies in such a way for the long-term risks were well known now and the costs to the community high.

A tall figure suddenly appeared from around the corner and strode towards the scuffling men, grabbing both by the scruff of the neck in each of his hands. 'OK, guys, let's cool it,' Sergeant Marc Di Angelo said, 'otherwise someone might get hurt.'

One of the men spat at Marc and the other tried to take a swipe but Marc's hold was too firm and his arms too long for the guy to reach his face. 'You don't want to go down for assaulting a police officer, do you?' Marc asked.

The younger of the two men was a patient Gemma had seen a few weeks ago for stomach pain, which had turned out to be a nasty case of gastritis. She had warned him then of the dangers of heavy drinking but it seemed her warning had gone unheeded. Darren Slateford was heavily inebriated as his words were slurred when he spoke. 'S-sorry, m-mate,' he said, staggering a little as Marc released him. 'I didn't realise who you were.'

The other man was only slightly less under the weather. Gemma could now see through the covering of dust and blood that it was Trent Bates, who at the best of times was a bit of a troublemaker in town. But on this occasion he must have realised he was outmatched and held up his hands in a gesture of surrender. 'It's cool, it's over,' he said.

Marc let him go just as Gemma approached to see if she could help Darren, who had a nasty split in his lip, which was bleeding profusely.

It all happened so fast Gemma didn't quite understand why she was suddenly flat on her back on the ground with her head thrumming like a bell struck with an anvil.

A short, sharp swear word from Marc cut the air like a knife. He lunged for Trent and had him with his arms behind his back, issuing a warning of arrest just as Ray Grant came on the scene. Marc handed Trent over with a grim statement to charge him. And then he was on his knees in the dust, leaning over Gemma, concern etched on his face. 'Are you all right, Gemma?' he asked, brushing the hair back from her forehead.

'I…I think so…' She put up her hand and felt the stickiness of blood on her forehead. 'Ouch.'

'That jerk hit you instead of me,' Marc said. 'I should have seen it coming but I didn't realise you were so close. Are you sure you're OK? Not dizzy or seeing double?'

'Are my pupils even?' Gemma asked, wincing at the pain in her head.

He peered into her eyes. 'Yep, they're even, a bit large, though.'

'That's OK, then,' she said, trying to sit up.

'Here, let me help you,' he said, scooping her up out of the dirt as if she weighed next to nothing.

Gemma wasn't quite sure if she was seeing stars because she was being carried in Marc's strongly muscled arms or because she had taken a punch to the head. It felt amazing to be held against his fit, toned body. He was all hard muscle and she could smell his distinctive smell of lemon and the musk of afternoon sweat. Her breast was rubbing up against him with each stride he took, a delicious sensation that made her already spinning head spin some more.

Narelle was at the clinic when Marc carried Gemma through the door. 'Oh, my God, what happened?' she asked.

'A stray punch hit her in the head,' Marc said grimly.

'I'm fine, really I am,' Gemma said. 'Stop making such a fuss.'

'I'd better dress that for you,' Narelle said, inspecting the wound. 'It doesn't look like it needs stitching. A Steri-Strip ought to do the trick.'

'She's already bruising,' Marc put in as he laid her down on the examination table.

Gemma breathed in his breath as it skated over her face. It was minty and fresh with just a hint of coffee. 'I feel such a fool about this,' she said. 'I should have stayed well clear. I know what Trent's like. He's got authority issues.'

'Yeah, well, he's going to be seeing a little more of authority figures if I have my way,' Marc said as he stepped aside for Narelle to set to work. 'I'd better give Ray a hand back at the station. Will you be OK until I get back?'

'Of course I will. Ouch!' Gemma said as Narelle applied Betadine to the wound.

'Look after her,' Marc said to Narelle as he headed out.

'I will,' Narelle trilled, giving Gemma an up-and-down movement of her brows once he had left the clinic. 'My, my, my, I do believe you have a knight in shining armour at your beck and call.'

'Don't you start,' Gemma grumbled, wincing again as the Steri-Strip was eased in place.

'Seriously, Gemma,' Narelle said as she took off her gloves. 'When was the last time a handsome man swept you off your feet? He's absolutely gorgeous. I'm so-o-o jealous. I wish someone would come and carry me off into the sunset. Mind you, he'd have to be pretty strong since I'm carrying twenty pounds I shouldn't be carrying.'

'He carried me to the clinic,' Gemma said with a note of pragmatism. 'And it was my own stupid fault.'

'Are you sure you feel all right?' Narelle asked, gently feeling over the back of Gemma's skull for any signs of haematoma.

'I'm fine except for a bit of a headache,' Gemma said. 'I think I'll go home and lie down.'

'Ah-ah-ah.' Narelle shook her finger at her admonishingly. 'No driving for twenty-four hours after a head injury, remember?'

Gemma scowled as she swung her legs over the examination table. 'I can see I've trained you a little too well.'

'You have to be careful, Gemma,' Narelle said, her expression serious again. 'You've got a nasty bruise forming. I'll get an ice pack to put on while we wait for Sergeant Di Angelo to come back to take you home. I'll get one of the guys to drop your car around tonight.'

There was that word again: home, Gemma thought. Now the whole town would be talking about her and the sexy sergeant getting it on. It wasn't that it wasn't a tempting thought. It was, perhaps too much so. But her pride was on the line here. He was only in town temporarily. What would be the point in having a fling, as Janine had advised, when her heart could get broken when it ended, as it most surely would? She wanted much more than an affair. She longed for companionship and commitment, for loyalty and love. It was a tall order in today's climate of casual relationships but she couldn't help feeling the way she did. She wanted to be a mother. She wanted to have it all—the career and the children and the husband. A husband she could trust with her life and her love.

She gave a heavy sigh and laid her aching head back down on the pillow. Did such a man even exist these days?

CHAPTER FIVE

'How are you feeling?' Marc asked a little while later when he returned.

Gemma began to sit up and he supported her by the arm as she hopped down from the examination table. He was struck again at how petite she was compared to him. He towered over her, especially when she wasn't wearing shoes. He could smell her perfume. It had lingered on his clothes from when he had carried her across the street. Holding her so close had made him regret the bet he had made with her. He wasn't keen on losing anything in life, but a bet was a bet. It would be interesting to see who broke it first.

Her mouth fascinated him. It had a little upward curve of the top lip, like a bee sting. Her lower lip was full too, soft and pillowy and utterly kissable. He could just imagine what it would feel like under the pressure of his. He had spent most of the night before thinking about it, which certainly made a change from having vivid nightmares about Simon. Who would have thought someone as attractive as her would be out here in this wasteland of a town? An affair would pass the time certainly, but she looked like the type of girl who wanted to play for keeps. He had once been the sort of man who would have done so. He had wanted what Simon had had. He had been actively searching for it…

But that had been before.

'I'm fine except for a slight headache,' she said as she hunted for her shoes.

Marc found them and lined them up for her to slip her narrow feet with their pink-painted toenails into.

She looked up at him sheepishly. 'I hope you didn't arrest Trent. He didn't mean to hit me.'

'No, but he meant to hit me,' Marc said. 'That's an offence that will be dealt with by the court. I'm sending him to Roma with Constable Grant. He will be probably be fined and given a good-behaviour bond.'

'Was Ray OK with that?' she asked with a frown.

'Constable Grant is no longer in charge,' Marc said as he helped her get off the table. 'I am.'

She didn't answer but meekly took his arm as he led her out to his car. It was an intoxicating feeling, having her lean on him; it made him want to draw her closer, to pull her up against his body and feel her softer contours mould against his harder ones. She smelt divine, some sort of light, flowery, fresh fragrance that teased his nostrils. Even with her clothes dusty and with a colourful bruise on her forehead she looked gorgeous. She was exactly the girl-next-door type his mother had her heart set on him finding and keeping. He quickly pushed the thought aside. He wasn't playing for keeps. He couldn't play for keeps.

'Thanks for coming to my rescue like that,' she said

as he helped her into the passenger seat. 'But I was concerned about Darren's lip. That's why I came over when I did. I could see he was bleeding badly. Narelle had to stitch it for him. He came into the clinic after you left.'

'You should know better than to approach a situation like that,' Marc said. His gut still churned when he thought about how a single punch could have killed her. He had seen too many tragic deaths caused by the effects of excessive alcohol. People often lost control and hit out, not stopping to think of the consequences. Sometimes they didn't even remember their actions the following day. The lives of both victims and their assailants were ruined. It was a lose-lose situation and it frustrated him that it seemed to be getting worse, not better.

'I know,' she said on an expelled breath.

He sent her a quick glance as he put the car into gear. 'As long as you're all right,' he said. 'That's quite some bruise you've got there. How's the one on your behind?'

Her cheeks took on a rosy hue and she turned to look out of the window. 'It's perfectly fine, thank you.'

Marc suppressed a smile as he drove out of town towards Huntingdon Lodge. He would have loved to check it out for himself but he wasn't going to make things any harder for himself than they already were.

Gemma woke after a long sleep. Marc had insisted she rest and she had obeyed, feeling relieved she could legitimately have a few hours off. She came downstairs to the smell of food, some sort of meat dish that was aromatic with Thai herbs and spices.

'I hope you're hungry,' Marc said as she came in. 'I took the liberty of taking over the kitchen. I hope you don't mind.'

She perched on the nearest stool. 'Of course I don't mind. I just feel a bit embarrassed you've had to fend for yourself. Gladys would be turning in her grave.'

'I am sure she would think it perfectly acceptable for me to take care of you after such an incident,' he said. 'You could have been killed, you know.'

Gemma bit down on her lip. 'Yes, I know. I treated a patient in Melbourne who died after a pub brawl. He was only nineteen. It was such a tragic waste of a young life. The guy who hit him wasn't even a bad guy. He had never offended before. He'd just had too much to drink.'

'Not all victims end up in the morgue,' he said.

Gemma saw the shadow pass over his features again and the grim tightness about his mouth. What horrors had he seen in the course of his work? Was that why he was out here in the bush? Was he suffering from some form of post-traumatic stress disorder? Should she ask or just leave it to him to tell her in his own time? She had hated talking about her break-up in the early days. It had taken some months before she could speak without tearing up. But after a while she had moved on. Maybe Marc too just needed some time.

The meal was delicious and although Gemma had decided against drinking any wine, she still ended up feeling light-headed after sitting opposite Marc while they ate and chatted about inconsequential things. He offered to make coffee while she sat on the veranda to watch the moon come up over the horizon.

Gemma breathed in the cooler night air. The sound of crickets and frogs around the tank stand reminded her of how far away she was from her previous life in the city. She loved it out here, but as she drew closer to her thirtieth birthday she couldn't deny feeling a little restless. Returning to Melbourne didn't really appeal—she felt as if she didn't fit in any more. Her father was busy with his second family and most of her friends had moved on with their lives, some of them busy juggling careers and children. Her time out in the bush had changed her. She had grown to appreciate the wide open spaces, the fresh air, the rhythm of the land, the turning of the seasons, the scorching heat and the precious rain, the dust and the flies, but most of all the friends she had made. She was needed out here, not just for her skills as a doctor but as a member of the community. But it worried her that by staying out here she might miss out on what she wanted most.

Marc came out with a tray bearing coffee. 'Is your head still hurting?'

Gemma straightened on her seat. 'No, not at all now.'

He put the tray on the table next to her. 'You were frowning.'

'I often frown when I'm thinking.'

'What were you thinking?' he asked as he poured the coffee.

'Nothing important.'

Marc sat on the other chair and picked up his coffee. 'I forgot to tell you I met your odd-job man, Rob Foster,' he said. 'He and another local guy came round while you were sleeping to drop off your car. He didn't stay long. He didn't want to disturb you while you were resting. He put some poison down for your mouse and he set a couple of traps before he left.'

Gemma suppressed a little shiver. 'I always feel a little guilty about using poison and traps. It seems so cruel.'

'Life is cruel, Gemma,' he said as he took a sip of coffee.

She looked at him in the light of the moon. There was a frown pulling at his brow, and his jaw had tensed up again, as if he was clenching his teeth but trying his best to disguise it. 'Why did you take this post, Marc?' she asked.

His eyes were hard and impenetrable when they met hers. 'Why do you ask?'

'I could be wrong but I get the feeling you're not here because you really want to be.'

He raised one of his brows mockingly. 'So you fancy yourself as a bit of a detective, do you, Dr Kendall?' he asked. 'What else have you decided about me?'

'You're cynical and you automatically think everyone is a criminal.'

'I would be a fool to take everything and everyone at face value,' he said, 'even someone as convincing as you.'

Gemma stood up and went to the railing. She gripped it so tightly her fingers ached. She took a deep breath before turning back to face him. 'So you still think I somehow manipulated Gladys into changing her will, don't you? Do you trust anyone, Sergeant Di Angelo?'

His gaze remained steady on hers but his expression gave nothing away. 'There have been many cases recently of elderly people being exploited by their relatives,' he said. 'Children who think that once they've got guardianship over a parent with dementia or age-related memory loss they can take every asset and use it for themselves.'

'Gladys did not have dementia,' Gemma said tightly. 'She knew exactly what she was doing. Anyway, I didn't know a thing about what she had written in her will.'

'There are other even more disturbing cases where the elderly person is persuaded by a non-relative to hand over all of their assets or remake their will in their favour,' he said as if she hadn't spoken. 'Sometimes the person deliberately sets the elderly person against their family or even their lifelong partner. There was a case where a guy inveigled his way between a husband and wife who had been married for over fifty years. The husband was dying of cancer so this guy moved in and promised the old lady he would help with running their small farm. The family, who lived interstate, could do nothing as the old woman had acted while in control of her faculties. She continually handed over large sums of money to this guy until there was nothing left.'

'Just what exactly are you implying?' Gemma asked with a combative glare.

'I'm not implying anything,' he said. 'Everyone in

town speaks very highly of you. You would be the last person anyone would suspect of devious motives.'

She folded her arms across her chest and sent him a cynical look. 'Apart from you.'

'I didn't say that.'

'I think you should find somewhere else to stay, Sergeant Di Angelo,' Gemma said dropping her arms to swing away to go back inside. 'You're no longer welcome here.'

Marc caught her arm on the way past, stalling her. 'Wait, Gemma.'

Gemma felt her skin tingle all the way up to her armpit as his fingers tightened to hold her securely. Heat rushed through her legs. She looked into his dark brown eyes and her belly turned over. His gaze moved from hers to her mouth and then back again. His tongue moved out over the dry landscape of his lips, signalling his desire to kiss her. She felt the tightening of the night air, the magnetism of his touch, how it drew her closer without her even knowing it. She felt the brush of his hard thighs first, and then the evidence of his growing arousal as the seconds throbbed past. His other hand had taken hold of her right arm as well as her left, his fingers like a pair of handcuffs around her wrists, his thumbs moving in a slow-moving caress that sent exploding fireworks of reaction down her spine. His eyes went to her mouth again, and then slowly his head began to come down…

'You're going to lose the bet,' she said, although her voice sounded like someone else's. It was husky and soft, breathy.

He paused just above her mouth, so close she could feel the subtle breeze of his breath on her parted lips. 'I haven't kissed you yet,' he said in an equally husky tone.

'No,' she said, running her tongue out over her bone-dry lips in a nervous, anticipatory gesture. 'But you were going to.'

He smiled a crooked half-smile that did serious damage to Gemma's heart rate, quite possibly putting it in the training zone for the first time in several months. 'Maybe I will, maybe I won't,' he said, his thumbs still working their mesmerising magic on her wrists.

Go on, do it, Gemma silently pleaded. Her whole body was teetering on a precipice of longing to feel that sensual mouth commandeering hers. Her breasts were aching as they were pressed against his chest, her tight nipples abraded by the lace of her bra. Her stomach quivered with excitement. It had been so long since she had been kissed. Her lips trembled in expectation, with longing and heart-stopping need.

He slowly straightened and released her hands, stepping back from her. 'I guess I'd better go and pack my things,' he said, and made to go inside.

Gemma caught him by the arm, just as he had done to her only moments earlier. His forearm was warm and strong with lean corded muscles, the covering of masculine hair tickling her fingertips and palm. 'No,' she said softly. 'Please…please don't leave.'

One of his brows rose questioningly. 'You want me to stay?'

She moistened her lips again and lowered her gaze

from the burning heat of his. 'I'm…I'm not asking you to sleep with me, Sergeant Di Angelo,' she said.

He tipped up her chin and looked deeply into her eyes. 'What are you asking me to do?'

She held his penetrating gaze. 'I'm asking you to trust me,' she said, 'to believe me incapable of exploiting an old woman for monetary gain.'

His eyes dropped to her mouth for a pulsing beat before coming back to hers. 'Trust is an important issue for you, isn't it?' he asked.

'Yes, yes, it is,' she said.

He brushed his thumb over her bottom lip, making every nerve ending scream for more. 'You have a beautiful mouth, Gemma,' he said, 'just made for kissing.'

Then do it, for pity's sake!

'I could so easily lean down and kiss you,' he said, still caressing her bottom lip as his eyes held hers.

'What's stopping you?' she asked throatily.

He gave another one of his crooked half-smiles. 'I don't like losing.'

'Call off the bet, then,' she said.

He trailed a fingertip down the curve of her cheek. 'That's as good as losing in my book.'

'Are you always so good at self-control?' Gemma asked.

'I've trained myself to think beyond the heat of the moment,' he said. 'Self-control and discipline are hammered into us as cops. You can't lose control in a life-and-death situation.'

'This is hardly a life-and-death situation,' she said with a wry look.

'No, perhaps not,' he said, dropping his hands to his sides, a mask slipping over his features once more. 'You should go to bed. I'll clear this stuff away.'

'I thought I was the doctor and you were the guest,' Gemma said. 'Somehow today we seem to have switched places.'

'You're not used to having anyone to look after you, are you?' he asked.

Gemma looked away from his all-seeing gaze. 'I like being independent,' she said. 'I figure I'm less likely to be let down that way.'

'Who let you down?' he asked. 'A lover?'

She looked out over the paddocks and to the ghostly silhouette of the willows down by the river. 'I had a fiancé back in Melbourne,' she said after a moment. 'He found someone else but forgot to tell me. I was still wearing his ring when she got pregnant. They're married now.'

'That would have been pretty tough to deal with.'

'It was, but I got over it.'

'Well done, you.' There was a touch of wryness to his tone.

She turned back around to face him. 'Maybe I will go to bed and let you clear things up down here. It's been a long day. Goodnight.'

'Gemma?'

She stopped in mid-stride and looked at him again. 'Yes?'

His eyes seemed to hold hers for an eon before he spoke. 'Why don't you call the bet off?' he asked.

Gemma felt a tremor of need rocket through her but she quickly squashed it. 'I'll think about it,' she said, and left him standing alone in the moonlight.

CHAPTER SIX

MARC had already left Huntingdon Lodge when Gemma came downstairs the following morning. She had taken the precaution of sleeping in one of the guest rooms rather than chance being disturbed by the mice again. She had slept fitfully, her head had ached a bit when she'd turned in her sleep, but the bruising was less noticeable this morning now she had covered it with some make-up. And thankfully she had heard no more squeaking.

Rob drove up the driveway as she was making a cup of tea. She waved to him as he got out and limped over to the house, taking off his akubra hat as he came indoors. 'I heard you got yourself punched,' he said, grimacing in empathy as he looked at the side of her forehead.

'It was my own fault for getting in the way,' Gemma said. Quickly changing the subject, she asked, 'Do you want a cuppa before you start on the hall?'

Rob gave his lower back a rub with one of his hands, his face screwing up in discomfort. 'Yeah, that'd be good.'

'Are you in a lot of pain today, Rob?'

'Same as usual,' he said.

Gemma felt for him. Chronic pain was debilitating and could affect mood and motivation. Rob was mostly stoic about it, but now and again he would seem depressed and lacking in focus. It didn't help that he had no partner or family to take his mind off his pain. He was only in his middle forties, far too young to be living like an old man. She knew he hated being a pension. He had been born and bred on the land so to have to give up hard physical labour was like a blow to his masculine pride. She had prescribed painkillers from time to time for him but he often soldiered on without them, insisting he didn't want to become dependent on drugs.

'How long's the sergeant staying here with you?' Rob asked as he took the cup of tea Gemma had poured for him.

'I'm not entirely sure.'

'Seems a nice enough chap,' he said, and, winking at her, added, 'good-looking too.'

Gemma gave him a mock glare. 'If one more person says how nice it would be for me to hook up with Sergeant Di Angelo I swear I'll scream.'

'Speaking of screaming, the sergeant told me you heard a mouse behind the wall in your room,' Rob said. 'I put some poison in the attic and set a couple of traps in the cupboard under the stairs. I'll check on them before I leave.'

'Thanks, Rob,' she said. 'I really appreciate it. Oh, and thanks for bringing my car out last night.'

'That's all right,' he said, blowing on the surface of his tea to cool it down. 'Any news on Nick Goglin?'

'I called while I was waiting for Sergeant Di Angelo to drive me home from the clinic yesterday,' she said. 'He's still in a coma but some preliminary scans have offered some hope. It will be a while before we know what to expect in terms of recovery.'

'It's hard on Meg and the kids,' Rob said. 'Narelle mentioned you were planning some sort of charity-bash ball to raise some funds for her while Nick's out of action.'

'Yes, that's right,' Gemma said. 'I thought we could have a bush dance out here in the old shearing shed. All the shed needs is a good brush out with a broom and a few decorations. We can have a barbeque and a raffle of some sort.'

'Sounds good,' Rob said, putting his cup down. 'Well, I'd better get started on that hall.'

'Don't work too hard, Rob,' Gemma said when she saw him wince as he reached for his hat.

He twirled the brim round and round in his hands before he looked up to meet her gaze. 'It's not the same without her, is it?' he asked.

She put her cup down on the table. 'No, it's not,' she said softly.

Rob gave a deep sigh. 'I really miss the old bird. She was always so good to me. I sometimes wonder what I would have done without her over the years, especially since my father died.'

'She adored you, Rob,' Gemma said. 'Anyone could see that.'

He smiled a sad sort of smile. 'She was like a mother to me, Gemma. My own mother took off when I was four years old. What sort of mother does that to a little kid?'

'Oh, Rob, I didn't know that. How awful for you.'

'My dad and I had to do what we could to run the property,' he said. 'I know for a fact that's why my back's the way it is. I worked too hard as a kid. I didn't have a childhood, not really. I don't blame my dad, he was just trying to make ends meet by cutting down on labour costs. But in the end we had to sell off half our land to get the bank off our backs after the drought.'

'Have you ever seen your mother since she left?'

He shook his head. 'No, she took off with some travelling salesman and went to live in the city—Sydney, I think it was.'

Gemma felt for the little boy he had once been. She had lost her mother to a freak road accident and even though she had been well past childhood she still felt the loss keenly. How much worse to be left behind at such a young and tender age? No wonder Rob cut such a lonely figure at times. Worn down by pain and hurts that were decades old. 'Rob…' She hesitated and began to chew at her lip.

'I know what you're going to say,' Rob said.

'You do?'

'Gladys wanted you to have Huntingdon Lodge. She wanted to keep you here in Jingilly Creek. It was her way of making sure you never left us.'

'So she talked to you about it before she died?' Gemma asked with a frown of surprise.

'Not in so many words but I could see how much she longed for you to stay,' he said. 'It's what everyone wants. You belong here, Gemma.' He gave her a smile. 'Besides, if you sell up and leave I might not have a job to come to. The new owners might not want someone like me limping about the place.'

Gemma gave his arm a squeeze. 'I'm not going any time soon,' she said. 'Anyway, I have Flossie to think about, remember?'

Rob bent down and stroked the old dog's head. 'She misses her too, don't you, Floss?'

Gemma didn't get a chance to draw a breath before lunchtime. The clinic had been busy that morning with a rush of patients keen to get their flu vaccinations as well as one or two more seriously ill patients who needed some extra time with her to discuss their treatment options. But finally the last patient left and she was able to close the front door. She took a deep breath and walked to the small kitchen area where tea- and coffee-making facilities were set up, along with a microwave and toaster oven.

Narelle looked up as she came in. 'Poor Ellice is going downhill rapidly, isn't she?'

'Yes, she certainly is,' Gemma said, thinking of how devoted Ellice Peterson's family were to support her the way they did through her long battle with leukaemia. She had a particularly aggressive form that had resisted all forms of treatment. Ellice had decided to come home from her long stints in a Brisbane hospital to die in peace surrounded by the family she loved.

'You have something else on your mind,' Narelle said, regarding her with a musing look. 'I can always tell. What's up? Is the sexy sergeant getting too hot to handle? Don't tell me he's kissed you. Oh, my God, he has, hasn't he?'

Gemma felt that familiar rush of heat go through her body whenever Marc's name was mentioned. 'No, of course not,' she said. 'Anyway, we made a bet.'

'A bet?' Narelle's eyes bugged. 'On what?'

'On not kissing each other,' Gemma said, flushing.

'I can't believe I'm hearing this.' Narelle gave the side of her head a couple of taps. 'You mean to tell me you made some sort of bet with Sergeant Marc Di Angelo over not kissing him? Are you out of your mind?'

Gemma set her mouth into a flat line. 'I had to put some sort of boundary up. He's living at Huntingdon with me for an unspecified time. It would be too easy to fall into a relationship just for the heck of it.'

'So?' Narelle said. 'Come on, Gemma, you haven't had a relationship since that jerk two-timed you back in Melbourne. Isn't it time to put that behind you and enjoy life a little bit?'

'Why is everyone so determined to run my life for me?' Gemma asked, reaching for a cup. It seemed there wasn't a person in the district who didn't think Marc Di Angelo was a perfect match for her. She'd had to field comments and ignore speculative looks all morning as each patient had wanted to know how she was getting on with the handsome city sergeant. She had enough trouble keeping him out of her head, without others reminding her constantly of how gorgeous he was and what an excellent husband he would make for her. She felt embarrassed that she was perceived as such a lonely heart. She hadn't realised she had been showing any outward signs of the deep inner yearnings she felt at times.

'Because we care about you, Gemma,' Narelle said. 'You do so much for this community but no one expects you to give up everything. You're entitled to have a life, you know.'

'I know. It's just that I'm not sure if I should make my life here or not.'

Narelle's hand froze on the cupboard door she had opened. 'You're not thinking of leaving us?'

Gemma bit her lip. 'I don't know…I feel so confused,' she said. 'I probably wouldn't have stayed this long if it hadn't been for Gladys, and now she's left me Huntingdon Lodge I'm worried it would look avaricious of me to suddenly sell up and leave.'

'I can understand how you would feel like that but you have to do what is right for you, Gemma,' Narelle said. 'Are you truly not happy out here?'

'Of course I'm happy here,' Gemma said. 'I love this place. You of all people know that.'

'But you still feel like you're missing something.'

'I guess I'm still trying to work out what I want,' Gemma said with yet another sigh.

'Aren't we all?' Narelle agreed as she handed over the chocolate biscuits.

The heat of the day had intensified rather than lessened by the time Gemma drove back to Huntingdon Lodge.

There was no sign of Marc's car and Rob had already left for the day. The swimming hole was just the place to unwind. She put a bikini on under her trackpants and T-shirt and slipping her feet into sandals walked down to the river. Flossie had walked with her as far as the house gate but then gave an exhausted doggy sigh and returned to the house, away from the heat beating down on her thick coat.

The water was deep and cold and Gemma breathed out a long sigh of pure bliss as it covered her from head to foot. She surfaced to swim a few lengths of her make-shift pool, using the willow branches as a guide before she deftly turned back to go the other way. The sound of the water being shifted by her body and the gentle rustle of the breeze through the trees were a tonic for her after the difficulties of the last couple of days.

The alarm notes of a bird calling from the trees further along the bank made Gemma take pause. She trod water for a moment, peering through the limbs of the willows to see what had startled the bird.

Marc appeared from the dappled shade. He was wearing jeans and a T-shirt, which was damp and clinging to his chest from perspiration. Her heart gave a little stumble and her belly fluttered when he took off his sunglasses to lock his gaze on hers. 'This looks like the place to be on a day like this,' he said.

'How did you know I was here?' Gemma asked, keeping her legs moving under the water to stay afloat.

'I saw you just as I was turning into the driveway,' he said. 'How's the water?'

'Wet.'

His lips twitched. 'Fancy some company?'

Her eyes flicked briefly to his jeans-clad legs. 'Have you got bathers with you?'

'Do I need them?' he asked with an unfathomable look.

Gemma's belly did a flip turn similar to the one she had done only minutes before as she had swum back and forth. 'Um…I was about to get out anyway…' she said, making a move towards the bank.

'Don't let me spoil your fun,' he said, hauling his T-shirt over his head and tossing it onto a sun-warmed rock. 'It looks like there's room enough for two in there.'

Gemma's hands slipped off the reeds she had intended to use to get out of the water hole as his hands went to the fastener on his jeans. Her eyes flared and her heart rate went full throttle as she heard the metallic glide of his zip go down. He heeled off his shoes and pulled off his socks, and then he stepped out of his jeans. He was wearing close-fitting black underwear, the sort that left you in no doubt of how he was made. She had to grasp at a low-lying branch to keep herself afloat, her eyes feasting on him, devouring every delicious inch of him before he slipped into the water beside her.

'Mmm, that's better,' he said, before submerging completely.

Gemma kicked herself away from the bank, going to the middle of the water hole to give him some room.

When he surfaced right next to her, one of his legs brushed against hers under the water. It was the merest touch of flesh against flesh but it sent shockwaves of feeling right through her body. She moved backwards but he came too, treading water just in front of her, his dark eyes with their thick water-spiked lashes holding hers in a mesmerising lockdown. 'Do you fancy a race to the fourth willow and back?' he asked.

Gemma was nothing if not competitive. She felt her muscles already switching on for the challenge. 'Sure, why not?'

'You call the start,' he said, positioning himself level alongside her. 'Do you want a couple of metres' head start?'

She gave him an are-you-kidding-me look. 'Ready, set, go!'

Of course, in the end he beat her easily, but Gemma gave it everything she had. It was exhilarating to fight it out stroke for stroke, metre for metre until he pulled away with a burst of speed and strength she had no match for. The light of victory shone in his eyes as he trod water near her and she noticed with annoyance his breathing rate had barely changed while she felt like her lungs were going to explode.

'Handicap next time?' he suggested.

'No way,' she said, trying to cover her gasping breathing. 'When I beat you, I'll do it fair and square.'

'You say that as if it's a given,' he said with a playful half-smile.

'Confidence is the key to success,' she said. 'If you think you can win something, you'll actively work towards it. If you think you're going to fail, it's like a self-fulfilling prophecy.'

His dark eyes took on a smouldering look as they

held hers. 'So you haven't changed your mind about our little bet?'

Gemma put up her chin. 'Why should I have?'

His eyes flicked to her mouth, and then back to her gaze. 'Because I think we both want to take this one step further.'

Gemma felt her insides clench with desire, an on-off sensation that radiated out from her core. She ran the tip of her tongue out over her lips, tasting the brackish water and her own clamouring need for his kiss. Her eyes dropped to his mouth, her insides kicking again with excitement and anticipation as he too moistened his lips with his tongue.

It was a tense, enthralling moment.

Would he or wouldn't he?

Or would she throw caution to the winds and move forward and press her mouth to his sensual one just for the heck of it, just for the taste of it, just for the sheer thrill of having a man want her?

But then she remembered his arrogant confidence, his assurance that she would be the first to give in. She didn't like being that predictable. She gave him a coquettish smile and disappeared under the water, swimming away with strong underwater sculling and kicking motions.

When she resurfaced Marc was swimming with long leisurely strokes in the opposite direction. She swam over to the bank and climbed up on one of the larger rocks to watch him, her arms wrapped around her bent knees.

After a while he swam over and hauled himself out

of the water with a lot more strength and grace than she had earlier, Gemma noted a little ruefully. She had the grazes on her knees to prove it. Water droplets from his body landed on her as he settled down beside her, his long, hair-roughened legs making hers look pale and milky in comparison.

'Hasn't anyone ever told you it's not advisable to swim alone?' he asked as he finger-combed his wet hair back off his face.

'I'm a capable swimmer.'

'Tree roots and submerged limbs make no allowances for competence,' he said. 'You should always have someone with you.'

'You may not have noticed but there aren't too many lifeguards out here, Sergeant,' she said.

'Then the very least you should do is tell someone where you're going.'

'Once a cop, always a cop.'

'What's that supposed to mean?'

'You think it's your responsibility to keep everyone safe all the time,' Gemma said, resting the side of her face on one knee as she looked at him. 'Don't you ever switch off?'

'Do you?' There was a brooding intensity in his gaze as it collided with hers.

'I'm aware of the dangers of burning myself out,' she said after a tiny tense pause. 'It's one of the dangers of working in an isolated community. There's no downtime unless you actively seek it. Someone always needs you.'

He looked into the distance, his dark eyes narrowed

against the slanting glare of the setting sun. After a long moment he got to his feet and reached for his clothes. 'We should get back before the mosquitoes start.'

Gemma stood up and went to where her clothes were lying. She got dressed and joined Marc on the path that led out of the willow glade. About halfway back to the house Marc's mobile rang and he took it out of the pocket of his jeans to answer it. She walked on ahead in case it was a personal call. Within a few minutes he had caught up to her, his expression grim as she turned to look at him. 'What's wrong?' she asked.

'Have you got your phone with you?'

'No, I left it at the house,' she said. 'Why? Is someone trying to contact me?'

'There's been an accident out at Jingilly gorge,' he said. 'A woman has fallen six metres. No one can get to her without abseiling equipment. The husband isn't sure if she's dead or alive.'

'Has the ambulance been called?' Gemma asked as she broke into a run.

'Ray's done that,' he said. 'They're already on their way. How far is the gorge from here?'

'Not far. We can be there in fifteen minutes, ten if we step on it.'

As soon as they got to the house Gemma grabbed her doctor's bag and joined Marc in his car. She gave him directions to the gorge and they drove out there with considerable speed, certainly faster than she would have done if she had been behind the wheel. Marc had put his portable siren on and the distinctive sound made Gemma's adrenalin surge all the more.

They arrived at the gorge just seconds before the ambulance. The husband of the victim was threatening to go down the rock face to rescue his young wife but Ray was doing his best to restrain him. 'Wait until we get the gear to bring her up, mate,' he said. 'The ambulance is here now and the doctor. Just stay calm, OK?'

The poor man was distraught, sobbing and tearing at his hair. 'We've only been married a week,' he choked. 'We're on a camping honeymoon. She was posing for a photo. I should have realised it wasn't safe. I tried to catch her but she slipped out of my hold.'

Gemma rushed over with her bag while Marc assessed the scene. 'I need to get down there to her,' she said. 'What are my chances?'

He let out a breath as he studied the terrain. 'Have you ever abseiled before?' he asked, swinging his gaze to hers.

'No, but if you've got the equipment I could probably give it a go,' she said, already feeling the flutter of nerves at the thought of going down that cliff face.

'I'll go down with you,' Marc said. 'But I think we'll need a chopper for the victim—that is, if she's still alive.'

Gemma swallowed as she looked down at the young woman lying in a crumpled heap so far below. 'How long has it been since she fell?' she asked.

'Half an hour,' Marc said, glancing towards the distraught husband, who was sitting on a log with his head in his hands.

'I'll call the chopper rescue just to be on the safe side,' she said, pulling out her phone and checking for a signal. 'It will take them time to get here in any case. Either way, it would be better if she was brought up via a winch.'

Marc didn't answer. He was already on his way to speak to Ray at the police vehicle, stopping briefly to place his hand on the bonnet of the husband's car, for what reason Gemma could not immediately fathom. Within a few minutes he had brought back some abseiling gear from the back of Ray's four-wheel drive. 'I'll help you down,' he said, uncoiling the ropes and assembling the clips.

It was a nerve-racking experience, going down the cliff, but with Marc by her side as Ray supervised the feed out of the equipment, Gemma felt as safe as anyone could feel given the circumstances. She bumped against the rocks a few times on the way down, but after a while she got the hang of using her feet to keep herself steady.

Feeling the solid ground under her feet when she finally made it to the bottom of the gorge was a relief, but she didn't have a moment to think about what she had just done. Marc had brought her doctor's bag down with him and handed it to her as they knelt beside the victim. The young woman, called Kate Barnes, was bleeding from a head wound and it was obvious from the unnatural angle of her right leg and left ankle that they were broken.

Gemma searched for a pulse and to her surprise and relief found a faint one. 'She's alive. You'd better let the husband know while I assess her condition,' she said, quickly donning gloves.

Marc called Ray on his phone, which seemed to Gemma a rather unusual thing to do when he could have just as easily given a shout to the top of the cliff face.

'How's she doing?' he asked as he came back and reached for gloves.

'Her airway is clear and breathing OK but I'm worried about that head wound,' Gemma said, as she worked on controlling the bleeding. 'She could have internal bleeding as well as a head injury. It's a heck of a long way to fall.'

'She must have broken the fall in a couple of places otherwise there's no way she could have survived that drop,' he said, glancing back up at the cliff.

'It's a miracle, that's for sure, but she's not out of the woods yet,' Gemma said as she went through her primary survey—airway clear, breathing twenty per minute, pulse about eighty, BP weak but palpable, GCS five or six, responding slightly to pain, exposure, possibly hypothermic. From her doctor's bag, Gemma retrieved a hard collar, adjusted it to small, and with Marc's help fitted it snugly to stabilise the neck. An oxygen cylinder, bag and mask were lowered down from the ambulance, with which Gemma was able to administer high-flow oxygen, with the patient breathing spontaneously. IV insertion came next, and a couple of bags of saline were lowered down in a bag from the ambulance supplies. Gemma's secondary survey had revealed an absent pulse in the right foot, certainly as a result of the tibial fracture above. She called for an inflatable splint from the ambulance, and had Marc stabilise the patient while she reduced the fracture and applied the splint, and breathed a sigh of relief at feeling the pulse return in the lower limb. Next a spine board was lowered, and with Marc's assistance the woman was carefully log-rolled onto it, sandbags coming down next and packed against each side of the neck. A space blanket was then applied to try to counter the hypothermia, and then it was a matter of maintaining oxygenation and circulation while waiting for the chopper.

The sound of the chopper arriving was an enormous relief. Gemma wasn't sure Kate was going to survive but her best chance would be to get her to Brisbane as soon as possible. While the chopper crew winched down the stretcher and a paramedic, Gemma was patched into the trauma centre via a handpiece to the chopper radio to fill them in on Kate's condition and vital signs.

It was almost dark by the time the chopper lifted Kate's shattered body up out of the gorge. Ray had set up some lighting from the top to guide Marc and Gemma back up, but it was a lot slower going up than going down.

'Don't look down,' Marc said at one point when Gemma froze when her foot lost its grip. 'Come on, sweetheart. You're doing great. Just keep looking at the next bit of the cliff. Concentrate on that.'

Gemma took a deep breath to control her panic. She felt beads of perspiration trickling down her shoulder blades, and her hands were sticky inside the climbing gloves Marc had given her to wear. Her heart was going like a piston. She felt dizzy and nauseous; terrified beyond anything she had ever felt.

'Come on, sweetheart,' Marc coaxed her again; his voice calm and soothing, just like a lover's. 'You can do it. One step at a time.'

'I can't do it,' she said, looking at him in despair. 'Marc, I don't think I can do it. It was so much easier going down.'

He bounced off the rock wall with his feet and held out his hand to her. 'That's because going down all you were thinking about was rescuing Kate,' he said with a smile. 'Come on, hold my hand. We'll go up together.'

Gemma slipped her trembling hand into the solid warm grasp of his, and slowly but surely he helped her to the top of the cliff face.

'Nice job,' he said, still holding her hand as she found her feet. 'I knew you could do it.'

'Sorry about the helpless female routine,' she said, giving him a sheepish look. 'I don't know what came over me. I just froze.'

'It was a tough climb for a beginner,' he said, releasing her hand and removing his helmet. He raked his fingers through his sweat-slicked hair before he helped Ray gather the equipment.

Ray came over to Gemma when the four wheel drive was loaded. 'I sent the husband, Jason, with the chopper,' he said. 'I thought he was going to go over that cliff as well.'

'What a dreadful thing to happen on your honeymoon,' she said. 'Are they from around here, do you know?'

'No, up from Sydney,' Ray said. 'Do you reckon she's going to survive?'

'It's hard to say,' Gemma said. 'She's got a pretty major head injury. But we got here pretty quickly so she's in with a much better chance than if it had been hours since she fell.'

Marc came to where they were standing. 'What time did you get the call from the husband, Ray?' he asked the junior constable.

'Five-thirty,' Ray answered. 'I was at the station when the call came through from the radio control room. I called you straight after. Then I tried both of Gemma's phones but she wasn't answering.'

'I forgot to take my mobile with me,' Gemma said, biting her lip.

'You can't be on call all the time,' Ray said. 'You work too damn hard as it is around here.'

'I'd like to interview the husband at some point,' Marc interjected. 'Did you get much of a statement from him?'

'Not much,' Ray said. 'He was barely coherent when I got here. I managed to establish that he and his wife pulled into the gorge just before five-thirty.'

'How did he react when you told him his wife was still alive?' Marc asked.

Gemma felt a ghost hand at the back of her neck. She wasn't sure where Marc was going with his line of enquiry. Did he really think Kate's fall hadn't been an accident? Was that why he had called Ray instead of shouting out, because he wanted to warn him to observe the husband's reaction? And was that why he had felt the warmth of the car on the way to collect the equipment?

'He was shocked but in a good way,' Ray said. 'The guy was beside himself. He was convinced she was dead. He was struck dumb with relief to find out she was still alive.'

Marc didn't answer. He had a look of concentration on his face as his dark gaze swept over the scene.

Gemma exchanged a quick glance with Ray but he just shrugged his shoulders in a beats-me gesture.

Marc had by now walked back over to where the couple's car was parked. He circled it a couple of times, crouching down to look at the pattern of footprints presumably. Gemma watched him move back to the edge of the cliff, shining his torch down over the area.

'What are you suggesting, Marc?' she asked when he came back to where she and Ray were standing.

'I want this place sealed off for a thorough investigation at first light,' he said. 'I'll get the Minnigarra guys in for back-up.'

Ray blinked as if he had missed something somewhere. 'What, so you think this wasn't an accident, Sarge?'

Marc gave him a grim look as he reached for his phone. 'I will decide that once all the evidence is examined, including the wife's statement, if she survives.'

'You think the husband…' Gemma gulped '…pushed her over the edge?'

'I think it's a possibility,' he said. 'That car's engine is stone cold. It was cold before we went down to do the retrieval. It's been here much longer than from five-thirty this afternoon.'

'You mean you think he…he waited before he called for help?' she asked. 'But why would he do that? If he wanted to kill her and make it look like an accident, why not just call for help as soon as he'd done the deed?'

Marc's expression was grave. 'Because he wanted to make sure she was already dead by the time help got here.' His mouth went tight before he added, 'That young woman was probably still conscious when she hit the ground.'

CHAPTER SEVEN

GEMMA hugged her arms around her body while she watched from the sidelines as the police from Minnigarra joined Marc and Ray as they worked on sealing the area. Two hours had passed since the chopper had left but there was no news on Kate's condition as yet. Gemma shivered in the cool night air as she thought about Marc's theory on what had actually happened. He was working tirelessly with the other officers, guiding them through the sophisticated investigation that would not have occurred without his powers of observation and mental acuity. She could see Ray was still trying to catch up, no doubt feeling a little out of his depth. The only criminal activity he'd had to deal with over the time he had been in Jingilly Creek had been the occasional robbery or drunken assault. Attempted murder was totally new territory for him.

Marc organised for the two officers from Minnigarra to stay on site and then he came over to where Gemma was waiting. 'I'll drive you home now,' he said. 'I'm sorry it's taken so long.'

'That's OK,' she said as she followed him to the car.

'Do you really think the husband pushed her? What if she just tripped and fell? It wouldn't be the first time. We had a local boy break his leg here last year when he fell while throwing rocks into the gorge. He was lucky he was able to break his fall by grabbing one of the tree roots, but it was a near thing.'

'All possibilities will be examined,' he said as he opened the car door for her.

Gemma slipped into the seat and waited until he took his place behind the steering-wheel before she asked, 'What made you suspicious?'

He glanced at her as he gunned the engine. 'I'm a cop. It's my job to be suspicious.'

'But what if you're wrong?' she asked. 'That poor man will go through twice as much hell if he's wrongfully accused.'

'No one is accusing anyone of anything,' he said. 'I'm just looking at this from several angles. It's what I'm trained to do.'

'Ray didn't seem to think anything was untoward,' she pointed out. 'Neither did the Minnigarra officers.'

'I've worked in Homicide for close to a decade,' Marc said. 'I have a lot of experience in assessing situations like this. I'm not saying for a moment that Ray and the others aren't good cops. They just haven't had the level of experience I've had.'

'What will you do now?' she asked. 'Will you have to go to Brisbane to interview the husband?'

'I'll speak to my colleagues there and set up an interview to get an official statement from him,' he said. 'We'll have to do a check on his background. Find out if he has any priors, how long he's been married, what insurance policies he has taken out on the wife, that sort of thing.'

Gemma raised her brows at him. 'Wow, you really are amazingly cynical, aren't you?'

'Motive, Gemma,' he said as he turned the car towards Huntingdon Lodge. 'It's what you have to look for. I'm not always right. Sometimes things look suspicious but in the end turn out to be all above board.'

'Does that mean you might change your opinion on whether or not I influenced Gladys into leaving me her property?' she asked.

He met her gaze briefly before he turned the car in the direction of Huntingdon Lodge. 'You don't seem the type to exploit people for your own gain.'

'Are you going on gut feeling here or on evidence?' she asked.

He stopped at the cattle grid on the driveway, his gaze drifting over her in a smouldering manner. 'I haven't finished examining all the evidence,' he said. He sent the car over the grid and added, 'But I have a feeling it won't be long before I do.'

Gemma felt a tantalising little shiver race up her spine at his words. 'Are you flirting with me, Sergeant Di Angelo?' she asked.

A smile kicked up the corners of his mouth. 'Maybe.'

'What about the bet?' she asked.

'I'm not going to lose the bet.'

'You sound very confident.'

'I am.'

'Aren't you even a little bit tempted?' she asked.

He brought the car to a halt and looked at her. 'Are you?'

She pressed her lips together, not sure she wanted to admit just how tempted she was. 'Maybe.'

He got out of the car and came around to her side to open her door. Gemma got out on legs that suddenly felt like pipe cleaners. He closed the door with the flat of his hand but kept it there, like a blockade for her body. She felt the brush of his strongly muscled arm against her shoulder, every nerve in her body starting to tingle with anticipation. She sent the tip of her tongue out over her lips, watching him follow the movement with those dark melted-chocolate eyes of his. Her belly quivered like a partially set jelly as he put his other hand on the car on the other side of her body, enclosing her like a pair of brackets. 'Um…what are you doing?' she asked in a thready voice.

'How much have we got riding on this bet again?' he asked, looking down at her mouth the whole time he spoke.

She moistened her lips again. 'I don't think we came up with an actual figure.'

'So if I were to kiss you right now, it would only be my pride that would take a hit, not my wallet,' he said, still looking at her mouth.

Gemma's heart picked up its pace and her breathing became uneven. 'Some people value their pride more than their money,' she said.

His eyes met hers, holding them with searing heat. 'I have my share of pride but I wouldn't let it get in the way of me doing something I really wanted to do.' He moved closer, his lower body brushing against hers, setting off spot fires in her pelvis. He brought his mouth down, but not to her mouth, instead brushing his lips along the line of her jaw, a feather-light caress that sent a hot spurt of desire straight to her core.

'Um…isn't that a kiss of sorts?' she asked in a breathless voice.

'Believe me, sweetheart,' he drawled laconically, 'you'll know it when I kiss you.'

Gemma felt a shiver of delight ripple over her flesh. Her body was quivering with escalating need, her lips tingling for the press of his mouth. It was like a form of torture to have his mouth so close without possessing hers. Was he doing it deliberately to see if she would break the bet first? He moved in closer as he caressed the sensitive skin of her neck with his lips, and even at one point with the raspy tip of his tongue. She felt the hard bulge of his aroused body against her, the unmistakable signal of his desire for her, and her spine all but melted back against the car. 'Y-you're bending the rules,' she gasped.

'So book me,' he said gruffly, moving up to nibble on her earlobe.

He nudged her legs apart with one of his muscled thighs, imprinting his desire for her on her flesh until she forgot to breathe. She had never been so powerfully aware of her femininity, of her need and desire for a mate. It was a force beyond her control. It was an urge that had started with a slow burn but was now an inferno. She couldn't damp down the flames—they were licking through her at breakneck speed, consuming common sense in their wake.

In the end she didn't really know who lost the bet. She turned her head at the same time he did and somehow their lips met in the middle in a blaze of heat that spread through her body like wildfire. It was like an explosion, a combustion of built-up energy that consumed everything in its wake. She felt the skyrocketing of her pulse as he increased the pressure, his hands moving from where they were leaning on the car to slip behind her lower back and pull her closer. Her spine loosened, making her feel woolly and soft and limbless as his mouth continued its sensual feast on hers.

His tongue brushed across the seam of her lips and she gave a little whimpering sigh of submission as he drove through. His tongue probed and then darted, dancing with hers in a sexy tangle of growing need. He tasted so male and so delicious, unlike anything she had tasted before. It was like tasting a potent drug, and she couldn't get enough of him. Her arms looped around his neck as he moved even closer, his pelvis grinding against hers, the barrier of their clothes hardly a barrier for she could feel the pounding of his blood against her, the thickness of his body sending hers into a frenzy of want. He seemed to have unlocked something inside her. Now it had been let loose, she couldn't contain it. It was unbearable, unthinkable to stop, to pull back and act with the common sense and reason she had always prided herself on in the past.

He made a sound in the back of his throat, something between a growl and a groan, as she laced her fingers through his hair. His tongue swept over hers again, teasing it, cajoling it into another sexy tango that sent shivers trickling like a waterfall of champagne bubbles down her spine.

Her breasts tingled as they got crushed against the hard wall of his chest, the tight nipples pinpoints of sensation. A fire was burning between her legs. Hot sparks licking at her flesh, the network of sensitive nerves leaping and dancing and firing off in anticipation for more of his magical touch.

One of his hands moved from behind her back to cup her breast, a light touch, not tentative but neither was it possessive or grasping. It was experimental, exploring, and utterly irresistible. He brushed his thumb over her nipple, back and forth, sending another shockwave of feeling through her stunned body. How had her body survived this long without such heady pleasure? She ached to have him touch her without the barrier of clothes, to feel his warm fingers trace her contours, to feel his hot, masterful mouth sucking on her, drawing her into his sensual orbit.

Marc slowly drew back from her, holding her by the upper arms, his breathing not quite steady. 'Not sure who started that, are you?' he said.

Gemma gave him an arch look. 'You did.'

His mouth formed a rueful smile. 'Let's call it a draw, shall we?'

'We shouldn't have made such a stupid bet in the first place,' she said.

'Why?' he asked, his eyes glinting with something

very male and very tempting. 'Because you knew right from the first day something like this would happen?'

Gemma pressed her lips together to stop them too from tingling, but if anything it made her more aware of how swollen and sensitive they were. 'It was just a kiss, Sergeant Di Angelo,' she said in a crisp tone. 'It's nothing to get too stirred up about.'

His hands moved from her arms to her wrists, his thumbs stroking her still leaping pulse. 'You think by switching back to the "Doctor" and "Sergeant" formalities, this will go away?' he asked.

Gemma swallowed as his warm breath caressed her face. 'It has to go away,' she said. 'We have to be sensible about this. We're both professionals in a small community. It could get tricky if we were to become involved.'

'Half the town thinks we already are involved,' he said as his eyes flicked down to her mouth as his head slowly lowered. 'May as well be hung for a sheep as well as a lamb, as they say.'

If she'd had any sense of self-respect or self-discipline, Gemma would have ducked out from under that tempting pressure and got away while she still could. But as soon as his mouth covered hers she was lost. She told herself it was because he was so darned good at it. He knew how to kiss with just the right amount of pressure, just the right amount of passionate intent to make her senses go into freefall. The heat inside her turned into a blaze of longing that sent hot, licking flames all over her body as each nerve reacted to his intimate embrace. His body was pressed up against her, his arousal so thick and strong she felt her spine wobble again as if someone had undone all her ligaments and tendons, leaving her vertebrae in a precarious house-of-cards pile that could topple at any moment.

He intensified the kiss, his mouth feeding hungrily off hers, making her realise with a little frisson of pleasure that he wasn't as in control as he had made out. She felt the tension in him building with each stab and thrust of his tongue against hers, the shockingly intimate mimic of what he really wanted. What she wanted. What their bodies both craved.

He lifted his mouth off hers, his breathing even more unsteady as he looked down at her. 'I really want to sleep with you,' he said. 'I want you in bed under me, on top of me, every which way I can have you. I think you need to know where I stand on that. I'm not the settling-down type. If we get involved, it will be an affair for a limited time.'

Gemma hesitated before she responded. She moistened her lips, caught in that moment of uncertainty she knew probably made her appear like a prudish relic from another time. 'You must think I am very out of touch.'

He picked up a stray strand of her hair and tucked it behind her ear. 'No, I don't think that at all,' he said. 'I think you are a nice girl who needs a man who can give you what you're looking for. I'm not that man.'

'How do you know what I'm looking for?' she asked.

His mouth went back into a rueful line. 'Sweetheart, what you want is normal—marriage and kids, the whole deal. I'm not interested in any of that for myself. You need to accept that.'

'Just because we kissed it doesn't mean I'm about to have you rushed off to be fitted for a morning suit,' Gemma said tetchily. 'Do you see every woman nudging thirty as some sort of ticking biological time bomb?'

He let out a long breath and scraped a hand through his hair. 'Look, I admit you pack a pretty awesome punch. I would love nothing more than a sizzling-hot affair with you. But within a month or two I'll be gone. I don't plan to stay out here for ever. This is just an interim thing for me.'

'I'm surely adult enough to deal with it,' she said. 'If I wanted to indulge in an affair with you—which you are arrogantly assuming I do—then surely it's up to me to deal with the consequences when it ends, as it inevitably would.'

'I'm not arrogantly assuming anything, Gemma,' Marc said. 'I realise there is pressure on you from the locals to settle down because they want to keep you here. That is totally understandable because you're gorgeous and sweet and would make someone a fabulous wife. But I wouldn't want you or anyone else to get the wrong idea if we were to engage in a short-term relationship. It would be just that—an affair, not a promise of for ever.'

'Fine,' she said. 'I'll keep that in mind if I should be tempted to be so stupid as to agree to such a thing. Now, if you will excuse me, I need to go inside and have a shower.'

* * *

Gemma blasted herself with hot water but it did nothing to wash away her sense of shame at how easily Marc had read her heartfelt desires. She felt gauche and too country for his city sophistication. He obviously saw her as a homespun type, the almost-thirty-year-old spinster desperate for a suitable husband before the clock struck midnight, with the whole local community cheering her on from the sidelines. Argggh! How embarrassing! He was being sized up by everyone. No wonder he wanted to make things perfectly clear from the outset. He was used to slick city girls who went in for casual hook-ups. He would not be interested in a woman who dreamed about sweet-smelling babies and a happy future with a man who loved and respected her.

She came downstairs only because hunger demanded it. There was Flossie to see to as well, not to mention her lodger, who would be expecting what exactly? Did he think she would agree to his no-string terms? Did he think her so needy and desperate she would gobble up the crumbs he tossed her way? She bit her lip as she searched the fridge for ingredients.

It would be so much easier if she wasn't tempted.

It would be so much easier if she had more experience.

It would be so much easier if she wasn't already halfway to being in love with him.

Gemma chopped onions with a savagery born out of frustration. The celery and carrots too were in for the same fate. Within minutes she had a stir-fry and rice on the simmer along with her temper.

Marc stepped into the kitchen. He too had showered

and changed. His hair was still damp. It looked like glossy black satin and Gemma could see the track marks of his comb. 'Is there anything you would like me to do?' he asked.

'You can pour the wine if you like,' she said stiffly.

She heard the glug-glug-glug of the wine being poured into two glasses. She kept her head down, concentrating on keeping the ingredients from sticking on the bottom of the electric wok.

'Gemma.'

'Don't,' she said, looking up at him through a cloud of steam as she clanged the lid back in place.

He raised his brows a fraction. 'You're really angry.'

'Why would I be angry?' she asked, flashing him a quick glare from beneath her lashes.

'Why don't you tell me?'

She put down the wooden spoon on the bench next to the wok. 'I suppose you think I should be grateful that you've been so upfront about all this,' she said. 'I realise most men would have taken what was on offer and delivered the sorry-it's-me-not-you-speech later.'

'I'm just telling you it how it is, Gemma.'

'How can you be so confident you don't want what your parents and sisters have?' she asked. 'What makes you so different?'

Something flickered behind his dark gaze. 'I've never said I don't believe in marriage and family. I just don't want it for myself.'

She gave him a long, studied look. 'You know something, Sergeant? I don't believe you. I think you do want more for your life.'

'Stick to your day job, Dr Kendall,' he said with a curl of his lip as he reached for his glass. 'Leave the detective work to the experts.'

'I think that's why you're out here now,' she went on. 'You're at a crossroads. Why else would a hot-shot city sergeant come out here to this isolated community?'

A muscle beat like a pulse in his jaw. 'The same reason a city GP would come out, to do their bit for the bush.'

'I came out here to get over a broken heart,' Gemma said flatly. 'I was running away. Is that what you're doing, Marc?'

He put his glass down with meticulous precision, and then his eyes hit hers. 'I have never run away from anything in my life,' he said. 'Now, if you'll excuse me, I have some work to do down at the station.'

She turned and frowned at him as he moved to the door. 'But what about dinner?'

'I'll get something later,' he said. 'Don't wait up. I have a key.'

Gemma let out a sigh as he strode out of the room. She heard his car roar as it started and then growl as it drove down the driveway. She looked down at Flossie, who was looking at her with empathy in her wise old eyes. 'You don't need to say I told you so, Flossie,' she said. 'I know I'm in over my head. I knew it the moment he walked into my consulting room. The thing is, what am I going to do about it?'

CHAPTER EIGHT

As soon as Gemma walked into the clinic Narelle raised her brows. 'Had a bit of a late night, did we?' she asked.

Gemma felt a blush steal over her cheeks. 'There was an accident out at the gorge. A woman fell six metres. We had to call in the chopper.'

'I heard about that from Ray,' Narelle said. 'But he said you were finished out there by nine, which kind of makes me wonder what you and the sexy sergeant got up to afterwards to give you those shadows under your eyes.'

'Nothing.'

'Liar,' Narelle said, leaning forward to peer at her. 'You kissed, didn't you?'

Gemma lifted her shoulder in a careless manner. 'So what if we did?'

Narelle's eyes bugged. 'Who lost the bet?'

'The jury's still out on that,' Gemma said. 'It sort of…happened.'

'So what was it like?'

'I'm not going to discuss such a personal thing with you, even if you are a close friend,' Gemma said.

Narelle gave a mock pout. 'Spoilsport.'

'Don't go ordering the invitations, Narelle,' Gemma said as she put her bag away. 'Sergeant Di Angelo has made his intentions clear. He isn't going to stay here for much longer than a month or two. This is just a fill-in post for him.'

Narelle clicked a ballpoint pen on and off. 'I wonder if he's had his heart broken,' she said. 'What do you reckon, Gemma? Perhaps he's come out here, like you did, to lick his wounds in private.'

Gemma frowned as she thought of the stony mask that had come over his face the evening before when she had pressed him about why he had taken the post. He hadn't even come back during the night. He hadn't even spoken to her by phone. Instead, he had sent her a text message early that morning saying he was going straight out to the gorge to continue the investigation into the accident. 'I don't know why he's here,' she said. 'But I do know it would be stupid of me to get my hopes up.'

'Ray thinks he's an excellent cop,' Narelle said. 'He said Marc put them all to shame with his assessment of the incident out at the gorge. No one was even thinking of anything suspicious until Marc put a red flag up.'

'I'm still not convinced it wasn't an accident,' Gemma said. 'The locals have been pushing for a safety fence ever since Jarrod Tenterfield broke his leg out there.'

'I know, but it can't hurt to ask some questions, can it?' Narelle said. 'If it wasn't an accident and this guy got away with it, think how awful that would be. Some other poor woman might have the same thing happen to her, or so Ray says.'

Gemma cocked her head. 'Since when have you and Ray been exchanging cosy little chats?' she asked.

This time it was Narelle's turn to blush. 'We're just friends,' she said. 'We've known each other for ever. Lyle and he used to be in the same class at school.'

'It's great that you've got someone to watch out for you,' Gemma said. 'Ray's a great guy.'

'I know but I don't want to rush things,' Narelle said. 'I have to consider Ben and Ruby. They still miss their father terribly. I don't want them to think I've forgotten all about him. I will never forget him, but he would want me to move on with my life. I would have wanted that for him if the tables were turned.'

'I'm happy for you, Narelle,' Gemma said as the clinic door opened with the arrival of the first patient. 'I hope it works out.'

Gemma was coming out of the bakery next to the general store at lunchtime when she saw Ron from the pub. 'Ron, I have a bone to pick with you,' she said, giving him a stern frown. 'I would have said something the other day but that drunken brawl distracted me.'

He grinned at her. 'What? Is Sergeant Di Angelo not paying his way?'

She narrowed her eyes at him. 'Do you realise how embarrassing this is?' she asked, lowering her voice in case anyone inside the bakery was listening. 'Everyone thinks we're having a relationship.'

'You could do a lot worse, Gemma,' Ron said. 'You

never know, you might be able to change his mind about making his appointment here permanent.'

'I don't think so, Ron,' she said with a trace of despondency. 'He's not the small-town type.'

'Yeah, well, that's what you used to say but look at you now,' Ron said. 'You're one of us. We can't do without you and you can't do without us. We're a team.'

Gemma chewed at her lip. 'Ron...I know everyone expects me to stay here for ever, especially since Gladys left me her property, but what if I did want to move back to the city at some point?'

Ron's bushy brows moved together. 'You're not thinking of leaving us?'

'I don't know...' She let out a sigh. 'Sometimes I wonder if I am missing out by staying out here.'

'You don't strike me as the flash restaurants and nightclub type, Gemma,' Ron said.

Just then a tall figure came across the road towards the bakery. Ron's weathered face broke into a grin. 'How's it going, Sarge?' he said. 'Is Gemma doing the right thing by you out at the lodge?'

Marc took off his police hat as he stepped onto the veranda. 'No complaints so far,' he said. 'She's gone out of her way to make me welcome.'

Gemma sent him a slit-eyed glare.

Ron just smiled and, tipping his hat at both of them, left to go back to the pub.

'Sorry I didn't make it back last night,' Marc said. 'I should have called you earlier to let you know.'

She raised her chin haughtily. 'It's no business of

mine, Sergeant. You're a paying guest. You're free to come and go as you please.'

He scored a pathway through his thick hair with the fingers of one hand. 'I'm going to be away in Brisbane for a couple of days,' he said. 'I have an interview lined up with Kate Barnes's husband, Jason.'

'Is there any news on her condition?' Gemma asked. 'I should have phoned by now but I've been caught up all morning with patients at the clinic.'

'She's still in a coma,' he said. 'The doctors are still very guarded about her chances of surviving.'

'Has the husband given a formal statement?'

'Yes, but there are some inconsistencies with what we've found out at the gorge,' he said. 'I want to do some further investigation.'

'The locals have been pushing the Minnigarra council for a safety fence at the gorge for years,' Gemma said. 'If you ask me, it was an accident waiting to happen.'

His mouth lifted in a mocking smile. 'Still flying the innocent until proven guilty banner, eh, Gemma?'

She arched a brow at him. 'I thought that was your job as an officer of the law?'

His mouth lost its curve. 'It's my job to see the guilty are punished for their crimes.'

The door of the bakery opened and Marc stepped aside to let the person pass.

'Hello, Gemma, dear,' Maggie Innes said. 'Is this your handsome sergeant everyone is talking about?'

'Er…'

'Good afternoon, Sergeant,' Maggie said, beaming up at Marc. 'I can't tell you how excited we all are out here to have a fully qualified sergeant to look after us. How long are you staying with us?'

'I'm not sure,' Marc said. 'A month or two perhaps.'

Maggie's smile made her china-blue eyes twinkle. 'Maybe our gorgeous little Gemma will be able to change your mind. I believe you're staying out at the lodge with her. Is she a lovely hostess?'

'Very lovely,' he said.

'We're very proud of our Gemma,' Maggie said. 'She's the best doctor this place has ever had. We're terrified she might pack up and head back to the city. You'll have to collude with us to make her stay.'

'I'll do what I can,' he said, still with that deadpan expression.

Maggie gave them both a fingertip wave and waddled off in the direction of the general store.

'You've got yourself quite a fan club,' Marc said.

'Please don't feel under any obligation to join.'

He held her look for a beat or two. 'So what's in the bag?' he asked.

She put the paper bag she was carrying behind her back. 'Calories.'

He felt a smile tug at his mouth. 'How many?'

'Don't ask.' Her colour rose, making her look young and vulnerable, far too young and vulnerable for someone as jaded and cynical as him.

'I guess I'll see you when I get back,' he said after a noticeable pause. 'Is there anything you'd like me to bring back from the city?'

She shook her head. 'No, but thanks for asking.' She

stepped down off the veranda. 'I have to go. I have patients waiting.'

Marc watched her walk back to the clinic, his eyes
narrowed against the glare of the unforgiving sun. He
waited until she had disappeared from sight before he
let out a sigh that snagged on something deep inside his
chest.

A week went past and Gemma heard nothing from
Marc. Any news she had of the investigation over the
fall at the gorge she'd got via Narelle, who had spoken
to Ray. There had even been a couple of reports on the
television news. Jason Barnes was under suspicion and
had engaged a top-notch lawyer to defend his plea of
innocence, and his family had rallied, offering up character references to clear his name. Gemma still couldn't
decide what to believe about it all. It wasn't the first time
a probably innocent person had been tried by the media,
and the police didn't always get it right either.

The news on Nick Goglin was good but it would
be quite some time before he would be back on the
farm and able to work. The plans for the bush dance to
raise funds to help the family were in full swing. In between seeing patients and a quick run out to Hindmarsh
Downs to check on Elizabeth, Gemma put up flyers all
over town about the fundraising dance. It was one of
the things she loved most about living in such a small
isolated community. Everyone chipped in to help each
other. She had so many offers of donations of food and
drink. Ron had donated beer and soft drinks and ice, and
others such as Maggie Innes had offered to bake cakes

and cookies for the supper. With Rob's help Gemma had cleaned out the shearing shed and Narelle and the kids had volunteered to help put up streamers and balloons for the event that coming Saturday.

On the Friday night before the dance Gemma was down putting the finishing touches to the shearing shed. Narelle and the children had left, which was probably why she hadn't registered the sound of a car pulling up. Even Flossie didn't prick up her ears, which gave Gemma absolutely no warning she was no longer alone.

She stepped back to survey her work and bumped into a tall hard figure. Her heart leapt to her throat as she swung round, her chest heaving in panic until she realised it was Marc. 'You scared the living daylights out of me!' she gasped. 'Couldn't you have called out or something?'

'I thought you would have heard my car,' he said. 'I gave Narelle a toot on the horn at the gate when she was leaving.'

Gemma brushed a lank strand of hair out of her face. She felt dusty and dirty and dishevelled, and a little put out he hadn't made any contact with her, not even a text message to say when he would be back. 'I didn't realise you were coming back this evening,' she said, trying not to sound too churlish.

'I left a message on your landline,' he said. His gaze swept over the shearing shed. 'Nice job.'

'Thanks,' she said. 'It's been a lot of work but I think everyone is looking forward to it.'

'Do you need a hand with anything?'

'I was just going to move some of those hay bales

closer for people to sit on,' she said pointing to a stack in the corner. 'Rob was supposed to help me but his back was playing up. I was going to get one of the men to do it tomorrow but as you're here now… That is, if you don't mind?'

'Not at all.' He put his keys down on one of the trestle tables Gemma had set up and got to work.

She watched as he lifted each bale as if it was a hand weight, positioning them around the area marked out as the dance floor. She could see the bunching of his muscles beneath his close-fitting T-shirt, each one taut and toned to perfection. Her belly gave a little shuffle as he came over to her once he had finished. He had some hay in his hair and dust on his shoulder. His eyes looked darker than normal, his thick lashes shielding his gaze as he looked down at her mouth. She felt the urge to moisten her lips but resisted it. She didn't want him to think her desperate for a repeat of their explosive kiss of a week ago.

'You have hay in your hair,' Marc said, and reached out a hand to retrieve it.

Gemma felt her scalp tingle at his touch, the slow drag of his fingers through her hair making her ache with want. 'You have too,' she said in a raspy voice.

His mouth kicked up at one corner. 'As long as I don't have it between my teeth,' he said. 'I can't quite see myself as a country yokel.'

She gave him a reproachful look. 'Is that how you see everyone who lives out in the bush?'

His eyes held hers in a little tussle. 'Don't get me wrong, Gemma. There are good people out here. I can see that. But I don't intend to stay around long enough to get too attached to the place. I'm a city boy born and bred.'

'I used to think the same thing,' Gemma said. 'I was determined I was only going to be out here for six months.'

'So why did you stay?' he asked.

She frowned as she thought about it. 'I don't know what or who changed my mind,' she said, kicking at a piece of hay on the floor. 'It was a gradual thing, I guess. I was hurting when I came out here. I thought my life was over. I couldn't see how my future was going to pan out without Stuart in it. We'd been together since med school.' She looked back up at him. 'I thought I was in love with him. I would have staked my life on it at the time but it was only after some time out here that I got some perspective. I had drifted into my engagement to Stuart. In fact, I don't think he even formally asked me. It was a sort of given. I was so used to us being a couple I gradually lost sight of who I was and what I wanted.'

'It can happen,' Marc said.

'Gladys was so lovely to me,' Gemma said. 'She was like a mother or really a grandmother, I suppose I should say. She helped me to see how much I had to offer in my own right. Having the responsibility of the practice really helped to build my professional confidence. It was something I never thought I would have been able to do. I would never have stretched myself in the city. It's too easy to send patients off to a specialist or for another opinion if you're not certain about a diagnosis or management. But out here I have had to deal with things I would never have seen in a city practice.'

'If you hadn't inherited Huntingdon Lodge from her, would you have gone back to the city by now?' he asked.

Gemma pressed her lips together before she answered. 'I'm not sure… Maybe. I think that's why she left it to me. She wanted me to take my time to think about it.'

'I can see there's quite a bit of pressure on you to stay,' Marc said. 'Everyone I have spoken to even in passing has told me what an asset you are to the place.'

She gave him a rueful look. 'The fan club.'

'Don't be embarrassed,' he said. 'It's a compliment to your dedication and commitment to the community.'

Gemma moved to straighten the paper cloth on the trestle table. 'Will you be coming to the dance tomorrow night or do you have other plans?' she asked. She turned and faced him again. 'Perhaps it won't be sophisticated enough for your city taste.'

His eyes stayed locked on hers for two heartbeats. 'I hate to tell you this but I have two left feet.'

She angled her head at him. 'I don't believe you.'

He held out his arms. 'Try me. I'll show you. I can't even do a waltz. Both of my sisters have tried to teach me over the years but I trod on their toes so much they quit in disgust.'

Gemma pushed her lips forward, wondering if it was a ruse. He was the most physically capable man she had ever met. 'All right,' she said stepping up to him. 'Put your hand in the small of my back. Yes, that's right.

Now give me your other hand.' She covered her reaction but only just. His warm, broad palm felt like a hot pack against her skin, and the fingers of his other hand as they grasped hers radiated warmth up along her arm.

'There's no music,' he said as he moved in close to her body.

'We don't need music,' Gemma said as a shiver cascaded down her spine. 'Just concentrate on your own internal rhythm. Now, you lead with your left foot and I take a step back. That's it… Ouch!'

'Sorry, I did warn you about my feet.'

'Never mind,' she said. 'Let's try that again. Step, step, glide, step, step, glide and turn. Yes, that's better. I think you're getting it.'

They did a circuit of the shearing-shed dance floor. She got her toes stepped on a couple more times but after a while he seemed to get the hang of it and began to lead with more competence.

'How am I doing?' he asked against her ear as he expertly turned her.

'You're a very fast learner,' Gemma said. 'Do you want to try a barn dance now? It's not hard. You've already got the waltz part. There's just the progression section to learn.'

'I'm game if you are.'

'Right, then,' she said, positioning him to her left with right arm around the back of her shoulders. 'We take three steps forward and kick and then three steps backwards and then…'

It took a couple of attempts but he managed to get through the sequence without too much damage to her feet. 'Well done,' she said, smiling up at him. 'You have just officially graduated with flying colours from the Gemma Kendall School of Dance. Your sisters will be very proud of you.'

Marc was still holding her hands, his fingers warm and firm around hers. His eyes were dark, as dark as Gemma had ever seen them. She felt the magnetic pull of his body, the way it was drawing her closer to his hot, hard ridges and contours, even though he was standing rock steady.

The air suddenly tightened like a wire.

Then in slow motion his head came down, lower and lower until his warm breath skated over the surface of her lips in that immeasurable moment before he finally touched down, evoking a soft whimper of pleasure from her as his mouth sealed hers.

It was a dreamy kiss, the sort of kiss where she totally forgot everything but the moment. The sheer sensation of having his lips move against hers, in tenderness and then with increasing pressure, as if something inside him that had been tightly controlled was slowly being unleashed. She felt it in the first stroke and glide of his tongue, the gentle urgency shifting up through the gears to full throttle want. His tongue danced with hers, but this was no slow waltz. This was a sexy tango that had an intimate progression in mind. She could feel the way his body spoke to her in the language of lovers, the aroused heat of him making longing seep through her body.

His hands moved from holding hers to gather her closer, one at the small of her back, the other cupping the curve of her cheek. The kiss went on and on, deeper and more sensual, drawing from her a response and need she had not known she was capable of.

His hand left her face to drift over the curve of her breast, a tentative touch, a teasing hint of how he wanted to explore her in more detail. She pressed herself against him, wanting more, aching for the cup of his palm and the caress of his fingers, the hot swirl of his tongue and the gentle nip of his teeth.

He walked her backwards in a parody of the dance steps she had taught him, one of his thighs moving between hers, tantalising her with its weight and strength, a potent reminder of how his body would feel driving inside hers.

Her back came up against the shearing-shed wall, the corrugations of the iron not unlike the ripples of feeling coursing through her. She kissed him back with wet, hot purpose, with hungry little nips and sucks of his bottom lip and greedy little pokes and darts with her tongue. She heard him groan as he pressed her up against the wall, his hands tugging at her shirt to free it from her jeans.

She felt the warm glide of his hand as it cupped her breast. Even through the lace of her bra it felt deliciously erotic, her nipple so tight it ached and burned. He bent his head and sucked on it through the flimsy fabric, the sensation of his hot mouth making her spine arch and her toes curl up inside her work boots.

He lifted his head and meshed his glittering gaze with hers. 'Do you want to finish this here or inside?' he asked.

Gemma suddenly realised what she was doing, or at least allowing him to do. She felt like a milkmaid being ravished by one of the farmhands.

A roll in the hay, so to speak. That was all it was to Marc. It was just another sexual encounter of which he had probably had hundreds. This wasn't about love or even liking. It was lust. There was no way of prettying it up.

He cocked an eyebrow questioningly. 'Gemma?'

She felt a blush moving up from her neck and had to shift her gaze. 'I'm sorry,' she said, ducking under his arm to put a safe distance between the temptation of his body and hers.

'Was it something I said?'

She bit her lip, wincing as it felt swollen and ravaged from his passionate kiss. 'I can't do this, Marc, not like this,' she said, waving her hand to encompass the rustic surroundings. 'It doesn't feel…right.'

'If you want roses and champagne then you'll have to move back to the city.'

'You don't strike me as a roses and champagne guy,' she threw back.

'You're right. I'm not.'

'I'm sorry for leading you on,' Gemma said after a tight silence. 'I got caught up in the moment. I've…I've never been kissed like that before.'

His eyes lost their hard glitter for a moment. 'It was a pretty awesome kiss, wasn't it?'

She felt a smile tug at her mouth. 'It was right up there.'

He smiled back, a lopsided half-smile that turned

her insides over. 'You know something? I've never had a woman say no to me before.'

'My heart bleeds for you.'

He came up to her and slipped a hand beneath the curtain of her hair, locking his gaze with hers. 'Thanks for the dancing lesson.'

'You're welcome.'

His eyes flicked to her mouth and lingered there. 'I hope I didn't break any of your toes,' he said.

'No.' Only I think you might be well on your way to breaking my heart, Gemma thought.

His hand dropped from her nape as he took a step backwards. 'Have you had dinner?' he asked.

'No, but I can rustle up something for us,' she said. 'I'm just about done here.'

'I'll see you inside,' Marc said. 'I just have to get my things from the car.'

Flossie heaved herself up from the floor and limped over to follow him out into the night.

'Traitor,' Gemma said under her breath as she bent to pick up the wrinkled skin of a burst balloon that was not unlike how her chest felt right at that point.

CHAPTER NINE

GEMMA had a quiche and salad ready when Marc came downstairs after a shower. The homely feel to the kitchen, complete with elderly dog asleep on the floor under one of the chairs, clutched at his insides like a hand. It reminded him of his parents' house when he'd been growing up. It reminded him of Simon and Julie's house—before.

'Would you like a drink?' Gemma asked.

'Better not,' Marc said with a rueful look. 'I only just managed to control myself in the barn.'

Her cheeks turned a delicate shade of pink. 'I'm sorry…'

'Don't be.' He pulled out a chair.

She looked at him once they were both seated. 'How is the investigation going in Brisbane? I heard a few snippets on the news a day or so after it happened but nothing since.'

'Jason Barnes has lawyered up, as I suspected he would,' Marc said.

'But wouldn't anyone do that?' she asked. 'I know I would. I wouldn't want to be accused of something without having legal representation. People can twist your words and misquote you. It's too dangerous to go it alone.'

'Fair enough, but this guy has guilt written all over him,' Marc said. 'He took an insurance policy out on his wife three months before they married. They'd only been dating six months prior to that. She comes from a wealthy background. Loads of family money. Her parents are not keen to point the finger but one of her sisters spoke to Kate since the wedding and thought she was having some trouble with her marriage.'

'What sort of trouble?'

'Apparently Kate didn't say anything outright—it was just an impression the sister got at the time.'

'All marriages have a teething period,' Gemma said. 'Maybe Kate was just letting off steam.'

'Maybe,' Marc said.

'Have you ever got it wrong?' she asked, passing him the salad.

'Of course,' he said. 'Policing isn't an exact science. Even DNA can be planted—or contaminated. We have to be meticulous in investigating all lines of enquiry in an incident such as this. That's what really gets me about the bush. How many people are getting away with murder out here because of the lack of police or qualified officers conducting investigations?'

'Maybe you should think about extending your stay out here,' she suggested. 'Ray and the others could really learn from your experience.'

Marc frowned as he helped himself to salad. 'I've told the department a month, two at the most.'

'And you won't change your mind?'

'No,' he said, his expression closed. 'Why would I?'

She gave him a tight smile. 'Why indeed?'

Gemma let Marc clear away as she had to deal with a call from Janine Hindmarsh. Elizabeth had fallen and Janine was worried she had broken a rib or two. 'I'll come out and see her,' Gemma said.

'What, now?' Janine said. 'It's nearly ten at night.'

'That doesn't matter,' Gemma said. 'If she has hurt herself it would be best to get her to hospital sooner rather than later.'

'I feel terrible for putting you out like this.'

'Think nothing of it. I'll be there in twenty.'

Marc dried his hands on a tea-towel. 'Want some company?'

'How are you at handling difficult old ladies?' Gemma asked.

'I have a grandmother still living,' he said. 'She won't do anything for anyone else but she eats out of my hand. My sisters and mother hate me for it.'

'You're in.' Gemma tossed her keys to him.

As they drove out of the driveway, just to be on the safe side Gemma organised for the volunteer ambulance to join them at the homestead.

'Do you do this often?' Marc asked.

'What? Come out at night on calls?'

'It seems a big workload for one person.'

'I know but everyone pitches in out here,' Gemma said. 'My car broke down a while back and Joe

Hindmarsh was the first on the scene to get me going again. It's how it works in the bush.'

'Here's your ambulance,' he said as a flash of lights appeared in the rear-view mirror just as he turned into the Hindmarsh property.

After brief introductions were out of the way Gemma went straight to see Elizabeth, who was sitting in an awkward position in a recliner chair.

'I told you I'm all right,' the old woman grumbled. 'I wouldn't have fallen at all if it hadn't been for Janine leaving those boots near the back door. In my day I kept this place spotless. Not a thing out of place and everything in its place.'

Gemma exchanged a look with Janine, who was looking even wearier. 'Is Joe around?'

Janine shook her head. 'No, he's gone to Charleville to look at a new bull. He won't be back till tomorrow.'

'I think it might be best if we send Elizabeth to Roma for a few tests,' Gemma said. 'She might have fallen because of a TI.'

'You mean she might have had a stroke?' Janine asked.

'Only a minor one,' Gemma said. 'Elderly people with arterial sclerosis can have lots of mini-strokes without even realising it. They have funny turns, fall over or black out for a moment. It can be very upsetting, of course, and dangerous if they fall and hurt themselves.'

'I don't think she's going to agree to go to hospital,' Janine said, glancing at the stony-faced old woman sitting muttering in her chair.

'I'll see what I can do to convince her,' Gemma said. 'I'm concerned she might have broken a couple of ribs when she fell. She seemed rather tender when I examined her. And in any case, I think you could do with a few days of respite.'

'You mean you don't want me to go with her in the ambulance?' Janine asked.

'No, you stay here,' Gemma said. 'Dave and Malcolm can manage things between them. If you just pack a few of her things—a nightgown or two and her toiletries bag—that would be great.'

After a volley of protestations that got more and more vitriolic, Elizabeth Hindmarsh was finally loaded into the back of the ambulance, but only after Marc took control. He handled the old woman like a dream, charming her into agreeing that the best place for her was hospital, where she could be looked after around the clock.

'Don't know how you did that, mate,' Dave said as he closed the door of the ambulance.

'Piece of cake,' Marc said dryly.

'You owe me for this, Gemma,' Dave said as he took his place behind the wheel, with Malcolm riding shotgun.

Gemma smiled sweetly. 'Have a nice trip.'

Janine was all for offering them supper, but Gemma didn't want to expose Marc to any more obvious attempts at matchmaking. She could see the way Janine's eyes had been dancing with delight from the moment Marc had stepped into the homestead.

'Thanks, Janine, but it's late and we really should be

in bed,' Gemma said, and then blushed to the roots of her hair. 'I mean, he should be in his bed and I should be in mine.'

Janine smiled a wide smile. 'How are you enjoying staying at Huntingdon Lodge, Sergeant Di Angelo?'

'I'm having a great time,' he said with a glinting smile. 'Gemma's even given me dancing lessons.'

Janine's brows lifted. 'Has she now? How delightful. So you'll be at the bush dance tomorrow night?'

'Wild horses couldn't keep me away,' he said.

Gemma rolled her eyes at him on the way to the car. 'Do you realise what you've just done?' she asked.

'Pardon me, sweetheart, but you were the one who was talking about going home to bed,' he pointed out wryly.

'A mere slip of the tongue,' she said, wrenching the door open. She glared at him over the roof of the car. 'You might as well have broadcast it all over town that we…that we…'

'That we what?'

'Never mind.' She got in and shut the door, frowning crossly.

'You worry too much about what people think,' Marc said as he drove out of the property. 'So what if you have a red-hot affair with a fly-in?'

'That's exactly my point,' Gemma said. 'I'm not look-ing for something temporary or casual. I'm not built that way.'

'What? So you're going to spend the rest of your life out here in this dead-end town, waiting until Mr Ticks-All-The-Boxes-For-You comes along?' he asked. 'Come on, Gemma. Get into the real world. You're going to throw your life away before you know it.'

'I could say the same about you,' she tossed back.

He shot her a cutting look. 'I'm fine with my life just the way it is.'

'Sure you are,' she said, folding her arms across her body. 'Flitting in and out of casual hook-ups with no promises of commitment, no lasting love, no kids and no growing old together. Yes, I can see how that could work for you.'

'You don't know what the hell you're talking about,' he muttered darkly.

'I do know,' Gemma said. 'I see couples out here who have lived their entire lives together. They've lived through heartbreak and happiness, all the highs and lows of life, and yet they've survived and stayed together. That is what life is about. It's not about living as an individual. It's about relationships. It's about community.'

'Not everyone survives,' he said. 'Not everyone gets their happy-ever-after.'

'I know that,' Gemma said. 'But that's where other relationships count. They support you through those rough times.'

'Good luck with it, Gemma,' he said. 'I hope you get what you want. I really do.'

I hope so too, Gemma thought dispiritedly.

Marc left early the next morning to do the day shift at the station. He had been up and gone for a run even before Gemma got out of bed. They crossed paths over breakfast but he didn't hang around for idle chit-chat.

He seemed preoccupied and restless but, then, so was she. She had spent a couple of hours lying awake the previous night thinking about him, wondering if she had burned her bridges by rejecting his offer of a short-term affair. She had heard him moving about his room as if he too hadn't been able to sleep. Would it be so wrong to indulge in a steamy liaison, even if it didn't last? Was she being too much of an idealist, waiting for all the planets to align? Would she regret this one day in the future? Marc thought she was in danger of throwing away her life out here in the bush. She worried about that too.

It had never been in her plans to stay out here indefinitely. But what was to say her life would be any more fulfilling back in the city? She had a sense of purpose out here. She belonged to a much larger family than her own. It was a nice feeling to be needed and appreciated, but would it be enough to satisfy her in the longer term?

Marc hadn't yet returned when the first of the cars arrived. Gemma welcomed everyone and handed around food and drinks while Ron, Rob and Ray organised the music system. After a few hiccups the music started to pump out of the speakers and several couples got up to dance.

'I see the three Rs have got things under control,' Narelle said to Gemma as she passed around a platter of cheese cubes, olives and home-made pickled onions.

Gemma smiled. 'Yes, thank God for testosterone.'

'Speaking of which, where is your Marc?'

Her smile faded. 'He's not my Marc.'

'Not progressed past kissing, then, huh?' Narelle asked.

'I don't want to talk about it.'

'Ah, here he is now,' Narelle said, nodding towards the shearing-shed door. 'If you don't ask him to dance, I will.'

'He'll crush your toes,' Gemma warned.

'It'll be worth it,' Narelle said, and sashayed off with her tray of nibbles.

Gemma turned away to help serve some drinks to the children who had accompanied their parents. 'Here you go, Amy,' she said to the blond-haired five-year-old who had eyes as blue as the summer sky.

'Fanks,' the little girl said shyly.

'Does the new sergeant have a real gun?' Thomas Bentwood, Amy's older brother, asked as Gemma poured him some orangeade.

Gemma was wondering how best to answer when Marc appeared at the drinks table. 'Um… Hi,' she said. 'Thomas and Amy, this is Sergeant Di Angelo. Sergeant, this is Thomas and Amy Bentwood.'

Thomas put out his hand and after a brief hesitation Marc took it and gave it a solemn shake. 'Nice to meet you, Thomas,' he said. He smiled at Amy. 'You too, Amy. That's a really pretty dress you're wearing.'

'It's new,' Amy said proudly. 'My mummy made it for me specially.'

'Have you ever killed anyone?' Thomas asked Marc.

Gemma saw a flicker of something pass through Marc's eyes but he covered it quickly. His smile as he looked down at the children seemed a little forced, however. 'Not intentionally,' he said. 'But sometimes police officers have to do things they would prefer not to do in order to keep other people safe.'

'I want to be a policeman when I grow up,' Thomas said. 'I want to shoot people.' He shaped his hand like a gun and aiming it at his sister said, 'Bang, bang, you're dead.'

'Thomas.' Gemma laid a gentle hand on the eight-year-old's shoulder. 'Why don't you take your sister over to Mrs Innes's cupcakes stall? I think I saw her with some lolly bags earlier.'

The children scampered off and Gemma looked up at Marc. 'Kids,' she said.

'Yeah.' He thrust his hands in his jeans and surveyed the couples on the dance floor for a long moment. 'You've got a good turnout.'

'Yes, I think just about everyone in town is here,' she said. 'It'll be a good chance for you to meet everyone.'

He swung his gaze back to her. 'I suppose I should ask you to dance.'

She gave him a churlish look. 'No one is twisting your arm.'

His lips twitched. 'I'd like to. I want to make sure I can still do it, with the music this time.'

'I'm sure you'll be fine,' Gemma said. 'It's like riding a bike.'

'You reckon?'

She smiled as he took her hand and led her to the dance floor. 'Just keep your big clumsy feet away from mine,' she said, and melted into his arms.

Gemma knew everyone was watching them but somehow it didn't matter. Being in Marc's arms was an experience she wanted to savour for as long as she could. She was finding it harder and harder to think of reasons why she shouldn't take things to the next level. For her it was not so much about lust. It was ironic that she had dated Stuart for years without being entirely certain of her feelings for him, and yet with Marc it had only been a matter of days and she felt her love for him blossoming like a flower opening to the sun.

'How am I doing?' Marc asked as he weaved them out of the way of another couple.

'Impressive,' Gemma said. 'You've only stepped on my toes once.'

'There's hope for me yet.'

'Hey, can I steal your partner, Sarge?' Rob asked as he approached them. 'Sorry, Gemma, but one of the kids has taken a tumble outside. I thought you might want to check it out.'

'Sure,' she said, slipping out of Marc's hold. 'Who is it and what happened?'

'Young Matthew Avery,' Rob said. 'You know what a daredevil he is. He jumped off the top of the tank and gave himself a gash in the leg.'

Gemma went to the young boy, who was putting on a very brave front. There was a lot of blood but on examination it looked as if a couple of stitches would soon sort things out. Marc carried him inside for her and she set up her equipment in one of the downstairs rooms.

Matthew's mother came in, carrying her youngest on her hip, her other tearaway son's hand clasped firmly in her other hand. 'What's he done now?' she asked wearily.

'Nothing too serious,' Gemma said. 'I'll pop a couple of stitches in and if you bring him to see me on Monday I'll check that all is going as it should.'

The wound was soon attended to and Matthew and his mother went back outside to the shearing shed, Matthew proudly showing off his starkly white bandage on his tanned shin.

'Do you ever get a break out here?' Marc asked as Gemma cleared away the dressings and swabs. 'You seem to be at everyone's beck and call all the time.'

'I guess I'm used to it now,' Gemma said. 'At first I was a bit taken aback by the kerbside consultations, but after a while I realised it was because I was accepted by everyone. They feel comfortable approaching me. I like that. It makes me feel needed.'

'You should set some limits,' he said, frowning. 'You'll burn out before your time.'

'I was thinking about taking a holiday when Gladys got sick,' she said. 'Now with Flossie to take care of, I've had to rethink my time frame.'

'Where were you planning on going?'

She straightened the cover on the bed. 'I hadn't really got that far. I guess somewhere where there's a beach and those fancy cocktails with an umbrella and tropical fruit on a stick in the glass.'

'You're making me drool,' he said.

Gemma smiled. 'When was your last holiday?'

'I took a month off late last year. I visited my sister in Sicily and then I did a bit of a tour around Europe.'

'Did you go alone?'

'That's the best way to travel, in my opinion. You get to do what you want when you want. No detours to look at stuff that is of no interest to you.'

'Have you always been such a lone wolf, Marc?' she asked.

His expression became shuttered. 'We should get back to the dance,' he said, holding the door for her.

She held his look for a moment. 'Tell me what happened, Marc. Tell me what happened to you to make you lock yourself away from everyone.'

His jaw tensed, making the edges of his mouth whiten. 'Leave it, Gemma,' he said. 'Just leave it, OK?'

She let out a sigh as he strode out of the room ahead of her, his long, strong back like a drawbridge pulled up on the moat of the emotions she had caught a glimpse of earlier. Just what lay at the bottom of that deep, dark moat that haunted him so much?

The bush dance was declared a fabulous success. Several hundred dollars had been raised and promises of more support for Nick and Meg and the kids were assured as the night drew to a close. Gemma hadn't seen much of Marc since he had left her earlier. She wondered if he had made himself scarce so as not to intimidate the more enthusiastic revellers who were enjoying a last beer or two before they headed home. She had seen Ray cautioning a couple of the men about driving under the influence, but mostly everyone had acted responsibly.

Gemma was tidying up the kitchen at close to one in the morning when Marc came in from outside. 'Oh,

I thought you must have gone to bed or something,' she said. 'I haven't seen you around.'

'I went for a walk,' he said, picking up a fresh glass and pouring in some wine from an opened bottle.

She gave the bench another wipe, her eyes downcast. 'I hope I didn't upset you earlier,' she said. 'I was probably stepping over the line with the trust-me-I'm-a-doctor routine. I'm so used to people telling me all their stuff I didn't respect your need for privacy.'

'It's OK,' Marc said taking a sip of the wine before putting it down on the bench.

She turned and faced him. 'No, really, Marc, I'm sorry. It's none of my business what's going on in your life.'

Marc looked at his glass but pushed it away rather than picking it up again. There had been a time when the only way he'd been able to block out his past had been to down glass after glass of alcohol. It hadn't made it any easier. It hadn't absolved his guilt. It hadn't taken Simon's wife Julie's shattered expression out of his head, neither had it taken the lost and bewildered look of Simon's little boy Sam, who had been used to his father bringing Marc home with him for a meal after a shift. Arriving that evening to tell Julie and Sam that Simon was not coming home had been the hardest thing he had ever had to do. Ever since the funeral he'd barely been able to bring himself to visit them. Just to be reminded of all they had lost and how he had lost it for them was too hard for him to face. His superiors had stepped in by giving him an ultimatum. He'd taken it because he'd wanted to see if he could still be a good cop. It was his life, his calling, and yet there were times when he wondered if he still had what it took.

'Marc?' Gemma's soft voice brought his head up and his eyes to her grey-blue ones.

'I watched my best mate get gunned down in front of me,' he said. 'We were on a job. I was heading the operation. Simon was following my orders when he lost his life. I can never forgive myself that it was him and not me in the way of that bullet.'

Her face fell. 'Oh, Marc…'

'Simon's wife and son have lost their world,' he said. 'One day they were a happy family unit and the next it was ripped away from them. Sam will grow up without a father, Julie without the husband she'd loved since she was a schoolgirl.'

'It wasn't your fault,' Gemma said. 'You can't blame yourself. You didn't fire the bullet.'

He gave her the humourless movement of his lips that had lately become his way of smiling. 'No, I know that. The guy who did it is locked away for life but it doesn't make it any easier. I've been given a life sentence too.'

Gemma came around to his side of the bench and laid her hand on his arm. 'You're the one who's given yourself a life sentence,' she said. 'You're denying yourself as a way to punish yourself. Surely Simon wouldn't have wanted you to do that. Would you have wanted him to do that if things had turned out the other way around?'

Marc looked at the soft bow of her mouth. Kissing her had been a big mistake. He had crossed the line and it couldn't be uncrossed. She wasn't like the other women he had been involved with in the past. She had an air of fresh innocence about her that was engaging and delightful. He thought of all the jaded types he had lost himself in for brief moments of physical release. He could barely recall their names. Not one of them had made his body throb with such heady desire after sharing just a kiss. He could feel it even now; the way his lips still tingled from being pressed to her mouth, even though more than twenty-four hours had passed. She had tasted unlike any other woman he had kissed and he had kissed plenty.

Gemma had tasted of strawberries and warm summer nights, of sunsets and sun-showers. It was a shock to realise how much he wanted to kiss her again. How he wanted to feel that electrifying passion again and again. But kissing her wasn't enough. He wanted more than that. He wanted to feel his body moving within hers, taking them both to paradise.

He laid his hand over hers, his darker skin making hers appear all the lighter. He felt the nervous flutter of her pulse and a wild stallion kicked him in the groin. 'God, I didn't want this to happen,' he said, bringing her towards him.

She softened like butter under the glow of a blowtorch as she came to him. His body kick-started against her, the leap of his pulse and the rocket fuel of his blood as it surged through his veins sending his rational mind to some far-off place way out of his reach. His mouth came down hard on hers, his nostrils flaring as he breathed in the scent of her and his tongue relishing the exqui-site taste of her as the kiss went on and on and on. She moved against him in an instinctive request, a silent plea for the pleasure she was seeking from him and him from her.

It was an unstoppable force that had captivated them both. Long, tight, hot wires of need coiled around them, pulling them closer and closer. His body, her body, the combined heat and need lifting the hairs on his scalp as he thought of sinking into her. It was what he wanted. It was what she wanted. It was pointless trying to resist. They were both adults. They were old enough and re-sponsible enough to take what they wanted without anyone getting hurt.

Gemma lost herself in his drugging kiss. If anything, it was even more sizzling and heart-stopping than the previous ones. She felt it in the way he pressed his mouth against hers, taking his time, not using his tongue until she opened her mouth to him on a breathless little gasp. It was like lightning striking when his tongue curled around hers. She even jolted against his body, her nerves singing in reaction as he deepened the kiss. He kissed her hungrily, passionately, purposefully, as if he had come to some decision in his head about her that he was not quite ready to put into words. The kiss went on and on, ramping up her desire for him inexorably. She felt the moistening of her body, the intimate dew of feminine desire in response to her mate. Her breasts too were tight and aching with need, the sensitive nipples tortured by the hard plane of his chest as he held her to him with hot, hard urgency.

He wrenched his mouth off hers and looked down at her with eyes glazed with heat and longing. 'This is

Marc carried her to his bedroom, shouldering open the door and dropping her on the bed with urgency rather than finesse. She lay there looking all feminine and soft and dewy-eyed and his groin gave him another zap of longing. He couldn't think of a time when he'd wanted someone more than her. It was like a fire in the river of his veins; they surged and pumped with it, sweeping away all sense and reason. He tore off his T-shirt and heeled himself out of his shoes before putting his hands to the waistband of his jeans. She was still lying there, looking up at him with a soft little smile playing about her mouth, but her chest was rising and falling at much the same hectic rate as his. 'You sure you want to take it this far?' he asked.

She looked him square in the eye. 'I'm sure.'

He dropped his jeans but kept his underwear on. He came over to her and lay down on the bed, half over her, his body leaping in excitement when her legs opened to make room for him. 'You're beautiful,' he said, lifting up the curtain of her hair to kiss her scented neck.

She turned her head so her mouth could find his, her soft lips parting as he drove through with his tongue. She tasted so damn good, so sweet and fresh he had trouble keeping his head. It was like making love for the first time. Everything felt so new and exciting: the touch of her hands as she explored his chest; the way her fingertips danced over him, brushing over his flat nipples before moving up to thread through his hair.

Marc gently worked on her clothes, taking his time over it, relishing every time another part of her was exposed to his vision. She had glorious skin, creamy and soft, just kissed by the sun, not burnt or heavily tanned.

He brought his mouth to the curve of her lace-clad breast, sucking on it through the delicate fabric, delighting in the way she arched under him at his touch. 'You like that?' he asked.

She answered him with a hot, moist kiss that nearly took the top of his head off. He tangled his tongue with hers, duelling with it, teasing it until she was moving beneath him restlessly.

He deftly removed her bra and feasted his eyes on her small but perfectly shaped breasts. They felt so soft to his touch, so feminine and delicate with their rosy pink peaks. He took each one in his mouth by turn, enjoying the way she melted as he worked his tongue around each nipple until it was as tight and erect as its twin.

He moved down her body, kissing her sternum, each side of her ribcage and then the shallow pool of her belly button. She arched up again and he settled her with a hand on her hip. 'Relax, sweetheart,' he said. 'I'm not going to rush you.'

She made a soft whimpering sound as he kissed her through the lace of her matching knickers. She was so responsive it made him feel as if he was in totally new territory. She moved against his hand when he peeled back the lace shielding her, her body asking him for more.

He gave it.

He parted her gently and explored the humid heart of her, the scent of her filling his senses. He brought his mouth down, tasting her, teasing her with his lips and tongue until she was gasping out little breathless sobs of release.

'I didn't… I thought… I haven't…' She blushed when his eyes met hers.

Marc stroked a long finger down her cherry-red cheek. 'You're not a virgin, are you?'

'No, it's just that I haven't done that… I mean, it didn't feel right…before now…' Her eyes fell away from his.

He tipped up her chin to make them come back to his. 'Hey, that's not something to be embarrassed about. Sex is all about chemistry. What feels right for one couple won't be right for another.'

She compressed her lips for a moment. 'I expect you're much more experienced than I am.'

'Is that a problem?' he asked.

'No, of course not.' She chewed at her bottom lip, this time reminding him of a shy child who was way out of her depth and knew it.

He brushed his thumb like a paintbrush over her lip where her teeth had left an indentation. 'I always practise safe sex,' he said. 'Is that what is worrying you?'

'I'm not worried,' she said, but he wondered if that was true.

'We don't have to go through with this if you're not ready,' Marc said, easing off her.

She grasped at his forearms to stop him from moving away. 'Don't go…please?'

He held her grey-blue gaze for a beat or two. 'I want you,' he said. 'I don't think I've ever wanted someone as much as I want you. Does that sound like a hackneyed line to you?'

She linked her arms around his neck and brought his head down. 'It sounds wonderful to me,' she said, and pressed her soft mouth against his.

This time there was no stopping him. Marc felt the rush of his blood as she tugged at his underwear, her fingers soft but worshipful as they uncovered him. He sucked in a breath as she curled her fingers around his length, the pressure of her grip just right. He reached past her to find a condom in the drawer where he had left his wallet and his gun. It was a bit of an effort but she was keeping herself busy in the meantime. He came back with the foil packet and got it on before she took him over the edge.

That first thrust, gentle as it was, took him totally by surprise. The feeling of her slim, tight body clenching around him, welcoming him into her, was mind-blowing. He increased his pace, slowly, careful not to rush her, but the control it took was costly. She was keeping up though with soft little gasps of pleasure as his body moved within hers, delighting him anew. He played her with his fingers, softly, coaxing her back towards paradise and she came willingly and enthusiastically. Her ripples of release triggered the switch on his control, and with a burst of blinding white light he emptied himself, collapsing as if he had run a marathon when it was over.

Her hands danced over his back and shoulders, her soft fingertips like fairy feet as she explored the knobs of his vertebrae. She moved up to curl her fingers in the back of his hair, tugging and stroking until he felt his skin pepper in goose-bumps of sensory pleasure. He felt her press a soft-as-air kiss to his jaw, then to his cheek and then she went in search of his mouth.

He met her more than halfway, drowning again in the damp heat of her lips and shy but still playful tongue. Her lips felt swollen beneath his and he eased off the pressure, realising it had been a while since they had been subjected to this degree of attention. How long he wasn't quite sure. He didn't really want to know. He didn't want to think of where this would go, or could go. This was here and now and it felt good. It felt wonderfully good. So good he could feel himself filling again, ready for another round. She moved against him, her body soft and pliable and scented with sex and sensuality.

He lifted his head and looked down at her. 'Hold that thought while I change the condom,' he said.

She gave him a shy smile. 'You're not too tired?'

'Not with you, sweetheart,' he said, deftly dealing with the condom exchange.

This time there was time to string out the pleasure of each caress. Marc explored her body all over again, taking her on a journey with him that was as exciting and as fulfilling as the last. When it was finally over he gathered her close in his arms and rested his chin on the top of her head as she drifted off to sleep. Sleep was not far off for him but there were still things he had on his mind...

Gemma woke up and stretched, and encountered a hair-roughened leg entwined with hers. Her heart gave a flying leap as she remembered what had happened earlier. She turned her head on the pillow and saw the sleeping form of Marc Di Angelo lying beside her. In sleep the hard angles and planes of his features softened, if anything making him look even more handsome. His mouth—her belly gave a little quiver when she recalled just where his mouth had been and how it had made her feel—was relaxed now as he breathed in and out evenly, his lips just slightly apart. He was in need of a shave. She had felt that when he had kissed her earlier. Her skin had reacted to the rough bristles, making her feel delightfully feminine. He had a tiny chickenpox scar just beneath his hairline and she placed her fingertip on it in a feather-light caress.

He opened one dark eye. 'Ready to play again?'

'You were playing possum!'

He rolled her over in one swift heart-stopping movement, his weight coming over her. 'I'm a light sleeper,' he said, dropping a hard, brief kiss to her mouth.

'Aren't you hungry?' Gemma asked.

'Starving,' he said, nibbling at her neck.

She shivered and gave herself up to his kiss. Food was suddenly the last thing on her mind.

But it must have been on his for after a few breathless moments he raised his mouth from hers. 'Let's eat and come back to bed and finish this.'

Gemma wrapped herself in a bathrobe, trying to disguise how shy she felt in front of him. It was one thing to sleep with a man but quite another to wander around without any clothes on. Thank God she'd shaved her legs.

Marc caught her by the tie of her bathrobe and tugged her back towards him where he was sitting on the bed, still naked. 'Hey,' he said, patting the bed beside him to indicate for her to sit down.

Gemma sat on the edge of the bed, clutching at the neck of the bathrobe to keep the edges together. 'Y-yes?'

He trailed a lazy finger down the curve of her terry-towelling-covered breast. 'You're beautiful. Every inch of you is beautiful.'

'Is that a line?'

'It's the truth.'

She looked into his darker-than-dark eyes. 'Thank you…'

He cupped her face and leaned in to kiss her again, a lingering kiss that set spot fires of wanting all through her being. 'You even taste beautiful,' he said, 'totally unforgettable, in fact.'

'So when you've gone back to Brisbane after your locum is done here, you might think of me now and again?' Gemma had intended it to sound light and flirty but instead it came out sounding petulant and needy.

He held her look for a heartbeat before he dropped his hands from her face and got off the bed and reached for his jeans.

'I'm sorry,' she said, chewing at her lips. 'I didn't mean that to sound quite the way it sounded.'

He zipped up his jeans with an action that had the dual effect of closing his fly as well as the conversation. 'I'll meet you downstairs,' he said. 'I have a couple of emails to check.'

Gemma sighed and flopped backwards on the bed, staring blindly at the ceiling. It seemed like she had a very long way to go before she had slick city sophistication down pat.

CHAPTER TEN

WHEN Gemma came downstairs Marc was dressed in his uniform and ready to leave for work. She wondered if he was rostered on or going out to avoid her. It was hard to tell what he was thinking. He had disclosed the tragic circumstances that had led him to take the post out here, but she still got the feeling he wasn't ready to have anyone get close to him other than physically.

'Gemma, we need to talk.'

She felt a wave of unease pass through her. 'It's all right, Marc,' she said. 'I understand the terms of our relationship. No one is holding a shotgun to your head.'

He came over to her and ran the back of his hand down her cheek, a soft caress that barely touched her but set every nerve alight. 'You deserve someone who can give you what you want,' he said. 'This is all I can give you. It's all I can give anyone.'

'I'm OK with that,' she said, even though she wasn't.

He looked at her for a long moment. 'If I had met you before…' He screwed his mouth up and his shoulders went down as he sighed.

'Before Simon's death?' Gemma asked.

He drew in a tight breath. 'I can't do that to you, Gemma. I can't destroy your life like Julie's was destroyed.'

'You're assuming something bad will happen,' Gemma said. 'That's a very cynical take on life, Marc. Not every cop gets killed on the job.'

His pain-filled eyes held hers for another long moment. 'When Julie opened the door that day she knew what I was going to say,' he said. 'She looked at me in that way that all victims of tragedy do. Her face sort of… collapsed. I see her face when I try and sleep at night. Not that I sleep, not properly. I lie there thinking of how I wish I could turn back the clock. It haunts me. I should have gone first. I should have known it was a serious domestic situation. I used to pride myself on picking them. I got it wrong. I got it so horribly wrong.'

'People aren't always predictable,' Gemma said. 'You had no way of knowing what was going to happen that day.'

'I see Sam's face too,' he went on, as if he wasn't listening to what Gemma was saying but was running a tape in his head that had been run time and time again. 'How am I going to tell him when he's older that I was the one who sent his father to his death? How can I go off and have a normal life when Julie's and Sam's lives have been destroyed?'

'Marc, you have to stop blaming yourself,' Gemma said. 'It's not helping you and it's not helping Julie and Sam. I don't think they would want you to be so unhappy and unfulfilled just because fate struck them a foul blow.'

'I was their best man,' he said, still on a roll. 'I can't bear the thought of getting married without Simon being there, as I was for him. I can't bear the thought of Julie and Sam standing in the pews, looking at the space where Simon should have been. I can't do it. I just can't do it.'

Gemma blinked back tears. 'You're being too hard on yourself, Marc.'

He breathed out another long deep sigh as he looked down at her. 'I guess I'll see you tonight.' He leaned down and pressed a kiss to her mouth, his dry lips clinging to hers as if they were not quite ready to let go.

Gemma touched her fingertips to her lips as she watched him drive away, her heart feeling as if it was being pressed together by two very large hands.

Narelle was one of the first to arrive to help with the clean-up. She had left Ben and Ruby with her mother so she could chip in, with Ray's help once he had finished his early shift. 'It was a fun night last night,' she said as she pulled down some streamers. 'Everyone seemed to have a good time, even your Marc.'

Gemma bundled up the paper tablecloth off the trestle. 'Mmm…'

Narelle came over and touched her on the arm. 'Hey, what's up? You seem preoccupied.'

'It's nothing,' Gemma said, forcing a smile. 'I'm just tired. It was a late night.'

Narelle wasn't fooled. 'OK, spill. What's going on with you and Marc?'

'Nothing… Well, nothing serious on his part.'

'But you're in love with him, right?' Narelle asked.

Gemma let out a deep sigh. 'If it's obvious to you, it must be obvious to everyone. I can't bear the thought of everyone feeling sorry for me when he finally leaves.'

'Maybe he'll stay or maybe you'll go with him,' Narelle said. 'No one would blame you for heading off to the city for love.'

Gemma gave her a despondent look. 'He won't ask me to go with him. He travels alone. No ties. No commitments. It's how he lives his life. He's got baggage.'

'He's a cop,' Narelle said with a roll of her eyes. 'They've all got baggage.'

'This is big stuff,' Gemma said. 'He's punishing himself for what happened to his partner. His partner was killed on a job. Marc blames himself.'

Narelle frowned. 'He told you that?'

'Yes, last night,' Gemma said. 'He's determined to deny himself a normal life to make up for Simon, his partner, losing his. I tried to talk to him about it but he's made up his mind. I can tell. It's as if he wants to suffer. I can't seem to help him to see how pointless it is to punish himself. It's not helping him move on. It's not helping anyone.'

'I guess you just have to go with it,' Narelle said. 'He's opened up to you, which is always a good sign. Maybe he just needs some time. Stop worrying about what you might not get and enjoy what you have while you still have it.'

'But how long will I have it?' Gemma asked. 'I can't help feeling he might pull the plug on our relationship at any time.'

'You don't know that,' Narelle said. 'You're projecting your insecurities because of what happened with Stuart. Enjoy what you have with Marc. Everyone can see how perfectly suited you are. Just go with the flow for now. That's all you can do.'

'You're right,' Gemma said on a sigh. 'I need to go with it. I need to enjoy the journey instead of worrying about the destination.'

'Attagirl,' Narelle said, grinning. 'Now, where do you want me to put these streamers?'

Gemma was doing the washing-up later that evening when Marc came in. 'Hi,' she said, keeping her tone light and carefree. 'I've kept some dinner for you.'

'Thanks.'

She smiled and made to move past him but he caught her by the arm and turned her to face him. 'I've missed you,' he said, sliding his hand down her arm to capture her wrist. He brought it up to his mouth and kissed the sensitive underside, his eyes holding hers in a mesmerising lockdown.

'That's nice to know,' she said softly.

His tongue traced a slow circle against her pulse, making her shiver. He lowered her arm and pulled her close against him. The muscled wall of his chest brushed against her breasts, and his strong thighs pressed against hers, making hers tremble in reaction. His head came down and her eyelashes fluttered and then closed as his mouth sealed hers.

It was a hungry kiss with a drugging intensity. It swept Gemma away on its turbulent tide, stirring her senses into a frenzied response that left her breathless and aching with want. His tongue slipped through her lips, taking control of the kiss with commanding expertise, leaving no part of her mouth unexplored or unconquered. She kissed him back with fevered urgency, need racing along her veins at breakneck speed. Her inner core pulsed with desire, a low, deep throb that silently begged for assuagement.

'I want you so badly,' Marc said as he dragged his mouth off hers. 'I thought of nothing else the whole time I was at work.'

'Me too,' Gemma said.

The journey up the stairs was peppered with breathless interludes until Gemma was almost jumping out of her skin by the time he laid her on his bed.

He came down beside her, covering his mouth with hers as his hands worked their way under her shirt to cup her breasts. 'Mmm,' he said as he lifted his head a fraction. 'You feel so nice, so soft and warm and feminine.'

Gemma undid the buttons on his shirt, trailing her fingers down his chest to rediscover him. He was powerfully aroused by the time she got to his pelvis. He groaned as her fingers danced over him, moulding him and stroking him until he had to pull her hand away.

'You're wearing too many clothes,' he said, and proceeded to get rid of them for her.

As each item was removed she gave another gasp of pleasure as his mouth burned like fire against her exposed skin. Her breasts were subjected to a hot, moist, sensual assault that left her flesh singing. Her belly quivered as he moved his hand down to press against her, cupping her gently before he stroked her apart to slide one broad finger into the moist tight cave of her body. Her spine loosened at the caress and she gave another little whimper of delight as he tantalised her on her most sensitive point. Little ripples started out from deep inside her, radiating out until there was no part of her that wasn't carried away on the racing wave of release. She arched her spine, trying to prolong the exquisite moment, but eventually it faded, leaving her boneless.

'You're the most responsive lover I've ever had,' Marc said as he kissed his way back up her body.

'I guess I must be making up for lost time,' Gemma said, trying to keep things light and playful.

He looked down at her for a moment with an inscrutable expression on his face. 'Or is it that you're making the most of it while it lasts?'

The smile she pasted on her face felt tight and unnatural. 'Could be.'

He brushed an imaginary strand of hair off her face. 'Gemma…'

Gemma pushed a finger against his lips. 'Let's not talk about what can never be. Let's just enjoy what's here for now.'

He captured her finger with his lips, drawing it into his mouth in an erotic motion, his eyes holding hers in a moment of passionate intensity. He released her finger and brought his mouth back down to hers, kissing her until she was restless again, needing him to take her to the heights of pleasure all over again.

He rummaged for a condom and she helped this time to put it on, stroking and caressing him as she went, delighting in the way he responded with such potency. He might think she was incredibly responsive but Gemma felt sure he was equally so. He was breathing hard and fast with each movement of her hands, his eyes glittering with need as he drove hard into her body.

She held him to her, each erotic stroke of his body within hers building her tension to a level she had not realised was possible. Every nerve in her body became taut, strung like wire stretched to snapping point. He pushed her over the edge with a deep groan against her neck, his body shuddering as hers quaked in the cataclysmic moments of heavenly, blissful, sexual pleasure.

Gemma listened to the sound of his heavy breathing, her arms still wrapped around him, holding her to him, wishing she never had to let him go. How soon would it be before he left town? Would she ever see him again? Would he look back at this time as just another notch on his bedpost or would he think of her as someone special, someone to be remembered as a perfect match physically? For that was what it felt like to her. He had shown her such passion, changing for ever how she would view intimacy. How could she ever find this with anyone else?

He rolled off her but brought her with him so she was lying over him. 'Hey.'

'Hey.'

He glanced at her mouth before going back to her eyes. 'Stay with me all night, Gemma,' he said. 'I'm not quite finished with you yet.'

Gemma gave him a coquettish look from beneath her lashes. 'Aren't we going to sleep?'

He swiftly turned her onto her back and covered her body with his. 'Eventually,' he said, and lowered his mouth to hers.

Gemma spent the next few days fielding comments from the locals on her relationship with the handsome sergeant. It was clear everyone was hoping Marc would stay and make an honest woman out of her. She laughed off their comments, trying desperately to keep things as casual as possible, even though daily she felt her love for him growing. It was the little things he did that made her realise what a special person he was and how much she was going to miss him when he moved on. She would come home after a long day of seeing patients to find he had cooked dinner, or he had bathed Flossie and picked all the grass seeds out of her coat. Another time he took Gemma on a picnic down to the swimming hole. It was one of the most romantic dates she had ever been on. He had brought wine and glasses and prepared the food himself. They swam together naked and then he made love to her while the sun sank in the west.

He never spoke of the future. He never spoke of his feelings. And although he was a sensitive and considerate lover, Gemma always felt he kept a part of himself separate. He was involved physically, but on an emotional level he wasn't touched, or certainly not as much as she was.

After another couple of weeks the investigation into the cliff accident took an interesting turn when Kate woke up from her coma. She was able to tell the police how her husband had asked her to pose for a photo close to the edge. She had been nervous about it as she didn't like heights. As to whether or not she had lost her footing or been pushed she was unable to say as her memory was affected from the cerebral swelling. She was determined to stick by her husband, however. She was furious about him being investigated and refused to assist the police any more with their enquiries.

'What do you think happened?' Gemma asked Marc when he had filled her in over dinner.

'It's hard to say,' he said. 'A lot of wives cover up for their husbands in difficult relationships. It wouldn't be the first time it's happened. She might genuinely believe he wasn't capable of it or she just can't remember.'

'Does it frustrate you that there's no clear-cut answer?' Gemma asked.

He toyed with the stem of his glass. 'A bit, but that's the job. Sometimes things don't work out the way you want them to.'

A little silence ticked past.

Marc looked across the table at her. 'Gemma, there's something I need to say to you.'

Gemma swallowed a tight restriction in her throat. 'Yes?'

His eyes looked shadowed and there was a frown pulling at his brow. 'I'm going back to Brisbane at the end of next week. I know it seems a bit sudden but I've been offered a new position. I've decided to take it.'

'You're leaving?' she asked, her heart thudding sickeningly. 'Just like that?'

He gave her a frustrated look. 'I've always been clear about my intention to return to the city,' he said. 'You can't say I didn't warn you.'

'But you've only been here just over a month,' she said.

'I've been here long enough to know this is not for me,' he said. 'It was always an interim appointment. Nothing has changed that.'

She gave him an embittered look. 'What you really mean is you've been here long enough to know I am not for you. Isn't that more accurate?'

The line of his mouth became tense. 'Don't take it personally, Gemma. It's been fun but I have to get back to my life.'

'Your life?' She threw the words at him in scorn. 'What life is that? The one with the one-night stands and the one-too-many drinks and where you work ridiculous hours to somehow try and relieve your survivor guilt?'

His eyes narrowed to dark slits. 'You don't know what you're talking about.'

Gemma banged her hand on the table. 'Damn it, Marc, I do know what I'm talking about. You think I don't have regrets? You think I don't feel guilty about some of the patients I've lost or couldn't get to in time? It's life. It sucks. It sucks big time. We work in jobs that ask a lot of us, and we give it. We give it because it's not a career, it's a calling.'

He got up from the table, tossing down his napkin as if it was something distasteful. 'I didn't want things to end this way between us, Gemma,' he said.

She glared at him with eyes burning with banked-up tears. 'How were you going to end it, Marc?' she asked. 'By leaving a note on my pillow one morning? Or maybe a simple text message when you were safely at a distance? Is that more your style?'

He raked his fingers through his hair, leaving deep grooves. 'Don't make this any harder than it already is,' he said.

Gemma forced the words out through stiff lips. 'Is there someone else?'

His frown deepened. 'No, of course there isn't. This is about me, Gemma. It's not your fault. I want you to know that.'

'You have to forgive yourself, Marc,' Gemma said. 'You have to forgive yourself for not being the one that died that day.'

'Thanks for the tip,' he said coldly. 'I'll keep it in mind.'

She tightened her mouth. 'Maybe you should think about staying the rest of the time at the pub.'

'I've already spoken to Ron about it,' he said.

Gemma felt as if she had been punched in the stomach. 'Then don't let me keep you,' she said.

His eyes held hers for a tense moment. 'If ever you're in Brisbane—'

'I don't think so, Marc,' she said with a plastic smile. 'I think it's better if we make this a clean break.'

'As you wish.'

Gemma waited until he left before she allowed herself to cry. She felt foolish for being so hurt when all along she had known something like this would happen. But she loved him. She had hoped and hoped he would love her back. It didn't seem fair that he could walk away with such ease. He had walked out of her life without a backward glance. It was what he did best: walk away before he got too involved. It tore her heart out to think she would never see him again. He was letting his guilt ruin his life and hers too. She had never felt more helpless in her life. She couldn't reach him. For all the love she had for him she still hadn't been able to soothe the deep ache of his soul. Could anyone?

Flossie came over with a subdued look on her old face and Gemma dropped to her knees and wrapped her arms around the old dog's neck. 'Why does loving someone have to hurt so much?' she asked.

'Don't look at me like that,' Gemma said when she walked into the clinic. 'I'm sick of everyone looking at me as if I'm about to fall apart.'

'Oh, Gemma,' Narelle said. 'It's just that everyone is so worried about you. It's been three weeks since Marc left and you're still crying yourself to sleep at night.'

Gemma thrust her bag into the drawer under the desk. 'I do not cry myself to sleep at night.'

'You've got red eyes.'

'It's an allergy to dust.'

'Since when have you had a dust allergy?'

Gemma swung away to her consulting room. 'I don't want to be disturbed unless it's urgent. I haven't got anyone booked in until ten. I have some paperwork to sort out.'

'Hey, did you hear about Kate Barnes?' Narelle called out.

Gemma stopped and turned around. 'No. What's been going on?'

'She's accusing her husband of attempted murder.'

Gemma's eyes went wide. 'But I thought—'

'Marc was right,' Narelle said gravely. 'Jason Barnes waited for over two hours before he called for help. He thought Kate was dead. His plan was to kill her and collect the insurance. If it hadn't been for Marc's suspicion, Jason Barnes would have got away with it.'

'Did Kate remember more about that day or did the husband confess?'

'Kate overheard him talking to a friend about how his attempt on her life had failed but he was going to try again once the police backed off,' Narelle said.

Gemma bit her lip. 'That's awful... That poor girl...'

'Yeah, but how cool that Marc was on the money from the start,' Narelle said. 'We could do with more cops like him out in the bush. Surely the city could spare one or two now and again.'

Gemma gave an evasive nod and turned back to her consulting room. 'Nothing unless it's absolutely urgent, OK?'

Narelle swung the chair around and plonked her bottom down. 'Got it.'

Gemma had only worked through one pile of notes and could already hear the waiting room filling with patients when Narelle popped her head around the door. 'Sorry to disturb you but the waiting room is full, and you also have a visitor,' she said.

Gemma gave her a narrowed-eyed look. 'Is it an emergency?'

'Looks like it,' Narelle said. 'Will I send them in?'

'Can't be all that serious if they can walk to my office,' Gemma grumbled as she hauled herself to her feet.

The door opened and a tall figure stepped into the room. Gemma's heart did a stop start and her stomach dropped like an elevator. Her palms felt moist and yet her mouth was completely dry, so dry she couldn't speak.

'Hello, Gemma,' Marc said.

She swallowed to clear her blocked throat. 'Marc...'

His dark eyes ran over her. 'You've lost weight.'

'Yeah, cool, isn't it?' she said dryly. 'I've been trying to shift half a stone for three years. Just shows what a bit of discipline will do.'

His lips moved in a semblance of a smile. 'How's Flossie?'

'She's fine.'

'And you?'

She set her mouth. 'Can we get past this bit and go straight to why you're here?' she asked.

'I know you're still angry at me and I don't blame you, but if you'll just hear me out I'll try and—'

'I'm not angry at you,' she said. 'I'm angry at myself. You told me the terms and I still went ahead and fell in love with you. I know it was my fault. You never made any promises. I'm the stupid romantic, remember? I was the one who was caught up in the romantic fantasy of falling for the handsome stranger who strode into town. Congratulations on the case, by the way. Narelle told me you finally got your guy.'

'Thank you, but I would much rather get my girl.'

She looked at him with her mouth open, unable to speak for a moment or two. 'Wh-what did you say?'

His dark eyes softened as they held hers. 'I was worried you would hate me by now,' he said. 'God knows, I deserve it, walking out on you like that.'

'I don't hate you, Marc,' she said. 'I wish I could. Maybe I wouldn't be the object of everyone's pity if I stomped around town telling everyone how much I hate you.'

'I got the impression I wasn't exactly welcome around here any more,' Marc said. 'Ron just gave me a serve and so did Maggie Innes. She told me in no uncertain terms that if I didn't do the right thing by you, she would run me out of town herself.'

'It's been a very long time since Maggie was able to run anywhere,' Gemma said with a wry smile.

His eyes softened even more. 'I've missed that.'

She frowned. 'What?'

Marc stepped up close and traced a fingertip over her

lips. 'Your smile,' he said. 'It's like sunshine. It lightens up the dark corners of my soul.'

Gemma had tried to keep her hopes in check but they kept filling up the space inside her chest until she could barely breathe. 'Why are you here, Marc?' she asked.

He took both of her hands in his. 'Because I wanted to see you again,' he said. 'I wanted to tell you how much I love you.'

Gemma just stared at him, her mouth falling open again.

He squeezed her hands and continued, 'I went back to Brisbane determined to throw myself at my new job but a week in I knew I had made a mistake. I toughed it out for another week, and then I went and saw Simon's wife Julie. I'd been avoiding her and Sam for months. I know she was hurt by it but I just couldn't bear being around them in their grief. It made mine so much more unbearable, the guilt too.'

'What did she say?' Gemma asked.

'Much the same as you said—I was punishing myself and it wouldn't bring Simon back. It was taking away two lives instead of one. She told me Simon had always told her he was prepared for the worst. He wanted her to get on with her life if the worst happened. She's taking baby steps to do that. She told me I wasn't helping anyone by blaming myself for something that so easily could have gone the other way.'

'Sensible girl.'

He smiled at her. 'Yes, she is, and she's looking forward to meeting you at the wedding.'

Gemma frowned again. 'Wedding? What wedding?'

He brought her hands up to his chest and held them against his thudding heart. 'Our wedding, sweetheart,' he said. 'You'll marry me, won't you? I've travelled all this way to ask you in person. You can't possibly say no to me.'

Gemma pursed her lips in a mock muse. 'Hmm… Not sure about the proposal,' she said. 'I think maybe I need a second opinion.'

'Where are we going?' Marc asked as she dragged him by the hand out of her consulting room to the waiting room, where it seemed half of Jingilly Creek was gathered.

'Ask me again,' Gemma said. 'I need witnesses. I need to know I wasn't just imagining it.'

Marc looked at the sea of faces, the previously buzzing waiting room suddenly silent, and then back at the woman he loved with every cell of his being. 'Gemma Kendall, will you marry me and live as my wife in Jingilly Creek, serving this community for as long as we both shall live?' he asked.

Gemma's smile lit up the room as well as Marc's heart. 'Sergeant Marc Di Angelo,' she said as she stepped up on tip-toe to reach his mouth, 'I thought you'd never ask.'

EPILOGUE

IT WAS a beautiful day for late winter, bright and sunny with fluffy white clouds drifting over the cerulean blue sky. The shearing shed was decked out with flowers flown in from the city—roses and jasmine, their fragrance heavy and spicy in the air.

Marc waited at the makeshift altar, his eyes going to Julie, who was standing with little Sam's hand in hers, her face beaming. He winked at Sam, who grinned back, and then he turned to look at his family. His mother was crying but that was what she always did at weddings, christenings, birthdays and even a barbeque on one occasion. His father smiled an I'm-proud-of-you-son smile that made Marc's heart swell. His sisters were craning their necks to catch the first glimpse of Gemma. They weren't at all interested in him now they were soon to have a much-adored sister-in-law to fuss over. They adored her as much as she adored them. His nephews and nieces too had taken to her like she was the best thing that had ever happened since toys were invented.

And then his bride stepped into view. His breath

caught in his throat as he saw Gemma walk towards him, step by step, her beautiful face shining with love for him. It had been her idea to get married in the shearing shed. And it was her idea not to have attendants but for them to come together in marriage alone. It was another one of the things he loved most about her. She was so sensitive and understanding, always letting him have the time he needed to heal and move on. He wasn't totally there yet but he was close. So very close.

The pastor had travelled all the way from Minnigarra to conduct the service and it was as meaningful and sacred as any city cathedral could have offered. The solemn vows were exchanged in voices that wobbled and cracked in places but somehow that just made it all the more special. Marc knew firsthand what 'till death do us part' meant. But, then, so did Gemma. At times her job was dangerous and that was something he'd had to come to terms with. They were on a journey together and no one could predict the future, but that wasn't what was important. The here and now was important: the journey, not the destination.

'You may kiss the bride.'

The words drew a collective indulgent sigh from the congregation as Marc brought his mouth down to Gemma's, sealing their commitment with a kiss that was full of love and hope for the future.

Gemma looked up at him once the kiss was over, her eyes glistening with happy tears. 'Is this a good time to tell you I love you?' she asked.

He smiled down at her. 'It's a great time,' he said, not in the least surprised or embarrassed that his voice broke over the words. Emotion was something else Gemma had patiently waited for him to embrace. He said it all the time now and it felt so good. 'I love you too.'

She gave him a sheepish look from beneath her lashes. 'I have to tell you something else but maybe now is not the right time...'

Marc felt a flutter of excitement inside. 'Sweetheart, you can tell me anything any time, you know that.'

She smiled with joy as she looked into his eyes. 'I'm having a baby,' she said. She did a little happy dance in front of him. 'Can you believe it?'

Marc felt his eyes go moist. 'Are you sure?'

Her eyes were bright with happiness. 'I did the test this morning.'

He squeezed her hands, holding them close to his heart. 'Is this a good time to tell our guests?' he said with a proud smile.

Gemma's eyes twinkled as she and Marc turned to face their friends and family. Marc opened his mouth to speak but before he could get out a word the congregation erupted in rapturous deafening applause.

Marc looked down at his beautiful bride, his eyes crinkled in amusement. 'I guess they must have already known.'

Gemma smiled. 'Some things are just plain obvious, don't you think?'

SOCIALITE...
OR NURSE
IN A MILLION?

BY
MOLLY EVANS

First published in Great Britain 2011
Harlequin Mills & Boon Limited,
Eton House, 18-24 Paradise Road, Richmond, Surrey TW9 1SR

© Brenda Schetnan 2011

ISBN: 978 0 263 88581 1

Harlequin Mills & Boon policy is to use papers that are natural, renewable and recyclable products and made from wood grown in sustainable forests. The logging and manufacturing process conform to the legal environmental regulations of the country of origin.

Printed and bound in Spain
by Litografia Rosés, S.A., Barcelona

Dear Reader

Thank you so much for picking up a copy of SOCIALITE... OR NURSE IN A MILLION? This is the second book I've set in the city where I live—Albuquerque, New Mexico. When I came to New Mexico for the first time as a travel nurse I didn't fall in love with it right away, but I found that I kept returning for more assignments and staying for longer periods of time.

The high desert is high-altitude living, at over 5000 feet. The textures, the colours, the scents are incredible—and very different from where I grew up. Each walk out into the desert brings a new breathtaking sight. I've tried to infuse some of my love for the high desert into this book. It was a surprise to me that I fell so in love with the culture and landscape here, and I hope that you enjoy reading about it.

Falling in love in and with New Mexico is easy. This state is called the Land of Enchantment for good reason, and I hope that you find the romance between Vicky and Miguel as enchanting as I do.

Love

Molly

Molly Evans has worked as a nurse from the age of nineteen. She's worked in small rural hospitals, the Indian Health Service, and large research facilities all over the United States. After spending eight years as a Traveling Nurse, she settled down to write in her favourite place: Albuquerque, New Mexico. In days she met her husband, and has been there ever since. With twenty-two years of nursing experience, she's got a lot of material to use in her writing. She lives in the high desert, with her family, three chameleons, two dogs and a passion for quilting in whatever spare time she has. Visit Molly at: www.mollyevans.com

Recent titles by the same author:

CHILDREN'S DOCTOR, SHY NURSE
ONE SUMMER IN SANTA FE
THE GREEK DOCTOR'S PROPOSAL
THE EMERGENCY DOCTOR'S CHOSEN WIFE

Dedication:

*This book is dedicated to healthcare workers
in the trenches, who get the job done every day*

Although she was an experienced nurse, this was a venture out of her comfort zone. Her father's chiding words and her brother's laughter still stung her pride. Determined to prove them wrong and, more importantly, to prove to herself that she could handle it, she had deliberately chosen this clinic far from her usual world of controlled, private hospitals and clinics. The mission statement here was closer to what her original goals in nursing had been. The time had come to make it happen.

For too many years she'd lived with the influence of her family hanging around her shoulders like a too-tight scarf she couldn't take off. Now she just wanted to be a nurse who took care of people. That's all.

She approached the glass door and opened it.

The clinic was packed with people. Some sat, some paced, some comforted small children, and they were all waiting for appointments. She'd never seen so many people lined up before a clinic even opened. That spoke silently of the great need of this community, but also of the quality of care they received there. Even though her nerves still tingled with anticipation, she knew this was the right move for her. She hadn't taken her career choice lightly when she'd entered nursing school despite the protests of her family, and she wasn't stopping now. Anyone who stood in her way could just get lost, including her family. Helping people who needed it gave her satisfaction that matched nothing else in her world. Somehow she saw parts of her mother in each patient she took care of. For her mother it had been too late, even before she'd been diagnosed. Cancer had invaded before she'd even known what had been wrong. Vicki wanted to help keep others from experiencing the same loss that had changed her life as a teenager. But this atmosphere was at complete odds with the type of hospital she had been working in for the past five years.

Looking around, she quickly found the nurses' station. "Hi, I'm Vicky, your new nurse." She hoped the woman remembered her from the interview last month.

A thin, gray-haired woman, who looked as if she might have known Florence Nightingale personally, peered up at Vicky over half-moon magnifier glasses. "Yes, Vicky Sterling-Thorne?" she asked in a cheerful and kindly voice.

"Yes. I prefer just Thorne, though. Makes the paperwork easier."

"Right. Just to refresh you, I'm Tilly McGee. Come on back, and I'll show ya round." She rolled her wheeled desk chair back and opened a side door for Vicky to enter. "As you can see, we've got a full docket today, so you may have to work on your own some, check vitals here and there, that sort of thing. Orientation could be a little unorthodox." She shook her head, as if knowing something that Vicky didn't.

"That's okay. I'll try to be helpful where I can. That's why I'm here." She turned and bumped into someone who had entered the station right behind her. "Oh, sorry." She looked at the handsome man, who took a step back from her. The blue scrubs failed to identify his status at the clinic. "Are you one of the nurses?"

A crooked smile crossed his face, and his deep brown eyes lit up for a second. "Some days I'm everything. Nurse, unit secretary, lab tech and clinic doctor all rolled into one." The smile he tossed her way was brief but welcoming.

Vicky blinked. "That's an impressive job description," she said, intrigued at his response. Here was a man who could multitask.

"It is." The welcoming smile faded away to what could only be an expression of mistrust. What had she done already to invite that? He sighed. "I guess you're the new nurse, aren't you?"

"Yes. You look disappointed already."

"I wouldn't call it disappointment."

Wariness stirred inside her. Had her family reputation preceded her so quickly? She gave a sigh of her own and hoped to head off any bias from the get-go. "My name is Vicky and, despite what you may think, I'm a nurse, that's all."

He nodded. "Just to let you know, quickly, our last nurse didn't return from maternity leave, and we've been shorthanded for weeks."

"The agency nurses worked for a while, but we need a full-time nurse, not a stopgap." Tilly grumbled her words without looking up from the computer.

Vicky nodded and gave a tight smile, understanding some of the man's reluctance. Despite the glowing references she had sent over, he had no confidence in her skills as a nurse. Time would change all that. "Well, I'm here to help. Where do we start?"

"Introductions, I guess." He glanced around. "Carlos is around here somewhere. He's the assistant extraordinaire, don't know what we'd do without him. And I'm Dr. Miguel Torres. We're not too formal, so call me Miguel."

Reluctantly, he stretched a hand out and shook hers in a firm but brief grasp. His hand was warm and not soft, like most of the men she knew who made money with their hands, but nothing else. The texture of Miguel's hand made her think he used his hands for building things and a slight shiver rocked her. She hoped that wasn't an omen. Work was her reason for being there and she hoped that she didn't have to remind herself that the boss was a hands-off relationship.

"Glad to be here."

Stepping back from her, Miguel glanced at the purse and lunch bag in her hands. "Tilly, can you set her up with a locker? By the look of that bag, she's going to need one."

She watched Miguel stride toward the triage area and wondered if there was anything behind that comment or was she just too wary of new people based on the experiences of her past?

"Come on, honey. I'll get you set up." The two women completed the task in a few minutes. Tilly returned to the desk to organize the patients, and Vicky noticed Miguel engaged in what looked like an urgent situation. He was trying to take a blue-faced baby from a young mother.

"He's not breathing, he's not breathing!" the woman cried, and clutched the infant more tightly, not knowing she was harming him further.

"Let's have a look," Miguel said, his soothing voice trying to gain control over the situation, but the anxiety of the mother was overwhelming.

Vicky rushed forward. Unable to interrupt the conversation, she leaned closer to the baby and blew a puff of air onto his face.

Startled, the infant jumped and took in a breath. And then another. And in seconds it turned from a ghastly blue to a lovely, normal shade of pink.

Openmouthed, the mother gaped at Vicky. Miguel raised amused eyes at her and gave a surprised look. The situation lost its tension in just a few seconds.

"What?" she asked as she looked between them. Had she done something wrong already? Seemed as if she was always stepping in it somewhere, but she didn't want to do that her first day on the job. This was a job she wanted and needed. Messing up was not an option, no matter how much money her family had. It wasn't hers. She paid her own way based on her nurse's salary.

"What did you do to him?" the mother asked, her demeanor much calmer than it had been moments ago, though she still breathed rapidly.

"I just stimulated his breathing reflex. Something I learned in my first rotation in the nursery at my previous hospital." She gave Miguel a concerned look. "Once in a while newborns just forget to breathe, and if you blow a puff of air on their faces it startles them, and they take a breath. That's what baby reflexes are for." Vicky reached a hand out to the mother and patted her back in a soothing manner, trying to ignore the intense way that Miguel watched her, but the fluttering in her stomach wasn't going away. The intensity of him was going to take some getting used to. "Is it okay if we take a look now?"

"Yes, yes, yes. Dr. Torres, I'm so sorry!" Tears now

poured down the mother's face as she relinquished the baby to Vicky.

"It's okay," Miguel said, and squeezed her shoulder. "We'll take a look and make sure everything is okay, just to be sure."

Vicky handed the baby boy over to Miguel and engaged the mother in small talk to help calm her down and give herself a moment to beat her nerves down. "What's your name?"

"Tina."

"Why don't you have a seat for a second? I'm sure that you're worn-out." Vicky guided her to a nearby chair.

"I am. I'm shaking." She rubbed her hands up and down her arms, as if she felt chilled from the experience. "I thought he was going to die."

"He's okay now." Vicky raised her eyes to Miguel, who gave her a reassuring nod, which calmed her own nerves a bit. Having such a strong team leader who didn't get ruffled was going to be a wonderful experience. "It's scary when babies do that, isn't it?"

"Yeah, it is. Still, I bet this boy's going to be a champ one day." He wrapped the baby up in the soft blue blankets and tucked him against his body, talking to the infant as if they were old friends.

Vicky tried not to stare. The man was gorgeous with those incredibly dark eyes of his and hair to match, but coupled with a smile and a soft voice when talking to a baby? Absolutely stunning. Nothing like the men she knew in her part of the world far away from this clinic. Something cramped inside her chest, maybe a long-lost hope or dream of having a family. Since her divorce two years ago she'd not allowed herself to dredge up those forgotten dreams. A man with a baby was an intoxicating sight, but she'd learned long ago that not every beautiful man had a heart to match. And not one could be taken at his word. She finally had to look away when Tina asked her a question.

Miguel had seen infants like this come and go since he had taken over the clinic a few years ago. Some stayed healthy and survived, some didn't. His hope was that when they grew up, none of them would succumb to the influence of gangs and drugs, like his younger brother, Emilio, had done, but he knew that was probably unrealistic. Emilio's death at the hands of a gang was one of the reasons he himself fought so hard for every child that entered his clinic. Each battle to save a life was a battle with a gang or disease and every one was a battle he intended to win. Death was not going to defeat him or take the life of his patients. Not if he could help it. Back then he hadn't had the skills to save his brother, but he was different now. One day, maybe some of his patients could get the education they deserved and would live long, healthy lives far away from the tragedies of life. If he had some small part in helping that happen, all the better. It would help pay back the debt of honor he owed. Family was everything, and he owed much to them.

With the infant sleeping in the crook of his arm, he knelt beside Tina. "He's okay now. You did the right thing by bringing him in. The nasal congestion should go away in a few days with some medication I'll give you, but if it doesn't, bring him back."

"Seriously?" She looked at him, her eyes wide with

shock, and tears welled again in her eyes. "That's all it is?"

"Seriously." He patted her shoulder again and gave her a smile. "That's all it is."

With a nod, Tina accepted the baby back. By watching her, how she continued to look at his face, the way she stroked his cheek with her finger, she had certainly bonded well with him and that was half the battle with very young mothers.

"You'll be fine. You just need to rest a little more and worry a little less," Vicky said.

"Thank you. You don't know how much that relieves my mind." She let out a shaky breath and brushed away the tears. "I always think the worst."

"Me, too. That way, if it doesn't happen, then it's good, right?" Vicky said, and gave Tina an encouraging smile.

"You're right. I guess that's what I do, too."

"There are times you will need to think with your mind and not your heart, even though it's really hard. I learned that a long time ago. You can try that little trick I showed you if he decides to stop breathing again."

"I will. Thank you."

Miguel watched the exchange with interest, wondering what the princess of the Sterling-Thorne vineyards was talking about. Surely she'd never had to suffer a day in her life, so he couldn't understand her words. As he watched her, though, she seemed to genuinely believe what she was saying to the young mother. Somehow these two had found a common bond that allowed Tina to relax a little. So very different, light and dark, they were a visual contrast to each other. Miguel could see by simple observation that Vicky wasn't from this part of town. Knowing her family history, he imagined she lived in a castle with an ivory tower. But if she fit into the clinic, he didn't care as long as she was a good nurse, and that was the reason she was there. Most people with her financial status simply made charitable donations. What she was doing there in the flesh was anyone's guess. Right now, none of it mattered when he had a waiting room full of patients. People with real needs were why he was here.

"Did you come by yourself or is there someone here with you?" Miguel asked Tina, and stood, directing his gaze away from Vicky's distracting beauty.

"My mother is in the waiting room."

"That's good. Is she helping you out at all?" Vicky asked as she walked with them out to the front.

"Yes. She helps me every day. I don't know what I'd do without her."

"Why don't you bring him back in a few days so we can do a well-baby checkup?" Vicky asked, then paused with a quick glance at Miguel. "Sorry. I should ask first. Do you actually have a well-baby clinic or something here?"

"Yes, we actually have one," he said with a little starch in his voice. "We're really a full-service clinic, though it may not look like it. One day a week we have a nurse practitioner come in. I'm hoping to increase her clinic to two days a week, but for now it's just one." He touched the sleeping baby again and marveled at the softness of his skin. They started out so innocent.

Wariness eased into Vicky's eyes, but she spoke kindly to Tina. "Oh, good. I'll look forward to seeing this little guy again. Let's have Tilly make an appointment for you." Vicky smiled, looking up at Miguel for confirmation. He nodded, his voice suddenly stuck. When Vicky smiled, it went all the way to her eyes and the outer corners turned up, making him wonder what secrets lay in their dark blue depths. He stepped back and cleared his throat, surprised by the attraction that surfaced in him. Now was not the time to be attracted to a coworker. Especially not one with a background that was totally at odds with his. In his experience, that sort of situation never turned out right. "Go ahead. I think he's fine now. See if she can make your appointment for about a week from now."

"Okay." She turned with Vicky and released a tremulous sigh.

Miguel watched them go and then prepared himself for the next patient of the day.

CHAPTER TWO

"So, is that your typical emergency around here?" Vicky asked Miguel as she followed him down the hall and around the corner to the staff lounge, which looked as if it had once been a large closet.

"We really see anything and everything here," he said, and put two cups of water in the microwave. "Coffee?"

"Sure."

In minutes he had heated water for the both of them and as Vicky watched, he opened a jar of instant coffee, spooning an uncertain amount in each cup. Hiding a grimace, she accepted the offering from him.

"Here's to your first day." He sipped and then sat at the small table. "We've only got a few minutes before we have every room full, so I'll give you the orientation of how I do things as we go. It'll be easier that way, rather than just telling you about it."

"I learn better that way, too." Vicky sipped from the cup, anticipating a vile brew. She wasn't disappointed. She tryied to hide her revulsion then reached for the sweetener on the table. "I think this needs a little sugar."

Miguel chucked. "You're being too kind. It needs a lot more than that, but my taste buds were nearly destroyed by residency. If you're wanting good coffee, you'll have to bring your own in a thermos or something. The coffee fund went away with the budget cuts."

The stuff was despicable beyond description. Reaching into her jacket pocket, she pulled out a pack of mints and popped one in her mouth, hoping that it would kill the taste. "Oh. No worries. I'll figure something out, but I hope you won't be offended if I don't drink this," she said, and started to pour it into the sink.

"Wait, I'll take it." Miguel reached for the cup.

The poor man. No coffee fund? Horrors. She thought a second about a friend who had a coffee delivery business. She was going to have to talk to him. "So, tell me some more about the clinic."

"Oh, right." In just a few minutes Miguel had given her the quick history of the clinic, how he had taken it over on the brink of closure and brought it to life again. "The really unfortunate part is that our grant money is ending and the city is uncertain whether they can find money for this place. The state of the economy has hit them, too." He tugged at the lapel of his lab coat, and his lips pressed together firmly for a second. "I'm working every angle I can but it's just not coming together yet. There's got to be something else that will help."

She could see the worry etched on his lean face. He put a lot of energy and probably his heart into this clinic. "What about having a fundraiser?"

"The only fundraiser I've held myself is a bake sale, and we can't have enough of them to fund the clinic. The community has put together some car washes, stuff like that, but it's just not going to be good enough for long-term funding."

"No, I mean a big fundraiser where people and corporations donate large amounts of money for tax deductions. That's the kind you need." She'd put together a few of them herself and knew what it was all about. At least that's how things got done in her family's world. Things just snapped into place when a Sterling-Thorne wanted something done. You called your wealthy friends for donations or put on dinners and gave everyone a good time for their money. Couldn't that be done in this community, as well? Though it was foreign to her, there had to be some common ground.

Miguel heaved a sigh that spoke of long frustration and Vicky sensed that she'd unwittingly brought up something she shouldn't have. "I'm sorry. I didn't know the clinic was in a bind."

"You couldn't know." He gave an unhappy smile. "We've fortunately had a benefactor for several years. He died last year and the family has decided not to continue his charity work. The city might come through, but maybe not. We won't know until July or so what they can do, when their budget is finalized."

Anger surfaced in her at the injustice. She'd just started there and now it was in danger of closing. "That's just wrong. Is this a historic building or something?" Vicky asked, wondering how she could help save this little clinic.

"Good idea, but no. It's not old enough to be considered of historical significance, so there's no help there either."

The door to the tiny lounge burst open and a young

man popped his head through the doorway. "Chest-pain patient coming."

"Chest pain trumps everything else," Miguel said, and they rushed out the door.

They dashed into a patient room where the young man she assumed was Carlos had disappeared into. Miguel was a man of energy, each movement strong, self-assured and confident, even though the patient looked quite gray. Vicky gritted her teeth and prepared herself, immediately switching on the E.R. nurse in her. Now was not the time for nerves.

"Get the crash cart ready," he said, his voice low, "and then get a line in him. Two if you can manage it."

Tilly hurried into the room. "I've called 911 for transport."

"Thanks, Tilly," Miguel replied. "He's going to need hospital care for sure. We'll get him as stable as possible first."

"Code cart is ready, Doctor," Vicky said, after tugging the massive tool kit on wheels to the patient's bedside. "Do you want to start a nitro drip?" Knowing her emergency medicine drills by heart, she hoped that she could anticipate Miguel's needs, as he hadn't been able to do any orientation with her yet.

"Yes."

The other two in the room seemed to know their roles well. Carlos hooked up the heart monitor, which looked as if it had come from an old hospital supply house. It was practically an antique, but it worked, and that was probably all Miguel wanted out of it. Next, he applied the automatic blood-pressure cuff. Tilly inserted an IV with a sure hand and hooked up the nitro drip that Vicky had prepared.

"The medication we're giving you should ease your pain quite a bit," she said to the male patient, who appeared to be in his mid-sixties. With one hand, she adjusted the oxygen mask over his face. His breathing was shallow and grunting, which was extremely worrying. She glanced at the monitor, interpreting the squiggles immediately. "Looks like he's having an infarct right now."

Miguel also looked at the monitor then at Vicky with surprise at her precise interpretation. "You're right. Start a potassium drip and give him an amp of magnesium." Leaning over the patient, he said, "Try to slow your breathing down."

"I'll do the mag—you get the drip ready," Tilly said, and together they got the medications prepared and into the patient.

Soon they heard the sound of sirens. "I'll go and get them," Carlos said, and dashed to the door. Vicky called out vital signs now and then so Miguel didn't have to keep looking up at the monitor.

Miguel remained focused on the patient situation, not being distracted by the other activity. "Keep the fluids going, increase the nitro drip."

"Yes, Doctor," Vicky responded, and although her hands trembled slightly, she changed the setting on the IV pump to the next level. "I hope it opens his vessels a little. He needs better circulation than he's got."

"Agreed." Miguel hit the print button on the old monitor that hung on the wall and a segment of the ECG appeared on paper, which he tore off. "He's got some serious S-T segment changes."

"Should we send that strip with him to the hospital?" she asked, knowing that the E.R. doctor there might appreciate that additional information to compare with further ECG interpretations.

"Yes." He pushed the print button again and a second strip printed from the machine.

The E.R. crew arrived, following Carlos, and in just a few minutes they had the patient transferred to their stretcher and he was out the door.

Vicky took a few deep breaths and placed a hand on her chest. "Wow. That was something."

Miguel's lips compressed into a line momentarily then he nodded, as if conceding something. "That *was* something. A trial by fire on your first day. Good job, everyone."

A flush of pleasure pulsed through her. Compliments certainly were unexpected at this point, especially after some of his earlier comments. "Why don't I get the room ready for the next patient?" she asked. A few minutes alone would do her some good, and she hoped that her limbs would stop shaking. She hadn't been prepared for such an urgent situation on her first day.

"I'll get the next few patients lined up," Tilly said, and returned to the nurses' station.

"Sounds good." He stepped out the door with Tilly and after a glance back he paused. "I'll just wash up first," he said, and returned to the room.

This was usually the time she collected her thoughts, after the scary stuff was over. A time she could allow herself to mentally go over the situation, make sure she'd done everything she could have and settle her churning stomach.

Miguel cleared his throat and looked at her, then his glance bounced away. "You were fine, Vicky," he said, startling her. She hadn't realized that he'd finished and was standing so close to her.

"I always second-guess myself, you know? Did we do everything and do it right?"

"I do know, and that's good, not bad. Reviewing a situation with a team member is always good to do. Emergencies like that don't come through the door every day, so it can be a little nerve-racking."

"I'm just thankful I didn't forget anything in the middle of it all, you know?" She opened the top drawer of the code cart. "I suppose you have replacement medications somewhere?"

"In the med room. Tilly can show you where." Vicky stopped and looked up at him. He was a head or so taller than her, and she was pretty long and leggy. She wore her pale blonde hair in a swingy bob that just grazed her collar. She was trim and had the look of a runner. Her eyes were a startlingly clear blue, and she had a nearly flawless complexion. There was a small scar on her left cheek that he wouldn't have noticed had he not been so close to her. It was probably from childhood chicken pox or something. Without it, he would have called her delicate, but the mark saved her from being too perfect. At least on the outside.

And he wondered again what this woman, who came from nearly unprecedented wealth, was doing in his humble clinic. The monthly income from the family business could probably finance his entire clinic for ten years. It boggled his mind to see her behaving just like any other nurse he could have hired. Frankly, he'd been against hiring her, but due to desperate measures he'd given in and offered her the job. Tilly had supported the idea of hiring her, and though his instinct had protested, he trusted Tilly implicitly. Vicky had looked good on paper, but that didn't mean she could hold up under the kind of pressure they sometimes got in the clinic, though she certainly had today. He hadn't changed his opinion in a few hours. Only time would tell, but he didn't totally mistrust her.

"What's wrong?" She held his gaze, and nothing but curiosity swirled there. "You're looking at me strangely."

Miguel met her gaze and held it for a few moments before answering. "What are you doing here?"

"You hired me."

Frowning, he shook his head. That hadn't come out right. "I mean, what is someone from your background doing at a clinic like this? Shouldn't you be working at a private hospital somewhere?"

"I *could* doesn't mean I *should* or that I even *want to*."

The light in her eyes faded, and she stepped back a pace. A frown flitted across her face, but he supposed he'd surprised her by his question. He ignored the squirm that it caused in his stomach. He'd learned the hard way, too, that people were hardly ever what they seemed.

"On the surface things are different than they really are. You must know that."

Wariness appeared in her eyes and her lips compressed. "I see. You don't think I'm capable of handling this job despite my excellent references and my performance during the crisis we just went through?"

"I know you're capable of it, but I don't know why you want to do it. With your family background—"

"Forget my background. Please. I'm here for the same reason as you, Doctor. I'm here to help people who really need it, not putting ice packs on someone who's had too much plastic surgery." She huffed out a sigh.

"Seriously, what makes you want to do this kind of work?" That was the big question. What made anyone want to do this kind of work? He had his reasons, which were private, very personal, and he wasn't about to share them with Vicky.

"If you're through being prejudicial, I'd like to get back to work. Tilly can orient me for a while if you need a break from someone like me." She turned to leave the room.

"Listen, that's not what I meant." Dammit. He hadn't intended to have this conversation and now that he was it was coming out badly.

"I think it's exactly what you meant, Doctor." Pausing, she looked over her shoulder with a tight smile.

"Vicky, this isn't coming out right." He tugged on his lab coat and straightened it, giving himself a moment to think. "I simply don't understand why someone who has all the opportunities in the world would choose to settle for a small clinic in the middle of nowhere."

"Maybe I don't consider it settling. I consider it an opportunity to expand my knowledge and skill base as a nurse." She shrugged and the steam seemed to fade out of her. "In nursing, if you don't keep your skills up you get stale and forget things. I don't want to forget things."

He'd have to accept that at face value, because at the moment he could find no other obvious motivation. "That's true for doctors, as well." He flipped his stethoscope around his neck and shoved his hands into his pockets. "Guess I'll get out of your way and let you finish up."

"Won't take long now." Vicky flashed a look at her watch and gave a surprised laugh. It was a nice sound, and one he didn't hear often yet. "Wow. It's only eleven. Feels like it's quitting time already."

"I know that feeling of strange time passage when you're in the midst of a code or something." He'd had that feeling even before his residency. When he'd held his dying brother in his arms so long ago. That had been the first time, and he'd never forgotten it.

CHAPTER THREE

THE rest of the day passed by in a rush of patients, most with minor complaints, upper respiratory issues and someone who had flattened a finger with a hammer. She and Miguel reverted back to their professional roles after the short exchange in the patient room. There was safety in her role, and it was one she knew well. She'd performed it often.

In her family, she'd been forced to play a role that she'd been desperate to escape for years. There had been various reprieves during nursing school and her short marriage. Now that she lived in the caretaker's cottage on her family estate and not under her father's thumb, she had found some relief. Living under her father's roof again was not an option. Only by helping others who needed it and being a nurse did she truly escape the artifice of her family's reputation, which always seemed to be more important than she was. When she entered the family domain, she was once again Victoria Sterling-Thorne, name before nursing.

Nursing was too personal, they thought, too hands-on. Just donate money from a distance and be done with it was their philosophy, and she didn't agree with it. There was simply something within her that wouldn't allow her to do that. A sigh eased out of her. She wasn't going to fix them, and they weren't going to influence her any longer. So back to work for now was the only answer.

The clinic stopped taking new patients at 4:00 p.m., so they were out the door by five when the clinic officially closed.

"I gotta go, M. If I'm late for dinner again, my mother's going to have a fit." Carlos hefted a backpack over one shoulder.

Miguel smiled at the young man and nodded. "Get out of here. Tell her I said hello and it was all my fault."

"You've got it." Carlos strolled out the door and disappeared down the sidewalk into the early-evening shadows.

"Tilly, you ready to roll?" Miguel asked as other staff members filed out the door.

Tilly left the nurses' station and closed the door. "Yeah." She paused for a second, looking at Vicky, then directed a pointed glance at Miguel. "Good going, kid. See you tomorrow."

Vicky retrieved her purse from the locker and reveled in the tiny compliment that Tilly had given her. Although this was a new venture for her, she thought she might like it here. As she proceeded to the door, she realized that Miguel hadn't moved and she waited for him. "Aren't you coming?"

"I've got some notes to finish first," he said. "But I'll walk you out." He left the chart where it was and stood, but Vicky didn't move. She stayed rooted where she was, looking at him seriously, assessingly, making him a little curious as to what was going on in her mind. There was something about her that made him uncomfortable, and he had no idea what it was. He'd been around plenty of lovely women and many nurses before, so simple attraction wasn't the answer. Maybe it was the way her eyes seemed to penetrate right into him, trying to see what was going on inside. Maybe it was just bad lighting.

"Finding time to play helps balance the workload, Doctor."

"It certainly does. For other people." But it was one thing he hadn't been able to do. All playfulness and joy had seeped into the ground with his brother's blood the night that he had died. Part of Miguel had died that night, too. He hadn't been able to prevent Emilio from dying. His brother had lost his life, so what right *did he* have to one? Since that night he'd dedicated himself to serving others, saving others and sacrificing himself in the process. The clinic had become his family now, its patients his children. When one of them died, he experienced a small death, as well. Each loss was one he took personally. Each loss was one patient he'd never get back and meant the kind of endless suffering of a family that he knew all too well.

Looking at Vicky, he realized she was very observant and a little too insightful for his tastes at the moment. He'd do well to watch where those blue eyes roamed. A long time ago he might have been susceptible to their allure, but not now. For the sake of his career and community, his focus had to stay right where it was. No distractions allowed. Not even one as tempting as Victoria Sterling-Thorne. Not that he had any business associating with someone from her walk of life anyway. Worlds apart, though they lived only miles apart.

"My brother owns his own business, so I know a little about it. All work and no play usually makes people very unhappy."

He thought of his family and the Sunday dinners, baptisms, weddings and other gatherings that he missed on a regular basis. He had been close to his family, but the kind of work he had dedicated himself to came at a price. Unfortunately, his family paid it for him. He had so much to make up for, he knew he'd never live long enough to make things right with them. His family had never blamed him for Emilio's death, though it might have been easier on him if they had. Pushing back those thoughts, he escorted her to the door. "It works this way for me." He didn't want to admit aloud that it might not be the complete truth.

"You've hired me full-time, but how many hours do you put in per week?"

"I don't keep track." If he did, he'd have to take a long, hard look at what he was doing with his life, and he didn't want to go there. This was all he deserved. It was his fault that Emilio had died. End of story. Turning away from her momentarily, he hung his lab coat on the back of a door. "Ready?"

"Thanks." She proceeded out the door ahead of him. As she walked past, he caught a whiff of her perfume, a sweet but spicy mix, not too heavy, and very enticing. It reminded him of sandalwood and musk. Through the course of the day he'd been close enough to catch it, but now it seemed to be hooked deeply into his brain. He'd know that sweet and exotic scent anywhere now.

"I'm sorry if I offended you, Dr. Torres," she said, and shoved her hands into her pockets. As she spoke, she kept her eyes averted from him. "It wasn't my intention."

"It's Miguel, and you can't offend me." He'd been through so much over the years that life had hardened him to insult or injury with mere words, and he had the scars to prove it. Offend him? Not a chance.

Her head snapped up, and she looked closely at him, peering into his eyes as if looking for something that simply wasn't there. "I find that hard to believe. We all react to things. Things can hurt us if we let them."

"Then it's simple. I don't let them." He'd walk her to her car, ensure that she got safely away and go home. Discussions of emotions weren't on the agenda for this evening.

She let that comment go, but he could see that she didn't like the answer or believe it.

In silence they walked to her car at the far end of the parking lot, and she gasped. "Oh. There's a dent in the door." She leaned over to examine it and unknowingly gave him a lovely view of her equally lovely backside.

As a professional, he knew he should avert his eyes and focus on the car door, but some deep-seated male instinct allowed him one last wistful glance before he stooped beside her to examine the damage. He pressed his fingers to the dent. It looked as if someone had opened a door onto hers and caused the dent. "Cars aren't made the way they used to be. Sometimes the wind can take a door and throw it pretty hard." He looked over at her. "Sorry about that. Maybe the parking garage down the street would be a better option."

Though her car wasn't a showpiece, it was new and it showed.

"Nice idea, but it hardly does any good now."

The frown between her eyes made him want to do something to fix the situation. He was a doctor and a man and that was what he did. He fixed things. Running his fingers over the dent again, an idea surfaced. "Stay here for a minute. I'll be right back."

"Why? Do you have a dent-fixing kit in the clinic?"

"No, but I might be able to help." Despite his misgivings about Vicky, he couldn't not help her. It just wasn't in him to walk away from any situation that he could possibly fix, no matter what his personal feelings.

"I'll still have to take it to the shop, won't I?" she asked, worry clouding her eyes.

"Give me a minute, okay?" In just a few minutes he strolled across the parking lot back to Vicky and her pricey dent.

"What are you going to do?"

He swung the plunger off his shoulder to show her. "I'm going to apply a little physics to see if it will reverse your situation."

"With a plunger?" The expression on her face was full of understandable doubt. She raised her brows and stepped back. "I've got to see this."

"You'll learn to get creative if you work around here long enough." Turning to the car, he placed the plunger in the center of the dent and secured a good seal. Then he slowly pulled. The dent popped back into place with a thud, and Vicky jumped at the sound.

"You did it!" she said, and in her excitement clutched

his arm with her hand. "I can't believe you did it with a *plunger,* of all things. I *never* would have thought of that."

A grin he couldn't suppress surged across his face at her contagious enthusiasm. He didn't know plumbing supplies could so easily please someone. The warmth in his chest was a puzzling sensation, one he hadn't felt for a long time. And one he couldn't afford to feel now. Stowing the pleasure at her reaction in a compartment deep inside, he nodded. "Well, there you go. Newton's third law in action."

"Equal and opposite forces, right?" She was nearly giddy in her excitement.

In the dim twilight he could see her sparkling eyes, and his gaze dropped to her mouth. It was curved upward, and her full, sensual lips were made for a man to kiss, to lose himself in, and forget the troubles of the day. Some part of him yearned to respond to that, but he couldn't. Not now. Probably not ever, and he pushed away the desire to do so. He needed her as a nurse, not a lover. This was strictly a hands-off relationship, so he changed the subject and gave his libido a kick in the shins.

"You obviously paid attention in physics."

"A little, but it's really not my forte." She gave a quick laugh then released his arm, and he could draw a full breath again. "Thanks so much, Miguel. This saves me a trip to the shop. I always feel so stupid when I go there."

"You're welcome. And you should never feel stupid. You're bright." Very—and he'd do well to remember that.

"Thanks." She dropped her chin and looked away. "My family doesn't particularly think so."

"I'd say that's their problem, then, not yours." He took a safe step back from her, removed the plunger from the door, then opened it for her. "Still willing to tackle this job?"

"Absolutely."

"Then I'll see you in the morning."

Before she got in, she glanced around. "I just noticed that there's no other vehicle around. Where's yours? Dent-free in the garage?"

"I usually walk. Burns off the day for me." And the ghosts that haunted him every waking moment. No walk would be long enough to outdistance them.

"Do you want a lift?" she asked, and got into the vehicle. "Be happy to."

"No, thanks. The air will do me good." He closed the door and watched as the most intriguing woman he'd met in a very long time waved then drove away. Intriguing, yes. Within the scope of attainment? Not even on a good day. Eventually, the princess in her would come out, and then he'd see the real Vicky.

As he returned to the clinic, the mural painted on the side caught his attention. Local kids had covered the building with their art, their words and their love. It soothed his soul a little to see it. Life moved on around you, even if you were stuck in the past. Unfortunately, love wasn't going to be enough. He'd learned that the hard way long ago. No matter how much you loved someone, it simply wasn't enough. Life got in the way as it had when Emilio had been killed and his fiancée had left him. His own life had been on the fast track with medical school and a fiancée with golden plans for the future. That night, he'd nearly lost everything. Turning away from the sight of the building, he continued inside and stowed the plunger where it belonged.

He finished the remaining notes as quickly as possible, intending to go home and get ready for another day. As he strolled down the sidewalk, taking in the early-evening air and admiring the drawn-out sunset, thoughts of Vicky and, as much as he resented it, her words followed him home.

What was it about her that churned up the past that he'd thought had been tucked away? Maybe she reminded him of something, or of dreams let go, of an unrealized future. He didn't know and didn't want to spend another second thinking about the princess in his clinic. One day she'd walk off like everyone else had and he'd be stuck trying to replace her.

Normally, he would have walked past the photos on his wall without stopping, not allowing the memories to make him stop. Tonight he paused and really looked at the faces there as he hadn't in a long time. He paused longest in front of Emilio, who had been seventeen at the time of this photo, and he had never grown any older. In an unconscious movement he clasped the sterling-silver bracelet on his right wrist. Every time he touched it he thought of Emilio and he touched it often, scratching the surface of the memory that he could never allow to heal.

Miguel turned away from the image. He didn't need a photo. Emilio's face would be forever etched in his mind. The old cliché was that time healed all wounds.

Not for him it hadn't. He couldn't let it. He didn't deserve it.

He moved away and tried to find the usual pace of his evening, but it eluded him. Images and thoughts of Emilio plagued him. Staggering guilt filled his chest and burned a path straight through his heart. The boy never should have been there, never should have come looking for him, but he had, and it *was his* fault that Emilio had died.

He'd never forgive himself for allowing his brother to die. If only he'd been more skilled, or further in his career with enough skills, or better at convincing Emilio to leave the gang that was not a true family to him, that he had one of his own that loved him. If only he'd been a better brother, doctor, friend, Emilio would be alive right now and both their lives would be very different.

There was no fix, no absolution for that one unforgivable act. The mistake he couldn't take back and could never mend. Broken limbs he could fix. Broken lives were out of his realm. If he had minded his own business, Emilio might still be alive.

Determined not to give the entire night to the ghosts, he turned on the news, got on his stationary bike and pulled out a medical journal. One of the three were bound to distract him for a while.

CHAPTER FOUR

THE next morning Miguel strode through the front doors of the clinic, which were already unlocked, and past a waiting room full of patients. Dammit. He was late. After a restless night filled with unwanted and haunting dreams, he'd finally fallen into a deep sleep just before dawn and had apparently slept right through his alarm.

He strode to the nurses' station and shoved his hair back from his face. "Sorry, Tilly. Who do we have up first?" Trying to calm his irritation, he didn't want to be rattled when seeing patients. He could miss potential signs of illness if he were distracted. He couldn't allow himself even that small lapse. Someone's health, or life, could depend on it.

"First three rooms are full, Carlos is checking vitals and Vicky is triaging the next few," Tilly said, and glanced over her shoulder at him. "Relax, *mijo*. She's good and the world hasn't ended because you were five minutes late."

"Okay." Miguel let out a relieved breath. "Thanks, Tilly. You're a gem."

She cackled and returned to the computer screen. "More like a diamond stuck in the rough."

Still a little rattled, Miguel tended to his first two patients, with Carlos assisting. The third patient was going to require some labs and a chest X-ray that they couldn't do in the clinic. He'd have Vicky fill out the proper forms and send him to the lab and then radiology department.

The second he stepped out from the lengthy patient exam in room three, his mouth began to water, and he stopped in the doorway.

"You okay, Doc?" Carlos asked.

Miguel's gaze darted around the area. "What do I smell?"

With a chuckle Carlos clapped Miguel on the arm then pulled him out of the doorway so the patient could leave. "That would be coffee, my friend." Carlos pulled in a deep breath and sighed as if sniffing ambrosia.

"I know it's coffee. Why is it here, and why does it smell like that?" he asked, still stunned at the fragrance and his visceral reaction to it.

"Thanks to our new BFF, Vicky, we now have coffee for everyone. Really good coffee, too!" He laughed and led the way to a shiny new machine that emitted the most divine odor he'd ever smelled in this clinic.

Vicky stood beside three cases of prepackaged coffee. "I hope it's okay here. This way both the staff and patients can help themselves." Obviously pleased with the arrangement, the smile she gave was radiant.

Unfortunately, Miguel was about to wipe the smile right off of her face. "You have to send it back. I'm sorry, but I believe we talked yesterday about the budget shortfalls. We simply can't afford the luxury." He cleared his throat. "No matter what you're used to, around here money is tight and there are no unilateral decisions made."

As they spoke, an elderly patient walked by with a cup of the steaming brew in his hand. "Thanks for the coffee, miss. I sure needed a cup today." He continued on his way, oblivious to the conversation around him.

"But—"

"I'm sorry, Vicky. We can't have it."

"But—" she tried again.

"No. We can't do without medical supplies for the luxury of coffee."

Now Vicky's smile turned into an angry stare. "Your next three patients are in rooms four through six." She picked up her clipboard and entered the triage area again.

"You should listen to her, man. It's not what you think. She did a good thing for everyone." Carlos moved forward to assist a woman juggling her purse and a walker. "Let me help you with that," Carlos said to the woman, but kept his eyes on Miguel. He jerked his head in Vicky's direction and frowned at Miguel.

With a sigh, he waited until Vicky returned from the triage area. She avoided eye contact with him and walked briskly past. Damn. Late for work and now he'd offended his brand-new nurse. Could the day get any worse? "Vicky? Can I see you for a moment?" He led the way to the staff lounge and waited until she entered behind him then shut the door.

"What is it, Doctor? I have patients to see," she said, the fire still in her eyes.

"Despite my misgivings, Carlos tells me there's more to the coffee story than I know." He hated even starting this conversation, but the day was already shot to hell. One more delay wasn't going to make it any worse. Carlos had never led him astray. Yet.

"Yes, there is." She folded her arms across her chest and stared at him.

She wasn't going to make this easy on him, and he supposed he deserved her irritation for not listening to her in the first place. In his experience, his worst-case scenario was usually right. "Will you please tell me?"

"It's simple. Happy patients come back, and they tell their friends about the place that made them happy. A little gesture like *free coffee* goes a long way in public relations. You can't put a value on word-of-mouth advertising. It's priceless. You may not think much of me, but I know that to be a fact."

"I know all of that, but—"

"So I called a friend of mine that I went to high school with. He owns a coffee delivery service."

"But—"

"And I talked him into making a *charitable donation* to the clinic for the tax write-off. *He* was pleased with my suggestion." She turned away and reached for the door.

In a split second, before he could even think about what he was doing, Miguel reached over her head and slammed the door shut, trapping her between the door and his body.

With a gasp she whirled and raised her face to his, only inches away. "Open this door."

"No. Not until you listen to me."

"You didn't listen to me. Why should I listen to you now?" She continued to glare up at him, and he could see every speck, every detail of the irises of her eyes, and the way the pupils changed.

"I'm not letting you out of here until you let me apologize." Though it nearly choked him to say it, it was the right thing to do.

Surprise covered her face for an unguarded second, and her pupils dilated at the rush of pleasure his words caused. When her lips parted, they drew his attention. If he were a different man in a different situation, he wouldn't have hesitated to close the gap between them and find out how soft her lips were. If he were a different man, he'd take her in his arms and press her length against his. But he wasn't, and he didn't. He couldn't.

When she blinked and looked at him with a softening in her expression that made him want more than anything to take that step, he choked down that feeling of want that she unknowingly stirred in him. The muscles in his arms trembled from the effort of holding himself back. Sweat beaded on his forehead and he began to lean forward, began to make that move toward her. Something in him held back and he froze.

They remained locked in that position for a few more seconds until Miguel slid his hand down the door to the knob. If he didn't hold on to something he was going to make a move he'd likely regret.

"I'm sorry, Vicky. I should have listened to you before I jumped to conclusions. I was irritated at being late and starting out the day so far behind in patients. It won't happen again, I promise." He took a step back from her and drew in a deep breath, shaken by the memories that statement roused. "I overslept this morning, which always puts me in a foul mood."

"I accept your apology, but the coffee situation is totally your fault."

"What?" Now that certainly got his attention. "How?"

"After you fixed my car with the plunger, you said that when working around here you had to be creative." She let out a small laugh and the tension visibly left her shoulders. "After that awful coffee you made me yesterday, I decided to get creative with that first." A shrug lifted her shoulders. "Didn't hurt to ask my friend, you know?"

A grin split Miguel's face and he relaxed, too. "Okay. I'll take responsibility for that."

A light rap on the door made them both jump, as if they had been guilty of doing something other than talking.

"We've got patients out here," Carlos said through the door.

"Oh, dear." Vicky pulled the door open and nearly collided with the assistant. "Sorry, Carlos. We had to get something straightened out."

"Yeah. And thanks for the coffee," he said. "Everybody loves it."

"That's great."

"Think you could do something about doughnuts next?" The young man grinned and raced off to collect the next patient.

Vicky laughed. "He's a great kid, isn't he?" she asked Miguel as they left the lounge.

"He is. I hope he stays."

"Why wouldn't he stay?"

"He's got bigger dreams than this clinic. At this point he thinks he wants to be a doctor. He's got a long road ahead, if he really pursues it." Miguel sighed, having already walked the path that Carlos wanted to take.

"You did it, why couldn't Carlos?" she asked. "Seriously. There's the state-funded lottery program he could apply for. As long as he graduated from high school, it's guaranteed for college, right?"

"Yes. I just hope he doesn't get...distracted." The way his brother had, which had led to his demise.

"Well, guess we need to get back to the patients for now, and work on Carlos's future later, right?"

"Yes." He was pleased that they had solved the issue so quickly and so well and were right back to their professional roles. Contacting a coffee service for a donation wasn't something that would have occurred to him. Maybe someone who came from a different background could be beneficial to the clinic. Time would tell.

"Why don't you try the coffee?" she asked, and poured him a cup which he accepted, his fingers brushing over hers.

"I'm afraid my taste buds might keel over from exposure to real flavor," he said, but took a sip anyway. He groaned in reluctant delight. "Be sure to thank your friend for me. This is fabulous."

Vicky flushed with pleasure at his reaction. No man in her life had ever been as satisfied with something as simple as a cup of coffee. "I will." She dashed off into a patient room.

CHAPTER FIVE

ONLY after Vicky got home that evening did she allow herself to relive the moments when Miguel had trapped her in the lounge. She'd been horribly angry at him. At first it had seemed that he was treating her exactly the same way her father and brothers did, as if she didn't have a brain in her head. The same way her ex-husband had treated her. But then Miguel had changed and listened to her. He had been so close, so masculine, so very attractive and totally off-limits. He'd said it would never happen again. That's what had dissolved her anger. She wanted to believe him, but trust came so hard to her. After the life-changing experience with her former husband, trust was not something she handed out like candies. She'd put her trust and faith in a man, supposedly for the remainder of her life, and with that weapon he'd turned her world upside down.

Closing her eyes, she allowed her mind to take the image further than it had gone in the lounge. If she had raised her face just right, if he had reached out just so, it would only have taken an inch or two before their lips had met. Vicky melted into the dream for a second, wondering just what a kiss with Dr. Torres would be like.

The phone rang and she jumped, and the fantasy spiraled away. Before picking up the phone, she checked the caller ID. It was her brother, Edward.

"Hey, Eddy."

"You're the only one in the world that calls me that, you know."

She heard the affectionate irritation in his voice, and she smiled. "That's 'cos I'm your little sister. You'll always be Eddy to me, no matter how successful you are as a big-shot designer."

"Just, please, don't call me that around anyone in the business. I'd never live it down."

"Hey, I just had an idea. You could create a whole new line of clothing for kids called Eddy Wear, or something like that." How strange. That idea had never occurred to her before and a little bubble of pleasure rippled through her. Then she bit her lip, waiting for his response. He'd never taken suggestions from her before, so why would he now?

He chuckled. "That's funny, Victoria." He chuckled again. "Really funny, but I'll have to think about that one, if you don't mind."

She mentally sighed, knowing that she would always be the little sister with ideas that never went anywhere to him. "So, what's up? Why are you calling? I know it wasn't to get fashion advice."

"You are *so* right. I was wondering if you'd like to come to a little dinner engagement with me."

Another sigh escaped her. He always called on her when he needed a date. He was married to his design business, jetting off for meetings and shows in New York and Europe, so dating was a chore for him. "What, when, where and all that stuff?"

Edward gave her the details, and she checked her calendar. Two weeks' time on a Friday night. She certainly didn't have a date either. "Sure."

"Great! I'll send a few new designs for you to choose from, and the limo will pick you up at six-thirty." Always one to take advantage of publicity opportunities, Eddy insisted that she wear his designs at these outings of his and anytime they were at an event together. Fortunately, nothing was indecent or had too many frills, and always complimented her figure, so how could she argue with that?

"Will Daddy be there?" She hated asking that, but it was better for her to be prepared with her Victoria face on when he was near. That mantle she wore helped to protect her emotions from the pain that usually ensued. When she was unprepared, he always seemed to hurt her with his judgments and opinions of her life. Being on guard and prepared around him took the sting out of some of his comments.

"No, Charles was invited but has another engagement." For whatever reason, Eddy always called their father by his given name. "Secretly, I think he's seeing someone and doesn't want us to know about it," Eddy said in a dramatic whisper.

"Why not, for heaven's sake? We're adults, and Mother died a very long time ago." Perhaps if he had a romantic diversion, he'd take things easier on her. Running her life seemed to be a hobby for him, and he definitely could use some distraction.

"I think that he thinks that *we* think he's being disloyal to her memory by getting involved with someone, and you know how he is about loyalty."

Vicky could imagine the eye-roll that Eddy put on just then, and she laughed. "I do indeed." It was part of the reason they had fought so much when she had declared her major in college. She wanted to leave the family business behind for a hands-on career. It was the only battle she'd ever won with her father, but he'd by no means forgotten about it. He was so much prouder of his two sons than of his daughter, whom he viewed as a failure. Failed marriage, failed career, failed daughter.

"Well, I've got to go, Eddy. I'll see you at the event."

"See you there, baby sister. Can't wait for you to see the gowns I'm sending."

After hanging up the phone, she poured a glass of wine to settle the sudden nerves in her stomach. A simple Chablis, but it was her favorite wine from the family vineyard. New Mexico was the oldest wine-growing region in America, thanks to the Spanish settlers of long ago. Although her family was not of Spanish descent, they had purchased stock from the original vines and developed their own holdings, which had been in the family ever since. That was the loyalty that Eddy had been talking about. It ran as deep in her family as the vines in the ground.

The vineyard grew on acreage that had once been the bottom of a very large, very ancient ocean. The land left behind after the ocean had receded millions of years ago was some of the most fertile in the country. This location so close to the Rio Grande River provided the only thing lacking when Mother Nature didn't cooperate: fresh water.

Looking out the picture window of her little caretaker cottage, she enjoyed the lavish view of row upon row of grapes. As a child she'd raced and hidden among the lush canopy of leaves and vines, using her imagination to create stories that had taken her to exotic and wondrous lands where she had been queen.

Now the vineyards were waking up after being dormant all winter. New Mexico springs usually began in April and the growing season stretched out to the first frost, sometimes as late as October. This was her favorite time of year, when the earth renewed itself and grew to face another season of glorious bounty.

The cottage was her sanctuary. After her divorce she'd needed to be in the middle of the vineyard where nature soothed her, not in the bustle of the main house where every move she made was scrutinized and watched. There she could never truly relax and just be herself. This cottage was where she'd needed to be. It had provided the protection and safety she'd needed, and demanded nothing of her. If she had her choice, she'd never leave its secure walls unless she found something its equal.

Now, wine in hand, she opened her door and took an evening stroll through the vines, enjoying visualizing the journey of the grapes and drinking the end results. Life came full circle right there in front of her. Touching a leaf or vine here and there, she wondered if she could remember some of those stories she'd told herself as a child. It would be good to be queen again, if only for a while.

Miguel sighed as he looked at the prospectus in front of him. He'd had some mad idea about presenting it to potential private investors like their previous benefactor, but it was hopeless. The clinic lost money every year thanks to the economy, higher health costs and lack of reimbursement. No sane investor was going to put money on this dark horse. After a quick glance at the clock, he saved the file then closed the computer document. He'd fiddle with it some more later. Right now he had to get to the community center or he was going to be late for his standing Wednesday night basketball game. After a quick change from his scrubs into ratty exercise attire and filling a water bottle, he headed out.

In a few minutes he reached the community center that had saved his life more than once over the years. He and some of his cousins had practically grown up here, and he had a special affection for this building and the people who ran it. Blood and roots ran deep in the south valley of Albuquerque.

"M., you ready for a whooping?" his cousin Arturo asked, and tossed a ball to him. Miguel caught it and automatically began to dribble it, the thump of the ball on the floor corresponding with his heartbeat.

"After last week I don't think you have it in you." He grinned and tossed the ball back.

Arturo caught it, then made a quick spin and charged the net, catching Miguel off guard. "How's that?"

"Got me on that one," Miguel said with a grin, and the game began in earnest. They played and carried on for an hour before either one was willing to be the first to take a water break. Hot and sweaty and thoroughly drained, Miguel parked himself against the wall and caught his breath. Although they were cousins, he and Arturo were friends, too. Each knew the other's deep, dark secrets and was willing to keep them that way.

"Are you coming to the graduation party?" Arturo asked.

"What graduation party?" he asked, and frowned. Arturo didn't have any kids graduating.

"Don't you check your email? I sent it to you a couple of weeks ago. Cindy is graduating high school."

"*Cindy?*" Miguel cringed. "No way. Did I miss something? She's only a junior, right? She should have another year."

"You're behind the times, dude. She's been in an accelerated program all year, taking high school and beginning college classes at the same time. She's finishing a year early so we're having a big celebration."

"How did she get so smart?" No one in their family had been accelerated like that.

"Takes after her mother's side of the family," Arturo said, and drank some more water. "So how's the clinic? Still making a good wife?"

"What?"

"You're married to that clinic of yours. You don't date, you don't go out to meet anyone, all you do is work." He drained the contents of his water bottle. "You are turning into an old man way too soon, my friend."

Miguel turned suspicious eyes on Arturo. "Now you sound like my mother. Have you been talking to her?" That wouldn't surprise him. She'd been trying to match him up with someone, anyone, for years.

"Oh, no, not really." Arturo looked away, then back at Miguel, and shrugged. "She talked to my mother, who talked to me."

A laugh creaked out of Miguel as his suspicions were confirmed. "I knew she was in there somewhere. What's she up to now?"

"She worries. They both do. You need to get out a little more, M. She's afraid you're becoming an old man way before your time."

"No worries. I'll be fine." The concern in Arturo's face puzzled him. Didn't they know he could take care of himself, that he always had, and didn't depend on anyone? But later Miguel wondered if their fears were coming true. Was he turning into an old man while still in his early thirties? After his fiancée had left him years ago, he'd never really tried to get out there into the dating arena much. Too busy, too intense, too many things to do that didn't include leisure time spent on relationships. Oh, once in a while he'd hook up for a mutually temporary situation, but those were few and far between. His thoughts turned to Vicky and he wondered if she had any better luck at relationships than he did. With her looks and background she likely had men lined up for her. But, then, that could pose its own set of problems.

He showered, changed, ate something, all the while

wondering about Arturo's seemingly innocent statement. Was he right? Maybe that's why it wouldn't leave his mind and continued to nag him like an imminent case of flu coming on.

When *was* the last time he'd had a date or even gone out for coffee with a woman that wasn't business re-lated? He couldn't remember. Last year? Maybe the year before? Miguel blew out a long sigh. Arturo could be right. He *was* married to his work and hadn't even real-ized it. Based on principle alone, he was going to have to do something about it.

The next day passed smoothly, and the coffee service continued to be a huge success with staff as well as patients. Pastries magically appeared and Carlos was ecstatic.

Arturo's words followed Miguel around like a shadow. If he turned quickly enough, he thought he might actu-ally see them lurking behind him, goading him on.

He and Vicky continued to work efficiently together. At least that part of his life was going well. Until he had to close the clinic forever. He was beginning to think that Vicky's idea of a major fundraiser would be the only way to save it. But that was a topic for another day. First things first.

The afternoon wound down and the last patient had been seen. The familiar pattern, the flow of the day, had soothed him at one time. He could trust in the continuity of his work, but today it didn't seem to be working.

"You okay, Miguel?" Vicky asked, perceptive as ever. "You seem a bit off today."

"I'm good. Just got something on my mind."

She leaned against the desk and put her purse down. "I've got time to talk if you want to." She shrugged and her glance skittered away. "I mean, if you'd like to. It helps sometimes."

Miguel thought a second. Maybe she could help. Mirroring her position, he moved and leaned against the desk beside her. "Well, I have a problem. A woman problem."

"Oh," she said. "I didn't know you were involved with anyone." Her shoulders sagged a little. "Not that it's any of my business, but how can I help?"

A grin split his face at her reaction, though it shouldn't have pleased him. "It's a female *cousin* problem."

Vicky brightened and met his gaze. "What kind of problem is that?"

"She's graduating this weekend from high school. I need to figure out what kind of present to get her for her party on Saturday."

"Cash. It always works for kids that age." She shook her head. "My oldest brother has three kids, and that's what they always want. Cash, cash, cash. And you're off the hook from having to think too hard about it. A card, a check, they can buy whatever they want, and you don't have to feel bad if they didn't like what you got." She snapped her fingers. "Done."

Miguel narrowed his gaze on her. "I like the way you think." That would be the simplest solution and he was chagrined that he hadn't thought of it himself. Arturo was looking more right all the time.

"I was a teenage girl once. I have the inside scoop." For a few seconds their gazes locked, and Miguel thought about her as a teenager. "I'll bet you were pestered by all the boys in school, weren't you?"

A quick laugh chirped out of her. "Hardly. I was awkward, too tall, too skinny, introverted and…well, my mother died when I was sixteen, so that made life more difficult than it could have been, I guess."

The momentary flirtation in his gut evaporated at her words. "I didn't mean to pry, Vicky. I'm sorry."

"You're not prying and it's fine. It's been over ten years, so for the most part I've put it to rest."

He gave a mental sigh, feeling a connection to her that surprised him. "I also lost someone when I was young. My brother." He hadn't meant to tell her about Emilio, but the words just popped out.

"I'm so sorry. It's tough, isn't it?" she asked, offering unexpected sympathy. "I think sometimes it makes us better caregivers because we know what it's like to lose someone. Just wish that it had been different, you know?"

"Yeah, believe me, I know." Sadness crept into her eyes and something cramped in Miguel's chest. He knew that feeling exactly and he didn't want to share it with anyone, let alone Vicky. They were poles apart in so many ways. Finding common ground between them was impossible. At least, that's what he'd thought. Pain shared with another often took the sting out of it, but he couldn't imagine that happening with her.

"So, is your cousin having a big bash or just running off with her presents?"

The change of topic was a welcome one, and he returned to the present situation. "It's a big deal—family, an outdoor tent, the whole thing."

"Judging by your reaction, not one you're eager to attend?"

He frowned and crossed his arms over his chest. "It's not that I'm unhappy about it, it's good to be with family and all that."

"I sense a *but* coming."

A long-suffering sigh rolled out of him and he tried not to groan. "At these types of events, I get just hounded about being single. *Are you dating anyone, are you going to ever get married?* All that stuff. I'm sure it's not something you suffer at your own family events. Your family experience may be quite different than mine."

A snort was her only answer.

He shook his head then something occurred to him. If he took a date, everyone would back off and give him a breather. It had potential. Now, who could he get to go with him who wouldn't read anything into it?

"I suppose you're the only single man there, too."

"No. Just the grandson who hasn't fulfilled his family and reproductive obligations." He turned slightly toward her. "So, uh, what are you doing for the weekend?" Was he mad for even thinking of asking her to help him out? People like her didn't help people like him, but desperation pumped through him, and he was willing to risk nearly anything to get out of this.

"No plans, really. I'm just going to be in and out, errands and that kind of stuff." Then her gaze flashed to his and shock widened her eyes as she realized what he was up to. "Are you serious?"

"Dead serious. I need you to protect me."

She almost snorted out a laugh. "How am I going to protect you?"

"Well, at least people will think twice about grilling me about my future reproductive plans if I have a date on my arm."

"You're really serious?" The smile faded away. "Are you certain that I'm the right person for the job? Doesn't Carlos have sisters you can borrow or anything?"

"He does, but my family knows them, so they'd know it's a sham. You're the only one who can help me out." As much as he hated to admit it, she was the best person for the job. His family didn't know her and she wouldn't give him any unrealistic expectations about their relationship. Strictly business. "How about you wear a nice summer dress, bring your appetite, and pretend to be my date for an afternoon?" Asking her out was another thing he hadn't planned on doing, but now that it was out there between them, his heart sped up and his stomach clenched, waiting for her reply. Her gaze held his for a few seconds longer, considering, and he could almost hear her debating the issue mentally.

"Okay, I'll be your date and spare you from your family for an afternoon. But you're going to owe me one, buster."

"Totally. You have no idea how much I appreciate this."

She sighed. "I'm beginning to feel I'm forever the bridesmaid, never the bride. My brother always hits me up for functions, too."

They made arrangements to meet at the office and Miguel would drive from there. "See you tomorrow."

CHAPTER SIX

WELL, that hadn't been the kind of ending to her day that she'd expected. Who said miracles didn't happen anymore? Miguel had asked her out. Sort of. It wasn't really a date, but a pretend date, so she shouldn't get too excited about it. That wasn't something she'd ever have expected, especially after the rocky start to her job.

All the same, little flutters stirred in her stomach. The man was gorgeous and single. How much better could a day get than spending an afternoon with him, whether it was a real date or not? She'd never been to a graduation party as he'd described. Those sorts of functions in her family tended to be held at the country club, not the backyard at her cousin's house. The decorating and cleanup could be left to the staff, but then you missed the fun of it. Should be an enjoyable way to spend an afternoon, especially as she didn't have anything else do to and it was an opportunity to stay away from the homestead and her father's oppressive energy. Over the years she'd learned just to avoid him rather than engaging in endless arguments that she'd never win anyway. One day she hoped to mend her relationship with her father, but until he was open to it, it would never happen.

Miguel was so different from the men in her family. He put himself out there for others, and she couldn't imagine her father extending himself in the same way. Her ex-husband had been a carbon copy of her father and just as cold. A man who'd taken his money to bed instead of his wife. As a result their marriage had ended within months. Back then she'd deluded herself into thinking that the intimacy she craved in a relationship was something she could live without, that there were other things she could be happy with. She'd been so wrong about that and about the man she'd married. Her judgment in men had always been poor, but it had been totally missing when she'd agreed to marry Carl. In the end, she'd chosen to correct the mistake before bringing children into the picture. She and Carl had parted ways, with him happily counting the settlement money that had been more important than she had been. That had been the end of any romantic endeavors in the past few years. Sticking to being her brother's date now and then had gotten her out of the house but kept her safe enough from any awkward entanglements. Tomorrow was only one day out of her life, and she was doing a favor for her boss. That was simple, wasn't it?

That night Vicky slept with dreams disturbing the peace of the night. Dreams of unfulfilled longings stirred her body to a blistering heat that woke her. Images of Miguel, his face tantalizingly close to hers, teased her through the night. If only she had reached out to him the other day, her night might not be so restless. Until the early hour before dawn she slept fitfully, trying to ignore the call of her body, the yearning to hold another close.

Years had passed since she'd been intimate with anyone. Getting hot over her coworker was just a case of familiarity and having an attractive man right in front of her every day, right?

Her dreams and her subconscious knew otherwise.

As they drove to the party, Miguel ran through the extensive list of relatives she was most likely to encounter.

"You know I'll never remember all that," she said, and gave him a smile that looked more like a grimace. She didn't want to disappoint him, but she was afraid she was going to. And she had to keep reminding herself that this wasn't a date but a favor, so the same rules didn't apply. The little butterfly careening around in her stomach wasn't convinced.

"I know, I know. I have a huge family. If we stick close, I can refresh you as we go along. You'll be fine."

"I hope you know what you're doing, Miguel."

After a quick glance, he said, "I do, too." Then he patted her hand. "It'll be fine. No matter what happens. It's just one day, right? Then we go back to our lives and call it good."

Before Vicky could even think of what to say, Miguel pulled his truck up against the curb and parked behind a line of other vehicles. "We'll have to walk from here, but it's just a block or two."

In minutes they had arrived at a very large outdoor tent filled with people of all ages. She turned to stare at Miguel. "This isn't a party, this is an event. You could fill Isotopes Park with this many people."

"Now, that's a slight exaggeration, but I told you there

would be a mob of people here. Let's find the food. I'm dying for my cousin's enchiladas. His green-chili stew is outstanding." He grinned and took her hand.

The feel of her trim hand in his surprised him. The surprise was that it felt immediately comfortable, not in the size of her fingers or the silky softness of her skin or even the way her fingers naturally curled against his palm. It was the fit. A fit he hadn't expected and one that he wasn't sure he should even be thinking about, even in the loosest of terms. Guilt surfaced in him. Guilt that he wanted a life of his own to enjoy while leaving the memory of his brother behind. That couldn't happen. Tension knotted his shoulders, but he tried not to show it.

Today was all about getting him out of a jam, and Vicky was nice enough to help him out. That was all. He knew that there would never be any chance at things going beyond today because he wouldn't allow it.

Somehow they made it through the mob of people and to the food line. It just seemed natural to have Vicky in front of him and for him to place his hands on her shoulders, and he tried very hard not to feel the silky softness of her skin bared enticingly by the thin straps of her summer dress. The sun shone down on the day and it was a gorgeous afternoon. Miguel started to relax as he introduced Vicky to some of his family. When he got to his mother, he hugged her tight, then took Vicky's hand and introduced them.

"It's been so long since my son has brought a woman to meet the family." The woman with intelligent brown eyes, the same chocolate shade as Miguel's, took her hand from him. "It is good to see him socializing, but

I can see why he's kept you to himself." She started to lead Vicky away from Miguel.

The panicked look Vicky cast over her shoulder at him nearly broke his resolve. There was desperation in those eyes, which he worked hard to resist. Something, some protective male instinct he'd nearly forgotten about, surfaced strong and fast in him. Before he knew it he'd stepped forward without taking his eyes from Vicky. As much as he'd tried to ignore it, push it away or flat out deny it, there was something going on between them. Some attraction that he hadn't felt in years. Although it wasn't exactly welcome, he couldn't stop it. Walking away from that was going to be difficult, no matter what his head told him. His heart and the heat in his blood told him something entirely different. Aside from that, he couldn't let his mother take over or she'd find out their whole ruse in seconds. "We were going to eat first then catch up with everyone."

"See that you do, *mijo,* see that you do." She patted his cheek as her perceptive eyes watched him. "I've missed seeing you with the family."

He took Vicky's hand in his and led her to a row of chairs where they balanced their plates on their knees.

"This is quite the party, isn't it?" she asked, breaking the silence between them. She tucked her hair behind her ear, not wanting to let Miguel know that she'd never been to a party like this but that she was totally prepared to enjoy herself. The nerves she had now weren't at all like the nerves she had when she was at a society event. Now it was all because of Miguel's presence so close to her.

"Yes, it is. Cindy's the oldest of my cousin Arturo's

kids and is a really smart girl. She's graduating a year early and already taking university classes." Small talk helped break the tension in the air between them. "I was never that dedicated when I was her age."

"Wow, neither was I. I was lucky to get through some of my classes, let alone graduate early." Vicky shook her head. "Math was the bane of my existence."

"I'll take your word for that." He looked over at her as she sat with her plate on her knees. "Before anything else happens, I want to thank you for coming." If nothing else, he owed her his gratitude. He couldn't see behind her sunglasses, but he thought she winked at him. The sideways smile she gave him, with her lips just turned up, made his heart lurch. Vicky was simply gorgeous, and he wondered why she wasn't taken. If he'd been looking, he might have been looking at her. Yet there was that bloom of attraction between them that lay waiting to unfold.

"Just remember you owe me one." She laughed and shook her head, then tucked her hair behind her ear in a gesture he was beginning to realize was a nervous habit.

He laughed and suddenly felt much better, his heart lighter than it had been in years. It was a good feeling and one he didn't want to let go of just yet. It reminded him of the way he had lived a long time ago, before the death of Emilio and the ruining of his life. "I won't forget. Promise."

Arturo dropped into the seat beside Miguel. They spoke a moment in Spanish then Arturo turned to Vicky. "So, you're the new nurse, right?"

"Right."

"Has your mother met her yet?" Arturo asked with a big grin.

"Yes." Miguel nodded his head.

"She like?"

"Yes, I think so. But just so you know, Vicky's only helping me out for the day." As Miguel said the words, for a moment he wanted them not to be true. Watching Vicky sit beside him, seeing the sunlight glint off the highlights in her hair, he wanted to really have her in his life. But what could he do, fire her and then ask her out? That wasn't going to happen. The clinic was much more important than his pitiful social life. He needed her as a nurse, not a date right now, although unofficially Vicky was his date. For today.

"Yeah, right." Arturo leaned over and shook Vicky's hand. "Anyway, welcome to the party. Be sure to have a glass of wine or something before it's all gone."

"I will, thanks. By the way, your chili is fantastic—what do you do special to it? I don't do much cooking, but for this I'd learn."

"Oh, a little of this and that. I don't write anything down." He waved his hand as if waving away her request. "Have you ever seen the movie *Like Water For Chocolate?*"

"No." She'd never heard of it, but it sounded intriguing. Anything with chocolate in the title had to be good. She took a quick glance at Miguel, but he seemed to be paying close attention to his cousin. A little pang fluttered inside her. What had she been thinking, agreeing to this nondate? Was she thinking that Miguel would somehow put aside his biases, ignore the glaring chasm between their backgrounds? She refocused on Arturo. "What's it about?"

"Rent it sometime. My recipe is just like that. Passion in every ingredient."

Vicky narrowed her eyes. She was certain he was teasing her, but she wasn't really sure. "I'll do that."

"Stop teasing her, will you? You're no gourmet, you just won't give up that recipe that you stole from Grandma."

Arturo grinned, but didn't deny the friendly accusation. "I've gotta go anyway. It's tough, being the host." He gave a casual wave and wandered off through the crowd.

After they'd finished eating, Miguel stood. "I guess there's no way around it, I'm going to have to introduce you to people."

"I'm ready." She held her hands out to him, and he pulled her to her feet. With the uneven surface of the ground, she bobbled a little bit on her sandals, and Miguel placed a hand on her hip to steady her.

"Okay?"

For a second she didn't answer, just looked at him and swallowed. "Yeah, I'm good." If they had met in a different place and time or were from more similar backgrounds, maybe then they could have been on a more equal footing. The buzz of attraction that hung in the air every time they were near each other hadn't gone unnoticed by her. She simply didn't trust in herself or her judgment in men to be able to reach out to Miguel. The fire of her past had burned away any confidence she might have once had and she still had the singe marks to prove it. The idea of reaching out to another man had her quaking inside. Because of her upbringing and the need to keep up appearances, she didn't let her fears show. God forbid that anyone should see outright emotion in a Sterling-Thorne. Not that Miguel would believe her anyway. The man was the most fearless person she'd ever seen. Nothing scared him, and he wouldn't understand her fears, so it was best to hide them beneath a bright smile. With one last glance at his tempting mouth and mysterious eyes, she released her grip on his arm and let him lead her through the crowd on their nondate. "Let's go."

As they made the rounds, it seemed perfectly natural for Miguel to place his hand on her shoulder, touch her arm, take her hand and tuck it into his elbow. Although this started out as a way for him to keep his family from asking questions, he was allowing himself to fall deeply into the role he'd set up for himself. For the next few hours he enjoyed the luxury of touching her whenever he could, and she never pulled away from his touch but rather seemed to enjoy it. Each time Vicky turned her face up to his, he wanted to bring her closer, but knew that was the wrong thing to do—for both of them.

"You have a lovely family, but I think I'm ready for some wine or a spritzer now," she said, and fanned her face with her hand. "Whew."

"Let's go. Me, too. I've had about enough talking for a while." He glanced at his watch and was surprised at how much time had passed. He was enjoying himself more than he had thought he would. Thanks to Vicky. He certainly was going to owe her a big favor. They arrived at the refreshment table, which was tucked into a corner of the yard beneath a sprawling cottonwood tree that offered the welcome shelter of shade. He looked up into the branches, which seemed different than they had been in childhood. Perspective, he guessed. All things changed with time.

"What's up?" She gave his hand a squeeze.

"Nothing, really. I was just thinking of the times I climbed this tree." He looked down at Vicky. "This was my grandmother's house first, and I spent a lot of time here as a kid. Good memories…" He only wished that some of them could have been different.

"I didn't climb trees, but I spent a lot of time in the gardens and vineyards when I was a kid, just wandering and getting away, you know?" She looked away from him, then at the beverages. "I wonder what kind of wine they have."

"Arturo likes local wines, so it's hard to tell what's here." Miguel reached for a bottle and held it up. "This one's from Gruet Winery."

Vicky leaned over his arm and read the label. "Oh, that's lovely. I know that one."

"Isn't that one of your competitors?" he asked with a sly grin.

"Yes, they are, but what's business without competition? Makes everything taste better when the batch is done, you know?"

"Are you serious? Isn't the wine business as cutthroat as any other?"

"It can be, I guess, I just prefer to stay away from that part of it and focus on the results." She paused a second and then took the glass that he held out to her, not caring what it was at this point, just grateful for it and the breather it gave her. Having Miguel so close and allowing him to touch her was something she'd not normally have done. Each touch, each time his body grazed hers sent ripples of awareness through her. "So, where's your cousin's daughter? We haven't met her yet."

"I know. She must be holding court somewhere. I'm sure we'll see her pretty soon. She's not exactly the shy-and-retiring type."

A squeal announced the arrival of the party girl, Cindy.

"Miguel!" The teenager launched herself at him. He caught her but had to take a step back from the force and the wine in his hand sloshed over the rim.

"Wow. Is this my little Cindy?" he asked, and twirled her around in a quick circle.

"It's me. All grown up now!" With a laugh she stood beside him but kept her arm around his waist as he introduced her to Vicky. "I'm so glad you came."

"Wouldn't miss it." He ignored the twinge of guilt when the little voice inside him reminded him that he almost had, that his guilt had kept him away. "Where have you been?"

A dramatic roll of her eyes was all the answer he needed. "Got to make nice with the aunties before I can play, you know?"

"I know what you mean." He reached into his shirt pocket and extracted a long, slender envelope and held it out.

Cindy snatched it from his hand with another signature squeal. "Ooh! What is it, what is it, what is it?" She tore the envelope to shreds and extracted the card containing a check. "Thank you, thank you, thank you!" She hugged him again and dashed off.

"What a bundle of energy. No wonder she's an over-achiever," Vicky said with a laugh. "She adores you."

"It's mutual. Sometimes I feel bad that I haven't been around more." He looked away and then sipped his wine.

"Well, the good thing is that you're here now, right? Life gets in the way for us all." Hesitation in her move, she reached out and placed her hand on his forearm. There was strength there in the muscles covered by tawny skin, but there was steel that she sensed beneath the surface.

"I appreciate that," he said, and held her gaze for a moment. "There are a few more people I want to find then we can go."

CHAPTER SEVEN

AFTERNOON sun gave way to evening shadows. Vicky was enjoying herself immensely and felt the chains of anxiety relinquishing their hold on her. Even the chat with Miguel's mother wasn't as intimidating as she'd thought it was going to be. The woman was lovely, had raised a fine son and was very proud of his achievements. Though there was a touch of caution in her eyes when she looked at him, she obviously loved him. Emotions stirred inside her. Seeing the love of his mother reminded her of what she had lost so long ago. The grief that she'd dealt with at the loss of her mother surfaced briefly in her heart. The pang of her loss nearly brought tears to her eyes as she watched Miguel and his mother, but she choked them back, trying not to allow envy for something that could never be claim any of this day.

Just as she thought the party was going to wind down, a band began to play.

Excitement danced in Miguel's eyes and she was nearly mesmerized. "Part two—music. It's not a party without music and dancing, is it?" Miguel asked, grabbing her hand.

"I thought we were going to leave?" Panic set in. This wasn't the kind of music she knew.

"Sorry. Change in plan—do you mind?" He tugged on her hand.

"Wait! I don't know this stuff. I'm strictly ballroom. This is…I don't know what this is!" Although she protested, she was helpless to stop Miguel as he led the way to the makeshift dance floor. What if she embarrassed herself?

"That's okay. I'll lead."

And lead he did. Every move they made together was directed by Miguel. His hands spun her, led her through each step as if he were a dance instructor. Within a few minutes Vicky relaxed and just let him lead her. It was what she wanted anyway. Never in her life had she felt so feminine, so light, so enchanted by a man in the moonlight.

When the music finally slowed down, Vicky thought that Miguel was going to take her back to sit down, but he simply drew her closer to him. The tiny lights strung around the yard created interesting halos of light and deep pockets of shadowy darkness in the corners of the yard.

Miguel tucked Vicky close against him with his chin against her right temple. She felt a sigh roll through him, and she closed her eyes, letting go, letting the sensations of the day and the feel of Miguel's body be her guide. The flames that had singed her in the past gave way to a new heat source.

Each move they made together was guided by his hand in the small of her back. The man was an expert dancer, and Vicky found herself unwilling and unable to resist the desire that bubbled up inside her. What if, for once, she made a move unlike any she'd ever made? What if she reached out to Miguel? Would he hold on or would he burn her, the way every other man she'd known had burned her?

Leaning back slightly, she needed to see his face, to look into his eyes, to see if she was simply fooling herself into believing that something was going on between them. Could she have imagined the tenderness in every touch of his hand, the want in every move of his body toward her?

Now, looking up at his face, the way his eyes held her gaze then dropped to her mouth and lingered there, she knew she hadn't imagined anything. Automatically, her lips parted as Miguel guided them around to the music. Her heart raced and it wasn't from the exercise of the dancing. She wanted Miguel with everything she had in her. Shadows darkened around them as Miguel led her into a quiet sanctuary of the yard. The music faded to a dull rhythm far away as the roar of her heart crowded out all other sound.

The hand at her waist eased up her back until it cupped the back of her head. "Vicky," he whispered, and bent his head toward her. "This may be the worst move I'll ever make, but I want to kiss you."

Needing no encouragement, she raised her face and met his lips. The instant their lips touched, a shock of deep desire rolled through Vicky. She parted her lips and eagerly met his tongue with hers, melting against him and clasping his neck with her hands. He gathered her tight against his body and squeezed her, kissed her, as if ravenous for the taste and touch of her. As if she were the very thing he needed to sustain life.

No woman had ever felt this way to him. Miguel held on to her as if she were a dream, a wisp of smoke that would fly away if he didn't hold tight. This night was enchanted, and Vicky was the magic in his arms.

Heart racing, desire pulsed through him as he kissed her and held her. In less than a second he forgot where they were and lost himself in the feel of Vicky's curves against him. She was trim, but lush in all the right places. The feel of her soft breasts crushed against his chest made him wish they were somewhere else. Anywhere else.

When he finally lifted his head, his breathing was ragged, as if he'd run ten city blocks. Desire hung in the air, hot and heavy between them. They simply stared at each other as if in shock. Maybe they were. Maybe it was an enchanted evening and they were under the spell of the night.

"Wow." She brushed her hair back from her face with a hand that visibly trembled. "Wrong move or not, I certainly didn't expect that."

"Neither did I. I hope I haven't offended you?"

"Being offended never entered my mind," she said, and placed her palm on his chest over his heart. "I…feel…more alive right now than I think I've ever been." Then she looked away, as if embarrassed by her admission.

With a finger under her chin, he raised her face so that she looked at him again. "So am I," he whispered, and it was the biggest truth he'd faced in a long, long time.

Over the course of an afternoon he'd begun to fall for Vicky Sterling-Thorne.

At last they said their goodbyes and left the party. They drove back to the clinic in silence. Miguel maintained his loose hold on her hand as he drove. Pulling into the parking lot of the clinic, he stopped beside her car and didn't know what to say.

"Thanks for a lovely day." Vicky spoke first.

"I need to thank you. It was certainly more pleasant than I expected it to be."

She smiled at that. "I think there was one part that neither of us expected." Shyly, she glanced down and then curved a hand around one ear, tucking the hair back from her face.

"Definitely." That was an understatement. There was so much about today, about Vicky and himself, that he hadn't ever expected. There were things about her that were incredibly appealing, but as the bubble of the past returned to surround him, he didn't know if he could keep it at bay. "I definitely enjoyed that part, too."

"Well, I'll see you on Monday."

"See you Monday." Gripping the steering wheel, he held on as he watched her get out of the car and walk away from him. This was the best way for both of them. He didn't need a relationship with a woman like her and she definitely didn't need anything with a man like him. He wasn't capable of having a full relationship. He could only do temporary and it simply wasn't in her to have a casual affair, he knew that for certain. So the best thing was to let her go home alone, forget about how she had felt against him, and he would take a cold shower to wash away the demons of desire that circled around him now.

Before she closed her car door, he hurried around the front of his truck, ready to close it for her. She looked up with a startled expression that changed the instant her eyes met his. She rose from her seat and reached out to him. In seconds she was in his arms, and he kissed her again. He pressed his mouth to hers and parted her lips. Exploring, teasing, tasting, testing, he let go of any restraint, pressing her against her car. Her fragrance and the way it wrapped itself in his mind drew him closer. When her arms clutched his shoulders, he knew he could lose himself in her if he weren't careful. Each curve, each nuance of her was impressed on him for the last time and he knew it. It had to be this way.

Miguel's hard body against hers was right, and wonderful, and so masculine. There was no protest in her as he pressed her against her car. The way his mouth explored hers, the silken glide of his tongue against hers made her want more than just this embrace. The feel of his arousal revealed that he was more than able to take things to another level. She wished that she was more adventurous, but taking the lead in a relationship hadn't been her way. But surely a night in bed with Miguel would be worth any regrets she might face later?

The wind shifted and fluttered the hem of her dress against her leg, teased a tendril of her hair against her cheek and gave her a chance to catch her breath. She clutched his shoulders and hugged him against her, trying to catch her breath.

The rasp of his light beard teased the bare skin at her neck. Then the pain came, and she winced. "Ow."

"What's wrong?" Miguel stilled except for his harsh breathing.

"I think I got a little sun," she said, and placed a hand on her neck. The skin was hot to the touch, but she didn't know if it was from the sun or Miguel's influence.

"Let me see," he said, and opened her car door so the light shone on her. She bent down and Miguel eased one of the dress straps to the side. "Yep. I'd say you have sunburn that's going to get your attention tonight."

"I forgot about sunblock today." She hated sleeping with sunburn. "Does it look that bad?"

"Unfortunately. Why don't we go in the clinic and have a better look at it?"

"It'll be okay, Miguel. I ought to know better, though."

"Take a shower when you get home or a mild vinegar bath sometimes takes the sting out."

"Isn't that just old wives' tales?" she asked, smiling, liking the way he incorporated nontraditional treatments into his medical practice. That was probably from working in such a nontraditional setting.

"It's true, though."

"Okay, then, I'll give it a try." She faced him and took his hands in hers. "Even though this was a nondate, and I was just helping you out, I had a really good time. You have a wonderful family." She was a little envious of the closeness they shared. It was a far cry from the formality of hers, especially since her mother had died. Before that, things had been different.

"Thanks. I had a great time, too. One of these days you can drag me along to one of your family functions, and we'll call it even."

A snort nearly made it out of her, but she choked it down. "I'll spare you that, but maybe something else will come up." That would be the day that she voluntarily brought anyone home to meet her father. The last man she'd tried to introduce was likely scarred for life. "Anyway, I'll see you on Monday."

Miguel ran his hand over his face as if he was trying to think of something to say, but instead he sighed. "Monday, then."

She got into her car. With what she hoped was a casual wave she drove off and left him standing there, watching her go. The cold sweat that broke out on her didn't stop until she was miles away. Just the mention of him meeting her family was enough to inspire panic, and the insecurity of the past returned. Was she doing the right thing? Would she and Miguel really have a chance at something or was this just attraction for a bad boy from the south part of town?

Slowly, she relaxed her grip on the steering wheel and let out a breath she hadn't realized she'd been holding. Miguel's family and background were so different from hers. There wasn't a likely chance that even if they tried to make something of it, they'd be successful. People gravitated to the familiar, and they were simply poles apart in that. Although she'd not kept her family name off her job application, she had considered it. For once in her life she'd just wanted to be accepted on her own merits, not the reputation her family lineage brought with it.

He wasn't far from her thoughts as she peeled her clothing off and got into the shower. His touch and his scent clung to her until she entered the shower stall.

The water felt like a zillion cactus needles on her skin, piercing and poking at her, but she knew that if she could tolerate it for a little while, some of the sting would stop and her skin would be happier. After moisturizing heavily with cocoa butter, she finally got the relief she needed and the desire to sleep overwhelmed her. Crawling between the crisp, Egyptian cotton sheets on her platform bed was the most luxurious feeling. With the heat of her skin roaring like a bonfire, she settled down and closed her eyes.

The rest she craved came in bits and pieces, interrupted frequently by images of Miguel and memories of his touch.

CHAPTER EIGHT

ON MONDAY morning Vicky's nerves tightened. How would it be to work with Miguel again? Would things change or would they simply return to their work roles and forget about the stunning kisses they had shared?

Saturday seemed like a moment out of time and possibly a hallucination. If it hadn't been for the evidence burned onto her skin, she might have considered the passion between them part of her imagination or a lusty daydream.

There was only one way to find out. She had to go through the door to the clinic. Either way, she had a job to do.

"Mercy, girl!" Tilly said, and did a double take when Vicky walked into the nurses' station. "What happened to you?"

"Oh, I got some sun over the weekend," Vicky said, and tried not to let the butterflies in her stomach get away.

"I'll say. Looks like you got burned to a crisp. Are you okay?"

"Oh, yeah, I'm fine," Vicky said, and gave a quick laugh. "Just have to remember the sunblock next time."

"Be sure you do. And a hat. With your coloring, you're at risk for skin cancer if you don't watch out." Tilly clucked her tongue then went back to the computer.

"I will. I will." The small reprimand brought back thoughts of her mother's illness. She hadn't known how her cancer had started and it certainly could have been a melanoma. Her mother had been a sun worshiper as a young woman. She really would have to be extracareful with such an unknown family history. But work first.

Mondays always seemed to be the busiest of days and this one was no different. She only had time for a cursory greeting to the other staff and a nod to Miguel before patients flooded the clinic.

Each time she passed Miguel in a patient room or discussed a case, the tension knotted tighter in her gut. He wasn't meeting her eyes, and the smile he offered to others wasn't sent her way. Things had reverted back to the way they'd been before Saturday. Maybe Saturday had been a daydream after all.

So she fell back on her nursing role and decided she'd get depressed later. Too many people depended on her giving her best right now for her to indulge in personal feelings. If she was overly bright or her smile too big, only she knew why.

The last patient of the day was a heartbreaker. Or at least she would be in about ten years or so.

The huge tears that coursed down the little girl's cheeks nearly did Vicky in. She loved children and hated to see any of them suffering. She squatted down to be at eye level with the girl and cast a quick glance at the name on her clipboard.

"What happened to you, Trina?" she asked, seeing

quite well that blood oozed from a makeshift bandage her mother had applied to her injured knee.

"I fell...in the rocks," she said, her words interspersed with tearful gasps.

"I couldn't clean it up. I know there is dirt in there, but I just couldn't do it," the mother said, nearly as tearful as Trina, and pressed a hand to the bump of her belly.

"It's okay. Lots of women have sensitivities when they are pregnant." Vicky stood. "Can I pick you up, Trina, and we'll go get your knee all fixed up?"

Only a nod and more tears were the answer, but she held her arms up to Vicky.

"It's okay, darling. It'll be okay." Vicky closed her eyes as Trina's arms closed around her neck in silent trust and acceptance. For a second Vicky's breath caught. If only she had been this trusting as a child, had been encouraged to be, maybe she wouldn't have such trust issues as an adult, but the fact was that she had them. As she looked at Miguel entering the room with a bright smile, she nearly forgot to breathe again. She cleared her throat and gained control of her emotions.

Her stomach tightened when he peeled back the bandage. There certainly were bits of gravel embedded in the wound and she was going to need a few stitches for sure. "Ouch! That must have hurt," he said. "What happened, little one?"

Trina nodded and her chin began to tremble again. "I fell."

"I'm guessing irrigation and a few stitches?" Vicky asked, and patted Trina's back.

"You got it." Miguel paused, looking at how Trina

clung to Vicky. "Why don't you sit with her and I'll get the supplies?"

While Miguel got ready, Vicky sat on the exam table and brought Trina across her lap. "Just hold tight to me, darling, and this will be over before you know it."

In minutes the irrigation was over and Miguel had picked out a few remaining bits of dirt. After a quick injection of numbing medication, he was able to place a few stitches to close the wound. "That ought to do it."

When Miguel looked up, a lump formed in his throat and his heart skipped at least a few beats. Vicky sat with Trina folded across her lap. Vicky's eyes were closed, she had tucked her chin over the little girl's head and was humming softly. What a gorgeous picture they made. Vicky didn't move except to open her eyes. As her gaze held his, something stirred in him. The same something that had been stirred over the weekend when he'd held her in his arms now roared to life, but he struggled to control it. He swallowed then cleared his throat and tried to choke down the emotions that wanted to race out of him. Vicky was truly beautiful as the light of her heart shone through, but it would never be enough to bridge the gap between them. No, it was best to keep his distance. "All done here. How about a few stickers and a lollipop or two?"

Distraction. That was the ticket for Trina as well as himself. If he busied himself with the tasks at hand, he might forget the feelings Vicky brought out in him.

Vicky looked at her. "Ready now? All the nasty stuff is done." She hugged Trina. "Let's go find you a treat. You were very brave."

"I was, huh?" Trina held her leg up to look at the

stitches and then back at Vicky. Tears and questions brimmed in those big brown eyes.

"It's okay. They'll only be in for a little while and then we'll take them out when your skin grows together. Then you won't need them anymore."

"Can I have a lollipop now?" she asked.

"Absolutely, then we'll get you back to your mom."

Miguel entered his office just before the last of the staff left for the day. Vicky made sure that everyone was gone before she sealed her fate. She didn't need any witnesses to what she was about to do. Her heart thundered in her chest and her mouth went dry. Confrontation was not in her makeup, but she had to do this. Not knowing where things lay between her and Miguel was worse than knowing there was nothing. The truth might not set her free, but it could free her from unrealistic expectations and she could go on with her life.

She knocked on the doorframe and he looked up, surprise on his face, which quickly switched to a closed, guarded expression. "I thought you left with everyone else." The set of his shoulders was stiff and unyielding, unlike the way they had softened beneath her touch just days ago.

"Just had one detail to wrap up." If that's what you could call it.

"What's that?"

She entered the room and sat on the edge of the chair across from his desk. "It's about us."

"Us? There is no us, Vicky." He leaned forward and folded his hands together on top of the desk. "I'm sorry if I misled you, but any relationship between us is out of the question."

Any possible hope inside her deflated at his statement. "I see."

"I'll apologize now, because I can see with the clarity of hindsight that my behavior on Saturday was unacceptable."

"Unacceptable?" She gave a harsh laugh. "It was perfectly acceptable at the time. What changed in the last forty-eight hours?" Bitterness sizzled on the back of her tongue.

"I did." With a sigh, he leaned back. "I realized that it was inappropriate of me to behave the way I did and give you an impression that things could be different between us." A frown covered his face. "I can see that this makes you uncomfortable, so if you were to resign, I would totally understand."

"Resign? The idea never occurred to me, Dr. Torres. I'm made of sterner stuff than that." She pulled herself upright in the chair. "I'm not going anywhere. If you don't want me to show up tomorrow, you'll have to fire me now. I simply needed to know where things stood between us and now that I know, I'll head home." She rose from the chair. "I have to say that I disagree with your position. There was something magical between us and it wasn't due to the wine."

Miguel opened his mouth then closed it again and let her go out the door. Frustration and anger at himself burned in his gut. He'd handled that as poorly as he'd handled anything in his life. There was no way he'd fire her. After being here such as short time, the other staff and patients had already begun to depend on her and asked for her when they arrived. Dammit. He was beginning to depend on her too, way more than he'd ever expected or wanted to.

He didn't need the complication of any relationship, let alone one with a coworker who happened to be from the richest family in the city. Yeah, that was just what he needed to make his life complete. What could he bring to a woman like Vicky anyway? Grief, a family history to rival any fictional account and unrelenting misery? No, the best thing was for them to maintain their professional relationship, and he'd have to forget about how remarkable she had felt in his arms.

If he could.

The rest of the week passed in a blur, with the days running together, the patients melding one into another, and finally the week ended on a particularly sour note.

Their additional funding wasn't going to come through. The city was functioning at a massive deficit and couldn't find the money to assist the clinic. It simply wasn't going to happen this year and possibly not for the next few years. Layoffs and cuts were inevitable for the city and now probably for the clinic, too.

The staff sat in the waiting area after the last patient left on Friday night. Miguel looked around at the despondent group after he'd broken the news to them.

"I'm really sorry to have to tell you all this, but I just found out that the current funding will only last us through July. The city won't come through. After that, I can't see how we're going to be able to carry on."

"You've kept this place going for years, M. You can

keep it going now, can't you?" Carlos asked, his wide eyes reflecting the shock in everyone else's.

"It's not just what we do, but it's the cost of supplies, the building maintenance and rent, which has gone up in the last two years and is now expected to go up again this year." It was an endless source of frustration to him. No matter how hard he worked to keep the desperately needed clinic going, external forces seemed at odds with his plans.

"How about that private fundraiser?" Vicky asked, her eyes guarded. She was calm, but he could see that she was thinking very hard about this. "I have an idea for one that could potentially keep the clinic going for years."

"Potentially?" Miguel asked, and shook his head. "I'm sorry, Vicky, but for this we need a sure thing. These people aren't going to get paid on a 'maybe.'" He'd been disappointed so many times in the past by potential plans that never worked out. He didn't want to risk any false hope on another one. "Anyone else have a brainstorm they want to share?"

The rest of the staff perked up and there was an outcry among them. "Wait! Let's hear what the lady has to say," Carlos said. "She got us coffee and donuts, maybe she can help with this, too. You never know what kind of connections she could have."

"If there's any idea worth hearing, Miguel, I say let's hear it," Tilly said. "Come on, Vicky, what is it?"

She looked at Miguel and hesitated. He nodded. What the hell? "Okay, let's hear it."

Vicky stood and faced the small group of people she had come to know over the past month or so. They were friends now. She knew she could trust them. "Well, I've been involved in some fundraising events in the past and it's always easier to get a bunch of people to donate a small amount than it is to get fewer investors to commit to larger funds." She tucked her hair behind her left ear. "Carlos, you're partly right. My father knows some people and so does my brother. They're people who live in this city and who might be able to help us out. They simply need to know about us."

"What kind of fundraiser are you talking about? It's going to have to be big," Tilly said with a cluck of her tongue. "If we intend to save this clinic, we need a lot of money, not loose change from people's pockets."

"Insurance companies have dropped their reimbursements, the co-pays are going up and people are losing jobs, too. We all know how hard it is to make ends meet these days." She looked around at the faces in front of her and saw the desperation, the will and the strength in each of them, and she wouldn't want to let any of them, but especially Miguel, down. He'd been let down so many times that he needed someone to come through for him and she wanted to be that person, even if nothing else transpired between them. "If you can give me a couple of weeks, I can pull it together. I'm sure of it."

"We all expect you to give us jobs to do so you're not doing everything by yourself," Tilly said, and crossed her arms. "We're in this together, Vicky."

"Agreed. I'll do some preliminary planning and see what kind of numbers I can come up with then we'll go from there."

Applause broke out in the little group and Vicky couldn't keep the grin off her face. When she looked at Miguel, her heart nearly thumped its way out of her chest. The way he looked at her, the way his energy, his focus seemed to home in on her made her want to reach out to him, but he'd made his position clear.

"I'll give you two weeks. If it's not coming together by then, I think we'll need to make other plans."

Vicky stuck out her hand to Miguel. "Agreed."

"I say we head out. Not going to solve anything on a Friday night." Tilly fished her purse from beneath her chair and stood. "See you all next week."

There was a mass exodus of staff. For once Carlos didn't have a quick solution or a flip answer. In silence he slid out the door with the rest of them.

"Hey," Miguel said. "Can you give me an idea of what you're planning? It would help me if I could know the details as soon as possible."

"Sure. What you need to do for a fundraiser like this is give the people a good time, that's all. Music, food, some dancing. People enjoy getting dressed up for a good cause. Every year there are fundraisers in town that people look forward to, like the Chocolate Fantasy Ball. Maybe we could make this the first annual one for the clinic. I haven't got it all figured out yet, but it will come together, don't worry."

"There are so many things to worry about, Vicky. You don't know how hard I worked to turn this place around. There simply isn't money to purchase the building, and I'm afraid the owner won't work out something that is in our best interests."

"Your hard work has shown, otherwise it wouldn't be so full every day, right?"

"Yes."

"And you take people with and without insurance. The simple answer may be a nonprofit status." She got excited about that idea. "My older brother is an accountant, so I'll talk to him about it, too."

Letting out a long sigh, Miguel rubbed a hand over his face. "I'm too tired to think about it right now. If you're ready, I'll walk you out."

She wanted to be able to say something to him, something that would ease his mind, but right now she didn't have the words. She would have to prove it to him. "I'm ready." She shouldered her purse and started toward the door, but they paused as it opened unexpectedly.

Carlos burst into to the clinic with a surprised look on his face.

"What, did you forget your backpack again?" Miguel said, but then some instinct, some sick feeling of dread bubbled up in him from a dark place in the past. He knew that look.

"No." Carlos held out a hand to Miguel. Blood dripped from his fingers. "I…" His eyes rolling back in his head, Carlos crumbled.

Without even thinking about it, Miguel lunged forward to catch him before he hit the floor. A wave of adrenaline hit Miguel like a tsunami. Nothing else mattered. He had to save Carlos. Thank God Vicky hadn't left yet, or he would have been more desperate than he already was.

"Carlos!" Vicky screeched, and dived to the floor opposite Miguel. "What happened?" She fumbled in her pocket for her phone.

"I don't know, but he's bleeding badly."

"I'll get 911 on the way." After a short conversation with the 911 operator, Vicky put the phone on speaker and sat it on the floor beside them to keep the line open.

Every move Miguel made felt as if it was being made in slow motion and he were shrinking away into the past. Every instinct he possessed as a physician and a healer kicked in to overdrive, but seeing Carlos on the floor nearly paralyzed him. This scene was so familiar it sickened him and brought back the night that had forever changed him.

"What are his injuries?" Vicky asked, and snapped on a pair of gloves.

"I don't know. He's got blood on his shirt." So much about Carlos reminded him of his brother. Until now, he hadn't realized it. Looking down at Carlos was like looking down at Emilio dying in his arms again. Reaching out toward the shirt, his arms locked and his hands trembled.

"Miguel? Miguel!" Vicky reached out and shook his arm. "Whatever is going on inside you right now has to be put aside. We have to focus on Carlos."

The sound of her voice pulled him from the past and with a monumental effort he shoved away the images of his dead brother. Vicky reached out and pushed the shirt up to expose Carlos's torso.

CHAPTER NINE

THE sight of a knife wound below the left rib cage stirred Miguel to action. There was a similar wound above his navel. "Dammit." The blood flow from the larger wound was a dreadful sign. "He's been cut deep, possibly the spleen." That alone was life-threatening.

"I'll get the cart." Vicky rushed into the trauma room and brought out the crash cart. "Everything we need is in here. We'll save him, Miguel. We'll save him."

Despite her brave words, he heard the tremor in her voice. She was as uncertain as he.

"Get a couple of big lines in him and all the fluid you got. He needs blood and surgery." He reached up, snapped opened the drawer with dressing supplies in it and grabbed a handful of gauze. Applying pressure to the wound externally wasn't going to help much when the injury was likely as deep as the spleen, but he had to do something. Dammit, there was so little that they could do.

"Get some oxygen going, too," Vicky said, without looking up from the IV she had just put into Carlos's right arm. In seconds she had fluids going and was reaching for his left arm to put another in. Then she paused, hope surfacing in her eyes. "I know it's not much, but what about a tampon?"

"A tampon?" Miguel frowned, dumbfounded.

"I read about marines using them for field dressings."

In that instant Miguel saw exactly where she was going with that thought. The expansion of a tampon deep inside the wound could provide some internal pressure that might slow down the bleeding and absorb some of the blood. "Do you have any?"

"Purse." She put in the second IV.

Miguel grabbed her handbag, turned it upside down and shook everything out of it. He grabbed the three tampons that surfaced. "You'll have to do it. I don't know how to operate these things."

Without a word, Vicky handed the IV bags to Miguel and ripped open a tampon pack. With deft fingers, she inserted a tampon into the edge of the larger wound.

"Go deeper."

Vicky's trembling hands pushed the tampon an inch or two farther. "You have to push the tampon bit forward with the applicator." After that, Miguel used his gauze to mop up the blood that had leaked out. The flow slowed to a trickle.

He grinned, now feeling as if there was real hope for Carlos. "You did it!"

Sirens cut the stifling air between them and the crews from an ambulance and fire emergency crashed through the front doors. The silence and isolation was fractured as new energy and people with purpose poured around them. The overwhelming relief that flashed through Miguel was a kind he'd never known. Now the tremors began in his gut and in his limbs. "He's been stabbed, possibly into the spleen. Lots of bleeding."

"Has he roused?" the paramedic in charge asked, while the others tended to Carlos, taking over each task from Vicky and applying oxygen at a higher concentration.

"He walked in then lost consciousness right away."

"Did he hit the floor?"

"I caught him so he didn't hit his head." Miguel tugged on his lab coat then realized it was covered in blood and tore it off. "Look, I'll go with you and answer questions, but this kid needs blood, stat."

"We'll get him loaded, Doc."

The next few minutes were a flurry of activity as they loaded the still-unconscious Carlos onto a stretcher and hurried out the door with him.

As Miguel was about to step into the back of the ambulance, Vicky called to him. "Will you call his mother?" she asked, tears now rolling down her face. Worry clouded her eyes, but he couldn't take the time to comfort her now. He had to save Carlos first.

"I'll call her. Come to the E.R. after us." He needed her comforting presence with him. He was selfish enough to admit that.

"Go! I'll catch up."

The ambulance doors slammed shut and Miguel's last image of Vicky was of her racing across the parking lot to her car.

When Vicky found Miguel, he was sitting in a chair outside the surgery waiting room, his elbows on his knees, his face in his hands. He looked like a man filled with anguish. At first she hesitated, not sure whether to disturb his solitude, then something snapped inside her. He'd been alone too long.

She rushed to him and dropped to her knees. "Miguel." She threw her arms around his shoulders. "They've taken him to surgery already?"

"Yes."

After a second's hesitation his arms flashed out around her. She felt the desperation in them and clung to him harder, trying to infuse as much of her energy and comfort into him as she could. "Tell me."

"It's his spleen for sure and possibly a major vessel. The other one is uncertain."

"I'm so sorry. Oh, God, I'm so sorry." For a second or two they simply held each other, sharing their grief over their young friend. "Did you call his family?"

"They'll be here in a few minutes." Miguel pulled back from her but kept her between his knees.

"You love him like a brother, don't you?" She could see the agony in his eyes and knew it was true. Though she didn't know much about his past, she knew he'd lost his own brother.

"Yes. He's like the little brother I had and lost. His mother is my mother's best friend, so we've known each other a long, long time. If it hadn't been for that crazy tampon trick of yours, he would have died right in front of us." His eyes glittered but she didn't know if it was anger or from tears he couldn't allow himself to shed.

A puff of air escaped her throat and tears overflowed her eyes. "I don't know whether to laugh or cry about that."

"I don't either, but you certainly saved his life."

Vicky placed her hands on his face and made him look at her. She was no saint. "*We* saved his life. Together. Now it's up to God and the surgeons." She sniffed. "We can only pray and send good energy for him."

Nodding, Miguel pressed his face into the junction of her neck and shoulder. Tremors rolled through him, and he held on to her. For the first time she felt as if he truly needed her and she reveled in that sensation. And she knew that she certainly needed him. It wasn't the heat of the moment, it wasn't simply passion that came and went. She was falling in love with him. With everything she had in her, she was falling for him.

Tears coursed down her face as they held each other, oblivious to the noise of the hallway around them. The goings-on of the hospital simply ebbed and flowed around them. Together they were solid as a rock, and there was no separating them. If only she could convince Miguel of it.

Then chaos, the likes of which she'd never seen, descended on them. Cries of alarm and hysterical Spanish mixed with equally hysterical English bombarded them, and they drew apart. "Family's here," Miguel said, and stood, then pulled her to her feet. He kept her by his side until Carlos's mother separated herself from the group of people surrounding them.

Miguel didn't have to introduce them. Vicky knew from the tone of her voice and the tears rushing down her face that this was Carlos's mother. She was the matriarch of this family and everyone deferred to her.

Rushing forward, she nearly threw herself at Miguel. He held her and listened. With the smattering of Spanish that she knew, Vicky heard words that she understood, but she couldn't quite put it all together and she took a step back as the group surged around Miguel. In minutes they had calmed down a little, and Miguel switched to English. "He's in surgery now and is going to need lots of blood."

An immediate outcry came to donate for their brother, their cousin, their friend.

"Good idea. Some of you can go down to the blood bank right now. Tell them you want to give blood for a patient in surgery, then come back up and wait while some others of you do the same."

Vicky's gaze flashed to Miguel and she frowned, but didn't say anything. She knew that wasn't quite a correct interpretation, but he had to have reasons for making that statement.

"Vicky, this is Carlos's mother, Priscilla."

Before she knew what had happened, she found herself enveloped in a hug from Carlos's mother. Surprise made her eyes go wide then her arms went around the tearful woman. *"Gracias, gracias, gracias!"* She took a breath and pulled back from Vicky. "Miguel tells me of what you did to save *mijo*. Tampons, of all things!" She shook her head in disbelief. "You are truly an angel to save my son."

"Oh, but, really, Miguel—"

"He is an angel, too," she said. She patted Vicky's cheek and held a hand out to Miguel, bringing him closer. "The two of you will ever be in my prayers. Thank you. Thank you." She held her arms out to the two of them, and the family crowded around, adding their love and thanks.

Never in her life had she felt such an overpowering

sense of love and purpose. Although she was sorry about Carlos's injury, it certainly proved to her that she was where she needed to be and this was the kind of work she was meant to do. It didn't matter where she had been born, or how she had lived her life previously—this moment in time clarified it all.

"You're welcome seems so silly to say right now." She sniffed and wiped her cheek on a shoulder.

"It's not silly at all." Priscilla pulled herself upright and nodded. "You are right. Now is the time to be strong for Carlos. Thank you again, *hija*. I will always be indebted to you."

"Oh, no—"

"Please, *hija?* Allow me that?"

Vicky paused and looked at the faces of Carlos's family around her. They needed this, and she could give it to them. Nodding, she hugged Priscilla then moved to the background.

A few minutes later, after some of the family had left for the blood bank in the basement of the hospital, Miguel sat beside her. "You okay?"

"Yeah, sure." She offered a smile, but inside she was a mass of nerves. Clutching her hands in her lap, she tried to focus on something else. "How long do you think he'll be in surgery?"

"At least another hour. Getting the spleen out is first then checking the other areas for injury will take a while." Without another word Miguel leaned back in the chair, placed an arm around her shoulders and pulled her against him.

For a second she resisted, then the emotion and the

energy of the past hour or so caught up to her and she nearly melted.

"Do you know how he got stabbed in the first place? It hadn't occurred to me until now."

"No. We'll have to wait until he wakes up to find out. Even then he may not have any memory of the attack itself, just vague splotches of images. The brain protects us that way."

"Is that what you told his mother?"

"Yes. And as far as I know, it's the truth." His lips pressed together and there was a tension about him.

"But you have an idea, don't you?"

Miguel leaned toward her, cupped a hand on her left cheek and pulled her face closer to his. "I don't want to say anything with the family so close." He pulled back and placed a quick kiss on her forehead.

Nodding as he pulled back, she looked up, wishing that he would kiss her once more but afraid that she wasn't ever going to experience that again. Without thinking, she placed a hand on the back of his neck and closed the distance between them. It was only a chaste kiss on the lips, but one she needed to give him. "It's going to be okay, Miguel. It's going to be okay." Somehow she knew Carlos was going to pull through. "He's young and strong. He'll make it."

As he drew back, he took her hand in his and pressed a long kiss to her palm.

Some of the family returned from the blood bank and others went down to donate their blood. Everyone settled down into a somber group as they waited for the surgeons to give a report on Carlos's condition.

* * *

Two hours later, the surgical team, two male physicians, both of whom wore exhausted expressions, entered the waiting room. "Carlos's family?" one of them asked. Even before he finished looking around, the two men were surrounded by Carlos's eager relatives.

"He'll make it."

Cheers and tears erupted in the room. It was exactly what they wanted and needed to hear. Miguel reached out for Vicky and brought her against his side. He needed her there. At least for the moment he needed her. He'd allow himself to lean on her for a while then he'd stand on his own, as he always had.

Then her trembling touch and her fragrance wrapped themselves around him tight and he didn't know if he could ever let her go. Turning to face her, he held her even more tightly, allowing himself that indulgence.

"He's got a good heart, a young healthy body and an extreme run of good luck," the surgeon said to the group, then his gaze came to rest on Miguel. "Miguel? What are you doing here?"

Miguel moved forward, with Vicky still clinging to his side. He shook the surgeon's hand. "Hello, Craig. It's been a long time. Carlos is my employee…and a very good friend." His voice broke and he cleared his throat.

"I'm so sorry to have run into you this way," Craig said.

Miguel nodded and introductions were made. "I'm assuming he's headed for the surgical ICU?"

"Yes. He's doing well in Recovery, but we'll keep him sedated for the first twenty-four hours or so and limit visitors to immediate family only."

"Understood. He needs to hear his mama's voice."

Priscilla stepped forward with authority and held out both of her hands to the surgeons. "I'm his mother. Thank you both for saving my son's life."

Craig grinned. "You're welcome. We did the clean-up job, but whoever thought of the tampon trick really saved his life long enough for us to get the rest of the job done."

Priscilla turned to Miguel and Vicky and nodded. "It was those two."

Vicky turned a glorious shade of red and tried to move behind Miguel, but he wasn't having any of it. "Come out here, you, and accept the credit you deserve. It was brilliant."

"But I didn't do anything," she muttered, and her eyes were wide with panic.

"Don't ever say that, *mija*," Priscilla said. "You did save my son's life and for that I'll never forget it."

"Absolutely," Craig said. "The tampon expanded fast enough and applied enough compression internally to slow the bleeding. That couldn't have been accomplished with simple external pressure." He gave a chuckle and the tension in the room loosened its grip. "I think I'll ask the ambulance crews to stock tampons from now on."

Vicky looked up at Miguel, helpless, and then she burst out laughing. The family joined her as she covered her face with her hands.

CHAPTER TEN

SHE looked so beautiful standing there with the flush on her face and surrounded by people who had been strangers but, due to her selfless actions, were now life-long friends. And against his will Miguel was falling hard and fast for her. Much more than he'd ever thought possible. Guarding against the enticing Vicky Sterling-Thorne was much harder than he'd expected. She was so much more than he had thought in the beginning. Now he was going to have to rethink his beliefs.

Arrangements were made for Priscilla and Carlos's father to have visits in the ICU; other family members were sent home to start cooking. Relatives and friends were going to arrive at the house, and having a pot of beans and rice, as well as one full of *posolé,* a stew of pork or lamb and hominy, would feed everyone. At times like this the family came together.

The midnight hour approached, and Miguel felt the exhaustion of the day crowding in on his mind. Fatigue like he hadn't felt since his residency weighed his shoulders down.

"Are you ready to go?" Vicky asked. "I can give

you a lift home. Seems like everyone else has settled down now."

Unfortunately, one could function on adrenaline only for so long before one's body crashed. Miguel was on the crashing end now, and he knew it. If he didn't get home soon, he was going to keel over. "Yes. If you don't mind, I'd love a ride home."

"I don't mind at all." They said their goodbyes and in minutes were in Vicky's car on the nearly empty streets, headed west from the University of New Mexico Hospital. Silence filled the air between them, but Miguel reached over and took her right hand, needing just that little bit of a last connection between them. When he got home and they returned to work, the closeness between them would end. Again.

He directed her through the residential neighborhood to a small cul-de-sac that was almost hidden by sprawling oak trees nearly as old as the city itself. His bungalow was at the end of another property. "It started out as a caretaker's cottage or a mother-in-law's quarters or something. I bought it about five years ago."

"It's darling. Pretty similar to the house I live in. It was a caretaker's cottage a long time ago, too, but when I divorced my husband I took it over."

Miguel unbuckled his seat belt, but didn't have the energy to open the door just yet. "I didn't realize you were divorced. Not that it's my business."

"No problem. It was a mistake from the get-go, but I corrected it as soon as I realized what was going on."

"What do you mean?"

"I married a man who took his money to bed instead of his wife. Ambition and greed didn't leave any room for me." She snorted. "That still burns. I should have seen it sooner."

"At least you saw it."

"Yeah. Want me to walk you up?" she asked, changing the subject. The green glow of the instrument panel illuminated her face, and he could see the little smile flirting with her lips.

"I know it's late, but would like you like a cup of coffee or something before you head home? I know neither of us had dinner and I won't be able to settle down for hours."

"If all you have is instant coffee, I'll pass. I can grab something at home."

He patted her knee. "Come on. I'll fix you a sandwich or something."

While Miguel puttered around the kitchen, Vicky wandered the hallway with the glass of wine he'd poured for her and admired the photographs on the walls. "These are just gorgeous, Miguel. You do have a beautiful family."

"Thanks," he said. "There's a whole pile of pictures I need to put up, but just never seem to find the time to do it."

"More cousins?"

"Yes. My mother has eight siblings, my father nine, and I have four."

Vicky's eyes widened. "Wow. There's just my two brothers and I. Only the older brother has kids, two. The younger has his own business he's married to, so I doubt there will be any children from that union."

Miguel laughed. "Let's hope not." He pushed a sandwich on a paper plate over the breakfast bar toward her and together they sat on the bar stools and ate with their hands. There was something simple yet incredibly exotic about eating plain food with the hands.

As he watched Vicky pull grapes off the small bunch he'd given her, he found himself becoming aroused at the sight of her small fingers holding the fruit as if it were fragile then pressing a kiss to each grape before she put it in her mouth.

"Why are you doing that?"

"Doing what?"

"Giving each grape a kiss?" He watched her hands as she plucked another grape.

"I didn't realize I was. I must be tired. It was something that I heard of as a kid, giving thanks to the goddess of the vine for the bountiful harvest, or something like that," she said, and waved away the sentiment. "It's silly, I know, but it never hurts to give thanks."

"I like it." He pulled a grape from his own plate, kissed it and held it out to her. Her gaze flashed to him, suspicious yet curious, brimming with desire. Hesitation in every movement, she leaned forward and accepted the grape from his outstretched fingers. The soft touch of her lips against his skin inflamed his arousal.

Without taking her eyes away from him, she picked up a grape from her plate, kissed it then held it out to him. "I think they taste better this way. What do you think?"

A growl burned deep in him. It was animal instinct, something wild and untamed that he'd kept locked up for too long. He circled her wrist with his hand and took the grape from her fingers. Its sweet, tangy flavor nearly exploded in his mouth. "It is better." He moved closer to her. "I wonder if it's the same."

"What's the same?" Her gaze flashed to his mouth. She knew he wanted to kiss her, and she was obviously not displeased with the notion.

"If I kiss *you* and then eat a grape. Will it taste the same?" He edged a little closer to her, drawing her closer by her wrist.

"The only real way to tell is by testing, right?" She licked her lips, her breathing shallow and rapid, and allowed him to pull her closer, until only inches separated them.

"That would be the only proper scientific analysis."

Science couldn't wait for the answer and neither could Miguel. He closed the tiny gap between them, brought her lithe body against him and pressed his mouth to her parted lips. Heat seared him everywhere he touched her. Her skin, her hair, her breasts burned into him, and her hips tight against him roused him further.

It was the fresh, fruity taste of her that finally unchained the man-beast inside him. The taste of her silky tongue against his, infused with the freshness of the grape, blended with her own, made him want to throw away any personal ethics and strip her bare right then.

Her arms wound around his shoulders and held him tight. Each move she made renewed the scent of her in his mind and turned the key to the primitive male held captive inside him. He hadn't felt this moved by a woman in so long. She was precious and kind, and lovely beyond measure.

And he didn't deserve her. That was the problem.

He ended the kiss and hugged her tight. Her breathing

was just as rapid as his and he could feel the way their hearts raced in time, as if they beat as one in separate bodies. If he weren't who he was and if circumstances had been different, they might have made a go of this thing simmering between them. But he wasn't, and they couldn't. It was that simple. The words *if only* echoed through his heart and his soul.

"Grape?" she asked, and pulled back.

"What?" he blinked and tried to refocus on her.

"To finish the experiment, we need to eat a grape."

"Oh, yes. Right." Putting more space between them, he sat in his chair. He took a grape and handed her one. "Cheers."

"I'd say it's a hit and if it gets out, it might catch on worldwide."

He laughed. "You are such a nut." Then the smile faded away. "This has been a pretty crazy day, hasn't it?"

"That's the understatement of the year." She pushed her hair back from her face. "I can't think of a time I used up so much adrenaline in one day. I sure hope Carlos is going to be okay."

"Me, too." They were both aware of the ramifications of what could set in. ARDS, adult respiratory distress syndrome, could also hit him and make his recovery slower or permanently change him.

"I have to ask you, though, why did you send the family to the blood bank? The blood they donated wouldn't be used for Carlos. It has to be donated ahead of time, but you knew that."

Unable to resist the allure of her skin, he allowed his hand to stroke her cheek. "I knew. Carlos was going to use a lot of blood during surgery and possibly afterward, but the family needed something to do. It was a good way to fill up the blood bank's resources, too. I'm sure they were thrilled."

"I'm sure they were." She nodded. "It was a good thing to suggest. If you hear of any changes, let me know, okay?" She stood.

"I will."

"My brother is dragging me out to a formal dinner tomorrow night, so leave me a message if I don't answer."

"Your brother? It's okay to tell me if you have a date, Vicky. I don't have any claim on you." As his hands clenched, he tried to keep his face calm, keep the insane flash of jealousy hidden. He had no rights to Vicky. But, damn, he wanted them.

"Really, it's my brother Eddy. He's the one married to his work and doesn't take time for a social life. Once in a while he talks me into feeling sorry for him, so I go."

She shrugged, and he believed her. So many times in the past he'd been around women who thought nothing of lying to the man they were supposed to be involved with. That self-protective instinct had stuck with him over the years, but now he relaxed, trusting that Vicky was telling the truth. The warmth that hummed through him had nothing to do with fatigue and everything to do with the realization that she wasn't dating anyone else.

"I know you're tired, but try to have a good time."

She stood. "I'll try. If it weren't so late I'd try to find him a date. After tonight I'm exhausted."

"Maybe the outing will perk you up. You never know."

"I hope it's certainly less stimulating than today has been." A yawn overcame her, and she covered her mouth with one hand. "I guess I should head home now."

Miguel walked her to her car, the warm feeling lingering in his middle and migrating upward toward his heart. He knew he could never make a claim on Vicky, but he was glad that she wasn't dating anyone else. "I'll see you on Monday." He allowed himself to cup her face and bring her close for a small, chaste kiss. "Thank you for being there."

"You're welcome." She hesitated a moment, as if she wanted to say something, but didn't. He could see the questions surfacing in her eyes, and he knew he couldn't answer them. He didn't know what the hell was going on between them or how it was all going to pan out. He just knew he wanted more than he deserved.

CHAPTER ELEVEN

MIGUEL knew he had to do it, that there was no one else who could do it. His hands and his insides trembled as he unlocked the door to the clinic late Sunday morning.

The blood was still there.

The floor was covered with Carlos's blood.

The door opened against the pressure of his hand and he stepped inside, trying to control his breathing, but his heartbeat was unstoppable.

It was a mirror image of the night his brother had died.

Miguel had been determined to get Emilio out of the gang, which had been just as determined to keep him. The leader, Juan, was a kid he'd known all his life and one that had been in trouble as long as Miguel had known him. The brothers had fought earlier in the day and Emilio had run off in a rage. It seemed that the forces of the universe had been at odds that day, as well. Nothing had come together to help him and nothing had helped him save his younger brother.

Trying to ignore the rage building inside him, Miguel dragged the mop and bucket from the storage closet. He filled the bucket with steaming-hot water, added detergent and began the mop-up job. Back and forth, back and forth he went across the pool of Carlos's blood, which had dried on the floor. With each stroke of the mop memories poured into him, reminding him again of how he had failed to protect his brother and failed his family. He was the oldest. He was supposed to take care of Emilio. Even though he was a successful physician now and his clinic thrived, part of him would always be a failure.

If he hadn't tried to control Emilio, tried to force Juan to let go of his brother, Emilio might now be alive. Emilio had come home to find Miguel when Miguel had gone to find Juan. The gang leader hadn't been hard to locate. Miguel had known the neighborhood.

Emilio had arrived just as Juan had been about to put a bullet in his, Miguel's, back. Instead, Emilio had taken the slug that had been meant for him.

Everything had happened in unreal slow motion. He'd heard Emilio's warning too late. He'd turned, seen Emilio dive for Juan and they'd both fallen to the ground.

Emilio hadn't got up. In his mind, Miguel raced to where Emilio lay on the ground, a puddle of his blood pooling rapidly beneath him. The cheap white tiles on the floor had contrasted sharply with the blood.

Fear of that kind had never touched Miguel before. He'd slid to the slippery floor beside Emilio and turned him over.

"There! He's out of the gang. Now get his carcass off my floor," Juan had said.

"He needs help!" Miguel had cried, with tears of rage in his eyes. "Call 911."

"Get out." Two of Juan's assistants had hoisted Emilio up and dragged him out to the sidewalk. Though Miguel had wanted to kill Juan with his bare hands, he'd knelt beside his brother and gathered him into his arms. Even though he'd barely started medical school, he'd known that Emilio was dying, and had cursed himself for not being able to save his brother.

"Tell Mama…s-s-s-orry," Emilio had whispered, and then had closed his eyes for the last time.

The power of the memory overwhelmed Miguel, and he had to stop, close his eyes and take a minute before the images, the memory of his failure faded away. If he hadn't tried to force Emilio out of the gang, he might still be alive. But they would never know if he could have gotten out on his own.

Returning to the task, Miguel cleaned up the last of Carlos's blood, took the mop out to the Dumpster and threw it away.

Miguel arrived at the trauma-surgical ICU at the University Hospital and let himself in through the staff entrance. He'd done his resident training there and knew all of the ins and outs, the hidden exits and corridors for the staff to get around without being seen.

Although he knew and loved Carlos's family, he was still too raw to talk with anyone right now. He just needed to see Carlos and find out his condition, maybe find out what the hell had happened to him.

He opened the door from the stairwell and entered the SICU. Busy activity never stopped in a place like this. The lifeblood of the unit was the pace set, the energy, the ability for the staff to act immediately and save the next life that rolled through their doors.

Breathing deeply, he tried to suck in some of that atmosphere, that energy, and realized that he missed it, that he'd once been part of a unit like this, been part of the team that lived and thrived on emergencies. For a second he soaked it all in and good memories of his time there flooded over him. He'd once wanted to save the universe one sick patient at a time, and trauma had been his chosen method until the clinic in his community had called out to him for help. It had been a call he hadn't been able to ignore, but now he wished there was room in his life for more.

"Miguel!" A male voice brought him out of his reminiscences. "What the hell are you doing here, buddy?" The tall man dressed in surgical scrubs headed toward him, smiling widely.

"Jason!" Miguel held out his hand to the old friend striding toward him as a surge of warmth pulsed through him. "I sure didn't expect to see you still here."

"Can't pry me away." They shook hands and moved to the side of the hallway to allow staff to move past them. "What are you doing here?"

Miguel explained the situation with Carlos. "I'm responsible for the kid, and I need to know firsthand what's going on with him." It was way more than that, but he didn't want to go into any more detail at the moment.

"Just so happens he's doing great. Extubated this morning, breathing well on his own, no signs of ARDS, so I'd say he's on the mend, barring unexpected infection."

"That's great news." The tightness in Miguel's shoulders loosened and the relief pulsing through him was nearly tangible.

"He was awake a while ago, but I'm not sure now. Want to see him?"

"It's enough just to know he's been awake." The relief inside him was overwhelming.

"I hear your clinic's doing well. Still working for you?" Jason had always been observant and somehow had his finger on the pulse of gossip everywhere in this town.

"Most of the time." Miguel looked around at the bright lights of the unit and listened for a second to the rhythm beating a low hum. "I do miss this once in a while. I never realized how much until now."

"It's always been in your blood." Jason grinned. "All you have to do is apply and you can be back here in a month."

"The clinic—"

"Will run just fine if someone else takes over for you. Someone who is heading toward retirement, not a young surgeon with a passion like yours." He patted Miguel on the shoulder. "Carlos is in room fifteen. I've got to roll now, but think about it." He fished a business card out of his pocket. "Call me and let's go have a coffee."

"I will." Miguel took the card and stuck it in his pocket, wondering if he really would. When he'd left the hospital to take over the clinic, he hadn't thought he'd ever return. Now, taking in the sights and sounds around him, he wondered if that decision was written in stone.

He moved toward room fifteen, anticipating what he'd

see there. Seeing patients hooked up to tubing and drains was one thing, seeing a loved one in the same position was quite another. After just a quick look inside the room he could see that Carlos had his eyes closed, that his breathing was even and deep. The monitor displayed good vital signs and the tension in Miguel's shoulders eased another notch.

Dropping into the chair beside the bed, he let go of his emotional stranglehold and rested his face on his hands, his elbows resting on his knees.

Minutes passed as he sat there, listening to the monitors and being reassured by the consistent rhythm. The nurse came and went, but didn't disturb him. Jason must have given a heads-up to the staff that it was okay for him to stay.

Footsteps entered then stopped close by him. He figured it was the nurse again, and he remained in his position, not wanting to talk to anyone just yet. The touch of a hand on his back startled him, and he looked up. Vicky stood beside him, concern etched on her face. "What are you doing here?" he asked.

"I came to see Carlos. The nurse couldn't give me any information on the phone, so I came down to talk to the family and get an update." She glanced away. "You didn't answer your phone, so I figured you might be down here."

"I turned it off when I came in." He'd actually forgotten about it. "Are you okay?"

"Me? I'm fine, but you look like death warmed over. Did you get any sleep last night?"

"Not much." He stood and moved away a little from her. If he touched her, he was going to regret it. Although her concern for him was genuine, he couldn't tolerate the honesty in her touch right now. "I'm fine. You needn't be concerned about me."

A guarded look came into her eyes, and he knew he'd hurt her. "I'll be concerned about whom I wish." She cleared her throat and stood up a little straighter. "I've come about Carlos, so can you tell me how he's doing? Priscilla said he was off the ventilator, so that's very good news."

"Yes. He's breathing on his own. I've been sitting here for a while, but he's been sleeping the whole time."

"Sleep is restorative, and he sure needs it."

"Not…sleeping," Carlos said in a voice that crackled with dryness and fatigue.

Miguel spun around and leaned over the bed. "Hey, are you in there?" he asked, and placed his hand on Carlo's forehead, needing to touch him, to have that connection to the young man who meant so much to him.

"Yeah." He licked his lips and his eyelids fluttered.

Automatically, Vicky reached for the mouth sponge to moisten his lips and tongue. "Here you go. This ought to help."

"Do you know what happened to you?" Miguel asked.

"Mugging." He paused again. "Tried to help."

"Oh, Carlos," Vicky said, and tears ran down her face. "I'm so very glad you're still with us."

"That bad?" he asked, and looked at Miguel.

"Yeah." He didn't have to say anything else. Carlos had been around enough to know what that meant.

"Thanks." He glanced at both of them.

A sudden shock of pure joy shot through him. The kid was going to be okay. Somehow he knew it. "Vicky's the one who really saved your life."

"I did not! Will you quit giving me all the credit?" The flush on her neck gave away her pleasure, despite her words.

Miguel told Carlos what had happened and how the events had unfolded.

Carlos groaned and closed his eyes.

"Are you in pain? Do you need pain medication?" Vicky asked.

"A *tampon?* You let her put a *tampon* in me?" He paused for a breath. "I'm never going to live that down."

"At least you'll live long enough to not live it down, bro." Relief continued to overwhelm Miguel.

The nurse entered the room. "Sorry, folks. Time to rest up again," she said.

"It's okay. We've spent too long with him anyway." Miguel clasped Carlos's hand. "I'll see you soon."

"I'm so glad you're on the mend," Vicky said, and pressed a kiss to his forehead. "When you're taking fluids, I'll bring you some coffee."

"The good stuff." A sideways smile lifted one corner of his mouth and his eyes drifted down.

CHAPTER TWELVE

MONDAY morning was full of the blues. Everyone, staff and patients, at the clinic knew and loved Carlos. The mood was somber as they moved through their normal clinic duties without him.

"It's just not the same without that boy, is it?" Tilly asked during the silent lunch break in the staff room. There was an almost palpable heaviness in the air, anticipating word from the family, the waiting time.

"No, it isn't," Vicky said, as her appetite for her sandwich fled. She returned it to its wrapper and covered it up. Nothing was going to make her take another bite of that unfortunate excuse for a meal that she had made. If she couldn't make a proper sandwich, she was in sad shape. After the busy week, then the horrible incident with Carlos and then the very late night with her brother and his awful dinner engagement, no one would blame her if she was exhausted.

"There's a different vibe in the air when he's here." The older woman shook her head and looked away.

Vicky knew there were tears in Tilly's eyes. She'd heard the emotion in her voice and sympathized with her, but Vicky had had a bit longer to get used to the idea and to see Carlos for herself. Seeing him in person was different than simply getting a report about him.

"How about I order us all something for lunch?" Vicky said, and tossed her sandwich bag in the trash. "This isn't cutting it for me today."

"What did you have in mind?" Tilly asked, but the other staff in the lounge looked at her, too. Since she had suggested the idea, she was in charge of it.

"How about lunch burritos or something? I'll call in the order and go get some if anyone else wants to join in. My treat for today." The idea of it was suddenly much more appealing than anything she'd thought of all day long.

"Yeah, let's do it." Tilly balled up her lunch and tossed it, as well.

With a grin, Vicky grabbed some paper for everyone to write down what they wanted. In minutes her list was complete, with the exception of Miguel's order. He had closeted himself in his office. She knocked lightly in case he was on the phone.

"Come in."

Fatigue sounded heavy in his voice, and she was sorry it was there. Carlos's condition weighed heavily on him. "We're just sending out an impromptu lunch order and wanted to know if you want in on it, my treat." She handed him the takeout menu.

"Sure." He quickly scanned it, then handed it back. "I know this place. Give me a number five with extra cheese."

She took the menu back and looked at it. "Sounds good. Might have to try that myself sometime." As she turned to go, she hesitated. "Are you okay?"

"Yes."

"I mean really okay." She bit her lip and glanced away for a second. "You seem a little off today, but considering the last few days that's not totally unreasonable."

A sideways smile crossed his mouth briefly. "Don't worry about me, Vicky. I'll be fine."

This was a level of coolness she'd never seen from him. He'd totally pulled back from the closeness they'd started to have, even as coworkers. Maybe she had been wrong again. Maybe her judgment of men hadn't improved over the years and Miguel was just like the rest of them. Couldn't be trusted to have an honest relationship. "I see. Sorry to bother you. I'll just go get this and be right back."

She closed the door behind her and huffed out a deep breath. Whatever she had once thought possible between them was now obviously just a mistaken desire. Men who ran hot and cold with their emotions unnerved her, and she couldn't deal with the dishonesty of it. Tears clouded her vision on the way to the restaurant, and she had to pull over for a minute or risk getting into an accident.

Somehow she managed to get to the restaurant, pick up the order and return to the clinic without causing an accident or dropping the bags of lunch burritos. The cheery smile she pasted on her face was a farce and she knew it, but the staff responded and that was the important thing.

The food was a big hit and after consuming the fragrant and flavorful burritos, everyone returned to work with a bit more zip in their step.

"A little green chili goes a long way, doesn't it?" Tilly asked.

"What?" Vicky blinked.

"Just look at everyone. Back to their usual selves mostly. A little green chili helped. That was a great idea you had," she said, and squeezed Vicky's arm. "We all needed it."

"It's okay. It really wasn't anything." Somehow the morose atmosphere seemed to have lightened around her, but Vicky's heart still felt heavy.

"Yes, it was, girl. It was a great idea and it's time you accepted something." Tilly turned to face her fully, making Vicky feel as if she was back in nursing school.

"What's that?"

"You're a part of this group. You might have come here as an outsider, a stranger, but you've quickly been accepted as one of us here." Then Tilly smiled.

"I don't know, Tilly. Sometimes I feel like I'm at home here and other times I just think I'll always be an outsider no matter where I go." That was the bald truth of it.

"We all feel that way at times, but, just so you know, you're one of us." Tilly patted her arm. "Now, go and get the first three patients lined up or Miguel will toss us out on our ears."

Vicky laughed, her heart a little lighter, and called for the first three patients. She placed them in different rooms, and began the assessments for Miguel.

CHAPTER THIRTEEN

THE London Broil was fabulous as always, but it didn't matter what the chef served, it always stuck in her throat. Washing the meal down with more wine didn't make it any more palatable and simply wasted good wine. The only time she thought she was developing esophageal reflux disease was at her father's dinner table.

"Victoria's got some news," Edward said as he cut into his food.

The hair on Vicky's head actually stood on end. No matter how old she was, she'd always feel six years old when she sat at her father's formal dining table. Even though it had been in the family for generations, it would always be *his* table.

Turning his head, peppered with steel-gray hair, and focusing those brilliant blue eyes on her, Charles Sterling-Thorne raised his brows at his only daughter. "What sort of news, Victoria? Did you finally come to your senses and leave that ridiculous *career* of yours? It's about time."

"Hardly, Father. I'll always be a nurse." She nearly scoffed, but managed to choke it back. Insubordination was not tolerated at the table. "Eddy's referring to something else entirely." Managing to look calm and cool on the outside had always seen her through these tense meals, but now she knew the brittle veneer was beginning to crack.

"Edward," her brother snarled at her through gritted teeth. "She's talking about having a fundraiser for her little clinic. Seems their benefactor has died, and the rest of the family is too greedy to continue the endowments."

"Well, that's too bad," her father said, his eyes glittering with amusement and his I-told-you-so look. "Guess you'll have to quit now, won't you?"

That did it. She'd tolerated his snide comments and superior looks for too many years, allowing him to control her for most of her life. It ended there and right now. Carefully, she placed her fork on the table beside the plate rimmed in gold, wiped her mouth with the linen napkin and stood.

"Victoria, sit down. The meal isn't over."

"But I am, Father. I am through with this…" She gestured to all of them and the air. "This farce of a family."

"What are you talking about? You're overreacting again as usual. Sit down." He dismissed her with his eyes and returned to his meal.

"No, it's well past time I reacted this way and stood up for myself. You will never, *ever* again belittle me or my chosen career. I am a nurse, and a damned good one. Last Friday one of our staff nearly died, and I saved his life by using my brain and not waiting for someone else to swoop in and save the day. *I* did it. *I* worked with

Miguel, and together we saved this young man's life." She sniffed. "I'm very, very proud of the work I do."

Tears of rage at her father and pride in herself clouded her vision, but she was determined not to let him see her emotions because he would continue to think of her as weak. "He means everything to his family, and I gave him back to them." She stood straighter, not realizing those words had been bottled up inside her. Her father put his fork down and although his expression remained closed, he looked at her in silence.

"I demand that you treat me with respect and respect my career choice because it's not going away, ever. I'm not a corporate type, I'm not going to be a university professor, and I'm never going to enter the business other than in a peripheral manner, Father. It's well past time you accept who I am." She paused and looked at the faces around the table, all of whom stared at her with rapt attention. Having been accepted by the group at the clinic based on her personality, her skills and a little coffee, it had given her the courage to stand up to her father. Being accepted by her peers was something she hadn't realized she'd needed until she had it. Now she was never going to let go of it.

"Who exactly are you?" Charles asked, his tone serious, all sarcasm gone.

"I am a nurse. I will always be a nurse and this clinic is a very important part of our community." She sucked in another breath and held her father's gaze, although she spoke to them all. "And when the time comes, all of you are going to cough up a healthy donation to keep it going."

"I see." He rested his elbows on the table and tented

his fingers. That was always a bad sign. She knew it and sat down, still determined to hold her position. Charles was a businessman and a master manipulator, and she needed to be on her guard. "When will that time be?"

"I'm not sure yet, but soon. I've made the suggestion to put together a big fundraiser, and I've a preliminary plan, but Miguel is still working his numbers, too. The city was supposed to come through with additional funding, but they haven't." That was unfortunate for all of them.

"Who's been managing the money until now?" Arnold asked. He was the brother who made magic with numbers.

"Miguel has been doing everything, but it's simply too overwhelming for one person to be the director, the physician, the accountant and find more funding all at once."

"Well, Victoria, when you get the benefit together, you can count on me for assistance." Charles watched her.

Surprise and shock raced through her system, but at the same time a self-protective suspicion. "What are you playing at, Daddy? I'm not talking about loose change here. This clinic is a very worthy cause, and Miguel simply can't do it all by himself any longer. No one can." The light in him was rapidly burning out, and she was determined to help keep it going.

"I'll kick in some accounting help," her eldest brother, Arnold, said, and speared a bit of meat. "Set up a nonprofit or something for him."

"Me, too!" Jessica, her niece of ten, said. "My class has raised money before, and we can help, too."

Tears that she'd held back now gushed forth, and Vicky allowed them to roll down her cheeks. "Thank you, Jessy." She looked at her father, afraid to hope that he was really seeing her for the first time, acknowledging her as an independent adult with a life and agenda of her own. "Are you really serious or are you just amusing yourself at my expense?"

"I'm certain it will be at *my* expense," he said, and dropped his gaze with a clearing of his throat. "I'd forgotten what heart you have, Victoria, the passion you have for helping others. Please accept my apology and count on me to help out the clinic in any way I can."

Victoria leaned her elbows on the table and tented her fingers this time, while holding her father's gaze. "How about unrestricted access to your contact list?"

He roared in laughter and nearly tipped his chair over. "You are definitely my daughter!"

"I hope that's a compliment," she said as the family laughed, too.

"It is, Victoria, it is." He reached across the table and squeezed her hand, then picked up his fork. "Now, tell me what kind of ideas you have and how the rest of us can help you. Of course we'll provide the wine. Won't do to have a Sterling-Thorne fundraiser without the family label."

Victoria's appetite returned with gusto as she outlined the ideas she had for the fundraiser. Everyone engaged in a vigorous discussion, tossing out ideas and hashing them over until a brilliant plan emerged that Vicky was certain would work.

Now all she had to do was convince Miguel.

* * *

Between extra duties at the clinic and checking on Carlos, there was simply little time to spare to talk to Miguel until the end of the week. He was as personable with the patients as he had always been, but now he'd clearly withdrawn into some sort of bubble that protected him from everything and everyone else. He was simply burned-out.

She lingered after the staff left, hoping to catch him, to talk to him. She approached his office, where he was spending more and more time, and had raised her hand to knock when his office phone rang. Easing away, she didn't want to eavesdrop and waited a few minutes until she heard him hang up.

"Miguel?" she called, and knocked on the door. "Got a few minutes?"

"Sure. Come in."

Vicky entered the office and nearly gasped. He looked terrible in the fluorescent lighting overhead. "You're not sleeping, are you?"

Before answering, he rubbed his face with his hands, as if trying to wake up, though it was the end of the day. "Is that what you wanted to talk about, my sleeping habits?"

"No, of course not, but—"

"What did you want?"

Taken aback by the gruff tone of his voice, she frowned, trying to decide what to do. "I wanted to talk to you about the fundraiser. I've got some ideas and can get moving on things now that we know Carlos is going to get better." She sighed. "That's at least one less thing to worry about now."

"Yeah, it is. I hadn't expected him to do so well so quickly."

"I'm just glad he is. The resilience of the young, you know?" She cleared her throat. "However, the problem for the clinic remains."

"The clinic problems have changed since we last talked. It may have to close."

"What?" That was something she'd never expected to hear. "Why?"

"I've been offered a job at the hospital in the trauma unit. And I've spent the last week on the phone trying to find someone to take over the clinic, but no one wants to do what I do and there simply isn't the funding to hire more staff." He angrily got to his feet and cursed under his breath. "Until I laid it all out on paper, I hadn't realized how well we did with so little help. No one is going to do what I've done. No one!" He threaded his fingers in his hair and groaned aloud. "If I want a life I have to close the clinic. What choice is that?"

"Miguel, be straight with me. What's going on?"

"I either have to sacrifice the clinic and the community if I want to take the university job or I have to sacrifice my life to keep this clinic going. This isn't what I set out to do when I took over the clinic."

"You've done a marvelous job with so many things here. Tilly told me how you turned it around in just over a year. That's astonishing."

"Yeah, by working my ass off." He turned to face her. "Do you know I haven't had a true vacation in three years, nearly four? There are so many family events that I've missed because of some crisis or another." Anger snapped in his dark eyes, and she knew it was focused on himself.

"That's not good, Miguel." She shook her head. "No one should sacrifice all their time like that. You deserve to have a life, too."

"Do I really?" he turned away from her and swore again. "I don't know if I deserve anything."

"That's not true. You've put your heart and your blood into this place."

"My brother's blood, you mean."

"What are you talking about?" That didn't make sense.

"Never mind. I'll just have to decline the job offer and carry on as usual."

"You can't mean that," she said. "I saw you in the trauma unit with Carlos and when he was injured. You were at your best, weren't you?"

"No." He shook his head in denial, but she knew the truth of it.

"Yes, you were. I've been around enough to know when a physician is truly in his element, when he knows what he is doing and what feeds his soul. That was it for you, Miguel. I saw it. I saw you."

"It was one incident."

"But it changed you, didn't it?"

"No. It merely pointed out all my failings."

"How can you say that? Carlos would be dead if it weren't for you."

"It doesn't matter."

"It does matter. His family sure as hell thinks it matters." She approached him and invaded his personal space. She closed in on him and tried to ease his pain.

Carefully, she placed her hand on his forearm and squeezed. The muscles beneath her hand bunched and trembled, but she refused to release him. "Tell me what's bugging you."

"There's nothing to tell."

"That is an outright lie. Tell me." The gaze that met hers was devoid of life, of the passion she knew lived in him. She'd felt it, touched it, tasted it. "I'm not going anywhere until you talk to me."

"Vicky, it's none of your business. It's history, my history, and—"

"It's eating you alive," she whispered. Never in her life had she assaulted a man, but she was about to if he didn't start talking. Some sort of fearlessness came over her, and she placed her arms around his shoulders to bring him closer. His body was stiff and resisting.

Miguel clamped his hands around her wrists, intending to drag her arms away, but he didn't. Something about the way she moved, the way she smelled, the way she felt so close to him stopped him. Then he looked into her eyes, and he was done for.

"Vicky." His voice was a hoarse whisper. "Vicky."

"It's okay, Miguel. It's okay. I'm here for you."

He didn't know if things would ever be okay again, and right now he didn't care. Instead of putting her away from him, he grabbed her tight against him. Emotions and feelings that he'd kept locked up inside of him burst free. Right now, talking wasn't what he wanted.

He pulled back, cupped both hands around Vicky's face and kissed her. Hard and hungry, he wanted her. There was no hesitation in her response as she parted her lips to his tongue. Each stroke of her silky tongue met his and he put all of the pain, the emotion of his past into the kiss. With her arms linked tight around his neck, he pressed one hand to her back and allowed the other to drift down to that lovely backside he'd noticed the first day. He cupped one hand against her curved bottom and then brought the other hand down. Somehow he managed to move so that he pressed her against the wall. A groan of pure lust rumbled deep in his chest. If he didn't control himself right now, he might commit an act he'd likely regret.

Easing back, he gave her a little room, but didn't let go of her. She was a beauty inside and out, and he'd been an idiot for not seeing it. Although he wanted her, he didn't belong in her life any more than she belonged in his. They either needed to end this little flirtation of theirs or take it all the way and be done with it. As he looked at her flushed cheeks and the way her eyes went soft, the ruby lips, he doubted that making love to her for one night would ever be enough. If he jumped into that water, he'd certainly drown.

"Can you talk now?" she asked, and cupped her hand against his cheek. "I don't mean to pry into your life, but something's almost destroying you, and it might help to talk about it."

Easing back some more, he considered her words. "Nothing can help this." He'd never really tried, but the pain ran so deep, he couldn't conceive of anything ever releasing it. It was part of him.

"Tell me." She took his hand, led him out of the office and locked the door to the clinic. She made a pot of coffee and pulled out a packet of crackers and a jar of peanut butter from the cupboard. After things were ready, they sat on the floor of the waiting area.

"You really don't know what you're letting yourself in for," he said, trying to make light of the situation, but he also recognized the wisdom of her words. Who knew? Maybe something could help. If anyone could make it happen, he knew it would be Vicky.

"Just start talking. I know you were awfully worried about Carlos and rightfully so, but after he started to improve, you didn't."

Miguel closed his eyes and let the emotions of that day wash over him. Images of his brother and Carlos meshed together and blended until they nearly became one. "The incident with Carlos was nearly a replay of the night my brother, Emilio, died." Inside him a tremor started. His hand shook as he reached for a cracker.

"Miguel, I didn't know."

"I know." He patted her shoulder and tried not to fall too far into those blue eyes of hers. "You couldn't have. Carlos, of course, is Carlos, but he looks nearly identical to my brother."

Vicky's eyes widened. She knew the implications. "That brought it all back again, didn't it? I'd guess that's a case of PTSD you didn't expect."

"Yeah. It was like reliving it all over again, except that this time you were there, and Carlos survived." He huffed out a sigh filled with regrets he could never change. "Emilio died on the sidewalk in my arms. I had to tell my family that he'd been shot by the gang I'd been trying to get him away from." The irony of it hadn't eluded him.

"Oh, my God, Miguel. You've kept this inside until now?"

"I took responsibility for what was my fault." It was that simple to him. He was older, he was the responsible one.

"How could any of it be your fault? The gang pulled the trigger."

"I might as well have. I was trying to persuade the gang leader, Juan, to leave Emilio alone, and he was about to shoot me. Emilio dived in and took the bullet that was meant for me."

Tears filled her eyes as she watched him tell the story and she waited until he was finished speaking to ask questions. "How old were you when this happened?"

"Twenty-one. I was the oldest, responsible." He held up his wrist and pointed out the silver bracelet he wore. "I'd just finished college, was home on break before medical school. This was a present for Emilio, but I never got to give it to him."

"I've noticed it. It's beautiful."

"It reminds me every day of how I failed my family and my brother, that I was responsible for his death." He'd never taken it off.

"Where is this Juan now?"

"In jail. For another murder." He snorted in disgust. "At least they got him for that one."

"I'd say he's where he belongs, and so are you." She placed her hand over his. "Nothing you've told me changes the fact that you are doing very good things for your community. And no part of Emilio's death was your fault. You've got to know that."

"If I hadn't tried to get him out, he might be alive now."

"Or he might not. He could have been killed in another incident. You'll never know. But you have to let him go, Miguel. That's the only way you'll be free. You've been punishing yourself with this clinic, and now I know why. You think if you work yourself to death by saving others, it will pay for your crime, but it wasn't yours to pay for."

He looked at her and opened his mouth to deny everything, but he couldn't. The words just wouldn't come. Instead, he needed a change of pace. "Tell me what you have in mind for the fundraiser, and I'll tell you what I think."

"Change of topic won't get you off the hook," she said, but opened a folder filled with a lot of papers and numbers. "'A Night for a Life' is the tentative title I've given the event. If people spend one night bringing in money to the clinic, it will save a life." She paused and looked at him. "If we do this right, the clinic will run itself. My brother can set up the nonprofit part of it, and you'll have the freedom and the time to work at the hospital, too."

Fascinated, he listened to her give the minipresentation. No fancy computer programs, just a simple retelling of her plan for funding the clinic, for helping him to achieve his dream of returning to the trauma unit and keeping the clinic alive, as well.

He'd been so wrong about Vicky Sterling-Thorne.

CHAPTER FOURTEEN

MIGUEL lay in bed sleepless, restless, his mind racing as midnight approached. Spring eased its way into summer with bright beautiful days and evenings that were designed for sleeping with the windows open to catch any stray breeze that happened by. This was the beauty of living in the high desert: warm days, balmy nights.

Another week had passed, seeing Carlos's continued improvement. At least that was one worry off his mind. The days were full of patients and the evenings full of fundraising plans. Now that he was on board with the idea, he was really enjoying the process of putting together such an event. It was a far cry from the bake sales and car washes he'd envisioned. He and Vicky worked together, tirelessly caring for patients and planning for the event. In doing so, he was seeing her in a different light that was not as unflattering as he'd thought in the beginning. Now he had no regrets that he'd hired her.

He'd come to depend on her more than he'd ever thought he could and the ice surrounding his heart had begun to melt because of her. That was another thing he never thought he'd experience. She brought new life to the clinic and was slowly bringing new life to him.

The red numbers on the bedside clock showed it was midnight. Frustrated, he sat up and shook off the sheet. Before he knew it the phone was in his hand and he'd dialed Vicky's number. If she didn't answer in the first ring or two he'd hang up, but he just wanted to talk to her. Just had to hear her voice. Now.

"Hello?"

Miguel nearly dropped to his knees at the husky, sexy tone of her voice. "It's Miguel. Did I wake you?" He could just imagine her all rumpled with sleep, soft and sexy, as she reached for the phone in the dark.

"Sort of. I was resting but not really asleep. You know that in-between state?"

"I know it." He'd been in it.

"What's up besides us?"

He smiled at that. One of the things he'd come to love about her was the subtle sense of humour she had. The patients responded to it, and he found himself responding, as well. "I...I don't know. I just wanted to talk to you for a minute."

"Restless, huh? Usually when I'm restless a walk helps settle me down."

"A walk at midnight?" He'd never thought of that.

"Definitely. Why don't you come over, and I'll take you for a midnight stroll like you've never imagined."

Intriguing. "I'll get dressed."

"Me, too." She gave him her address and they hung up. Adrenaline and anticipation replaced the restlessness than ran through his veins. He didn't know what kind of midnight walk she had in mind, but anything had to be better than the current situation he was in.

In short order he made the trip to her home in the

north valley area of Albuquerque. Though not far away in distance, the area was far away, a throwback, in time. Huge trees and mature foliage hugged both sides of the road mixed with open fields for alfalfa and grazing horses. She lived in a caretaker's cottage in the middle of the vineyard, she had said. Someday he'd like to see this area during daylight. As beautiful as it was at night, he wanted to see it in the light of day. He made the turn onto a narrow lane, darkened by the dense cottonwood trees overhead. It almost put him in another land or era. No wonder she loved it here.

The porch light guided him and in minutes he saw her standing by the front door of a quaint cottage nearly enveloped with dark ivy and surrounded by rose bushes. He'd never seen her looking so casual, in a plain shirt, denim shorts and flimsy sandals. He'd never seen her looking so luscious, either. This was definitely where he wanted to be instead of rolling around in his bed.

"Made it okay?" she asked as he stepped out of the truck.

"No problem. Love that GPS."

With a sideways smile and eyes full of mystery, she held out her hand. "Let's walk." She led the way into the incredibly dark night, as if she'd taken this path many times. With only a tiny flashlight in her hand that hardly lent illumination, he followed her. Out here there were no streetlights. They were surrounded by acres and acres of vineyard and brilliant galaxies overhead.

In silence they strolled as the sounds of the night rose up around them. Crickets chimed their rhythmic songs, cicadas buzzed in the trees overhead, a delightful breeze stroked his skin, and he began to relax. The stress of the past two weeks was beginning to fade with the feel of her soft hand in his.

He took a deep breath, catching the fragrances of the night. Fresh dirt, the sweet scent of honeysuckle and Spanish broom bushes that had to be nearby. He'd know those scents anywhere. Large, lush leaves of the grapevines brushed his arms and legs, the foliage reaching out from the strength of the main vines.

"This is very nice."

"*Nice?* This is awesome." She gave his hand a squeeze. "I love this walk. There are times I just can't sleep and a stroll through the vines helps me to relax. You can't see it now, but over there is the river." She paused and pointed to the west. The unmistakable snort of a horse made him smile.

"I think we're disturbing someone's sleep."

"They'll get over it." They kept walking.

He was glad she had his hand or he would have been lost for certain. As they rounded a bend in the path, the glint of moonlight off the river caught his eye. The thought of her half-naked and wet was enough to set his imagine on fire. Right now, with her in the middle of the night, he wanted to set his imagination free. He wanted to stop and savor the night and everything it had to offer.

"You ever swim down here?"

"Not in the river. Too unpredictable for me." She tugged on his hand. "But there's a pool at the main house. We can slip in for a quick dip."

"If it's a bad idea, I'll understand." But the thought of getting her alone and naked and wet was more than he could resist.

"It's a great idea. My father's not home right now, but he won't mind, anyway."

Clenching his jaw, as a wave of desire hit him, he stopped there. Having a tryst in the middle of the night was something he'd have done in his younger days, but now having one with his coworker wasn't on the agenda. Things would never be the same between them, and he wasn't willing to ruin his relationship with Vicky just for sex. He'd have to reel in his libido as long as he continued to work with her. Once he left the clinic, things might be different, but there was no guarantee in that. "As much as I'd like to, I don't think we should."

"Why not? It's not like we'll be naked or anything."

"We won't?" That stopped him. "Uh, why not?"

She giggled. "Because I'll put on my swimsuit and you can borrow a pair of my brother's trunks, that's why. They're clean."

"Oh." So much for libido and a wet, naked woman.

She laughed again. "You sound so disappointed."

"I am." But he laughed and the feeling swirling inside his chest was a good one. One he hadn't let himself experience in way too long. "Maybe a cool swim is just what I need after all."

"Right this way."

Miguel changed first and eased into the pool. Submerging himself fully, he allowed the water to wash over him. This was a luxury he'd never imagined. He pushed off the bottom and swam as far as he could in one breath, then surfaced for air. Just as he came up, Vicky launched herself from the diving board. Though there were lights at the bottom of the pool, she hadn't seen him, and he couldn't get out of the way fast enough. He submerged beneath her and came up just inches away.

"Miguel! I didn't see you. Are you okay?" She reached out and placed her hands on his shoulders as they trod water.

It didn't matter what he told himself before and even if she wasn't naked, she was certainly wet and luscious in a barely-there bikini, and he wanted her. With one arm he snagged her around the waist and brought her fully against him, dragging her to the side of the pool. Now that the restraints had been loosened, he allowed himself to look down at her, to take in all that she was and enjoy his gaze wander over her. "I'm just fine." With her clinging to him, he approached the side of the pool where he could put his feet on the bottom.

Before he even knew what he was doing, he kissed her. Nothing was going to stop him from feeling every inch of her against him. He pressed her tight and the backs of his hands protected her delicate skin from rubbing against the side.

Slowly and deeply he took her, his lips, his mouth, his tongue, every breath he took seeming to become part of her. There was magic in the night and magic going on between them. The low groan in her throat made his desire flare higher and his arousal was both pleasurable and painful. He wanted her and as she raised her legs to wrap them around his hips, there was no doubt that she wanted him, too.

Lifting one hand, he slipped a thumb beneath the flimsy bikini top that clung to her skin and cupped her breast. The weight of her, the tight nipple in his hand felt so right. He wanted all of her filling his hands, filling his senses, and he tugged on the string that held the top together. In seconds it floated away to the bottom of the pool, like a leaf to the bottom of the river.

Dragging his mouth away from hers, he licked his way down her neck and over one collarbone. Scooping a nipple into his mouth, he suckled hard, stroking the tight flesh with his tongue, wanting to send her as far into the abyss as he already was.

Vicky had never felt as alive, as filled with desire as she was at this moment. The water licked her skin, adding to the delicious sensation of Miguel teasing her nipple. Her senses were on overload and there was only one way to fix it. Pulling his head up, she spread kisses over his neck, his face, his eyes, and settled on his mouth for a long slow drink. Groaning, he pressed her against the edge of the pool again and his arousal burned into her. She wanted him as she'd never wanted any man in her life. She'd never been a great judge of men, but in Miguel there was a hidden heart of gold. Somehow she knew it.

"Let's go to the cottage." She stroked her hand down his face and let it rest on his chest. "We need to get out of these wet clothes."

He dug his fingers into her hips, everything about him intense and aroused. Even in the dim lighting from around the pool she saw the desire burning in his eyes. She wanted him, too. There was nothing to hold either of them back. Any nagging doubts had faded away.

"I want that very much, but if we make love it will change everything between us." He took in a deep breath and held her gaze. "Not just some things. Everything."

"I think things have already changed between us. We've been circling this moment since we met." Feeling bolder than she ever had, she brought his hand back to her breast, loving the feel of his skin sliding against hers, needing to feel the vitality he infused into her with his touch. This was the way things were supposed to be between a man and a woman. This was the way it was supposed to feel, and she didn't want to let it go. "I want things to change between us, Miguel." She stroked his face again, loving the textures of him against her. "I want to make love to you."

Groaning, he hugged her close, then pressed her against the side again. He trembled in her arms. As she moved, he winced then pulled back.

"What is it?"

Cupping her face, he pressed a kiss to her mouth and eased her toward the steps. "I think the cement is chipped. Just scraped my hand on the side, but it's nothing."

Vicky pulled back. "Let me see. Doctors are the worst patients, you know."

"Seriously, it's just a scratch." He turned his hand over to show her, and she gasped at the blood streaming from several small wounds. "This isn't nothing." She looked back at the pool and saw the broken and chipped spot that she had avoided every time she swam lately. "Dammit. Daddy was supposed to have had that fixed by now." She grabbed a towel and wrapped it around her. Her breath came out in panting gasps as she stood trembling beside him. "Why don't we go get that fixed?" She held out her hand to him.

He took it and they returned to the cottage. With the

towel knotted in the front, Vicky tended to the abrasions that were really nothing, but he enjoyed the touch of her and the way she fussed over him.

With the gentle touch that he had seen her use count-less times on patients in the clinic, she tended to the small cuts as if they were the most urgent of injuries. That made him smile inside and the warmth of love pulsed out with each beat of his heart.

Unexpected moisture filled his eyes and the warmth began to burn in his lungs. He couldn't do it. He couldn't have a night of passion with Vicky and walk away from her. But he couldn't give her what she needed and what she deserved either.

Curling his hands into fists, he pulled away from her. He had to end it now, no matter how much it hurt him.

Vicky stared up at him, her eyes brimming with tears. "Miguel?" Her breath came in short gasps. "You're leav-ing, aren't you?"

The pain squeezed his throat shut. Though he opened his mouth, he couldn't speak. He'd never experienced such anguish tearing him apart. "I...have to."

"No, you don't. We can just talk or sleep."

A vulgar laugh opened his throat. "If I stayed, we wouldn't be sleeping."

"I can live with a sleepless night, Miguel." She took a step closer and some of the tears fell from her eyes. "I don't want to spend a sleepless night without you beside me."

"Vicky, you deserve so much better, so much more than what I can give you." He backed up and spun around in a circle. "I mean, just look at what you're used to. This is so far away from what I come from,

from who I am, it might as well be the other side of the world."

"I don't need this! I don't want this." She moved closer to him. "The outer shell of this life has cost me more than you'll ever know." Tears flowed as anger snapped in her eyes. "Existing in this environment isn't living. I've only begun to live, to grow, to love since I started at the clinic." She sucked in a ragged breath. "I want more of it. I *need* more of it. Of you."

"Vicky," he said, and his voice cracked. The emotion in the room nearly sizzled between them. "I'm broken inside. Whatever capacity I had to love another died a long time ago."

"That's not true. I saw you with your family, with Carlos's family. There was love and compassion in you then. It's not gone, it's just been in hiding for a long time."

"I'm sorry. If I were different, maybe things could have worked between us."

"If I wanted somebody different, I could have had them."

"I'm sorry." He cupped his hands around her face and pulled her close for one last hard kiss before he walked away from her forever.

CHAPTER FIFTEEN

VICKY sobbed the remainder of the night into her pillow. Around dawn she slept, but only for a few elusive hours. Erotic dreams of Miguel beside her melded into the nightmare of reality. Her life was destined for failure. If she'd hidden her identity from Miguel he'd have been furious when he'd found out. Not hiding her identity had turned out just as bad. Either way, her family name interfered with her ability to have a normal life and she was damned sick of it.

They still had to get through the next week together. The fundraiser was on Saturday night, and she didn't know how either of them would survive the week working together. After that she would turn in her resignation. There was no point in staying at the clinic. She had proved to her father and to herself that she could work in that environment. Maybe she would go to University Hospital, too. They were always looking for nurses and she'd be able to hide more easily among a larger staff.

Tears filled her eyes as she thought of leaving those patients and the staff she'd come to love. On Monday she would have to face Miguel again, and she didn't

know how she was going to do that without breaking
down and breaking her heart.

Monday morning arrived and Vicky strolled through
the doors a few minutes early. After putting on the first
pot of coffee, she chatted with Tilly and the other staff
members who arrived in the minutes before Miguel.
Trying to appear normal took a monumental effort.

There was a break in his stride as he came through the
door and saw her, then he continued on to his office.

As always, Mondays were the busiest of days and the
flow of patients didn't let up until noon. Miguel caught
her eye as she was about to enter the staff room for a
much-needed break. With a nod, he turned and headed
to his office. She followed, not sure what was going to
happen but she was determined to see it through. She
was a Sterling-Thorne after all, and they were made of
tough stuff.

She shut the door and stood inside his office, just
across the desk from the man who had held her in his
arms only two nights ago. "Did you need something?"
she asked.

"I didn't expect to see you this morning." There was
no warmth in his gaze, just cold indifference. Somehow
that was worse than his anger.

"Why not? Just because we had a philosophical difference on a personal level, it doesn't mean I quit my
job."

"It would be easier if you did."

She smiled at that. "I know it would, but I'm done
making things easier on people. I'm doing what's right
for me. I love this job and these people that I work with,

the staff as well as the patients." She huffed out a breath and realized that every word of it was true. She wasn't going anywhere. "If you don't want me to work here any more, you're going to have to fire me and then *you* get to tell everyone." Without waiting for his reaction, she left the office.

The trembling began in her arms and wound its way around to her stomach then down her legs. If she didn't sit soon, she was going to fall over. The conviction of her words surprised her, but as she'd told Miguel, she'd realized they were true. She turned down a hallway that led to a side door. She had to get outside for a breath of fresh air, just for a minute, then she'd head back inside and back to work.

Just as she opened the door, excited screams rang out behind her. "What in the world...?" she mumbled. The clinic closed for lunch, so there weren't any patients present at the moment. What could be going on? Reluctantly, she returned to the staff lounge and discovered people laughing and crying at the same time. They were grouped so that she couldn't see what they were looking at.

"Vicky?" Carlos called to her.

"Carlos!" She found herself enveloped in the young man's hug. "What are you doing here?" The joy at his recovery pushed away the sad feelings in her heart.

Too many emotions crowded around in her and tears fell from her eyes as she pressed her hands to her cheeks. But they were good tears, and she let them go. Hiding her emotions had never gotten her anything, so why waste the energy?

"I'm back for a visit. I go to therapy nearby, so I

wanted to stop and see if anyone had missed me."
He grinned and the room exploded in relieved laughter. Good wishes and gentle pats on the back were exchanged.

When Vicky looked up, Miguel stood across the room, his dark eyes intent on her for a second, then he looked at Carlos and his expression changed. In just a few steps he had crossed the room and enveloped the young man in his arms. "Why didn't you tell us you were coming?"

"That takes the surprise out of it," he said. They spoke in an excited mix of English and Spanish and Vicky could follow some of it, but it was obvious that everyone was glad to see Carlos upright and looking so well. Though he looked fit enough, there was a slight sheen of perspiration on his forehead and he hadn't quite lost his hospital pallor.

He placed a hand on the back of a chair, and Vicky noticed that it trembled.

"Sit down, why don't you?" She gestured for him to sit and took a chair herself, knowing that he'd never admit to feeling weak among his friends. Machismo ran deep in him, and he wasn't about to give it up now. "We were just about to have lunch. Did you want to join us?"

"Sure. Catch me up on what's going on around here. When's the fundraiser?" He looked across the small table at Miguel for the answer.

"We're going to have to cancel the event." He looked away and pressed his lips together.

A gasp rose in the room and worried glances were exchanged.

"No, we're not. The fundraiser is on Saturday night." Vicky focused on Miguel. What was he doing? "The clinic needs this."

"I've reconsidered. I won't leave. We'll just go on the way we were before."

"Leave? What are you talking about?" Confused, Carlos looked between the two. "What's going on?"

"Miguel's been offered a position at the trauma unit at University Hospital."

"That's great, man," he said, then frowned. "Oh, but not great for us, though."

"Exactly. Which is why I'm going to decline the offer. I can't walk away from everyone here."

She looked at Miguel and knew she loved him. "Don't make me do it, Miguel."

Now it was his turn to be confused. "Do what?"

She spoke to Carlos and the rest of the staff. "It's his dream to work in the trauma unit again. He was in his element when you were injured, and I've never seen him work better, though he's much too modest to admit that out loud. As much as he loves this place, his talent is wasted here."

"Vicky—"

Carlos simply looked at Miguel. "You have to, M. You saved my life and if you can save other people too, you have to do it."

"I'm not leaving here. I've made a commitment to the people in this community."

"And you won't be breaking it by going to the hospital," Vicky said.

Staff members stood up and gathered around the table, each of them placing a hand of encouragement on

Miguel. Good wishes and words of luck rang throughout
the room.

He cleared his throat and looked down. Tears welled
in Vicky's eyes at the emotion he struggled to hide. He
loved these people, and they loved him right back. He'd
never be far from them, far from this place where his
heart lived, but his dreams weren't going to wait. She
was sure of it.

The day seemed to struggle forward as much as Vicky
did. It was one of those painful afternoons where she
worked hard to put one foot in front of the other and
each movement was a chore.

Finally, all of the patients were seen and the clinic
had been put to rights for the next morning. A yawn
surprised her, and she covered it with her hand.

"Worn-out, are you?" Tilly asked as she gathered her
things.

"Definitely."

"You and Miguel have been working your tails off
to get things ready for Saturday night while working all
day long." She shook her head in amazement. "Good
thing you two are young."

They chatted another minute or two as the other
staff filed out. "It will be good when it's over, though.
The clinic will be its own nonprofit organization and it
will be able to almost run itself. Miguel will be able to
take the new position and everyone will be happy." She
sighed as she thought about it. His work and his presence
here would never be forgotten, she was certain of it.

"What about you?" Tilly asked.

"What about me?"

"You mentioned the clinic and Miguel, but not what you're going to do after it's all over. Will you still stay?"

For a second or two she thought about it. What was she going to do? She'd changed since she'd first arrived. "I'll be back on Monday, like the rest of you, ready for another round of taking care of people." She hugged the smaller woman's shoulders with one arm. "It's what people like you and me do, Tilly. We take care of people, right?"

Tilly patted her hand. "Right. See you in the morning."

Could it really be that simple? Miguel hadn't meant to listen in on the earlier conversation between Tilly and Vicky at the clinic, but he had. He arrived home and paused inside the door as emotions he'd held at bay now slammed into him. The sentiment in Vicky's voice was so sure, so filled with conviction that he wanted to believe in her in the same way that she believed in him.

Shoving his hands into his hair, he curled his fingers, pulling his hair until it hurt. He didn't know what to do. Giving in to the passion he felt for Vicky would be so very easy, but with nothing to offer her, nothing she didn't already have, how could he pursue her? Lying to himself would only get both of them into trouble and hurt Vicky more than he already had. Lies. They were what always got people into trouble, and he'd never tolerated them. Lies were what had gotten his brother killed.

He closed his eyes and images of his brother's death hit him, opened up the wound and let the pain flow. He'd

never gotten over it, he knew. Family events, the look
in people's eyes, the hugs that seemed to go on forever
all came back now to torture him. That was why he'd
wanted Vicky at the party with him, to provide a buffer
between his family and himself. That hadn't turned
out the way he'd planned. That had only given him
the opportunity to fall in love with a woman he could
never have.

The voice he hadn't heard in a decade whispered
into the room and enveloped him in a swirl of warm
comfort.

It wasn't your fault. It wasn't your fault, brother.

The pain in Miguel's heart felt as if he would die
from it and his breath ceased. If he had been shot with
an arrow, his heart couldn't have hurt any less. Tears
that he'd held back for so many years filled his eyes,
and he gasped for breath.

Let go, brother, just let me go.

He looked down at the bracelet on his right wrist and
blinked to clear his vision. The bracelet had been there
as a symbol to himself, and everyone who knew him,
of his guilt, his chain to the past. He'd never taken it
off. Not since that night so long ago. The metal that had
always burned hot against his skin now cooled, the heat
leaving it.

With the echo of Emilio's voice ringing in his ears, he
moved down the hallway to the pictures and stopped in
front of one of his brother. Memories of their childhood
flashed through him. He placed the fingers of his left
hand over the warm silver and pulled off the bracelet.
As he stared at the photograph, the pain in his chest
began to ease, replaced with a warm pulse he hadn't

felt for a long time. He hung the bracelet on a corner of the picture frame.

He didn't need it any longer.

CHAPTER SIXTEEN

VICKY had taken a room at the hotel for the night, as had been her custom for every fundraiser she'd ever attended. If she needed a break from the party she could go to her room, and when she was through for the night it was simpler to take the elevator than to try to negotiate driving in a fancy gown and flimsy shoes.

She'd made the final arrangements this evening then spent some time preparing herself. There were so many people that she'd see tonight that she had to have her Victoria face on for. That took preparation of a certain kind. And since the evening was for Miguel's clinic, he and her father were certain to meet. There were a few key introductions that she wanted to make to Miguel that could help with the future of the clinic, too.

That was anxiety of a completely different sort.

Whether Miguel would be warm or cool tonight, she had no idea. Either way, he'd see the woman behind the name tonight. So far she'd always been Vicky to him. Tonight Victoria would be on display. Tonight would reveal whether they truly had a chance to work things out. If he could accept who she was, that was one thing. If he couldn't, then things were well and truly over between them.

She stuck a few items plus the key card into a tiny purse that matched her dress and inspected herself in the mirror. The dress was another of her brother's creations and as usual he'd spared her no extra fabric.

After a calming breath, she turned on a dim light by the bed, then left the room to see what fate had in store for her in the ballroom.

The tux was too tight. And who in their right minds had invented the cummerbund? Dress shoes looked good, but other than that they were a waste, too. No wonder women had a love-hate relationship with high heels.

Miguel stood in the men's room, which was nearly as big as his entire bungalow. Looking in the mirror, he adjusted his tie a bit to the left then to the right. Right back where it wanted to go anyway. He'd arrived early to help Vicky with any final arrangements, but she had apparently already come and gone, leaving him with more minutes to spare than he cared to have. A stroll around the lush gardens killed a few minutes, but the nervousness and anxiety boiling inside him wouldn't be quieted so easily.

So many things were riding on the success of this night and any number of things could go wrong.

Maybe a quick trip to the bar would calm his nerves. He reentered the hallway, and his shoes made crisp sounds on the tile flooring.

"Dr. Torres!" A familiar woman's voice called to him. A smile seemed to grow from his chest and made its way to his face. Carlos and his parents had entered and his mother waved.

He greeted them and gave a peck on the cheek to Priscilla. "You know you don't have to call me Doctor. You're family."

"Oh, not on a night like this," she said, wide-eyed. "This is your night, *mijo,* and you deserve all the respect that comes to you." She looked up at her son with such affection and love that a lump formed in Miguel's throat. "You saved my son and there is nothing I won't do for you."

He shook Carlos's hand. "You're looking fit. How do you feel?"

"Great." He stuck a finger in his collar. "Tux is a little tight, but I'll live."

"Bah. Tight. He's lost twenty pounds since he was injured, and I think I've found them all!" Priscilla gave a laugh and patted her stomach.

"There will be plenty for him to eat tonight."

After that the guests began to arrive in earnest. People that he knew from the clinic and others he recognized from the community. Other people he didn't know but had to be among the wealthiest people he'd ever seen.

When a man in his mid-thirties entered the lobby with two clinging women dressed in haute couture, he hid a grin. That had to be the fashion-designer brother of Vicky's.

The entire group stopped in front of him and the man gave Miguel the once-over with his eyes. "You must be the doctor," he said, and held out his hand.

"I must be or I'm at the wrong party." Miguel shook the man's hand, liking him immediately.

"I'm Edward, Victoria's brother." One of the tall women with Edward gave a dramatic sigh.

"Quite the group you have here," Miguel said.

"Yes, isn't it?" Edward sported a woman on each arm. "I couldn't decide who to bring, so I brought both."

"Why limit yourself?" He grinned.

"Indeed. Do you know where Victoria is?"

"I haven't seen her, but she should be here some-where."

"Ladies, shall we go and see what sort of entertain-ment awaits us?" Without waiting for an answer, Edward strode forward and Miguel followed the small group.

"I'll catch you later," Carlos said, and walked beside Miguel. "Hey, what's with this 'Victoria' stuff? What's up with you and Vicky?"

Miguel paused inside the ballroom and pulled Carlos to the side. "Vicky...isn't who you think she is."

"What? What do you mean? You mean she's not a nurse?" His eyes went wide.

"Yes, she's a nurse—"

"Don't tell me she's a dude!"

"Carlos—"

"I saw that movie once, you know?" The man paled.

"No, just listen, will you?" He sighed, hating to break the news to Carlos. "She belongs to the family of Sterling-Thorne. She's Victoria Sterling-Thorne."

"Wow. You mean the wine people?" Carlos's eyes got very big at the mention of the name. He was obviously impressed.

"Exactly."

Carlos whistled. "I didn't know. I thought she was just a regular nurse. Way to go, man."

"What are you talking about?" Miguel frowned, not liking the implication of that.

"You hooking up with such a rich woman."

"Vicky and I aren't hooked up."

"Why not? You're perfect together."

"I don't think so." That comment was a small taste of what Vicky had been talking about, and this was coming from a trusted friend. Had he treated Vicky differently because he'd known who she was? He didn't know, but she had been right to be cautious.

Somehow something in the room changed, and he looked up. Scanning the crowd, he first saw a large group of people settling down at richly appointed tables, then his chest stopped moving and he couldn't draw breath.

Vicky stood across the room and stared at him. Just like in the movies, everything else faded away from his vision and he only saw her. Tall, lithe and elegant, she shimmered in the light. Sequins on the dress, patterned like an orchid, glinted with the slightest move she made. The dress hugged every curve and set her figure off magnificently. There were no sleeves, just small straps that disappeared against her skin.

Miguel was simply stunned stupid by the sight of her.

Someone placed a finger beneath his chin and pushed. "You look like a hound dog, man," Carlos said. "Try to look professional, will you?"

Right now, staring at Vicky, he felt like one. "I don't

know what you mean." He blinked and with an effort faced the younger man.

"You look like you want to take a bite out of her."

"That's not true."

"Well, if you don't, I will." He straightened his tie and took a step toward Vicky.

"Oh, no, you don't. You're entirely too young."

"A man needs practice, right?"

Carlos was teasing him, and he played right along. "Go practice on someone else."

"I knew there was something going on between you two. From the first day, I knew it."

"There's nothing going on between us."

Carlos looked at Vicky, then back at him. "If there isn't, there should be." He nudged Miguel. "Go talk to her, you know you want to. Just don't drool on her dress."

"I'll try to be civil."

"Good. I'm gonna check out the food. I'll catch you later." After a quick rap of his knuckles against Miguel's, Carlos left him alone. Unable to delay any longer, he made his way across the dance floor to where Vicky stood greeting people. The closer he got to her, the thicker his tongue felt, and he didn't even know if he could speak.

"Victoria!" An older gentleman, tall and upright, leaned over and kissed her on the cheek. "It's wonderful to see you doing good things again." He released her and his wife embraced Vicky.

"Charity was your mother's life after you children. She would be so proud of you."

"Thank you, both." She turned to Miguel and he

moved closer to her. That fragrance of hers sinuously invaded his mind and his heart, drawing him ever closer to her flame. "This is Dr. Miguel Torres, the medical director of the clinic. Dr. Torres, this is Mr. Thomas and and Mrs. Sally Hampton. They own the Hampton Inn chain."

"Pleasure to meet you," Miguel said, and he was certainly impressed at how casually Vicky introduced them. She was in her element here.

"Outstanding work you're doing in your clinic, Dr. Torres. Outstanding." They shook hands. "We need more physicians like you, not more hospital conglomerations that take you away from your patients."

"Thank you. You sound as if you have some experience in that arena."

"I'm an old adman, but two of my sons chose medicine." He raised his eyes skyward. "The stories they tell are shocking."

"Thank you very much for supporting the clinic. It means a lot to everyone involved."

"My sons are out of state, but they have sent along their regards," Mr. Hampton said, and retrieved a long envelope from his jacket. "Along with a donation. They grew up here and have a great fondness for the work you do at ground level."

Miguel took the envelope and tucked it inside his tux, humbled at the generosity of strangers. "Please give them my greatest thanks, sir." He'd never expected such a generous outpouring for the clinic. Never. He looked at Vicky, who wore an enigmatic smile.

"Lovely to see you again. Save me a dance later,"

Vicky said. She took Miguel's arm and maneuvered them toward another couple.

"Nicely done." Large crowds weren't within his comfort zone, but Vicky looked like a professional.

"Years of practice." She shrugged off the compliment. "Actually, he's like an uncle to me. I've known him my whole life."

Another couple of equal standing in the community approached them. Introductions were made and the interaction was repeated dozens of times over the course of the next two hours. Vicky truly knew how to charm people and share her wit so that everyone knew she saw them and heard what they had to say. He received several more private envelopes for the clinic.

"Dr. Torres, this is Dr. Flemming, a physician who might be interested in taking a hands-on role at the clinic."

Surprise filled Miguel. "Pleasure," he said, and shook the older man's hand. "I'd love to have you come visit and see what we do."

"Absolutely. I'm heading toward part-time employment, but I'm not ready to retire all the way yet." He smiled and creases appeared around his eyes. "I'll call you next week and we'll set something up."

"I'll look forward to it." Excitement pulsed through him. There were possibilities in a meeting like that. And it was all thanks to Vicky. "Would you like something to drink?" he asked. After so much time spent talking, he was parched.

"Yes. Champagne would be lovely." She surveyed the room. "Looks like everyone is settling down to eat. This is usually the time I have a little refreshment."

"It would be a shame to let all of that fabulous food go to waste."

"Absolutely." They sat at a reserved table and were served immediately by the attentive waitstaff. The food was incredible, but Vicky seemed to be more attentive to the goings-on at other tables than to what was on her plate.

"Not hungry?"

She sipped her champagne. "I'm okay. At functions like this my appetite usually spirals down to nothing. Too anxious to eat much."

"That's a shame. This is really good." He set his fork by his plate and took a closer look at her. She looked beautiful, her hair and makeup perfect, but beneath that she was pale and nervous. She'd hidden herself for so many years that she'd nearly fooled him. "What's really going on?"

The flash of her eyes down to her glass and then back at him told it all. This was the Victoria she'd talked about. And he understood it all. It wasn't just this event, it was every day of her life that wasn't at the clinic. This persona made it difficult to have a life that wasn't under a microscope all the time.

The part of him that had sworn not to empathize with her, to feel sorry for her seemed to have folded away with the feelings he'd had for his brother. The empty space that had held his pain was now slowly being filled with something else. Something unexpected and warm.

Without preamble, the music began. A medley of songs, old and new, faded away into a song that was certain to be an audience favorite. As Miguel watched, couples gathered on the dance floor. Many of them had obviously danced together for years. The way they moved together, flowed with each other, anticipating each move the other made, made it obvious.

This was a night like no other and he was realizing that Vicky was a woman like no other. When he left the clinic, he'd likely never see her again. Could he live with that? Could he walk away from her? Standing, he held out his hand to her, careful to keep his features controlled. This was not the time or place for any revelations, even if he had any. "Will you dance with me?" There was so much more than that one simple question.

The fatigue in her eyes lifted and a small smile tugged at the corners of her mouth. "I thought you'd never ask." She placed her hand in his and tonight it felt daintier, more fragile, than it ever had. That was an illusion, he knew, the same way that the magic of tonight was an illusion. He was going to take advantage of it as long as it lasted.

She turned to go to the dance floor, and Miguel felt as if someone had punched him in the stomach. Half of her dress was missing! At least, that's how it appeared at first glance. Somehow he'd only seen the front of her dress, and now that he'd seen how the dress revealed the long, elegant lines of her back, how the silken fabric fluttered delicately over her hips and down her legs, desire nearly incapacitated him. He made it to the dance floor just a few feet behind her, laboring with every step. He could delude himself all he wanted, but when Vicky turned to him, he knew this night was like no other.

And she knew it, too. It would be their last one together. After this, their lives would change forever.

The music filled his mind as Vicky stepped into his arms and filled his senses. Nothing compared to the way they fitted together. He cupped her hand in one of his and placed his other one in the small of her back. There was nowhere to place his hand where he didn't touch her skin.

It was warm and soft and silky beneath his fingers, and he itched to drag his hand over every inch of her. He looked into her eyes and stepped into the music.

They didn't speak. They didn't have to. Vicky closed her eyes and with a sigh pressed her temple against his jaw. Miguel nearly groaned. Every move, every sigh, every breath she took brought her closer to him, closer inside his heart.

The night moved forward and he didn't want to let go of her. The songs melted together the way he and Vicky melted together, until he received a tap on the shoulder, startling him out of his fantasy.

"Victoria, I believe you were going to save this particular dance for me." Mr. Hampton stood waiting with his wife, who looked at Miguel.

"Why don't we just switch partners for a few? That should shake things up a little." Mrs. Hampton held out her hand to him.

Unable to speak for the emotions strangling him, he simply nodded and made the change.

Victoria chatted with Thomas, but allowed her gaze to follow Miguel. He was such a handsome man and in a tux utterly delicious.

"He's quite the young man, isn't he?" Thomas asked with a knowing smile.

"Yes, he is." Vicky couldn't deny it. "Mother would have liked him."

"What does your father think?"

"Oh, he hasn't met Dr. Torres yet." The thought of it made Vicky cringe. When that happened, she'd likely need a sedative.

"Give you father a chance, Victoria. He might surprise you."

"That would be a novel experience."

"He only wants what's best for you."

"I know." It was his methods that Vicky didn't agree with, but that was an argument for another time.

Vicky didn't get to dance with Miguel any more, but she saw him dancing with Tilly. The woman looked so small and dainty compared to Miguel and she looked as if she was having a fabulous time in a silk-and-sequin dress that she had bought just for the event. Duties and small problems required Vicky's attention, and she kept her eye on Miguel as he made his way through the crowd, being drawn into conversations he probably didn't want to have.

She looked at him with pride pulsing in her chest. He smiled, he talked and he charmed everyone he came into contact with. Then the warmth in her chest was shoved away by an icy chill.

Miguel approached her father's table.

CHAPTER SEVENTEEN

Too late! She was too late! Her father was standing and holding his hand out to Miguel. From appearances, it was a friendly gesture, but her father measured a man by the strength of his handshake. Sometimes that was all it took to make or break a business deal.

"I hear good things about you and your clinic, Dr. Torres," Charles Sterling-Thorne said, and came around the table.

"Vicky...Victoria is being generous, I'm sure."

"Nonsense. She just put the idea out there. I do my own research before I put my money anywhere."

"And what did you find?" A muscle in Miguel's jaw twitched. She could see it from where she was, standing paralyzed, her heart racing as she watched the interaction between the two most important men in her life.

"Fabulous setup. You've taken a dying clinic and turned it around in just a few years. You should be proud of yourself."

Her eyes went wide, and her jaw went slack. A compliment from her father! Now she knew she needed that sedative.

Miguel grinned and the tension in his shoulders

eased. "Thank you. It's taken a lot of work, but I'm ready to move on now."

Tears filled her eyes at that statement. She was so proud of him.

"I'm certain there was more than a small sacrifice involved. With that kind of success there always is." He narrowed his eyes and gave Miguel a considering look. "Have you ever considered working in the wine industry?"

Miguel laughed. "No, sir. Medicine is where I need to be."

"You sound just like my daughter." He sighed.

The paralysis in her legs eased, and Vicky was finally able to move forward.

"Victoria, there you are, darling." Charles held out his arm to her, and she went to his side eagerly for the first time in a very long time. "You've put together a wonderful event here tonight."

"Thank you, Daddy. I see you've met Dr. Torres."

"Yes. And I have to say my money will indeed be well spent at your clinic."

"Thank you," she whispered, then pulled back. Losing control of emotions in front of Charles Sterling-Thorne was not something one did.

Edward stood and left his two companions at the table. "I believe the next dance is mine."

Vicky grinned. "Absolutely." Vicky looked at her father. "You behave yourself while I'm gone."

This time it was his jaw that dropped. "Me?"

She just grinned as Eddy led her away.

"I can't believe you said that," Eddy said.

"I can't believe I did either, but it felt good."

"I think our little Victoria has found her wings." He pulled her close and twirled her across the dance floor.

Miguel watched as Edward swirled and twirled Vicky. She was incredibly beautiful, and he knew he'd fallen for her. Despite all his reprimands to himself, he'd gone and done it.

"She's quite a beauty, isn't she?" Charles asked.

"Yes, she is. Inside and out."

"I'm finally beginning to see that." He sighed. "Congratulations, Dr. Torres. You've done fine things in your career, and I'm certain that you'll continue to do them in your future at University Hospital."

"Vicky mentioned it to you?" His brows twitched up at that.

His eyes glittered with amusement. "Research."

Miguel nodded. He was beginning to understand what Vicky had been talking about. There was no getting anything past Charles Sterling-Thorne.

Distracted with more conversations, he lost track of Vicky in minutes. Time seemed to move strangely this night, coming to a halt at precious moments and speeding by at others. Then Carlos and his parents approached.

"Hey, man. We're taking off. Mom's had enough fun for one night."

She gave him a playful glare. "Carlos is the one who needs to take it easy. He's been very active tonight and I don't want to him to have a relapse when he's been doing so well." She motioned for a hug and a kiss from Miguel, and he quickly obliged. "Thank you for a wonderful evening, *mijo*. Now go find your lady."

"My lady?"

"You know." She pulled back. "Good night." As they departed it seemed to be the beginning of a mass exodus, starting with the older folks. The younger ones would stay on the dance floor until the music stopped and they were shooed out of the ballroom.

His lady? Was that what Vicky was? Was that what he wanted her to be? He looked for Vicky and found her saying goodbye to several couples. What was it that she wanted? There was only one way to find out.

"Vicky?"

She turned toward him and he saw the fatigue in her. Although she stood straight and elegant, he knew her well enough now to know that she was exhausted.

"Are you leaving?" she asked, her eyes wide.

"No. I wanted to talk to you."

He took her elbow and walked with her to a side alcove where they could chat.

"Is something wrong?" she asked. "Seems like everyone had a good time and we've raised a boatload of money for the clinic."

"Yes, it's true. Thank you. Tonight could never have happened without you."

"I was happy to help out."

"Seems like I've gotten a lot out of tonight." He faced her, stepped a little closer to her and looked down into her eyes. Her pupils dilated a little and he knew he'd surprised her. "Is there anything you want out of tonight? Is there anything that you want?" That was as close as he could get at the moment to revealing the emotions that were about to swamp him. He'd hidden his feelings for so long that speaking them out loud wasn't possible at the moment.

A small gasp came from her, and then she took a deep breath, her gaze holding on to his. Carefully, she placed one of her hands on his arm, and the heat of her burned right through his sleeve. The air between them sparkled.

"I want tonight. I want you to hold me for one night. To pretend for just one night that there are no barriers between us. Nothing to hold us back. Just a man and a woman who might have cared about each other had the circumstances been different."

"Victoria," he said, his voice dark, husky, making her shiver. This was the first time he'd used her proper name. "I'll hold you tonight. I'll spend this night with you, make love to you, with you, because I want it, *and* you want it."

Her gaze flashed to him, wanting it to be true, hoping she'd not just imagined his words. If this was the end between them, she wanted to have everything out in the open. Raising her head and taking a deep, tremulous breath, she held her hand out to him. "I think I'm ready to leave, Dr. Torres. Will you join me upstairs?"

Without a word he took her hand in his and escorted her away from the crowd, the lights, the atmosphere that neither of them truly belonged in. In silence they walked away. With her hand still in his, he felt the tremors, the moisture of her palm, and knew she was as nervous, as excited as he was. Moments later, closed into the elevator with two other couples, he stood beside her, observing her statuesque, svelte form, and wondered how he had not seen the true Victoria. She had been everything then that she was now, just in different attire. Perhaps he hadn't wanted to see it. Perhaps he had chosen to close his eyes to what had been right in front of him the entire time she'd been working at the clinic. In the years he'd worked there he knew he had become more jaded, more disillusioned with life. Now he realized the depth of his despair if he had missed seeing the true Victoria in the simple clothes she'd hidden beneath.

After an interminable wait, the other couples got off the elevator at their floor and the doors slid closed silently, leaving them alone together. Trembling with need, with want, he turned his head and looked down at her.

There was nothing simple about Victoria Sterling-Thorne. She was the most gorgeous, compassionate, smartest woman he'd ever known, and he was an idiot for not recognizing what she was sooner.

Miguel didn't know how to feel, how to act, how to be inside. The knots in his stomach hadn't gone away all night, even though everything that had occurred was for the benefit of their clinic and the people in their community. He was humbled by the outpouring of support from people he didn't know and never would have turned to for help. All because of Vicky. Victoria.

With silence and sizzling tension between them, he escorted her out of the elevator and to her room. The hall was quiet, the dim lighting providing a smoky atmosphere where anything seemed possible. There was definitely magic in the air tonight.

"I'll...I'll just get the card...out of my purse." She didn't look at him, just opened her bag.

Without a word he watched her fumble with the silly little bit of fabric that could hardly be called a purse. Nothing more than lipstick and a key would fit in that thing. She had her back to him as she leaned toward the dim lighting.

Unable to avoid looking, unable to resist the temptation of her any longer, he allowed himself one long, lingering look at the silken length of her back, at what was revealed by the upsweep of her hair that bared the long, delicate curve of her neck. The hairpin decorated with diamonds that he hadn't noticed before twinkled like stars. The crisscrossed silken ties of the dress over her back revealed more of her than he'd ever seen and only whetted his appetite for more. He swallowed and tried to choke down the words that struggled to surface in him. He had to apologize, he needed to apologize. He'd been an idiot, but the words wouldn't come. Somehow, he would make it up to her. Somehow, he would make it right between them. Tonight.

"Dammit. It won't work," she said as she struggled with the key card.

He was just inches away and moved forward, placing his hand on her left thigh. She stilled instantly and stiffened, her breathing quick and shaky. Every sense he had was filled with her. "Shh. Shh. You have to take it slow, easy," he whispered close to her, and let his lips touch the outer curve of her ear, let the tip of his tongue trace the shape. She shivered, and didn't pull away from him. "Take it slow. Ease it in." In a precise move he placed his right hand over hers and guided the card into the narrow slot with a smooth movement of their hands joined together, and then pulled back with the same action.

Green light, a click and the door opened. With a ragged breath Vicky turned her face toward him and tilted it up, her eyes soft with the same want that raged inside of him. Her breath came in short pants, and she rested her head on his right shoulder.

"Miguel."

The whisper of her voice was a siren song that filled his mind, and he was powerless to resist the call. He felt the trembling muscles of her stomach, of her hips, as his fingers slid upward. Releasing her hand, he turned her face toward him and closed the gap.

As if knowing the moment had come between them, Vicky met his kiss with parted lips. Eager, anticipating, wanting. There was no longer any pretense between them. They wanted each other, and tonight was the night to bare secrets, souls and skin.

Clasping his arms around her, he brought her lithe body against him. Every curve, every line of her pressed against him as she answered his kiss. He cupped a hand against the back of her head while he plundered her mouth. Her tongue, soft and sweet, answered his call and desire raged through him. Somehow, he managed to walk them into the room before the lock snapped shut again. Turning with her, he pressed her against the door, trapping her with his body.

Vicky raised her arms and wrapped them around Miguel's neck. The feel of him against her was so strong, so right. Her heart thundered in her chest, and desire like she'd never known raced through her body. Tingles and memories of what her body wanted, what it could do, made her want Miguel naked. Now.

She pushed against the tux jacket and succeeded in getting his attention long enough to drop the thing to the floor. His hands ranged over her and then paused to cup her bottom, tipping her hips up against the heat and strength of his arousal. A groan caught in her throat.

Desire spiraled through her body, and moist heat flowed. The trembling inside grew as she cupped her hands around Miguel's face, pushing back slightly. "I want to undress you." She bit her lip. Such bold, wanton statements had never come from her. She was shy and an introvert, but with him aroused and wanting her so, shyness melted away to the truth. "I want to see you."

He planted a sweet kiss on her lips. "Are you positive you want this?" He looked at her, vulnerability that she'd never seen blatant in the warm eyes. "That you want this night and...me?" He swallowed.

She knew that she loved him, that the feelings in her heart were true. "I'm more sure than I've ever been about anything." She let her glance fall to his parted lips. His breath rushed in and out, and she felt the racing of his heart beneath her hand. He was as vulnerable as she.

With a groan, he pressed his lips to hers again, tugging and almost drawing her into him. Her trembling fingers released the cummerbund first then she turned her attention to the buttons of his shirt, releasing them one by one and revealing the smooth, tawny skin beneath. She shoved the shirt open. He was simply a beautiful man. And for this night he was hers.

Eyes watching her, ranging over her body, Miguel

stepped back long enough to remove his shirt. And she swallowed, her mouth nearly watering at the sight of him. Casually, he reached for his waistband and released the catch, removed his shoes then socks.

"Oh, my." She stilled as nerves that she'd thought had fled returned in full force. What if she didn't please him? What if...? So many haunts of the past tried to return, but she focused on the want in Miguel's eyes, vowed to live in the moment and shoved away the past. She reached out to him, but he caught her hand and pressed a kiss to the palm, his gaze never leaving hers.

"My turn."

He reached for her shoulders and turned her away from him. The hot feel of his wet mouth on her bare shoulder nearly dropped her to her knees. He pressed his arousal against her bottom, his hands drawing her hips back. One hand ranged upward over her stomach, and paused at a breast, testing and teasing it. Then his mouth moved to her ear. "How do you get this dress off?"

"It's kind of complicated," she whispered, and looked up at him. Desire shone hot in his eyes.

"I see that. How did you get it on?" Another kiss to her shoulder made her shiver.

"With difficulty," she said, and pressed her forehead against his cheek, settling now into the feelings, the essence of him, allowing the pleasure of the moment to wash over her, savoring every nuance of the moment that she knew was never going to come again.

"Let me see what I can do."

He placed his hands on her thighs and began to bunch the dress up into his hands, drawing the silken material up her legs, revealing more and more of her body to him. Allowing him to touch her, to let himself have free access to her was a glorious feeling. He eased the material up over her bottom and then stilled.

"Is something wrong? Is it stuck?" she asked.

"Oh, no. Not at all." Seconds later he pulled the dress upward, and she raised her arms as he removed it completely. It landed on the floor with a light clatter of sequins and swoosh of silk. "A thong is a beautiful thing. Seeing you in one is even better." He sighed and let his hand stroke over her perfectly shaped bottom. "You have the loveliest curves I've ever seen."

Heat suffused her at the compliment and shyness fell away. She turned to face him, the moment of truth revealed. The desire to run, to cover herself, raged within her, but when she looked up at him she was paralyzed by the beauty of him as he looked at her. In that moment she was absolutely lost in him.

Miguel swallowed as he turned her around and took her hand. He wanted this woman with everything he had in him. Allowing his gaze to wander, he looked at her from head to toe, memorizing everything revealed to him, for him. Her hair remained up, a necklace of gems gleaming around her neck. Lovely, pink-tipped breasts stood high. The inner curve of her narrow waist, the slight roundness of her abdomen and the scrap of tiny fabric called a thong made his mouth water. Long, endless silky-smooth legs that he wanted wrapped around his hips tapered down to trim feet and high-heeled sandals. He held her hand and stepped back from her, seeing her, watching her, appreciating the beauty of her from shoes to smile.

"As long as I live, I will never forget this moment, this

picture of you right now." He raised his gaze to hers, and his heart cramped from the beauty of all she was, inside and out. The anger, the resentment simply fell away from him. There was no place for it here tonight.

"Neither will I."

Unable to resist the temptation of her any longer and no longer willing to try, he moved in front of her, allowing her nipples to touch his chest. "I want to touch you, to taste you, to feel every inch of you against me."

"Yes." She reached for him, and he scooped her up and carried her to the bed. Turning, he fell backward with her sprawled on top of him. As much as he adored it, the thong had to go, and he tugged the thing off her then shoved away the remainder of his own clothing.

With his hot skin against hers, Miguel pressed her back into the silken softness of the cool bedding. His mouth plundered her and left her breathless and wanting more. His hands were all over her, the light rub of calluses stirring her more than she'd thought possible.

He eased away and used that hot mouth of his to blaze a trail down her neck, over her collarbone and to her breast. Teasing and sucking her nipple, he held her captive as he pressed the hot length of his erection against her leg. Every sense in her soared to life as he touched and teased and tested her ribs, her abdomen, her hips.

Squirming beneath him, she wanted him trembling as much as she was. "Come here. I need you."

He raised his head and met her eyes. She dug her fingers into his hair. "Soon. Very soon," he whispered, and pulled away from her, continuing to kiss and lick and tease his way over her body. The inside of her ankle, the inside of her knee fell victim to his kisses and caresses.

Her thighs fared the same as he made his way upward, pausing at the juncture to place hot, stirring kisses in each corner. When he opened his mouth over her core, she clutched the bedding and bit her lips together to stifle the scream in her throat.

The heat of his tongue traced over her tender woman's flesh, stirring her to heights she'd not known existed. Her body, stirred beyond comprehension, sizzled. When he eased a finger inside her, she crashed, her body no longer her own.

Then he was kissing her again and she held him tight, wanting to please him as much as he pleased her. He pulled back, breathless, and pressed his forehead against hers. "Are you on birth control?"

"No. Where's my purse?"

Turning, he looked around, then left the bed and returned with the tiny thing. "This won't help what I want to do."

She took it from him, extracted a condom and threw the purse across the bed. "This will." She tore the wrapping open and pulled out the little bit of magic inside.

"You came prepared," he said, and took it from her.

"No. I came with hope." With her hands over his, they eased the protective sheath down over him. "Love me," she said, and tears clouded her vision.

"I do," he whispered an instant before his mouth covered hers again.

The weight of him pressed her down, and she reveled in the textures and sensations of him against her, feeling delicate and protected all at once. He drew one of her knees up and eased it outward, giving him greater access. Her hands urged him on, and she tilted her hips up to receive him inside her.

Miguel pressed forward, the heat of him parting her flesh and filling her as far as he could go. This was the way love was supposed to be made.

He stilled, catching his breath, or the night was going to be over long before he intended. The feel of her hot flesh surrounding him, pressing on him, nearly made him cry out from the sheer pleasure of it.

Joined with her now, it was the most beautiful thing he'd ever experienced. Easing back, he wanted to prolong the pleasure for both of them. The pace he set was slow and designed for ultimate pleasure. When she locked her legs around his hips and squeezed, the time for slowness ended. He clasped her hips in his hands and fell hard into her, surging forward and back, letting his body take over, giving up any semblance of control.

Vicky dug her fingers into his upper arms, and she turned her face to the side. He pressed his mouth to her ear. "Don't hold it in. I want to hear you."

Turning back, she pressed her cheek to his and her breath warmed his skin. She gasped and clutched him tighter as her body responded to him again, and he lost all the control that he'd once thought he had.

Unable to suppress the wave that surged through him, he went with it, allowed it to take him under, and he drowned himself in the passion of the moment. Crying out his own pleasure, he held her tight as the final pulses of his body drifted away.

He rolled over, taking his weight off her, and, drawing her to his side, he held her against him.

CHAPTER EIGHTEEN

"ARE you okay?" he asked, and let his hand stroke its way down her back and over the curve of her hip.

"Oh, yeah. I'm good," she said, still marveling at the fire between them. Making love with Miguel was more than anything she'd imagined. "How about you?"

"I'm good, too." A sigh of contentment rolled out of him.

As his touch soothed her and stroked her skin she allowed herself to reciprocate and explored his chest and abdomen with her fingers. Intimacy with Miguel was an experience she'd never thought possible and here she was, right where she wanted to be. It was so much more than she'd hoped for.

They made love twice more and then showered together with strokes and sighs and kisses of desperation as their night of magic eased away with the breaking of dawn over the mountains.

"I guess this is it, then, isn't it?" she asked, tugging her robe more tightly around her. Though they'd recently left a very hot shower she felt cold and she hugged her arms around herself as she watched Miguel dress. The pain in her chest had begun when their last kiss had ended. It was over, and she knew it.

His jacket lay on the end of the rumpled bed with a bundle of envelopes sticking out of the inner pocket. That was the reason they were there, for the benefit of the clinic, not to satisfy her personal needs. The hope that she had come into this night with faded away. Even hope as strong as hers couldn't overcome some things.

"This has been a night I'll never forget." He pulled her closer and pressed a chaste kiss to her forehead. In a hurried movement he picked up his jacket and left the suite. The snap of the door closing shut ended any chance for a reconciliation between them. It was final.

Exhausted and anguished, she somehow made the drive home and brought her belongings in from the car, but dropped the suitcase by the front door and left it there. There was no name for the type of pain and numbness that overwhelmed her.

Although she'd left her cottage not twenty-four hours ago, it felt and smelled stale, as if a lifetime had passed. She opened several windows to catch the breeze from the river. Dressed in shorts, a plain shirt and flimsy sandals, she grabbed a bottle of water and her cell phone, and headed out to the vineyard.

This was her solace, where she would find the peace she needed, and hopefully the strength to go on after knowing what a night with Miguel was like, knowing she'd never have it again. After the past month of working and planning for the event, she was exhausted. She felt like Cinderella on the day after the ball. At least the event had been a wild success and Miguel would be able to move on knowing that the clinic was as solvent as it could be.

Her path seemed meandering, but it led her eventually to the bench swing that was tucked away in a secret part of the vineyard. She sat and put the swing into motion then tucked her legs beneath her, hoping the motion would soothe her battered soul.

The soft sounds of the breeze, the birds nesting in the nearby trees, the swish of the horses as they chased flies with their tails, all melded together in one blissful symphony of nature.

Then the tears came. In the privacy of her vineyard she allowed herself to let go and ease the tension that had been building in her for months. She loved Miguel, but now she was more certain than ever that there would be nothing between them. Last night had proved that. They'd shared a beautiful experience and then walked away from each other. Letting go was always painful. Being in such a beautiful, peaceful place helped. Only time would ease the pain, but she would never, ever forget him.

She'd had relationships in the past, but the breakups had never hurt her the way this one did. Not even her divorce had been this painful. Eventually, she calmed down and reconnected with the sounds of peace around her until the sound of footsteps on dirt penetrated her focus. One of the horses must have gotten out and decided to have a stroll through the vines. Wouldn't her father have a fit if that happened? She opened her eyes and down the row in front of her she found the source of the disturbance, and it wasn't a horse.

Miguel stood there.

Or perhaps against the afternoon sun the image was an illusion, a lame attempt by her heart to console her. Denial was a very powerful part of the grieving process. She knew that, but to have the full-blown figure of Miguel approaching her was something else. She blinked several times then held a hand up to shade the sun from her eyes. Nope. That was definitely Miguel getting closer to her, not an illusion. She swallowed and her heart pounded loud in her ears.

"What are you doing here?" She rubbed her hands over her face and dashed away any lingering moisture, but she was certain her face was red and puffy. He would notice.

"I needed to take a walk. I was restless." He shoved his hands down into the pockets of his khaki shorts and looked down at the ground then back up at her with an intensity that surprised her.

The nerves in the pit of her stomach clenched. What was he talking about? "There are plenty of places to walk in this town. There are the sidewalks, the parks, the Nature Center, the path down by the river." The implication was clear. Why here?

"I like this stretch of the river, but it's on private property, you know."

She stepped forward. "I know."

"I wanted to come ask one of the owners if I could take a walk here, in the vineyard." He stopped in front of her, just a foot away, and looked down at her, his eyes unreadable with the sun behind him. "I wanted to ask if she'd go along for a very long walk with me."

"Miguel, what are you talking about? What are you doing here?" She was so tired and confused she didn't know what to think, couldn't process what he was telling her.

He took her hand and led her back to the swing she had just left. They sat. "Leaving you this morning was the hardest thing I've ever had to do." He took her hands in his and squeezed. "That feeling, that pain, is something I never want to experience again." He cleared his throat and swallowed a few times. "This is so hard to say."

"I know. When you left and didn't look back, I knew things were over for us."

"Then when I thought of a future, I couldn't think of one without you in it, but I don't think I can do this." He raised a hand and indicated the mansion and vines.

"We don't need to do this. In fact, we need to do something else entirely. There's something you ought to know. Growing up in this environment was difficult and I know that's hard for some people to understand. I had few friends, no boyfriends through school because the boys I knew were afraid of my father. Then people only wanted to know me because of my name and my family's money." She shuddered and heaved out a trembling sigh. "The only thing I have of my own is my nursing career." Leaning her head back against the swing, she closed her eyes briefly. "Going to nursing school was the only time I've ever held my own against my father. Until now. Now I have a career and a job I love. Working at the clinic means everything to me, and I've discovered that I'm so much more capable than I've ever thought. It's because of the clinic. Because of you, Miguel."

"My past, my brother's death has haunted me through

my life. I never told you but I was engaged when Emilio was killed."

"No, I didn't know that." Compassion for the young man that he had been welled in her. He'd been so hurt by life at a young age and had only survived without caving in to the grief because of his personal strength, strength he didn't even know he had.

"When I didn't recover from Emilio's death, she broke things off. I couldn't give her what she needed and things just fell apart between us." He placed an arm on the back of the swing and teased her hair with his fingers.

"As you know, I'm divorced. It was a mistake from the start." She sighed and allowed the pain of her past to bubble up. "He was after connections with my family and the business. I was incidental to the relationship." Though it pained her to say it, it was the truth.

He froze as the white-hot heat of protectiveness struck him. "No one should be incidental in a relationship. You are precious and the man was a total idiot for not seeing it." As soon as the words left his mouth, he wondered if that was a statement about himself. "I should have seen it soon, too, Vicky. I'm sorry." He sighed and dropped his gaze. "I'm guilty of not seeing the real you in the beginning, too. But you've helped me to heal from Emilio's death and to learn to put the past behind me."

"You won't ever forget Emilio, but you can let go of the pain surrounding him." He'd begun the process and maybe some small part of that was due to her help. "If I've helped in any way, I'm very glad."

"I think from here we need to make a vow that the

future is ours and one that we make together. One that's our own."

She gasped, uncertain what he meant and not wanting to jump to conclusions. Did he mean at the clinic, to go to the hospital with him? What? Her heart raced and her mouth went dry. "Tell me what you mean by that."

Miguel squeezed her hands then dropped to the dirt in front of her. "Last night was filled with more magic and passion than I have a right to, but I don't want to let go of it, or let go of you." He placed his hands on her thighs. "I don't know what my future is going to hold, but I want you in whatever that is. I want us to build one together." He looked down at his hands then back up at her. "I don't know when or where, and there are probably a dozen reasons why you shouldn't, but, Victoria Sterling-Thorne, will you marry me?"

She launched herself from the swing with a squeal and wrapped her arms around his shoulders. Unprepared for the sudden weight of her, Miguel toppled over, and they crashed to the ground. She spread kisses over his face and ended with one long, hot kiss that left them both breathless.

"Is that a yes?" he asked when he could breathe again.

"Yes, that's a yes."

He hugged her tight. "Oh, good. If that had been a no, I was going to get worried."

They sat up and returned to the swing where Vicky curled against Miguel's side and they exchanged kisses that got longer and longer and nearly as hot as the sun overhead.

"How did you find me out here?" She pulled back with a frown.

"I stopped at the house."

"You did?" Her stomach clenched.

"Your father told me you'd probably be out here." Miguel winked. "He's actually not so bad when you get to know him a little."

This was a day of miracles if Charles was being civilized. "You actually spoke to my father?"

"Yes, when I told him I wanted to marry you."

Stunned, Vicky stared at him. "I love you."

"I love you right back."

EPILOGUE

VICKY looked at the schedule on Miguel's computer. There were too many holes in the physician side, but at least they were getting filled in one by one.

She grinned. Two months ago she'd never have imagined so many changes in the clinic. Now they seemed natural. With some additional brainstorming with Dr. Flemming, who had indeed taken over nearly half of Miguel's shifts, they had found extra physicians to put in time so that Miguel could in good conscience accept the position at University Hospital.

"Got a minute?" Tilly asked from the doorway.

"Sure. Come on in." Vicky sipped from her coffee cup. "How's Carlos doing on the computer?"

"Not too bad for a beginner," Tilly said, and grinned.

They'd made some changes in staffing. Since Carlos was officially on light duty, Tilly had trained him to take over the computer scheduling and answering phones so that her nursing skills could be better utilized triaging patients. Vicky was now the office manager and had given most of her duties over to Tilly.

"I'm just glad he could come back at all."

"There are a few things I wanted to ask you about. You may have done things differently when you were triaging, but I just wanted to see if this change is okay with you."

Although Tilly was the triage nurse and Vicky now the office manager, they had an equal relationship and interest in the clinic. "Let's see it." They looked over Tilly's proposed changes and Vicky had no issues with them. "Looks good. If something doesn't work, we can always try something else, right?"

"Sure. Just like always."

The phone rang and Tilly left as Vicky returned to her scheduling.

Hours had passed when she felt a presence in the doorway. When she looked up, her heart flipped and a smile crossed her face. "Hi, there. What are you doing here?"

Miguel crossed the room and leaned on the desk beside her. "It's quitting time. Got time for dinner?"

"Sure. Anything special?"

"I think it is. We're celebrating."

"I know I got most of the schedule filled, but is it worthy of a celebration?" She smiled.

"Not that—this." He placed two fingers in his shirt pocket and fished out a small wrapped package. Holding it in the palm of his hand, he waited for her to take it.

"Ooh. I see." She licked her lips. "I can't take it now."

"What?"

"I'm in work clothes at the end of the day. I should be wearing a dress and—"

"You were in work clothes when I met you and they don't detract at all from the way I feel about you."

"Miguel," she whispered, and tears filled her eyes. "I love you." Carefully, she took the box from his hand, unwrapped it and opened it. Her first sight of the ring made her breath hitch. "It's gorgeous."

"I hope it fits." He extracted it from the box and placed it on the tip of her finger. "Victoria Sterling-Thorne, will you do me the honor of being my wife sometime very soon?"

"I will."

He pushed the ring all the way onto her finger and it fit to perfection—just the way they fit together.

Medical Romance™

TAMING DR TEMPEST
by Meredith Webber

Annabelle Donne must survive working with womanising doc Nick Tempest in A&E. Surprisingly, Annabelle soon sees the reality, not the rumours, and now she's in real trouble…suddenly she's falling in love with Nick!

THE DOCTOR AND THE DEBUTANTE
by Anne Fraser

Lady Alice Granville is packing away her stilettos to volunteer in Africa—this could be her chance to impress the gorgeous Dr Dante Corsi. Does Alice have what it takes to show this Italian doctor that she's more than just a debutante in designer clothes…?

THE HONOURABLE MAVERICK
by Alison Roberts

Marriage is not for Max. But how can he turn away scared, pregnant nurse Ellie from his doorstep? Then, as he holds her tiny baby, Max's protective instinct kicks in, which makes him claim he's her husband.. a word that feels better than he *ever* expected!

THE UNSUNG HERO
by Alison Roberts

Renowned neurosurgeon and playboy Rick Wilson has set his sights o Sarah—until she drops a bombshell: he's father to her nephew—and the little boy needs his bone marrow… Rick is out of his depth— only Sarah can help him on the rocky road to fatherhood…

**On sale from 1st April 2011
Don't miss out!**

MILLS & BOON®

are proud to present our...

Book of the Month

Sins of the Flesh
by Eve Silver

from Mills & Boon® Nocturne™

Calliope and soul reaper Mal are enemies, but as
they unravel a tangle of clues, their attraction grows.
Now they must choose between loyalty to those
they love, or loyalty to each other—to the one
they each call enemy.

Available 4th March

Something to say about our Book of the Month?
Tell us what you think!

millsandboon.co.uk/community
facebook.com/romancehq
twitter.com/millsandboonuk

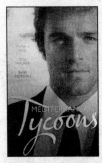

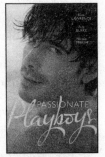

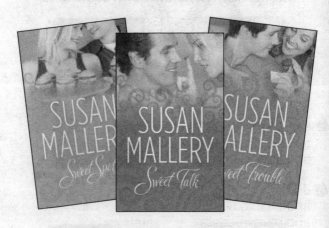